ANGORA FEVER

ANGORA FEVER

The Collected Short Stories Of Edward D. Wood, Jr.

Foreword by Bob Blackburn

BearManor Media

2019

Angora Fever: The Collected Stories of Edward D. Wood, Jr.

Foreword by Bob Blackburn © 2019

For information, address:

BearManor Media
P. O. Box 71426
Albany, GA 31708

bearmanorbare.com

Typesetting and layout by John Teehan

"Cover design by Marjan Dzin"

Published in the USA by BearManor Media

ISBN—978-1-62933-446-2

TABLE OF CONTENTS

FOREWORD

THIS IS THE SECOND VOLUME of short fiction by Ed Wood Jr. that I have been lucky enough to have been involved with over the last couple of years, the first was titled "Blood Splatters Quickly" released in Oct. 2014, a collection of 34 stories by Ed. This collection continues in that vein with many newly collected titles from various mens magazines from the early 1970's. This foreword and bio of Ed was included in that first collection, I am slightly revising it for this collection.

This includes a little bio of Ed Wood as well as how I came into the orbit of his widow Kathy Wood.

These stories originally were written to fill a few pages between buxom women in various states of undress and softcore sexual situations in what I call the "girlie" magazines of the late 1960's and early 1970's. Ed and his wife Kathy were struggling to pay the rent, put food on the table and have a bottle of booze to kill the pain and to inject a little fun into a life that had spiraled out of control for them from the late 1950's until Ed's passing in Dec. of 1978. They were forced to move from a house they loved but couldn't keep up the payments on to a series of apartments first in the Burbank, Ca. area back into Hollywood to what was a very dangerous part of the neighborhood back then.

Ed started writing for publisher Bernie Bloom in late 1968-'69, short stories and articles mainly about the sex trade, and the copy that went with the pictorials in the skin magazines published by Pendulum Publishing. Ed's time with Bernie was short lived he was fired for the final time in 1974, with some of his stories reprinted after that. This was a time when the porn trade was starting to show more skin but prior to full on hardcore which was opened up with the films such as "Deep Throat", "Behind the Green Door" even "I Was Curious (Yellow)". Ed had his own personal kinks, he was a known cross dresser who's female name was "Shirley", many of his short stories, articles and books dealt with transvestism as well as fetishism, . In fact his very first film "I Changed My Sex" aka "Glen or Glenda" dealt with this as well as Ed writing, directing and starring in it. Ed's biggest fetish was for angora, which appears in many of his novels, fiction and a few of his films.

Most of Ed's short fiction deals with Horror, Westerns, Crime, Human Sexuality and the Macabre as did most of his films. But with only 3-4 pages he had to get in and get out and have the stories make some sort of sense, you be the judge of that. This is a selection of stories all written by Edw. D. Wood Jr. which for the first time in over 40+ years are finally getting their just due. We hope you are entertained. So who was Ed Wood?

Edward Davis Wood J. was born in Poughkeepsie, NY. Oct. 10,1924. Growing up Ed loved movies, all types but mainly the "horse opera's" westerns starring William "Hopalong Cassidy" Boyd, Roy Rogers, Gene Autry, Buck Jones (Ed's personal favorite) as well as Kenne Duncan, Roy Barcroft & Ken Maynard all of whom made appearances in Ed's films. He also loved horror movies especially the Dracula films starring the legendary Hungarian actor Bela Lugosi with whom Ed would form a working relationship as well as a personal friendship over the last few years of the troubled actors life. Bela passed away in 1956 after starring in two of Ed's best known films, "Glen or Glenda" a.k.a. "I Changed My Sex", and "The Bride of the Monster", film footage shot of Bela would later be used in Ed's most well known film "Plan 9 From Outer Space" or as it was originally titled "Grave Robbers From Outer Space", (the title was changed at the urging of the Beverly Hills Baptist Church which had provided crucial funding for the film, plus the cast & crew were asked to be baptized prior to filming, another story for another day).

It was mentioned by Ed's late wife that Ed's mom had hoped for a little girl prior to Eds birth, and was wont to dress Ed up as such, which started a lifelong penchant for cross dressing as well as Ed's growing fetish for angora, a theme and fur that would show up in many of Ed's works, in fact Ed liked to dress as his alter-ego "Shirley" to write, not only on his film & TV scripts, but his large body of fiction, both pulp fiction as well as articles and his short fiction which appeared in many "girlie" magazines of the early 1970's, many of which are reprinted here.

For a short time Ed worked at a movie theater in Poughkeepsie, and when World War II began, a young 17 year old Ed lied about his age and joined the Marines. Ed's military service has been detailed in full in the recent book "The Unknown War of Edward D. Wood, Jr." By James Pontolillo. The apocryphal story of Ed wearing a bra & panties underneath his uniform may or may not be true, but I would like to believe it.

After his time in the service and being mustered out of the Marines in San Diego, Ca. and his eventual move to Hollywood in 1947 is an area of mystery. Ed was said to have joined a traveling carnival where he played the "half man-half woman" in the geek show, also he may have worked as a G-2 secret agent for the government while touring with the Ice Capades, and more, Ed was always vague about this period of his life.

After his move to Hollywood Ed tried to break into the movie business, he also wrote a play based upon his military service called "The Casual Company" which he also starred in which was panned by the few critics who took the time to see it, Ed also appeared in a couple of other plays. He tried to get a western TV show off the ground titled "Crossroads of Laredo", which failed to arouse any interest, he also directed a few television shows and produced some generic commercials he tried to sell but failed to do so. In 1952 he was introduced to Bela Lugosi by his then roommate Alex Gordon who would go on to fame and success as one of the creators of American International Pictures and co-write a couple of films with Ed. Ed persuaded George Weiss a low budget producer to let him make what was originally going to be an exploitation film about the recent sex change of Christine Jorgensen, but due to legal and financial reasons the picture was changed to one about cross dressing and societal taboo's, starring the one & only "Daniel Davis" our Ed, in the title role, with his live in girlfriend Dolores Fuller as his fiance and Bela Lugosi as the Godlike "puppet master". The film failed at the box office, but Ed persevered on. His next film "Jail Bait"(1954) a crime drama also failed, then came 1955's "Bride of the Monster" starring Bela Lugosi as a mad scientist bent on creating a race of super human's to take over the world, the film ends with Bela being killed by a giant octopus.... oh, and an atom bomb. Bela passed away in Aug. of 1956, prior to that Ed's girlfriend Delores left him. Ed's film career had barely gotten off the ground.

Ed and Kathleen O'Hara a recent transplant from Vancouver, Canada had passed a collection plate to each other at the religious Science of the Mind church at the Wiltern Theater in Hollywood on three separate occasions while attending services, but didn't actually meet, Kathy Wood told me this story years later. At a local bar, The Cameo Room that Kathy and a couple of her friends sometimes went to on Friday evenings after work, Kathy & Ed finally met and it was love at first sight, pretty much from that day in 1955 until Ed's alcohol related death in Dec. of 1978. through ups and downs, dreams realized then crashing back to earth, Kathy became a part of Ed's life.

The cast of characters that Ed gathered around him besides Bela and initially Dolores became a kind of "stock" acting company and drinking companions, including the wrestler Tor Johnson (The Swedish Angel), the television "psychic" "The Amazing Criswell" (a friend of Mae West), Paul Marco "Kelton the Cop", faded cowboy Kenne Duncan, Conrad Brooks, Dudley Manlove, Valda Hanson, Maila "Vampira" Nurmi and others.

Beset by debt and no work, Ed & Kathy moved from house to apartment to wherever they could find a place before the checks bounced and they were forced to leave. Ed's film career was sporadic at best thru the 1960's and early '70's, but he did work on a few films, sometimes writing scripts or dialog for A.C Stephens aka Stephen Apostolof a "T&A" exploitation film maker, and appearing as a bloated drunk in a few early "X" rated films, most lost to history.

In the early 1960's Ed began a long and prolific writing career to help make ends meet, he created a cross dressing hitman named "Glen Marker" who became "Glenda" featured in two of Ed's first novels, "Black Lace Drag" a.k.a. "Killer In Drag" and a sequel of sorts "Let Me Die In Drag", other titles include "Orgy of the Dead" (which was used as the title for one of Ed's later films), "Devil Girls", "Sexecutives", "Security Risk", "Mary-Go-Round", "Carnival Piece" , "The Fall of the Balcony Usher" (which I have never seen but LOVE the title), and many more, some dealing with the Occult, or Western themes but mainly with Sex as that was what would sell the best in adult book stores and through mail order. But surprisingly Ed also helped write & produce industrial films for Autonetics a division of North American Aviation for in-house training, the company worked on Air Force projects for which both Ed and Kathy had to pass security clearances which with Ed's history of transvestism is a minor miracle in a way. He also helped write speeches for the re-election campaign of L.A. Mayor Sam Yorty.

As Ed and Kathy Wood's lives slowly spiraled out of control due to drinking, pressures to pay the rent, etc. etc. Ed found work in the late 1960's for Bernie Bloom then the publisher for a "girlie" magazine publishing house called Pendulum Publishing, Ed was a very fast typist, with a fertile imagination who cranked out a lot of articles, "pictorial" descriptions, and short fiction primarily from 1970-1974. That is where the short story's in this compendium mainly come from. Ed would take a thermos of vodka to work with him and by the end of a work day be in his cups. Off and on over this time Bernie would fire, then re-hire Ed, until Ed just became to unreliable and was let go a final time.

Around 1976 Ed and Kathy moved to 6383 Yucca St, in Hollywood, a building known for drug dealers, hookers and others who had hit the lowest rung of the Hollywood Dream. Ed was known to hock his type-writer for money to purchase booze at the PlayBoy liquor store a block away (which is still there to this day).

On the morning of Thursday, Dec. 7, 1978 Ed and Kathy were evict-ed from this seedy run down apartment, all of their belongings that hadn't been put in a storage unit in North Hollywood, (which were later auc-tioned off due to non-payment of that bill), were thrown out on the side-walk, all they could scrounge up and carry fit in a small leather suitcase, that held one of Ed's un-produced film scripts titled "I Woke Up Early The Day I Died", as well as the manuscript for the "how-to-make-it-in-Hollywood" book, "The Hollywood Rat Race". The couple were taken in by their friend and sometimes bit actor Peter Coe in a small apartment in North Hollywood. The plan was to take Ed to the Veterans Hospital for medical help as he was dying slowly from alcohol, and malnutrition.

On the morning of Sunday Dec. 10th, 1978 only 3 days after their eviction, Ed Wood died of a heart attack. Kathy commented on how Ed's eyes were open and "looked as if he'd seen the face of death itself". Ed Wood was cremated and his remains were scattered off of the coast of the Pacific Ocean. Only a few friend attended a memorial service and wake for Ed shortly thereafter.

Ed's prolific, but unfulfilled life had come to a sad end, not even a mention in Daily Variety, he was that forgotten in Hollywood. Ed was only 54 years old. But did the story end there? No

Then only a couple of years after Ed's death, in 1980 Harry and Mi-chael Medved followed up their book "The Fifty Worst Films of All-Time" (which surprisingly does NOT include any of Ed's films, with what they ti-tled "The Golden Turkey Awards", which forever changed the public's per-ception of Ed Wood Jr. and the films and other works he created. Ed was named "The Worst Director" of all time and "Plan 9 From Outer Space" as the "Worst Film". Shortly after this book came out college campuses and art house's began to screen what few copies of Ed's films they could find, a growing audience for this type of notoriety started to swell, Ed Wood became a certified "cult hero" and then in 1994 it was announced that Tim Burton was starting work on a "bio-pic" about Ed Wood starring Johnny Depp. Which actually won two Academy Awards, one for Martin Landau for his portrayal of Bela Lugosi, and one for Rick Baker for his make up. Ed Wood became a household name in certain circles.

Today many of Ed's films have been restored and made available first on VHS tapes & Laserdiscs, now on Blu-Ray and Video On Demand, YouTube has many of what were thought lost Ed Wood films, TV shows, commercials and some of the documentaries made in the wake of Ed's notoriety and the Johnny Depp film. While most of Ed's writings have gone out of print a few have been re-printed or in the case of "Hollywood Rat Race" published for the first time during Kathy Woods lifetime... oh... what became of her? I'm glad you asked.

After Ed's death Kathy dealt with the Veterans Administration to secure Ed's military benefits, this took some time but eventually she received them, she had been a personal secretary during her early years in Hollywood including working for the oil company Bechtel Corporation as well as Muzak (yes that Muzak). Within a year after Ed's death she secured part time work and with one of their dogs, named McGinty she found an inexpensive studio apartment back in Hollywood almost directly behind their old Yucca street building, where she moved to in early 1980. because of the notoriety of the Golden Turkey awards, Kathy was sought out by cult film fans, the occasional documentarian, and book author Rudolph Grey who was working on an oral biography about Ed. Kathy Wood was a very private person and couldn't quite understand the growing fascination with Ed's work and the re-appraisal of his films and writings. She told me later on that Ed would have loved this, but it was too late for him to enjoy.

I moved from Seattle to Hollywood in March of 1989 to work in radio, not on the air but in production. I moved into the same building as Kathy Wood, whom I would see walking her dog in front of the building from time to time, and would say hello to her and on occasion walked with her down to Hollywood Blvd. where she would catch a bus to go shopping, and I to my job just a few blocks away, I had no idea she was Ed Woods widow.

In the summer of 1992 there was a series of "exploitation" films screened at a local run down movie theater in the bad part of Hollywood. One of those weekends was dedicated to Ed Wood, showing many of his films, his commercials and short features as well as a documentary filmed by the BBC called "The Incredibly Strange Film Show" hosted by presenter Jonathan Ross, originally filmed and aired in 1989. I was sitting with a couple of friends, one of whom played in a local rock band, and her boyfriend who worked in the film industry. During this documentary there were couple of short interview segments with Kathy Wood, Ed's widow, as I watched these I thought that the lady resembled the one who lived in my building, when I went home that evening I looked at the mail boxes and saw "K. Wood". It was her. About 2 weeks later I ran into her in the hall and asked if she was indeed Ed's widow, and she was a little nervous but answered yes, and why I wondered, I explained about the weekend film series which also had a talk back with some of the surviving people who had known or worked with Ed, including Vampira, Steve Apostoloph, Forrest Ackerman, Conrad Brooks, Paul Marco, Valda Hanson, Rudolph Grey, & make up artist Harry Thomas.

Not too long after that I ran into the friend who was at the screening and he asked if that was indeed Kathy Wood and I said yes, he told me that he had heard that Tim Burton was planning on making a film about Ed Wood starring Johnny Depp. I visited Kathy the next day and told her about this, she was fairly incredulous, she knew who both Tim Burton and Johnny Depp were but couldn't understand why anyone would be interested in making a film about "her Eddie".

Acting with her approval I approached the Tim Burton people and then helped her find an entertainment lawyer to deal with the complexities of the situation. The lawyer not only helped her with negotiations with the film company, but also in dealing with the changes affected by the attention now aimed at her and other areas of her life. Slowly I became Kathy's friend and took her to the market every week, sometimes to doctors appointments, we'd go see a movie every so often and visited or called nearly every day unless I was out of the country.

She passed away in the summer of 2006, and is interred at the Hollywood Forever Cemetery engraved on her plaque is "She Hitched Her Wagon To A Star", something she always said her father had told her as a young girl, and how she felt about her love and life with Edward D. Wood Jr.

From Nov. 2-Dec. 4, 2011 the Boo-Hooray art gallery in Lower Manhattan ran an exhibition titled "Ed Wood's Sleaze Paperbacks" curated by Johan Kugelberg & Michael P. Daley, which collected approximately 70 publications, books & short stories by and attributed to Ed Wood, I was lucky enough to be invited to speak about my friendship with Kathy Wood by Johan. It was amazing and impressive to see Ed's work taken seriously and at the end of the gallery run the entire collection was sold to the Rare Books & Manuscripts Collection at the Library at Cornell University as part of their "Human Sexuality Archive" a copy of this book will also be included there. Also in 2009 film historian Rob Craig published a book titled "Ed Wood,Mad Genius: A Critical Study of The Films". An in-depth scholarly look at the films of Ed. So he is finally getting his due for his place in the zeitgeist of the 20th century and into the future. Insert your own Criswell quote here.

I began collecting these short stories and articles following Kathy Wood's death, I was bequeathed some of Ed's paperbacks from his personal library, most signed. His writing's are scarce and very rare, a few of his books have been re-printed but even now those are out of print. It is nice to be able to help Ed Wood back into the public's eye and this collection fills a big hole of his long lost stories.

There are a few other projects in the works, one is a musical about Ed that I am helping along.

Enjoy the writings of one of the most unique and original, (and fast writers) of the late 20th Century. And just a word of warning, many of the themes in these stories are of an adult nature, there may a be a little violence and sexual situations, these are not bedtime stories for the kiddies, but I'll leave that up to you...

– Bob Blackburn

Friend of the Kathleen O'Hara Wood,
the late widow of Edward D. Wood Jr.

SPECIAL THANKS TO Ben Ohmart, Joe Blevins, Greg Dziawer, Jason Insalaco, Rick Tell, Steve Paul and Philip R. Frey.

And a very special thank you to the late Kathy Wood, for her friendship and trust, without her, this book would not see the light of day.

HITCHHIKE TO HELL

by Edw. D. Wood, Jr.

in One Plus One *Vol 4., No. 1 Jan/Feb 1971 on Ed's resume 1971*

FROM THE MOMENT he awoke that morning he knew he wanted to kill somebody. He hadn't done it in a long time… months… ever since the last full moon. He knew that the full moon had something to do with his murderous desires. He'd seen a lot of *wolfman* pictures and it was at the full moon when the man became the creature and killed. He didn't need any psychiatrist to tell him that the effects of the moon were what motivated his unnatural desires.

The last time the urge came over him he was able to securely lock himself in his room and within three days the mood had passed him by and he knew it wouldn't capture his mind and spirit at least until the next full moon. He would not lock himself in his room again!

It had always been so easy to find a likely victim. Naturally he preferred pretty young girls who had ventured out alone, after dark. They were the easiest and they always died so hard… fighting him all the way. Of course he always damaged their throat right at the start so they couldn't scream… could only make those horrified gurgling sounds. A quick jab with the heel of his hand to a spot on the neck just below the chin. They would make no intelligent sound from that moment until they died. Then it was too late to worry about sounds.

Harry Vincent had killed seven that way. Five beautiful young girls and two men. One man was rather young, but not a strong fellow who might have warded him off. The young fellow had coughed a lot in the cocktail bar where Harry had picked him up. It was a gay bar and very easy to make a pickup. Harry showed what looked like a good-sized bank-

1

roll, bought a few drinks then suggested his apartment. Only the boy never saw the apartment. Instead he only found a lonely road and the cold grass on his naked back after Harry had incapacitated him then stripped him naked and plunged the knife into him over and over again and again.

Harry didn't like that killing very much. The boy hadn't made a sound from the beginning… not even the gurgling… all he did was stare up at him with those big brown eyes, all horrified and disbelieving. Harry wanted his victims to attempt screaming and to kick and thrash around. The boy died like a limp dishrag. There was no fun in that. Harry couldn't get the excitement he needed when they didn't fight for their life.

The only other male was an old wino he found in an alley. That was the night Harry had almost given up and returned to his apartment. He really didn't like killing men very much. They were an entity which didn't give him much pleasure. It was the girls and their soft bodies and their lovely fronts. He could cut them up like a butcher in the meat shop and they would scream a lot longer and they would thrash around a lot longer.

But there were times when only some males happened to be on hand. After the first four killings, all young, luscious girls, and young women began staying in their homes, behind locked doors when the sun went down.

Harry Vincent had to be satisfied with what he could find. The urge to kill was so tremendously overpowering in him and his vital sex organs that the pressure had to be relieved.

The old wino was in an alley. It was the last place Harry was going to look that night. The weather had turned cold and he wasn't dressed for it. If he couldn't find a victim for his lust, then he would have to slip the needle into his arm and go off on a different kind of trip. He didn't like taking the needle. But there were times it was a relief.

However, he was not going to need the needle. He was only to need the surgical knife he kept up his sleeve with the extremely tight cuff.

The old bag of bones in the tattered overcoat had huddled in a packing crate near the end of the alley… a decaying crate hidden among the trash cans and alley crap. The stink of maggots was almost enough to make Harry turn back. But he knew that there was a live something in that crate. And that live something must necessarily become food for the maggots.

He approached cautiously. But he didn't really have to. The old bag of wino bones was so far gone in his wine deliriums he'd never have heard the slight movement. But when the final attack came, Harry had to make sure the old fart knew what was happening to him. It was the only way Harry could get his kicks. The man had to be fully awake. He didn't have to be in complete control of his faculties. But those faculties had to be sharp enough to know that the end was coming and that it was going to be a horrible, terrifying, tormented, painful end.

"Old man," he said hoarsely... "Old man," he repeated when the bag of bones simply moaned but did not stir.

Then Harry gave the old, ragged overcoat a stiff clout with the toe of his pointed shoe. The old man moaned and rolled over. In the move he knocked over his bottle of cheap wine and what was left began to spill out into the alley dirt. The old man became horrified... not at Harry's knife which was nearly pressed against his throat... but at the spilled bottle.

The old man darted his hand forward to save his liquid friend. It was the first cut he received. A long gash just below his left ear. Harry, that time, had not made a move. When the old man stabbed for the bottle he ran into the knife. It was all purely accidental. But the lust crazed eyes of Harry Vincent went wide at the sight of the blood and at the howl of pain from the old man as his hand flew to the injured spot.

Then the old man snapped his eyes up to Harry's face where the moonlight made a white oval with dark holes that were Harry's eyes, and saliva slobbering lips which glistened in the same half-light.

There were no real sentences from the old man. Only a word... then a jumble of words. He realized pain, but he couldn't understand where it came from. It was in the direction of his left ear... then there was something happening to his right shoulder. And when his left hand flew to that spot there was the sudden knowledge that two fingers dropped to his lap.

He was trying to scream. But the wine, puke, clogged throat only permitted stifled gasps and a choking sound which would attract no ones' attention. There was always some wino puking up his guts in that alley. No one would pay any attention. And if there were a few discorded, un-connected screams, again no one would pay any attention.

They were always going off into delirium horrors. No one would pay any attention. Harry took a long time to finish his job. The old man's puke finally clogged his windpipe and he choked to death. It was better to Harry's psyche watching him choke to death on his own puke than if he had cut his throat. But when the breathing ceased, he slit the throat anyway. Then there was a lot of cutting to do... after he had torn off the clothing, he had a naked bag of skin and bones to work on. The maggots would have their work that night also. And the newspapers would have another field day with their headlines about the mad slasher who was loose on the town.

But the moon was full again and Harry Vincent knew what he had to do. He was quite calm about it as he dressed and made all the other preparations there in his small apartment. He even hummed gaily to himself as he tied his tie extra tightly… around his neck. He knew what he had to do, and he knew, this time, that he was not going to come home unsatisfied. He'd not had a session in so long. There was a lot stored up in him. And he was wearing rubber panties… he found they were the best for what would happen to him as he slashed.

His only concern, as he stood at the mirror admiring the job he'd done with the tie, was just how to go about locating his victim this time. He really didn't feel like walking very much. It got so tiring. Sometimes it took a very long walk to find just the right victim. And he knew he didn't want another young boy. He didn't have any homosexual inclinations connected to his slasher thoughts at that moment as he had had with the boy those months before. And he didn't have the vengeance of the world against any old winos as he had in the alley.

He felt that it had to be a very pretty, and very young girl. Not a child! Children were innocent of all wrong doings. It had to be one of those that walked the streets with their pig of a boyfriend. Or one of those that stood around street corners looking for strangers whom they might roll, or prostitute themselves for. The scum of the earth. Those beauties walking around in such luscious bodies and all they were doing was ruining that body.

He'd show them exactly what a ruined body could look like. And they would die horribly in that knowledge. He would show them how to ruin a body fast. They might take years to ruin themselves. But eventually they would ruin themselves, and he was only the executioner who took care of the job much more swiftly for them. He was only doing a service to the world.

But which section would he haunt? Just which type of girl would he pick up?

He smiled inwardly as he realized exactly what steps his progression would take. He would find those broads who lived with the dirty ones. He would find them hitchhiking on any street corner. Their bearded boyfriends would stand far back so that they would not be noticed. Their pretty girlfriends would stand on the curb and flag down some unsuspecting driver, and when he stopped and opened the door she would be joined by the character. And he would be in the car before a change of gears could be made, and the girl would be in the front seat beside the driver.

They were all out to lure the unsuspecting into some dangerous position. And he knew that all of them were that way. There was no hitchhiker in the city who was not out to trap a guy, or perhaps another woman. They would rob them and beat them and in many cases murder them and toss them out of the car. They would drive off with the car and be long gone before the murder was discovered. He would be their unsuspecting lure.

He attached his surgical knife to his wrist with the usual elastic bands, then buttoned down the tight cuff and slipped into his usual dark business suit jacket. Then once more he hummed his little tune and made the last minute adjustments to his clothing in front of the mirror. And he felt the thoughts, the anticipation taking over, and the sexual heats burned in his groin and he felt the sweat already starting to gather in the thin rubber panties.

He knew he was going to have one of the best explosions he'd ever had before that night was over. It was going to be a night to remember.

Harry Vincent walked out of the apartment complex to the spot reserved for his car. And as he paused on the driver's side he looked up at the moon. It was full and round and it seemed to be laughing at him. No, not laughing *AT* him... laughing *WITH* him. He liked that feeling. The moon was on his side. When the moon was full it was his friend and he could do no wrong. He was like the avenging angel.

There would be no scum left on the earth. And he would enjoy himself while he cleaned up the mess. Then he was in the car and it rolled down the hill and into the main stream of traffic. He knew exactly the street he would cruise... and he cruised for more than an hour.

Not one hitchhiking girl was in evidence. He did see a couple of long haired boys. But it was not the boys he was interested in that night. It had to be a girl... preferably a sweater girl where he could see how well she was built because of the bulge at the front. He could always tell what kind of legs they had because most of them wore miniskirts. His girl would have to have beautiful legs as well as a pretty face and she must have titties which could honor a sweater.

Then the city streets were far behind him. It was a country road. He hadn't really realized until that moment that he had left the city. But there he was far out in the country, and he knew it was far out because he realized suddenly the area he was in. He'd been there many times. However, since he was already out there he figured he might just as well search a bit further. Sometimes these pretty young things were stranded along the road. He might find one before returning to town. He'd never taken on two in one evening. But that might be a different, better kind of thrill. He'd get one out there on the highway… the almost deserted highway… then return to town and complete his first plan.

It wasn't going to work that way. The motor of his car began making popping sounds, then loud explosions and suddenly, the whole radiator exploded in a cloud of steam and water. He would have been scalded badly if he had not had the window tightly closed on his side of the car. But there would be no more using that car that night.

There was only enough power to let it roll off to the side of the road.

He sat in the darkness for a long time cursing the elements which had taken him out of town… and the elements which would keep him from getting his own satisfaction that night… and cursing the fact that some dirty tramp would probably live to take her crap out on somebody else when he could have put such a clear end to it.

But the cursing had to stop. He knew he had to get back into town. He closed and locked the car, for whatever good that would do. If somebody wanted in they were going to get in… the tramps. Then he started walking back along the dark, deserted highway. He walked a long time and couldn't help but remember how he hadn't wanted to walk at all that night. But there he was walking… and it was cold… and he almost didn't hear the automobile as it pulled up behind him.

"Lift?" asked the sweet, musical voice.

He spun around, and after he got out of the headlights he saw her. She was luscious. More than he had hoped for. She was wearing a tight red angora sweater and a matching red miniskirt. She was beautiful and she was blonde. No good girl would stop for a man on the side of the road like that. She had to be one of those kind. And the old car she was driving certainly proved she was one of the tramps…. Not a high-class one or she would have been able to afford a much better car than that.

"Sure," he said and tried for a smile, but all that came out was a slobbering tear. He would get into the right-hand side of the car and he would wait a mile or two, then he would have a coughing fit and she would have to stop the car so that he could choke up whatever he feigned that he had to choke up.

It was an excellent plan and his rubber panties would not be denied after all. They would be filled with his own satisfaction and another one of those bitch-tramps would be sent to hell where she belonged.

It was such a good plan, only as he bent over to get into the right side, the heel of the girl's hand hit him just below the chin. It crushed his Adam's apple, and he fell back to the road. He thrashed and he clawed and he struck out and he kicked and he screamed each time her knife plunged into him…

"Road tramp. Road tramp…. Always out to take a girl… die… die… die…" It was the last thing he heard as the big black overtook his senses.

THE END

GORE IN THE ALLEY

by "Shirlee Lane"

in Horror Sex Tales *insert of* The Jumbo Book-Pendulum *1972 on Ed's resume 1971 (very similar to "Filth Is The Name For A Tramp")*

SHE WALKED!

She tried to walk silently, without her heels clicking on the cement alleyway. But the red, high-heeled shiny, plastic shoes sent echoing tattoos in the rhythm of her steps…. But then again, did she really care?

Abraham Lincoln Way with all its bright lights and topless, bottom-less bars and theatres showing skin-flicks was to the left and half a mile behind her. Carry Nation Street, another with bright lights, topless, bot-tomless bars and stag movie theatres was just to the right and ahead of her.

Her eyes looked to that vantage point which could not be seen at a distance because of the tall warehouse building, which appeared to be seen in miniature, blocked the entrance.

She really could care less!

The night had been bad!

Tricks! Johns! Clients! Only a few bums on Abraham Lincoln Way. Bums who certainly couldn't pay her price. She could always tell which pussy searcher had bread enough in his pouch. Knowing the score was no great distinction for a girl like Sandra who had been walking the streets just over two years…. If she couldn't figure the guy with a buck, she couldn't have stayed in business as long as she had. And it wasn't some-thing which could be learned overnight.

But there were nights like this. Abraham Lincoln Way was simply a *dead* issue. Sandra's thoughts drifted toward Carry Nation Street where there might be some action. The sweat around her pubic hairs melted into the crotch of her nylon panties, and even though there wasn't the slightest chill in the air, the dripping body juices felt cool... even more cool as they drained over the four-inch, razor sharp blade she had strapped to the inside of her right thigh.

She hated that alley. Every time she entered it she wanted to throw up. But the forces of evil were there... all around her... the forces of horror, the unknown in the ebony infinity a terror which excited her to the very marrow of her bones. But it wasn't quite the horror or the terror she attempted to make herself believe. Instead the horror and the terror manifested itself into a tingle of excitement which twisted her reasoning.

But then the panic overtook her. The dead of the night silence greeted her ears. The silence was so thick she could feel it... actually feel the flabby bulk of it.

She stopped dead in her tracks. Then she made a slow, complete turn. Nothing!

Nothing but the silence and the heavy air which seemed to threaten her very existence. She tried to stop breathing, but was unsuccessful because of nature's demands upon that life-giving process. She could remember that even when she was in a swimming pool, or the river or even the ocean she couldn't go under. She never could hold her breath. She'd go under the surface and pop right back up again. She simply wasn't one for holding her breath.

The soundless terror stalked her.

She did another slow turn. There was one dark spot... between two buildings which caught her attention. But why that particular portion of the area caught her senses she didn't know. There had been no movement. There was no human shape there. Just a blackness that appeared a bit more deep than all the others around her. Her eyes became fascinated upon it... and her mind drifted back to another time... another alley... another warehouse district... all of which seemed so long ago... but it really hadn't been that long ago... only a little more than two years... but it had been a terrifying experience.

The man she had picked up that night was tall and ruggedly handsome. In the beginning he had been tender and kind and he met her asking price without faltering. She had never received under thirty-five dollars a trick since she had started in the business. He was to give her seventy-five dollars for one half hour of her time... and he would furnish the room.

Only it wasn't a room.

It was the back seat of his car and he didn't even bother to take off his trousers. He only unzipped his fly. But she had to take off her skirt and panties and toss them to the right front seat.

There was no harm in that. She had been in the back seat of automobiles many times before… especially in high school when she had first learned of sex. Lots of the guys never took their trousers off. But most of them insisted that at least she remove her panties and pull up the skirt.

There was little difference in taking both the panties and the skirt off. Besides, the guy was paying her seventy-five bucks… for… a trip around the world… a trip along the delights of the female frame.

The warehouse district they had parked in was little different than the alley in which she now stood. A bit colder because of the time of year. But the heated affair in the back seat warmed her up. She actually liked the guy. He had the most educated tongue and fingers she had ever come across… up to that time. She cooed and sobbed… she had never sobbed before… but she had sobbed that time, and she clung to his neck as if it might fly away from his own shoulders.

Then it was all over. She lounged back on the seat, her left leg still flung over the top of the front seats. She had often done that when she was thoroughly satisfied. And the guy got up, opened the backdoor, zipped up his fly, then with the strongest arm she had ever felt, pulled her up from the seat and threw her to the alley floor, then sped off in the car.

Her skirt and panties went with him. She was nude to the waist… her cardigan sweater was completely opened down the front… she wore no brassiere. There was no crying over spilled milk. Others on the street, in her profession, had told her always collect your money in advance. She had not done so that time and she stood in the cold alley, her sweater opened down the front.

With shaking hands she had buttoned the sweater up to her neck and attempted to pull it down over her thighs and naked pubic region… a short knit mini dress. She wished she had a belt to keep the bottom in place. Perhaps she could find some length of discarded rope in the alley. She would look. But she wouldn't look for long.

The figure had dashed out of the shadows and she was felled to the filthy alley floor and she was taken with all the syphilitic gusto the scabby faced man could throw to her. And when her sweater was pushed up around her neck, his scarred hands took her breasts with the violence of a clawing cat.

She didn't pass out from the violence... but the maggot smelling breath brought on the delights of unconsciousness from which she didn't recover until the first signs of dawn crept over the eastern end of the alley.

She was bruised, cut and her box felt as if a steamroller had entered it and left it flat and raw... then there was the taxi driver who was kind enough to trust her until she could pay him when he left her off at her apartment... and then there was the treatment for the syphilis which had been transferred to her... and there were the endless weeks she dared not work... and the torture to her body when the next few men took her... until she was healed again.

Then there were the alleys... and there was the alley in which she now stood and there was that one dark space... a dark space which once more seemed to threaten her very existence.

She couldn't see him!

But she knew he was there!

It wouldn't be the same one who had taken her so long ago. But it would be another just like him. And he would smell of maggots and he would be full of syph or clap. And she would take him. And she would enjoy taking him with all her heart. She would give him everything she had, and then she would lash out to give him more.

But there was no movement. Only the dark spot and the shadows that didn't move... and there was the soundless stir. The expectancy of something... yet a something that did not emerge the way it should. Even the distant automobile motors from both Abraham Lincoln Way and Carry Nation Street ceased to exist in that vacuum.

There was no prowling cat... no scavenging mice. All alleys had cats and mice and even sometimes a stray dog. But the alley held nothing that gave any semblance of life. It was as if she had entered her grave and pulled the dirt and the silence in over her.

But she was not dead!

The one part of sanity she still possessed was her sight. She could see. Her eyes became as sharp as those of a cat. She could see into the very darkness... but she could not see the darker, human shadow which should be lurking there in the black of the building corner.

"You're in there," she ventured through strained vocal cords. But the sound traveling across the ether waves was only greeted by the silence and the slight echo of her ringing tones.

She could be wrong!

She had never been wrong before!

She had been in many alleys since that time two years before and she had never been wrong. They were always there lurking in the shadows… always lurking, ready to spring on their prey the moment they felt the prey was completely unsuspecting. The shadows themselves could creep over one, enfold one, suffocate one like a shroud. They were always there lurking in the ebony of an everlasting, foreboding, nothingness.

"Why don't you come and take me? Is it because I have my panties on this time?" She lifted her skirt, but made sure the blade on the inside of her thigh was hidden from any view. Then in one swift movement she pulled her panties down and stepped out of them. She wed these down into the "V" between her tight little breasts. They would remain there, held by the tight pink angora sweater she wore.

"See…" she suddenly screamed. Then she pulled her pink skirt up high around her waist. "See! There is nothing to protect it now. It's wide open and my juicy pink thing is winking at you. It's all yours for the taking." Then she was hoarse from the sudden violence she had commanded of her voice and she stood out of breath from the forced use of stored up air in her lungs.

However, again there was no sound from the deep shadows where she knew terror lurked. She squinted… she frowned. Then disgustedly she let her skirt drop back into place. She took the panties from the "V" between her breasts and slipped them on over her legs again. Once more she lifted her skirt so as to adjust the panties then let it drop into place again. The shadows were as deep and as silent as they had been since she first looked to them.

She was not to score!

Slowly she turned and moved forward… ever so slowly she moved forward. And then she didn't care how much noise her clicking heels made on the cement… she liked the rhythmic clicking… she fell in love with it. The shadows were broken by the sounds… and the end of the alley was in sight… not more than a quarter of a mile ahead of her. Then there would be the bright lights of Carry Nation Street and the John's who could pay her price and it would be tender hands which would remove the pink panties the next time. It would not be her hands as she faced some unknown horror in the forbidding shadows.

She shivered in that delightful thought!

A tender man with his hands running all over her body… his lips and his tongue moving over the nipples of her breasts… she had had some who would take an entire breast into their mouth and still be able to lick the nipple with his tongue. And there would be the hands all over the rest of her body... probing... pulling... sucking... tickling... and there would be that final insertion which would send her to Heaven, but recall her once more just before the gates closed behind her. And she would return to earth and the bed and the man so that she could repeat the motion again whenever she wanted....

And she felt the hot breath on the back of her neck. There still was no sound... no sound of a second set of footsteps behind the clicking of her red high-heeled shoes. But there was the hot breath and it stabbed through the sweat which had suddenly appeared on the back of her neck which originated from the roots of her hair.

She didn't turn!

There was no need to turn!

And she hadn't been wrong. There was that even darker *human* bulk in the ebony shadow of the building. And that *human* shadow had detached itself. And that *human* shadow was right behind her... creeping ever forward... always forward for the attack.

She wished she had left her panties off. The moisture was cold as it soaked again into the nylon crotch and remained there. Soon all the pubic hairs would be as soaked as if she had been swimming, or taking a bath, or taking a shower.... It would be wet, moist and inviting. She knew how it would be taken care of... where the relief would come from...

And the hot breath grew nearer... and there was the smell of cheap wine as all the others had produced... All the others who lurked in alleyways and in those dark corners of the warehouse districts. Maggots... always maggots.

He stunk and she hated him!

But she would take him!

It was the only way she could be completely satisfied and she could continue on to Carry Nation Street and a comfortable bed and a sweet smelling man with his pockets full of cash.

And she knew what the shadow creep held in his hands. They, like the fellow in the back seat, never took off their trousers... they only pulled open the buttons or unzipped the fly and held it in their hands... all stiff and throbbing... they would hold it erect and pointed like an arrow and they would always smash her to the filth of the alley floor... they waddled in filth and they wanted to take their prey in filth... and they would hold it in their hands and when they had torn her panties off they would drive that shaft home.

But that's what they wanted to do!

Sandra was more quick!

As she had always done before, she snapped forward and the four-inch blade came free into her hand and in the same instant she spun around and what the creep from the shadows was holding in his hand came off from his lower quarters and was held like a bleeding, dead worm in his hand. But that was all he was permitted to see. Sandra's hand and blade left that lower portion of the anatomy and shot upward and once more in a trained slice, the throat was cut from ear to ear.

She didn't bother to wait for the creature of the darkness to fall. She turned and slowly walked away… down the alley toward the renewed sounds of Carry Nation Street… and when she reached the warehouse at the mouth of the alley she bent low to the street and picked up a discarded cloth with which she wiped the blade clean and once more attached it to the rubber band around her leg.

The blade secured on the inside of her right thigh again she leaned against the warehouse wall and breathed lightly. It was such a delightful evening. And only a few more steps and she could find that delightful man who would sponsor her to a clean bed and a clean sexual affair.

But her eyes looked back along the dark alley!

She smiled broadly!

It was still such a long time until daylight!

Her footsteps turned and once more she entered into the blackness of the alley. Perhaps there was another client lurking somewhere in those dark shadows.

Another client for her special brand of thrills!

THE END

THE HAZARDS OF THE GAME

by "Dick Trent"

in Garter Girls *vol.6 no.1, Feb./Mar. 1972 on Ed's resume 1971*

GEORGIA NEARLY CUT Pete's nose off when she snapped her garter. She didn't have any panties on… in fact, she didn't have anything on except her high, sheer black nylons and the frilly pink garter belt. They had made the scene three times that night and the sun was already sending grey-red flares through the partially open window across the room. There was just barely enough pink light to see the stack of Pete's clothes which had been tossed into a corner earlier… like around midnight. Georgia's sweater, miniskirt and brassiere were, however, neatly draped across a white fur covered chair. The sweater was white angora and seemed to melt into the fur of the chair. She loved fur. It was a thing with her. She wore anything of fur whenever possible, even angora and fur skirts. Her fur mules were beside the bed awaiting her dainty feet… feet which had been washed clean by the ardent caresses and tongue licking they had received so many times during the foreplay action of the night.

Pete's hand flew up swiftly to capture and rub his injured, smarting nose at the same time he was jerking away. "Now that was a hell of a thing to do," he moaned, "after I've given you so many thrills tonight."

Georgia giggled. "Thought I'd give you a thrill back, honey love."

"Sadist!" He rolled his feet off the edge of the bed and they sunk deep into the white fur rug. The soft strands felt good between his toes. He gave the nose one more tweek, then stood up, looked toward the coming sunrise and stretched broadly, and yawned deep and long. His wilted ego hung limp, worn, useless between his legs. Useless except to urinate which he did a moment later when he entered the bathroom. And upon completing that business he started the shower.

"Bet the damned thing will swell up like a balloon," he yelled at Georgia over the roar of the shower and the flush of the toilet water.

"So tell anybody it is the wounds of battle," she called just as loudly.

A few minutes later Pete came out of the bathroom wearing her blue terry cloth robe, open down the front. Georgia made no notice of it. He'd worn it many times before, any time he came by and they laid up and he took a shower.

"Who's on the spot today?"

He cocked his eye at her while he lit up a cigarette, inhaled deeply and then let the smoke drift up around his head, heading for the ceiling.

"What's it to you?"

"Oh, I kind of get a morbid curiosity about the people you kill."

"That ain't a nice word… kill. I get a contract and the contract says take care of them. It's a business. The victim is like a commodity. Somebody's got something I want… and they got somebody they don't want. So I get what I want and they get rid of somebody they don't want around."

"I didn't ask for the operation, doctor."

"Honey… you're a great lay but you're also too damned nosey. Like all those somebodies that nobody wants… they got nosey… so they get into bad trouble… like from which there ain't no turning back."

"I like being nosey. I learn things that way."

"I bet you do, honey." He poured a shot of whiskey from the nearly empty bottle and slugged it down. "How long we been layin' up together, Georgia?"

"A long time."

"How long?"

"Six, eight months."

"Exactly?"

"Seven and a half months and that's as close as I can come to the exact time."

"That's close enough."

"You getting tired of me?"

"I could never get tired of you."

She rolled her luscious naked body off the bed and slipped into her fur mules. She crossed to him and closed her arms around his middle from the back. "That's nice to hear." She let her right hand slowly move down the length of his body until she had his soft dork closed in her dainty fist. "I like that very much."

Pete grinned. "Me... or it?"

She grinned behind his back and snuggled her cheek deep into the back of his neck. "It's all a part of you, honey lover."

"Well, it ain't going to be workable for a long time. You damned near wore it out."

"You're the one that kept coming after me.... You took me like I was going out of style."

"You're just a hot little tomato. Ain't you never satisfied, Georgia?"

"Not since I was six years old. Maybe before that. I was raped by a lawyer about that time you know."

"You told me."

"He hurt me bad that first time. But after that I got to like everything about doing it."

"I bet you'd of made a beautiful virgin." He laughed and poured the last shot of whiskey.

Georgia slapped him playfully on the rump then went back to the bed and sat on the edge of it. She indicated the bottle of whiskey. "There's another in the kitchen."

Pete downed the drink and threw the empty bottle in the trash can, then turned to a closet. He took down a black marabou trimmed negligee which he tossed to her. "Don't catch cold waiting for me," then he left the room as she started to slip into the negligee.

She was lying back on the bed which she had made up in his absence. It too was blanketed with a white fur coverlet into which her sexy body sunk neatly. "I missed you," she cooed as he started to pour another shot of whiskey.

"In five minutes?" He tipped the glass in her direction. "Want one?"

"Not now." She closed her eyes dreamily and a light, contented smile crossed her features. "I just want to lie back here, in this beautiful soft fur and think about last night... dream about it... relive the whole time."

"You're a crazy broad."

"I hope so. I'd hate to think I was sane and do the things I like to do."

"You're also a nymph."

"Which is only right when you figure I like being a nymph."

"Crazy broad!"

"Who are you sending out of this world today?"

"I didn't say anybody was on a contract."

"I know when you get a contract."

"How do you know? True, you always seem to, but how do you really tell?"

"Last night."

"All we did is screw last night… among other things that is."

"You get twice as hot when you've got your work on your mind. It's like you're trying to forget the whole thing and you're taking it out on my pussy."

"Do I hurt you?"

"Some… but I like it any way you do it, honey lover. You got what it takes to turn a broad on and keep her motor going all year around." She sighed. "Too bad neither of us are the marrying kind."

"Yeah! I can just see us getting married and settling down and having a flock of kids…. What do you do for a living, daddy…? I kill people, young son or daughter… that's what I do, and I make a lot of money, that's why you can go to all these fine private schools…. And soon I'll teach you my business." He looked to her with a cocked eye. "That way I could save a lot of money. They could quit school early and learn my trade." He laughed heartily and Georgia joined him.

"You know, Pete. I bet you could have made a lot of money being a comedian."

"But I wouldn't have as much fun as I do now."

"You really like killing, don't you?"

"It ain't the killing so much. It's the thrill of the hunt and the chase. That's the part that gets me. When I get my quarry right down on its heels and I'm all sweaty all over and I know it's been a long chase… only sometimes it ain't so long a chase. Sometimes the victim is right there in front of me. But they all have the same look in their eyes when they know they're heading into eternity the hard, painful way."

"Now who's the sadist'?"

"I suppose I gotta be… in a way. But I don't just go around hurting people. It's got to be on the job. There has to be a reason. Then I don't mind it… and I guess I do get sort of a kick out of it."

"Don't get me wrong, Pete. But I don't think I could kill anybody for any reason. 'Course I've got nothing against you and your… business… but for myself. I'm glad I'm just a panty and brassiere model." She let her hand sweep the interior of the room. "I live pretty well."

"You always have, Georgia… ever since I've known you, you have."

"Modeling pays good. I might even go into figure modeling one of these days… you know… nude and all that."

"Get into the pornographic films. That would be really in your line. Maybe you'd get all the screwing you could use."

"And all the clap and syph I could use, too."

"The hazards of the game, dear girl, the hazards of the game. I got them in my business too. Remember there's a cop's bullet which already has my name written on it... Or maybe one of my unsatisfied clients might wait up for me one night. It's all in the game. The hazards of the game. But that's all the thrill too... keeping those hazards from your doorstep."

"You know, Pete. Sometimes when you talk, you sound just like a writer. Did you ever think about yourself being a writer someday when you're too old to keep on with your business?"

"I'll never live to be that old. And there is no quitting in this business. But maybe I'll put down some notes one of these days. Only I can't put one word in front of another when I got a pencil in my hands."

"Try a typewriter."

"Type? Ha. I couldn't even finish the seventh grade in school. It's just lucky there are still some big paying jobs for grade school dropouts."

"You shouldn't always be building yourself down."

Pete took another drink then walked across the fur rug and sat down on the bed beside her. He put his hand on the inside of her thighs and she moved her hand over to take his limp worm.

"Do... do... you ever get sexually excited when you kill someone, Pete?"

"You mean like get a rod on? Yeah... sometimes when something turns me on. Like when it's a beautiful doll in front of my sights and she's got something sexy on. I don't like to kill dolls when they ain't got no clothes on. But when they're sexy dressed. Yeah, old Jacob rises up in the undershorts."

"That's when you always come back to me."

"That's when I've always come back to you."

"And I take care of you."

"And you've always taken care of me."

"I love you for saying that."

"I wish I could say more."

"You don't have to." She squeezed his dork and felt it growing in her hand. "You're getting ready for something," she giggled.

"Yes. I am getting ready for something." He took her in his arms and kissed her a hot tongue licking, then quickly he lifted the black, marabou trimmed nightie up around her neck. He took a longtime in kissing each of her nipples and Georgia moaned in ecstasy all the time. Then he lowered the nightie, pulling it down around her ankles.

"Aren't you… going to… to do me?"

"I need a drink."

"I could give you another kind of drink."

"I know, baby. I know. But I got terrible things on my mind right now." He got up and crossed to the stand with the bottle and glass on it. He dropped down three quick shots.

"You must have. I've never seen you go at the booze so fast before."

"Sometimes, in this life, you've got to do things you don't like to do."

"You don't like your contract?"

"Not very much."

"Then why go through with it."

"In my business you've got to go through with it. It's part of our creed. No contract is too big or too small, and there is never the point of turning a contract down. It is offered and you accept. You just don't turn any down."

"I didn't know that."

"I suppose there's a lot of things you don't know about."

"I suppose."

"It's just too bad there isn't time to teach you so much more."

"I'm young, honey lover." She started to play with herself.

And because she was playing with herself she didn't notice Pete take the pistol with the silencer from the pocket of his coat jacket which hung over the back of the chair. He aimed it at her head. "You sure must have made somebody awfully angry at you, Georgia…"

Her terrified eyes saw the gun and his hardened penis all at the same time…. "Me… no… Pete… For God sake not me… not me…."

Then he fired three times and she died with all three bullets in her forehead and her eyes wide open… staring. Then he lowered the gun and looked to his hardened muscle. "Damn," he said. "I wonder where I can go to be taken care of now?"

THE END

THE HOOKER

by "Ann Gora"

in Pussy Willow *Vol.4 no.2 Aug./Sept. 1972 on Ed's resume*

SHE WAS WEARING A THICK red cardigan sweater, buttoned down the front and it lay neatly over blue slacks which melted over the tops of red high healed shoes. It wasn't the most inventive outfit for a hooker... even as young and lovely a one as Shirley... But it was all she had... all she had until she could raise the ten dollars for her room rent... so she could pay for the room and have the landlord unplug the keyhole. She didn't have much, but all she did have was in that shabby hotel room... a place she never thought she'd ever have to live in.

Could it have only been three months since she left the comfort of her home in Tall Pine, Wyoming and ventured into the wilds of Hollywood? It seemed like an eternity. She couldn't see how it was she had failed. She was beautiful and she felt she had real talent... the movies should have gobbled her up like a Monroe or a Russell. But all she had ever gotten was the cold shoulder or the promise of something if she'd strip down and visit a casting couch with some cheap producer or assistant director.

She had been a virgin and she wanted that status until she found Mr. Right Guy.

Naturally, even before leaving Wyoming she had heard how tough it was in Hollywood. She'd even met a few girls going through the state who were returning to their own home towns after the big failure in Hollywood. But they were other girls... they were not her. After all, they probably didn't have the talent she had. There had to be something wrong with them otherwise they would not have failed. She was different... she knew that... and she couldn't possibly fail.

But when she did, she couldn't face the fact of returning to Tall Pine in that capacity. How she had bragged. And how they would laugh at her… all the gang she had hung out with in those beautiful early days of her life… how they would laugh… and even if they didn't do it to her face she knew they would be laughing and talking behind her back. She knew she couldn't face up to that.

Nor did she feel she could call to her own parents for money. They would insist she come back home. They would send her bus fare, perhaps even plane fare, but they would not send her money to keep her in a place where she couldn't earn her own living. They loved her and they would worry.

"What do I do?" She had pleaded with the landlord that morning. "What do I do? I can't sleep in the park!"

"And you can't sleep here either…. not without paying for it."

"Even if I did get some kind of job it would be a week or two before I could get paid… where would I stay?"

"There's ways of getting quick dough… a cute little broad like you… broad with a set of tits and an ass like you got. You won't have no trouble gettin' quick dough."

"How dare you talk to me like that!"

"Bitch honey, I can talk to you any way I please… I got the door key… remember. Now if you was real sweet, you'd come into my place and let me unbutton your sweater and I could put my tongue right down inside your sweet smellin' brassiere…."

She slapped his face and fled through the double glass doors and entered the sun drenched, but chilly street… not a very likeable street… but one she could afford… a couple of weeks ago.

There were very few people on the street that time of day… but those, especially the men, who passed her couldn't help but turn their heads. She wore a brassiere which made definite separations of her breasts and the red sweater featured them with exotic overtones… the buttons went directly up the middle and sunk deeply between each of the breasts. It was like accentuating the positive.

Even through the chill she felt nervous, sweat gathering in the crotch of her pink nylon panties… at first warm but then as cold as the chilly air itself. She let her hand run down the front of the thin blue material of her slacks… and her hand felt good there. Actually, she didn't know she was making that kind of a move until a young leather jacket character made his snide remark in passing.

"I could do better for you than the hand, bitchie." Then he stopped a few steps from her and turned directly to face her as if waiting for her answer. She didn't bother to look back, but she did realize what her hand was doing.

But then it was almost as if it was too late. She was a virgin, but she had played with herself to erotic climaxes at times when she was alone or nervous. The nervousness which had prodded her on the street had caused the simple reactions. Her legs began to shake and she wished she could go someplace where she could finish what she knew she had to do.

It was a gas station with a private, locked door. The attendant gave her the key and she went into the ladies' john where she secured the inside bolt as well as the knob lock, then lowered the pants and sat down on the toilet seat. She didn't bother to take off her panties but she lined the crotch with toilet paper… and slowly started the revolving motion on the outside of the material.

She didn't have to work long. The fires of her body heats welled up and spurted toward her brain. Then all the problems, for the moment, left her and she saw nothing but the pink clouds of ecstasy. Her finger crept through the leg of the panties and she entered herself until the explosive completion rocked her body and sent her up to meet the pink cloud.

Shirley settled back then. She was still faced with her problems but they didn't seem that important any longer. The landlord had told her what she must do. But she couldn't think of doing it… not the first time… with some smelly old man like he was. There must be some younger guys with some money she could latch onto. She'd met a lot of girls in the past three months who had gone into such an affair when they got into her problem. They had told her what to do… what the approach was…

"Men," she muttered nearly aloud. "How I hate them. They run the world. I am forced to lay with them just in order to eat. I'll lay with them but I'll hate every one of them that takes me. I'll hate every one of them that walks the face of the earth."

She got up from the toilet and adjusted the blue pants, took off the locks and after giving the attendant back the keys she started off for the street. She unbuttoned her cardigan down to the third button which was about two inches below her breast line, and the breasts through the swelling brassiere threatened to pop out of either side. She made sure that the inside mounds could easily be detected by anyone who wanted to look.

She swayed her hips. She narrowed her eyes. She curled up the edge of her lips in the enticing smile she believed would be the best come-on.

Sundown faded toward night and the street became more popular for the pedestrians, she wouldn't have known another hooker if she had seen one… but she surmised the occupation to be connected to every young girl she passed… and none too few gave her the eye which confirmed her suspicions… and they were not all friendly eye treatments… many of them were looks of anger. She couldn't have known how much another hooker hates the new ones who are infringing upon their territory.

But Shirley was young… she had so much to learn. Perhaps one day she would not be so trusting of her fellow man… but at that point she really didn't know much better.

"How much?"

He wasn't very tall, but was taller than Shirley, and he had a clean cut face under blonde hair. He looked like a good college kid and she wondered what such a clean-cut fellow was doing in such a lousy part of town. But then that wasn't any of her business.

She stopped and faced him. Her hands went to her hips as she had seen the whores do in the movies and she swelled her front out as far as her young boobies could be forced. It was far enough to bring both sides of the sweater further apart and expose more of the brassiere and the roundness of the breasts beneath.

"What did you say?" She made an attempt at being coy. It was a very weak cry of the young.

The man approached her and let his hand run up and down the wool covering her arm. The touch sent bits of electricity through her body… the electricity of anticipation. She certainly hadn't wanted some old bastard… and it looked like she wasn't going to be saddled with one after all. This guy was real cool… she could feel herself snuggling up to him… kissing him as she had learned to kiss the boys back to school… after the kissing and the petting she wasn't sure what the feeling would be… but she did know what would happen… she wasn't that dumb.

"How much?"

The question startled her as much as anything else she was doing. She'd never given much thought about the price. What was a good price for her body… the first time it had been used?

"Ten dollars." It was the only thing which jumped into her mind. It was the price of unlocking the room. It didn't put food in her mouth…

but at least that door would open and she could get a good night's sleep…
out of the cold…when the time came… later.

"You look pretty new at this."

"I've been around." She tried for the hardened tones of the movie
whore. It wasn't working.

The blonde guy smiled. "I like 'em young."

"I'm young."

"How young?"

"Young enough."

"I don't want to get mixed up with any jail bait."

She knew what that word meant. "I'm nineteen."

"Just a ripe age."

"I guess I'm ripe all over."

"You bet you are. My place or yours?"

She didn't have to think that over. "Yours… if you don't mind."

"Locked out, huh?"

She couldn't figure out how he knew that. "Well… no… not that. I
just don't like to have people know where I live. I go there for sleeping."

"I get it. Okay. I got a place just a couple of blocks from here. I even
have a bottle in the room. Not the best place in the world. But they don't
ask too many questions. Let's go." He folded her arm through his and they
started off down the street. He patted her hand with his free one. "Makes
us look more legitimate this way… holding arms."

Then they were in the lobby of the sleazy hotel. A sleepy-looking
clerk did no more than briefly look up, then went back to snoozing. There
was no elevator and they mounted the steps for the two-flight climb. The
blonde man opened a door halfway down the hall and they entered. He
closed the door behind them.

"Take your clothes off and I'll get us a drink." He moved toward a
blanket hidden shelf.

Shirley walked to a mussed-up bed unbuttoning the rest of her
sweater on the move. She slipped out of it and carefully placed it over the
back of a faded easy chair. Then her slacks came off and took their place
neatly over the sweater. She turned to face him wearing only the pink
panties and the sheer pink brassiere which no longer did anything to hide
her breasts.

The blonde handed her a drink, then reached over and felt her
breasts. "Nice… very nice. Now let' see what the rest of you looks like."

Shirley put the drink on the nightstand. She really didn't want any of it. She never found a taste for booze. She would only go along with drinking it because it was part of the play she was acting in.

Slowly, sexily she thought, she slipped out of the brassiere and her lovely boobies stood out firm and young and ripe. Then her hands slipped down into the elastic top of her panties and she slowly lowered them and then stepped out of them. She put them and the brassiere with the sweater and slacks.

She turned to face him.

"You've got a dream of a body, young lady."

"I'm glad you like it. But there's something I've got to tell you before we get started."

"Why don't you let me do all the talking. Lay down on the bed and stretch out… stretch those luscious legs wide like you really mean what you're doing."

Shirley cautiously lay back on the bed, and stretched her legs wide apart. She had never had a man but she knew what they wanted and she felt she knew enough to give them what they wanted. "Aren't you going to undress?"

"Like I said, little lady, let me do the talking. I guess I'm in charge here." He took the money from his pocket and handed it to her. "I think payment in advance is customary."

She didn't know if it was or not, but she took the money and reached over to lay it on the chair with the slacks and the red sweater. "Yes… yes, thank you." Then she rolled over on the bed and spread her legs again as she looked up into the big gold badge the man held in his hand.

"I guess you know what this means?"

"But… but… I'm a virgin." She couldn't think of anything else to say at the moment.

"Well now," he said. "I guess everybody starts out in life that way. Put the money in your brassiere when you get dressed… I see the pants have no pocket… Get dressed, we'll be going downtown."

Shirley had fainted just after she was placed in the cell. But she couldn't have been out long. When she came around she felt the cool cloth soaked in water rubbing her head. The woman was much older than she, but she had a kind face and her hand with the cloth was rubbing her head…

"No need to talk," she said. "They told me all about you… and a virgin at that. Now ain't that just like men. You can't trust them no how, no way. They're all a bunch of tramps.

"They take a sweet thing like you and make you a street mess... and here you are ending up in the clink like this. Oh, don't worry, you'll be out of here in a few minutes, I've seen to that. Oh, how I like virgins... how very much I like virgins. I could eat you up one side and down the other, honey. No sir, I'm going to show you a life that you never dreamed of... and there won't be any men in it to mess you up no more... you just trust me and everything is going to be sky blue and roses pink...."

"Who are you?"

"Right now, the Mother Superior." Her hand went up under the buttoned cardigan and Shirley knew the woman was doing what men liked to do... feel her naked breasts... the hand dipped into the top of her brassiere... Shirley felt no resentment at the touch... it was rather warm... tender... her nipples hardened and her legs began to twitch and the moisture dampened the crotch of her panties again... she was feeling that demand for her kind of satisfaction... Her hand went down the front of the blue slacks, but the old butch stopped the movement.

"I'll do all of that kind of thing for you from now on you, little dearie," she said...

THE END

BUMS RUSH TERROR

by "Ann Gora"

In "Horror Sex Tales" The Jumbo Book 1972 on Ed's resume 1971

HE HATED EVERY STONE OF IT... every brick. He hated every car and every bus and truck which passed him on the street. He hated the buildings, tall, short, or caved in. But most of all he hated the people. He hated their unfriendly spirit. He hated the unanswered greetings he'd given on any morning. He hated the way the women ran from him at those friendly greetings when the sun sank low into the ocean and the dark shades of night began to fall. He hated the sounds of his own footsteps against the pavement and most of all he hated the unpaved sump of a street where his shack rested near the railroad tracks.

During the hottest day of the season he could only feel the cold of winter chilling his bones. A friendless, young derelict in an even unfriendlier city... he was worth no more than a grain of sand on a massive beach. He was lost to the infinity of the multitudes. If he met someone on the street and by chance they saw him, it was doubtful if they could remember his features after they had passed ten steps beyond.

For a time perhaps the passer-by might remember the odor which rushed up from that unwashed body, but that would pass and that would be about as much recognition he could ever receive from his fellow man.

He didn't give a good god-damn.

Or did he?

The streets kept him walking, walking all the time. The night found him in any doorway. A few times he found a crate large enough to hold him and he had the comfort of some construction over his head and a mass of newspapers surrounding his body. That had continued until he found an old abandoned tool shed down by the railroad yard. Nobody ever went there, and nobody ever bothered him. He took over the shack and it was his fort… his private world… and if anybody tried to put him out of it he knew he could protect it as well as any other animal protecting its cave.

Somewhere along the line, perhaps when he was hitching freights across the country and had met some winos, he'd got to like the taste of wine. It was no trick for wine to capture a man's body and soul. And it was no trick for wine to hold that victim. But it could be a hell of a trick much of the time for the victim to capture the wine.

Wine cost money and there was no work for a guy like him to get the money. Some of the older and weaker derelicts lost their hard earned bottle when he either followed them or came upon them in some lonely alley. A quick backhand and the babbling old fool would lay whimpering in the filth of the alley, realizing that he had lost his prize and there was no regaining it from the stronger. The stronger always took from the weak. That was something he'd learned from his father. And another was… "if somebody has something and you want it… take it. But you'd better be damned sure you can take it before you try, because if you can't, you're going to get knocked on your ass." He was always sure when he moved in on some old piece of human crud.

Some of his luckier days he not only captured the bottle of wine, but he found some change… a nickel, a dime, even some-times a quarter mixed in with a few pennies… in an old geezer's pockets. He always searched through the pockets of those he felled. They weren't going to tell anybody. And besides he always knew that the bottle would be gone long before he fell into any tortured sleep. He would need more, and more and more until oblivion took him into the black folds.

Most of the older bums knew how to panhandle a few coins out of the luckless ones they met on the street. And when they had enough it was the bottle and always a lonely alley. The best place for them to be waylaid. And a few pennies from each one he found added up to always another bottle.

The bad nights!

The really cold nights and the rain swept ones.

They were the worst!

All the rats crawled into their holes on nights like that. The victims were few and far between on such nights. Sometimes he had to hunt for hours before he found a single slug, creeping through the trash cans, and most of them were as bad off as he was. They had nothing! They searched the trash cans hoping to find a discarded bottle which still had *just a few drops* left… something to tide them over and keep up their hopes that just around the corner there would be somebody who would take a dime or quarter's worth of pity on them.

But he showed none of them any pity.

It was always the back of the hand, and when the bum was on the ground he soon would be stripped. The pockets from their ragged clothing would be torn out and the lining, if there was any, would disappear from the material. Bums kept their wealth in strange places.

Which brought him one dusk in sight of Helen Broderick, the very lovely, very shapely, extremely sexy young social worker. Not the social worker type of old, but the new and modern girl in her tight fitting sweater and short mini skirt… and her boobies bounced brassiereless under the thin sweater… a sight which alone was enough to turn him on…. But there was more to the vision that evening. He watched from his concealment as she took a couple of bills .. . money… from her shoulder purse and hand them carefully to an elderly bum who immediately ran off toward the nearest bottle store… and the smiling girl continued on her way… and he followed… and he watched as she came upon another of her regulars… that bum was also given a couple of bills.

It was then he reasoned… the bums could come later. That lovely dish had a purse full of money… and she had to pass his place of concealment. There might be a double reward in such a capture.

His arm was snake-like as it lashed around the dark corner of the alley. There would be no sound from the girl as his strong inner arm would close off the windpipe. The girl fell easily to his pressure and her eyes closed while he dragged her deep into the alley and into a large packing crate… but he could not himself get into the box so once more he pulled her back to the alley and stood lust crazed looking down at the silent form.

His hands shook with the lust heat which raced through his body. He pulled the sweater up over her head and tossed it to the alley grime, then he tore off the skirt. His blood strained eyes gazed at the lovely breasts, the pink-white figure in the near darkness. His tongue flicked over his dry, cracking lips. Her perfume drifted heavily through the stench of his own body and the alley waste.

Then with one animal-like lunge, his hand darted forward and tore the crotch out of her panties. He shoved it into his mouth and began to chew the material as if it were a bit of chewing gum. The material of his fly tore apart easily and his stiffened member shot like an arrow into its target. Unconsciously, the girl's legs flew up around his back, and although she was still completely unconscious, her arms and the rest of her body responded to the tremendous, sex-crazed humping he gave her....

His hands clawed at her face drawing blood. He was a sex crazed beast taking his prey in the only way he knew how. And when his ejaculation matched her violent climax they moaned into each other's mouth....

If only the girl hadn't have come to at that moment she might have lived.... But she did come to, and she stared at the beast with wide, terrified eyes....

He had to slit her throat, then drift off into the darkness.... He'd neglected to take the purse.

But it was the changing point to his entire life pattern of prowling.

Later he stretched out on some papers in an alley box. His lips were parched for a taste of the sweet red and his throat constricted with each dry swallow. Then his furtive eyes began to snap like a mad dog all around him.

That's when the newspaper sub-heading hit him between the eyes. He'd never learned to read very well. But there were certain words he could make out and if he took each word slowly, he could make out what the story was all about.

"It seems there was this old lady," he thought slowly to himself as he put the words together and translated them into his thought waves. "And she's dead. Like she was seventy-seven or thereabouts, because nobody really knew her right age. And she was a bum all her life. A street bum just like me. And she went around in these old ragged dresses and sweaters that almost fell off her wrinkled old body. And she always collected safety pins whenever she could find them. Lots of the bums on the street saved the pins for her because they thought she was just nuts for safety pins. Well since all of the bums are nuts in one way or another and for one thing or another, they humored her and gave her pins.

"But that wasn't the whole story. The old bitch did have a room. A real room in a flop house. But one with a door and a key. Not that the key was any good, but she had a big padlock put on the outside and one on the inside. When she went out the outside one was locked tight and she pinned the key to her long-john underwear. And when she was on the inside the padlock was locked from the inside and she never answered the door for nobody. If somebody wanted to see her they had to wait until she came outside. That door was always locked.

"So some of the street creeps thought she had something real valuable in that room and one time when she was away they broke in and tore the place apart. Only there wasn't nothing in there they could find that they could even sell for a ten cent bottle of wine. But the other part that mattered is the old hag came in on them just when they were leaving and they beat hell out of her and she died without ever muttering a sound. Old bitch was deader'n hell, and that's the way they left her.

"Only thing they didn't know and nobody discovered it until she got to the morgue was she had more than the key pinned to her long-johns. The whole inside was lined, pinned with fifty and hundred dollar bills. The old bitch was worth more'n a hundred thousand dollars and all pinned to her stinking long-johns."

He could only whistle at how dumb the clucks were who searched the dump. "Crazy people don't keep locks on their door for nothing. Other people put locks on crazy people's doors, but they never do such things themselves. Maybe she was a little crazy, but she sure knew about money. Old bags like that. They got all that loot and don't know what to do with it. Just live in shit all their lives and don't use any of it."

He pondered over this and couldn't help but think that there must be more of those old hags around and bums too. She wasn't any one of a kind. There had been stories along the street and he'd heard them all the time he'd been around. But there were all kinds of stories, and they were as insane as the crazy minds who invented them. Old shit-heads with money like that. Whoever heard of such things. He'd laughed them off the same as any other listener had laughed them off.

But the paper said such things were no laughing matter. And more than a hundred thousand dollars was a damned serious matter. A matter he knew he was going to look into. There would be no more torn pockets. From that point on there was going to be a bunch of stripped corpses laying in the alleys. All bums... and who cared about the corpses' of bums?

One more bum, more or less, meant little to those who could afford a newspaper.

With each drunken stupor came the mania for the next kill and the certainty that somebody's skivvies were going to be lined with cash. Even the sole of a hole-infected shoe could keep a few hundred dollars. A heel, if the bills were folded right, could hold even more. The mania was upon him with all the force of a tropical storm.

But he was smart enough to know he must work in the shadows. He could never follow a victim from the point of conception to the point of attack. He had to plot his moves. He had to spot a victim, then watch him for perhaps days, then make the strike... those victims he didn't just happen upon. The victim who had panhandled a few coins for a bottle of wine and had retired to the solitude of the protecting alley… the protector of the dead.

Nobody cares about another dead street bum. And such a death is seldom investigated, they simply dropped dead from the alcohol and that's all there was to it and the John Doe's record would go on file and potter's field would have another John Doe and a number for the grave marker.

He had no plans to be one of those kind of John Does'. Of course he didn't carry any identification. But that's the way he wanted it… until he got the cash, then he'd have a name and every son-of-a-bitch in the world would know it and look up to it when it was spoken.

There were always bums on the street. He was never without another victim. They came like the locusts in the wheat fields, and he mowed them down like the exterminator with a flit gun. And still only pennies which went for wine. And always at night, when there were none left on the street there was his shack and the restless, ever-turning night until the first light of dawn when he knew once again the liquor stores were open and the bums would start to come out of their holes like rats from the cracks.

Those who had money lined the pavements outside of the iron bar covered liquor stores waiting until the hours of six a.m. when they would open. And the creeps who didn't have the necessary change stood with the others hoping that some friend would come along and they could share the bottle. Sharing of wine was almost an unheard of thing among the bums except when they were too stoned to know they were giving away some of their prize… a prize which many would die for.

But to him, with his killer instinct, there was only the shadows and the waiting. The waiting for the first head to come around the corner of the alley, and to listen to the flapping shoe soles as they plodded through the junk and the trash, and then his leap out of the shadows and another would fall in front of him.

But the flopping he heard that morning had another ring to it. He couldn't really figure it out. The steps were much slower and perhaps one foot dragged… there was a slushing sound as if something was dragging. Then there was the shadowed outline in front of him and the ragged edges of the coat which looked like fuzz with the morning sun behind the figure. It was another bum, and he was dragging a foot, and it seemed that one arm was held just above his belt line as if paralyzed. But in the other hand there was the unmistakable form of the wine jug… only one of the big ones… one of the half-gallon size. Even if this wasn't the one with the big cash it sure as   hell was one with a big prize anyway. He could suck away on that bottle half the afternoon.

The figure passed him and he grabbed the arm and pulled him around in preparation for the backhand, the death-dealing blow. But the hand stopped in midair, frozen, unable to continue in the move. The face had turned into the sunlight. But there was little which could be called a face. The disease, if it was a disease, had torn most of it down to the bone, and the puss and the sores which hung there were being eaten by the flies. The scabs oozed, the white flow mixed with the continued flow of rotten blood.

It was a death head… nearly a skull… a rotting skull.

He was staring into the face of death… he dropped dead on the spot. Then the figure laughed… the whinny of a horse, and continued on along the alley. And as he moved a fifty-dollar bill dribbled down through his pants leg and fell to the alley floor near the dead John Doe's left foot.

THE END

Blood Drains Easily

by "Dick Trent"

In Flesh & Fantasy *vol.5 no.1 Mar./Apr. 1971, not on Ed's resume, but it is his work.*

I LIKE TO KILL PEOPLE. I mean I really do. I like to say to them, "Go ahead and scream your bloody head off," and then stick it to them. I don't like any of them that take it like a man, so to speak. Those creeps that look at you and at the gun or the knife or the ax or whatever I use and just stand there wide-eyed and say nothing, just gulp a few times and gasp a couple more until I get so bored I just let them have it right across the Adam's apple. After I do that it's too late for them to do or say anything, or to scream or anything like that.

But then there came that night, just around springtime I see this punk dude all dressed up in velvet pants and a bright purple velvet coat and I know he's one of those fairy bastards and I figure by the look of a ring on his finger that he's good for a "C" note at least… and he is worth my trouble. So I wait in an alley and snatch him right around the neck and pulled him off the street and with one little twitch of my inner arm I could have snapped his neck right off. And he was fat enough I figured he would be spilling blood for a month.

But he's one of the real screaming kind. He screamed like a wounded maggot… and I found I was starting to get my jollies, so I figured I'd like to listen to him scream and holler more and more… and I put the pressure on him more and more, and I only give him little cuts through the velvet coat… just enough so that he feels it and he feels the expensive coat getting all wet and sticky and cold right there next to his skin. I guess I cut him a couple of dozen times. And it was right after I nearly sliced off one of his wrists that he says something which gets to me.

He tells me he is second in command of a syndicate and that they need a guy like me. A cold-blooded killer like me who likes to see blood running all over the place. Now I don't know why I believed the creep, but he is actually crying and begging and pulling wads of dough out of his coat pocket with the arm that I didn't do nothin' to yet. And he's tossing that money all around and there must have been a grand or more. I never did count it. But later I did pick it up and jammed it into my own pocket. And when I let him go he didn't bother to go running out into the well-lighted street. He takes my arm with his good one and stumbling all the way he leads me down the rest of the dark alley and we come to the back door of a funeral parlor.

It was a real funeral parlor alright. And he was like the owner of the place. Well now I know them creeps make a lot of dough but not the kind of cash he was tossing around like so much pocket change. So I guess I'd give him a listen.

About six guys took me right after I got into the room and they give me a working over to where I wished I had killed the son-of-a-bitch when I had the chance back there in the alley. I'd of gotten his dough anyway. After all, I go through all their pockets after I put them out of the world no matter how much blood I have to fight my way through. This velvet dressed creep would have been no different. I'd have gotten the money anyway. And I would have saved myself that friggin' beating. Now I like all the blood and the gore but I sure don't like no beating myself and I ain't about to be shedding no blood of my own… only somebody else's, that's the way I like it. I don't get no jollies off if it's my blood that's going all over the floor.

So right from the first when the guys grabbed me in front of that table where they cut up the stiffs and let their blood run down the gullies, I figure I'm going to get that faggot bastard and I'm going to cut his balls off and make him eat them before I slit his throat and take them out again and shove them up his ass. That was one creep that was going to give me the best jollies off I was ever going to have in all my life. I knew that right from the time they knocked me toward that table. And I knew it right from the minute I felt the first hit on the head and everything started to go black… and

I was positive of it when the third hit whacked me on the side of my right ear and my head landed on the stone floor. I was going to get that bastard and he was going to be cut up into little pieces and I was going to feed him to the pigs, if I could find some pigs to feed him to.

Only then the big black came and I guess I didn't think of nothing more for a long time. Nothing but them bright lights flashing in front of my closed eyes… now how could the lights flash in front of my eyes when they was closed? I guess I mean they was flashing in all them bright colors behind my closed eyes. I guess that's what I mean. Anyway, I saw them and every time they blinked I felt a hurt. And the more hurt I felt the more I knew I wasn't dead. I don't think I was thinking much then, but I thought about it a lot when I came to and I was all tied up in that chair. An electric chair at that. They was going to burn my ass off because of what I did to their boss. And I didn't have none of the money left. It was all stacked up on the bottom of a coffin. The lid of the bottom. The top was open and all that shiny satin looked like it was blinking at me too.

I put a lot of bastards in them things, but them creeps standing around me with their whips and their chains and the straps… I'll be damned if they was going to lock me up in one. I'd see them all rotting in hell without no balls before I'd let them do that.

Then they turned on the juice and I was bouncing around in that steel electric chair like a chicken head in hot grease. But they wasn't out to kill me. Not just then they wasn't. They were just having a good time with me. But that wasn't no good time I liked to be having myself. And I yelled at them asking what they wanted and they didn't never answer me. They just kept making the juice hotter and hotter until I sure did think that I was going to fry for sure. And I knew I felt weaker and weaker every time they turned the juice off and I sank back against the ropes and the straps that chained me into the chair. I just felt like I was a little pussy cat and I couldn't take on the big bull dog. And maybe for a while there I thought I might just as well give up and get it over with. At least I wouldn't have that friggin' buzz going through me no more. That's what I thought. But it wasn't long I felt that way.

I didn't feel that way no more when the creep in the velvet suit came back into the casket room. Yeah, there was a lot of coffins all around the place. They was all over the place with thick velvet and satin drapes hanging behind each one. I guess it was some kind of a casket showroom, or something like that. But there was that shithead. Only he wasn't no longer in the fancy purple velvet suit. I guess I messed that one up pretty good with the blood I took out of him.

But he didn't look nonetheless for the loss of the blood. He was just as fat as ever. But the wrist I cut up was all bandaged, and there was a bandage around his throat. I didn't remember trying to cut his throat. But then if I had tried there wouldn't have been any trying at all. His head would have been rolling in the alley and I wouldn't be sitting in the god-damned hot seat.

He wasn't going to get away with it. I had sworn he wasn't going to get away with tricking me when they was hitting me over the head. I knew what I would do to that bastard the minute I got out of that hot seat.

Then he was yakking at me. Calling me every kind of a bastard there was. Only he didn't know all the names I did. I could have double matched him word for word if I had had the chance. But every time he threw one of those shit-eatin' words at me, the good hand, I wish to hell I had cut it off, hit me a good one across the face and the guy across the room would throw the switch and the electricity hit me in the ass and I went up in the air as far as my bounds would let me. Then the switch was turned off and I slammed back into the hot seat and the bastard hit me again... and up I went again. And the son-of-a-bitch kept it up for maybe half an hour. Then I guess his hand got tired because he took up the strap and started in with that.

I could taste the salty flow of blood, blood mixed with sweat that came out of the cuts on my cheek and my forehead. The blood and the sweat was coming from other places too. It was easy to tell that because I could still see, and I was naked and I could see every place that they hit me. But they didn't bother my balls and the other thing. They all came just short of that. I figured the faggot wanted that for something else. Maybe he did. I don't know. But he didn't let the cat-o-nine-tails hit it, or the straps or finally the chains. Big heavy chains with rough edges that really cut me up.

He broke my left arm the first time he hit out with that goddamned chain. But I wasn't going to scream my bloody head off like I made the creeps do when I was out to kill them.

All I ever wanted to be when I came out of that reform school was a hired killer. I loved to kill and I figured as a hired killer I could get my jollies... have my fun and still get paid for it. That would have been the best life of all.

But sitting in that chair didn't change things. As long as I could feel I knew I was alive and there was still a chance I could answer my calling... the hired killer... and I knew I wasn't dead even when the big black kept coming up momentarily in front of my eyes, because I could feel the hurt, the pain, the searing flame of the beating I was taking.

But the black started lasting longer, and longer and I didn't like that very much. I didn't like the dark very much. I never did. I never did ever since my old lady put me in a closet for breaking Sally Kendelsmith's arm. The little bitch lived next to us and she was always shoving down her panties and pulling up her dress in front of me. And I knew what she wanted and I gave it to her and when I got my jollies off she started in that friggin' screamin' and I had to hit her. I didn't have to, I just wanted to. I took her arm and I twisted it until it was hanging only by the skin. That was one arm that wasn't never going to be fixed up ever. I still laugh about it whenever I think of what she might be now... pretty... maybe even with a hell of a nice body. But there she would be going down the street with that friggin' arm just hanging there by the skin. That's a good laugh.

But the friggin' old lady won't be laughin'. Nobody ever found her from where I put her when I got out of that dark closet. Nobody ever will. They don't never tear up bridge supports once the cement has hardened. Besides, it was miles away from where we had lived. Nobody would never have thought to look there no way. No way would they ever think about that. She just was a lush who walked off one day and never came back. The old man didn't give a good shit either. He was well rid of her. And he wanted to continue on with the whores anyway. He picked her up when she was a bitch whore and some way, I never did know how, she got him to go to a bastard preacher with her and they tied the knot and then they slept together sometimes, only they didn't do much sleepin'. It was all fighting, and the bottle and the screwing... and then he'd get out of bed and go off with another tramp.

But the bitch sure found out she wasn't going to lock me in no dark closet. She got just what I figured on giving her just as soon as I got out of that closet and could get to the kitchen and get the meat ax and the butcher knife. She found out just how sharp the old man had made it. And there was always a bunch of bags around the house.

She must be pretty hard in that cement by this time. But I sure never liked the dark. And I didn't like it none the last time that electric shock shot through me and I fell back into the black. It was so black and lasted a lot longer. I remember that much. I remember that I wondered how long it would be that I was going to have to stay in that black. I can't tell for sure but I knew I was walking. I thought I was walking because I felt myself getting more and more tired and my legs felt like they were going to fall off. But then there was the bright lights behind my eyes again and there were the shooting stars which exploded right where I could see them. I didn't see the shooting stars the last time when they had hit me over the head. But the shooting stars hurt even more than the bright lights had. I didn't want to stay in the dark and I didn't want that kind of shooting star to light the way because it hurt.

Then it was cold… so very cold on my back. I don't know if it was that cold or the cold water that they threw over me that brought me around. But I knew I was blinking my eyes and the shooting star dissolved into the bright light which was directly over me. They had strapped me down to that bloodletting table, and all I could hear was that they were going to cut me up. Now that was something I didn't like at all, and I'll be damned if they were going to do that to me.

The fairy in the velvet suit… no, he had taken that off. All he had on was black pants and a white doctor's coat… well, he was standing there over me and he had them little knives that doctors use. The sharp little ones and he had it near my right arm which was stretched and tied down along my side. And it was held there right tight like.

Some other time I might have laughed right in his face. Who could do any kind of a decent job with a little knife like that? Why that wouldn't even go half an inch into a guy's skin. You want to get at the real blood and gore you got to have a good dagger, a butcher knife, a hunting knife, a machete, that's what a good bloodletter needs. Then when he gets his victim that victim knows he's been a victim and then will they scream their heads off.

I stopped killing them with one swift stroke a long time ago. It didn't give them time to scream their bloody heads off. They get that one swift stroke from an expert like me and they're dead… all dead and crumpled up on the ground. They don't never get a chance to scream their bloody head off. You got to take them a little at a time. Oh, cut their throat a little if you want. That's only to keep the screaming down to a medium roar. But to really get your jollies you got to cut them up slow and watch the blood run out and all over the place… seep right into their clothes and get all sopped up like a sponge. That's when the real jolly sport sends you off to the toilet.

But that fat ass in the white coat. What in hell did he think he could accomplish with that dinky little knife of his?

Son-of-a-bitch cut me right along the main vein of my arm, right from my shoulder right down to where my hand starts. He let that whole vein wide open then went around to the other side and did the same thing.

Now that ain't a nice sight watching your blood going down that gully of the table. That ain't no nice sight at all. And to make matters worse, one of them other creeps that put me to sleep came up, and he's got a white coat on too, and he's got a hose and he lets the water run up and down my arm, like he's keeping it clean of all the blood. And one of the others, he's got a white coat on too and he's taking up another hose and he's going to do the same thing. Like they're helping wash the blood right out of me.

Now like I said over and over again, I like to watch the blood and the gore when it comes out of somebody else, but I don't like being hurt, and one of these days when I get out of this nightmare I'm going to see that I cut his balls off and let his blood run all over the floor while I make him eat the goddamned things, and like I said then I'm going to slit his throat and take them out and shove them up his ass. That's exactly what I am going to do.

Only I know that he's cut mine off.

It was all done very swiftly and I can feel the blood running out of that spot and down over my ass and onto the table where there is another indentation. And I know I ain't never going to get to be the hired killer I always wanted to be, and I know I ain't going to see no more blood and gore, only my own until I get too tired to stay awake.

But I can't understand why he wanted to cut my things off. Except that he's a fairy bastard and fairy bastards like them things that a guy's got between his legs....

And this guy likes them a lot. It's kind of crazy but every time my eyes clear for a minute I can see the jars and jars of them that are on the shelves, all labeled with names and dates and times....

They all stand there on the shelves like squatty little fat men standing row on row, like soldiers in formation... all sizes inside the fat little glass shapes, all sizes and shapes... all sizes and shapes... and the one empty glass on the end which a third white coated man has gone to get and brings back to the shithead of a fairy bastard... who stands over me... ready to cut.

Damn... it gets so dark so quick in a mortuary these afternoons...

THE END

A Taste For Blood

by Edw.D. Wood Jr.

in ORGY *Vol.5 no.1 Jan./Feb. On Ed's resume 1972*

Tom Duke played with her titties, then his hand went down into the soft "V" region where the soft pubic hairs sent renewed electrical charges into his fingers, electrical charges which traveled through the fingers, into his hand and shot up his arm and smashed against his brain.

He'd had the lovely, red haired girl six times during the past twenty-four hours, but he was ready for another ride in her saddle; she was that good.

And moments later she was moaning with sexual heats and her lower quarters appeared as if they were trying desperately to get away from him. But that was far from the truth. All her kicking around, all her ass and thigh movements were for one thing and one thing only… to give her more of a kick. Her moans were nearly all lost into his throat, but what he couldn't hear he felt deep down into his groin and his body heats were turned so high he thought that his juices might be cooked before they could be shot into her.

However, that didn't happen. And like all the six times before he shot a load that might have sent her through the mattress if it had not been so thick.

Then they rolled away and lay back.

Tom Duke rolled over a moment later and captured a cigarette from the night stand. He lit it and let the smoke curl into the air above him.

"You sure got experience, that's one thing I'll say for you."

"I know my business."

"I bet you do."

"I size up a *JOHN* almost the minute I meet him. I don't have to have any pictures drawn for me."

"How long have you been on the street?"

"I've never been a streetwalker."

"High class whore, huh?"

"I hate that word."

"No offense meant."

"I was a high priced call girl. Only I think this kind of work is going to pay better."

"You can bet on it."

"When do I start?"

"You already have."

"You mean by laying you I'm already initiated?"

"Something like that. If I like a broad, I'm man enough to go after her. So what if I break you in to the racket. And you were certainly one that I wasn't going to pass up. I'd have to be queer or dead to pass up a stunning chick like you, Shirley."

"Of course, things like that are always nice to hear. Tell me more."

He rolled over and with his free hand he touched, then began to massage one of her breasts. "Those are about the most beautiful mounds I've ever seen… ever touched."

"What kind of slobs have you been training anyway?" She grinned then reached over and took the cigarette from his mouth.

He let his hand drop from her breast and twirl in her pussy hairs.

"I like what you do with your hands," she said in changing the subject.

"I do it much better with my tongue."

She sighed. "I know. Lord, how I know."

"Don't tell me you're ready again."

"I never stop being ready. For this sort of thing, I'm insatiable."

"My clients will like to hear that. But in the meantime, lay back and rest. Want a drink?"

"I didn't like the Scotch you gave me last night, Tom honey."

"How about whiskey?"

"How about some gin?"

"How about whiskey?"

"I guess it's going to be whiskey… and coke?"

"And water." He walked into the bathroom and she heard him urinate into the toilet from a standing position, then the toilet flushed. A moment later she heard the gurgle of whiskey being poured from a bottle to a glass, then tap water being poured into it.

He returned from the bathroom and handed one of the glasses to her. "Saves me a trip to the kitchen."

"Hope that was tap water you put in there."

"Good lord."

She eyed the light through the amber liquid. "Who could tell in this golden mixture." Then she downed a good portion of her drink.

"One of these days I've got to meet the guy who sent you to me."

"My connections have long arms when it comes to locating what I want."

"After these last seven sessions, Shirley, I'm not sure if I want to put you into the business… in where you're going to get laid by any client I want to send you to."

"You'd like me all for yourself, huh?"

"Something like that."

"I doubt if you could afford me, baby."

"I wouldn't be too sure of that."

"I come very expensive."

"Money has never been anything for me to raise. I make a lot of money in the work I do."

"You make a lot of money, but it isn't enough to keep me in perfume and perfumed soap. I take three baths a day… and in very expensive perfume."

"How do you know the kind of money I make? How can you be sure it's not enough?"

"Oh, I know. I get around."

"Look, I won't be their pimp all of my life. I've got plans… big plans."

"Tell me about them… the big plans."

"I don't think I'd better do that."

"Think you can't trust me?"

"It's not that. It's just that in keeping something to yourself it can't get out… accidentally."

"But you told me right off what you wanted me for… "

"That's because you told me what you came for… and it was the kind of work you wanted to do."

"Tell me again what I have to do."

"It's all very simple. The syndicate has its little games also. First of all, if they don't want some guy around any longer he is set up with a pretty doll like you… and when the time is right, you slip the arsenic into his glass… or you set him up in a spot where the executioners can get at him. All very simple and straight to the point. A guy on the run is frightened of every guy he meets, but never of a pretty girl. Even if he is frightened of such a girl he's more than willing to take a chance that she's straight. A guy doesn't like to think a girl can put anything over on him. The big boys are very smart when it comes to such things."

"Yes, I guess they are pretty smart."

"Only maybe they're not smart enough."

"Oh!"

"Sometimes, the bigger they come, the harder they fall."

"Yes, I've heard that one all my life."

"And it's true. Everybody can't be smart all the time. Sometimes they got to let their guard down. It's all human nature." -

"I guess it is at that."

"Why in the world do you want to be a syndicate moll? You should be able to make a good living as a call girl or with one of the other operations."

"Not the kind of money I want, darling. And I like a taste of blood. Don't think that it's only your male executioners that can do a job and walk away from it and not vomit all over the place. There's plenty of girls who would like to be in my spot. There's a lot of girls who have plenty of violence in them and they can get it off by sticking a shiv into some guy… or watch him curl up in horror after he has swallowed a measure of arsenic."

He finished off his drink and Shirley did likewise, but they held their empty glasses in their hands reflectively. "You know, honey. Maybe I should retract my statement."

"Which one?" she grinned.

"About keeping you on permanent. Maybe you have too much violence in your heart. Maybe there would come the day, even when I'm rich, that you'd get tired of me and you'd get your kicks watching me curl up in agony and die."

She took the empty glass from his hand and started for the bathroom. "But that could be a long time off, darling. Think of all the fun we could have in the meantime."

Then they both laughed. Shirley handed him the whiskey and water when she returned. "Ready for another one?"

He indicated the glass. "This or the bed routine?"

"How about both?"

She put her glass down on the nightstand and watched as he gulped down the entire glass of whiskey and water. He looked across to her and her legs were spread wide. His member had stiffened and with an animal like sound he climbed on top of her and slowly began the rhythmic movement which would give them both a charge.

"It was Manny," she said behind closed eyes and her arms tightened like a vice around his back.

"It was Manny what?" he questioned, almost not realizing what she had said, or what he was saying.

"Manny sent me to you. It seems he didn't like the idea of his pimp-runner thinking about taking over his operation. He thought that perhaps you had fulfilled your contract to him and the organization. He felt you were getting too big for your boots and that perhaps you should be replaced. Sorry, lover."

At which point, just as his explosive climax came Tom knew what she meant and as the arsenic closed off his heartbeat, Shirley grabbed him with all her might, all her strength and she exploded and exploded and exploded...

"Ohh, what a way to go," she sighed sometime later when she rolled his dead body from her.

THE END

THE LAST VOID

(no author listed) on Ed's resume, 1971 from Ecstasy
vol.3 no.1 Mar./Apr. 1971

HE DIDN'T GIVE A DAMN. He just stepped off the curb and plunged, determinedly out into traffic. He defied every car on the road to hit him. He slammed his fist on a fender as it flashed by, then took a stab with his toe at a speeding tire which careened away from the maniac. The brakes squealed and the horns blared as frustrated drivers took to the defensive in protecting their property as well as trying to avoid hitting the miserable nut who demanded the street for himself.

Rickey Torius wasn't always such a maniac. In fact, he generally thought of himself as pretty damned stable and calm in any situation. But damned if he was going to be screwed by some dirty bitch whom he trusted all the way. Witches like that could make any man go off his rocker. But this one had cheated him beyond redemption… that made the whole affair even more frustrating.

Rickey had stepped into the Ten High Bar which was in his neighborhood. He didn't frequent the bars in that section very often because he preferred to spend his money in the uptown places where maybe he could do some good. Stay in the low-class dives and that's just about where you end up. But that night he was tired, he was in the area and he didn't have a bottle in his apartment. So he decided to lift a couple of quick ones, then sack out. An early night once and awhile does a hell of a lot of good for a guy's constitution. Makes him kind of bright eyed the next morning and ready to look the world right in the face, and go out and get things done.

Only Rickey didn't know it, but the Ten High Bar wasn't about to turn him loose very early. Instead, almost immediately upon entering the bar, the place furnished him with some delightful female company. He'd never met the broad before, but when he sat down on the bar stool this sexy dish moves up to him and plocks down on the stool beside him.

There wasn't a lot of conversation right off, but it was apparent she had eyed him for an easy touch for some quick booze. She didn't have to put on much pressure because Rickey always had his eye out for a pretty female, and this was one damned pretty female. She said to call her Lila, and that was all which was necessary to strike up the acquaintance. She liked her liquor strong and in double shots, but it didn't seem to bother her much. That pleased Rickey. He didn't mind a broad drinking it up lush style, but he liked to slap the ass of those who couldn't handle their whiskey. He'd met too many of the loud mouthed, filthy tongued characters and that night he wasn't in any mood for such nonsense.

Damned if she didn't turn out to be a smart broad too. She knew something about everything: Maybe she didn't know everything about everything, but she knew enough to keep up with any conversation that got started. Then too she didn't talk just to be talking or to hear herself talk. She spoke it like it was, then sat back and let somebody else get his two cents in. She listened with sparkling eyes… as blue as the short satin dress she wore. Her breasts popped out of the lowcut dress front almost to the nipples, and what he saw made him want to see more.

It wasn't long before the subject came up. What the hell did he have to lose. He'd never seen the broad before, and he'd probably never see her again, so why not make the pitch and get it over with?

Much of the tired feeling had left his body with the thoughts of making it with Lila… but if she turned him down, he was sure the tired muscles would return. It was just thinking about seeing the rest of that luscious, pink body which turned him on so hard. He crossed his legs under the bar to keep what was happening to him as much of a secret as possible… at least until he was sure which way she'd go. He prolonged the inevitable only through one more tall cocktail, then came directly to the point. He liked what he saw and wanted to take it home with him and unwrap the package.

She giggled at his approach, but there was no holding out on her part. She'd go with him. She had planned to all along, ever since he first came into the bar. Rickey was to learn quickly that was not all she had planned all along. She had a wicked, evil mind and all the cunning devices for using it to her own ends.

They stopped at a liquor store and got a bottle of good whiskey and some ice… Rickey's small refrigerator didn't have room for ice… then they walked the block and a half to his walk-up apartment. It was a dive of a building, but Rickey didn't keep his place in the rundown condition as most of the other tenants did. He prided himself on cleanliness… that went for the furniture as well as his own personal being. Lila marveled at such a place in such a destitute disaster area. The place even had a private bedroom… not one of those pulldown affairs. Rickey showed her that before he poured the drinks into sparkling clear hi-ball glasses.

They were in the middle of their second cocktail when she suddenly turned around and lifted her long hair so that his fingers could easily find the zipper. Rickey made quick work of the operation and when she lowered her arms, the dress simply slid down then and crumpled into her lap. She lifted up her fanny and pulled the dress free, and her panties came off with the dress.

"My God," thought Rickey. "She's a real, honest to love, redhead." A real redhead with blue eyes… something he didn't run across very often… but then he knew Lila was going to be spectacular in every way… that's why he took to her in the first place… her perfume drove him a little dizzy, but it was the expectation more than the scent. His manhood had risen to a great bulge in the front of his pants and he knew there was no way she could miss it. But she took a long time letting her hands rove tenderly over her own skin, mainly her breasts, before she reached over and unbuckled his belt, unzipped the front then kneeled down in front of him to pull the trousers free.

Damn if she wasn't an expert at everything she did. The way she had so swiftly slipped out of her dress… then the removing of his pants. It was like no effort at all was being displayed. It was like everything just came natural as the normal course of events. Then they had their first affair by candle light on Rickey's soft bed. It was all that he hoped for. But when it was over she offered to stay overnight… again, more than he hoped for. The overnight turned into a weekend and they continued uninterrupted, except for bouts with sleep which was simply to renew their energy.

Rickey didn't mind if she stayed on for a month. But there would come a time he'd have to go out and replenish the dwindling food supplies. And there was always the possibility his call service would have something for him. When his call service got the message he had to work fast. That was the nature of his business… working fast and sure. His kind of clients didn't wait. Most of them were much to anxious too have their particular job done quickly. Rickey was noted in his closed little world for being one of the fastest in that line of work. He'd never had a complaint. But he knew what it would be like if the answering service got a call for him and he couldn't be reached. He never gave anyone his apartment phone number. A few of the dishes had it because they took it when his back was turned, but he never gave it vocally. He'd bet right on the spot Lila had stashed it during the first couple of hours of her stay. But what the hell. None of the broads could hurt him. None of them knew the kind of business he was in, and it was none of their business. Somebody could be in a heap of real trouble if they tried prying too deeply in the things he didn't want known. They would only pry once, then they learned their lesson the hard way. Rickey especially didn't like doing things the hard way. He figured life was much too short and things should be handled swiftly and with as much ease as possible.

He didn't mind if Lila took the number. She didn't seem like the type who would ever become any trouble for him. Right from the beginning she'd played it straight down the line with him, and when a woman does that, he liked to put all his trust in her. She played a good game, that Lila. She played it to the hilt. She was smart, and she expounded words which told everyone just how smart she was. Every word meant something. Also, every word brought her closer to the truth in her situation.

Rickey Torius was no simple pick up. She didn't know where he lived, but she knew the neighborhood. She didn't know he didn't frequent the bars in that neighborhood very often either. But it was a chance. And after five nights in the Ten High Saloon her chance paid off with the entrance of her prey. She knew what he looked like. The only inquiry she had ever made in the bar about him was if he ever came by. The "occasionally" answer gave all the hope she needed. She'd simply wait him out. When she saw him she knew it was all in knowing who she wanted and how to go about getting him.

The rest of her plan… like getting him to buy the drinks… steam him up in his pants and the next part was easier than any of the others. She hadn't met any man who didn't want to take her to his place and see what goodies her panties held. Rickey Torius was no different than any of the others. She proved that quickly enough.

She hadn't been in any hurry in finding Rickey… she took her time, and in so doing she knew there was little chance of the fish leaving the bait.

It was the same way in remaining at his apartment the whole weekend, and considering the thought of staying perhaps longer. There was no real hurry. She had her quarry in the dock and he wasn't going anyplace.

But she couldn't know Rickey Torius didn't like to be trapped… shut in. At any time he felt such he broke out with a fury that no one better be standing in his way. It hadn't happened very many times in his young life, but when it did he only knew one law of survival. He made the play, and stayed on top. However, for a time, Rickey didn't realize that he'd been trapped by the woman. It had all been a simple meeting and a gracious friendship with the intervention of sexual relations between them to enhance the friendship.

Rickey started feeling the steel claws of the trap closing around him when she couldn't understand why he had to go out, why he couldn't simply call his answering service and take the message over the telephone. It would save so much time and they wouldn't have to be separated. Rickey, however, turned a deaf ear to her dialogue and continued dressing… and he might have continued had she not come right down to the point.

She knew all about him and his business. She knew why he had the call service instead of direct service. And she knew why he housed an assortment of pistols and rifles in the bedroom closet. Rickey had to give his full attention when such words began to spew out of her mouth. No one knew him. No one could connect his name with his business. He was simply a number at an answering service. Even the answering service didn't know his name. There was the monthly bill, always paid by money order and signed by the same number he'd been known as. The bill never varied from month to month, so the envelope, the money order… all was dropped into a corner mail box… seldom the same one. There was no way in the world of tracing him.

Lila had done it. She had connected his name and his business and that was bad business for him. Somewhere there had been a leak… that wasn't good. He knew he had to plug up that leak. But he had to hear her out first. Why in hell had she gone to so much trouble locating him? If it was for a job, all she had to do was call the answering service and leave a message. That number was always available. He knew she'd made a bad mistake no matter what she wanted in searching him out like she did. Lila had to go, but first, what in hell did she want?

Her demands were simple. She wanted him dead! And she had a small pistol in her purse which backed up her words.

Strange, that was exactly the way he wanted her. She couldn't go around breathing, knowing all she knew about him. But for the moment she had the upper hand. The gun may have been small... dainty, in her dainty hand, but it could spew mighty hard bullets. No one in the world knew more about what a bullet could do than Rickey Torius. He knew every caliber of bullet made, and he could tell exactly how much damage each could do. He was an expert in his field... he'd proved it over and over. He also wasn't going to let some blue-eyed broad put an end to such a lucrative career. He didn't actually know of anyone who could completely take his place. What a void would be left in the community if he were suddenly taken from it. The idea didn't suit his way of thinking at all, and he was going to do something about it. Now on the other hand, what kind of a void would the blue-eyed bitch make in the community? She was simply a piece that could be replaced from any saloon in the city... the whole world. A piece of fluff which could be blown away like some lesser zypher. Why in hell had she come into his otherwise peaceful life? He never hated anyone. He simply had a job to do, and he did it to the best of his ability. They were all strangers to him... just faces passing in the night... never to be seen again... and he was nothing more than a number to the interested clients.

Rickey Torius, the hired gun... the assassin for pay wasn't about to end his days seated on the foot of his bed, and certainly not by a little gun, held in the petite hands of a pretty bar squawk... who had been the daughter of a man some client wanted disposed of. Rickey had always been careful not to be seen when on one of his jobs. But on that particular case he was seen by the girl, then six years younger and a very young girl. The job had been done at night while the victim was reading by a nightlight near the swing in which he sat. It was one clear shot through the head, then he was off over the back fence like a shot. Who could have known a little girl was playing hide and seek on her father. The hedge had been a good cover for her... and her wide, big blue eyes saw everything... and her mind retained everything she saw.

Lila Sanders didn't have to go through any secret society to find out the man's phone number. She kept watching the faces around her and one day Rickey Torius walked in her direction. From there the rest was easy. His name. Approximately where he lived. And the only time his guard was down was when he was in the company of a pretty woman. Lila Sanders had grown up to be mean and vicious. She'd held the hatred of the man who killed her father so long, that it boiled hatred all through her for every man. She took them right up until she took Rickey Torius. She actually hoped the hatred would stop flowing in her veins when his heart stopped beating… but even after she had fired so many times, his heart didn't stop. He kept lunging at her, his strong fingers around her throat. Her heart stopped long before his, and she would take the hatred to her grave.

But Rickey Torius held to the life he cherished so deeply for a long, tortured few minutes. His massive frame, and twisted handsome features stumbled down the stairs and out into the traffic where he screamed and cursed every car… every human… he wanted only to destroy that which he would never see again. He was frightened of the void he was going to leave behind. Why he ran he didn't know. But he ran, and he pounded, and he cursed all women with real red hair and blue-eyes, and the blood drained steadily from his gut… spurting harder as he choked and cursed.

It was a big, black, shiny Cadillac which finished the job Lila's little gun couldn't accomplish. It tore into him from the left side and left him prone in the street where there had been somewhat of a void… waiting for him….

THE END

SUPER WHO?

by "Ann Gora"

from Fetish Annual *on Ed's resume dated 1972.*

SHE WORE AN EXTREMELY tight-fighting, short-sleeved green sweater and as equally a tight-fitting miniskirt of the same shade. Then there were the long, leg clinging panty hose which fitted tightly down into nearly knee high white boots. She carried a shoulder purse of white, very small and very dainty, and her walk was as graceful as an Angel... but she was no Angel.

Her face was well made up, the lips pouted in their deep redness, and her blue eyes were enhanced by the light blue makeup over the upper eyelids... the face of an Angel... but she was no Angel.

She hugged the corner of a building and her eyes darted to the left, down along the nearly deserted street to where an armored truck was parked in front of the loan office. One man stood guard while the other took out two sacks from the rear, then when the door was securely closed and locked again the first man joined the second and they moved into the loan office.

The girl kept up the vigil and her keen eyes watched carefully as a few moments later the two guards came out, got into the truck and drove off. Her eyes narrowed, and a slight smile crossed the red lips as she watched the truck amble past her and off into the distance.

Slowly she turned and made her way past the vacant lot which housed a single outside telephone booth, then continued on past several store fronts until she came to the front door of the loan company. She entered. The money bags were still visible on top of the manager's desk. It would seem that he was going over some receipts since he had not gotten to the money business at hand. He briefly looked up to the lovely girl who had entered the office, then his eyes went back to the papers in front of him, little realizing at that point that the money business would be promptly at hand.

A lovely young girl in a white angora minidress moved to the front counter. She smiled broadly. "Hello," she cooed, and was answered with the girl in green reaching into her shoulder purse and bringing out a small pistol... small but deadly... and it held a full six shots. The girl in the angora backed off, she didn't stop her movement until she stood beside the manager's desk. The manager looked up to the girl, then to the newcomer... he blinked... he started to raise his hands but quickly put them back on the desk as the girl in green indicated that that should be his movement.

Then there was another movement with the pistol... one which indicated that the girl in the angora dress should pick up the two sacks of money and bring them forward. This was done and there was a further movement with the pistol.

The manager and the girl in the angora dress were marched back to a windowless lavatory. They were locked inside and as further security the girl in green propped a chair up under the handle, then calmly walked back across the room, picked up the money bags, put them in a paper sack which she took from her purse and calmly left the premises.

Detective Lieutenant Art Reason propped his feet up on his shoe-scarred desk and sipped of some hot, black coffee and directed his words to Detective Rance Clanton.

"How many does that make?"

"Started last month with the candy store... then there was the office of the big cleaning establishment, followed with, in order, two retail stores, a grocery, small, the dime store and the latest the loan office yesterday. That was the biggest hall of all. Seven I make it..."

"And there's no doubt that the same dame did them all."

"Always a tight-fitting sweater and miniskirt. The color changes but the style never does. The only thing that never changes is the white boots and the white purse."

Reason put the coffee cup on the far side of the desk and lit up a cigarette. He let the smoke ring his head then drift off into nothingness. "I want that broad. I want her on our most wanted list."

"We got some harder customers around which rate that spot."

"Not the way I figure it."

"How's that?"

"She carries a gun. My guess is it's loaded. And sooner or later that loaded gun is going to go off and our thief will become a killer. Got me?"

The detective nodded in agreement. "She goes on the most wanted list."

"Put as any men on it as you need. Give me a map of the entire area around each of the victimized establishments… the stores around them, lots, possible escape routes, alleys, the works."

"You got it."

Then the telephone on Reason's desk rang. He swung his feet to the floor and captured the receiver in the hand which held the cigarette. He listened intently, then slammed up the receiver.

"Put *wanted for murder* on that poster."

Moments later the two detectives stood facing Mr. Dobbs and two young lady secretaries who were sobbing softly, their hysterical crying having subsided earlier. Back by the toilet area, lay the uncovered body of a third lady, much older, who lay face up on the floor, her body in the grotesque posture of sudden death… there was a small hole in the front of her once white blouse: directly over her left breast.

"She must have died instantly," remarked one of the uniformed police officers.

Reason nodded then went for a quick inspection of the body, then returned to Mr. Dobbs.

"I told the officers everything."

"So tell me again… I'm new here."

"She came in about fifteen minutes ago…"

Reason interrupted. "Just a minute." He turned to the uniformed officer who had spoken to him. "Get out there to the crowd and see if anybody saw this bitch running from here… Wait a minute." Again he turned to Mr. Dobbs.

"What was she wearing?"

"Tight pink sweater. White miniskirt, white boots and white purse. She had red hair."

He turned to the uniformed officer "See if anybody saw a dame of that description running from here. She undoubtedly would have been on the run… having just committed murder."

"Suspected of committing murder," corrected the officer.

"Yeah! Be sure to read her her rights when you grab her. Then come back here and read to that woman on the floor over there her rights."

Reason turned back to the manager. "Your window says you're a loan company."

"Yes, I'm Maxual Dobbs, the manager for the company. This is Miss Rice and Miss Featherstone." He blinked as he pointed to the body. "That was Miss Patterson, the bookkeeper. How often I've told employees… if we were ever held up, give them the money… just give them the money and no trouble… Miss Patterson didn't heed that warning. When the girl herded us back to the bathroom, I suppose to lock us in, Miss Patterson suddenly twisted around and tried to knock the gun from her hand. The person fired… and that was the result. How many times I've told them to just give over the money. The money isn't worth your life."

"The gun woman thinks so."

"But it was so all for nothing." He turned and indicated the single, but large, bank money sack on his desk…. "She didn't get away with the money. She seemed terrified when the gun went off. She just turned and sped out that door. Was… was it her first… first killing?"

Reason nodded, "It won't be her last. The first is always the hardest. Only next time, when the shooting becomes easier, she won't forget the money. And now that the gun has jumped in her hand for the first time she won't think twice about using it the next time… needed or not."

Lt. Reason was exhausted when Detective Clanton brought in the cartons of coffee and the lights had been turned on in his office to cut away some of the darkness which had fallen with the night. He was physically tired, and his brain was tired from going over the drawings and sketches that had been given him upon his return that afternoon.

He put his head in his hands as he looked up to his assistant… The man put down the coffee containers.

"See anything?"

"Something is bothering me, but it won't come to the front of my mind." He sipped of the coffee, then with a fresh cigarette, unlighted, he tapped on several drawings… "Every one of those places was about in the middle of the block. The stores next to them… all the way down the block on both sides are tight together… a cigarette paper couldn't pass between them… the same on the other side of the street. *But* again… and it's a large *but*… there is also a vacant lot about a block away in each case… then comes the *BUT* again… all the lots are backed up with buildings that are as close as those on the front of the street, and no way of scaling them."

"Which puts us at a dead end. The broad just melted off into the street people. Like the two witnesses that think they did see her... she came running out of the loan office and they didn't pay any more attention, and when the manager, Mr. Dobbs staggered out of the place, still shook up, and screamed for help, the broad had completely disappeared."

Reason looked back to the drawings. "They said she was running toward the west, huh?"

"Yes."

"Toward the vacant lot." His eyes suddenly lit up and he threw the unlighted cigarette to the desk. "By God, I think I've got something." He quickly reached for his phone and pushed the inter-office numbers.

The Angel which was no Angel had more of a sinister glint to her eyes as she ambled along the street. It was a bit busier than she would have liked. But there was no turning back. She had never turned back once her mind was made up to pull a job. After all, she had a foolproof plan... and she had killed. If anybody ever got in her way again she'd kill. They could only hang her once... hell, they didn't even do that anymore... another killing... what would be the difference? She even gave vent to the thought that she might do it once and awhile just for the hell of it... to keep the thrill alive... to keep her hand in practice.

The manager of the loan office himself greeted her as she entered. He glanced up and down the tight fitting white sweater and miniskirt. The white boots shined as if they had been polished. And there was that luscious smile on her face, even as she pulled the gun.

The manager had a right to smile because he was Lt. Reason and Detective Clanton who had been waiting outside came up behind her. In one quick move he had clamped his big fist around the dainty wrist and the gun clattered to the floor... Reason reached over and pulled the red wig from the young fellow's head.

"The purse was only big enough for that small pistol and the shopping bag. But anybody carries a shopping bag... perhaps not full of money and a wig... but it was a good gag... he had me going for a while. But those vacant lots had to be the key. Then I figured out that there was an outside telephone booth on each one of them. That's why I made the phone call at the office. I had every officer on the beat and in patrol cars look into every phone booth on every vacant lot. The one down the street held this guy's change of costume… men's clothes. All he had to do was make the telephone booth, slip on trousers over the tight skirt… a sweatshirt over the sweater, take off the wig… cold cream his face and he was on his way… a young fellow carrying a shopping bag… Bet he tells us he stood outside the victim's establishments even while the investigation was going on… but he isn't having the last laugh… is he?"

"The telephone booth," said Clanton… "just like Superman."

THE END

FLORENCE OF ARABIA

from An Illustrated Study of Voyeurism *Vol.2 No.3 Nov.Dec. 1971, credited to Edw. D. Wood, Jr.*

JOHNNY TORRANCE LOOKED at himself, naked in the mirror. He held his dick in his hand and watched it just lay there. He was handsome. He was rugged of build and stood nearly six feet. But he was lacking in the most important part of his physical make-up. He simply couldn't get an erection in the usual way. He could masturbate till the cows came home and the erection would elude him. He couldn't even make an ejaculation with the thing in its soft state. Under no circumstances could he work the thing up for the satisfaction his body cried for.

No way, except one and that was… it had to be a few minutes after he had seen some exciting happening. Some exciting sex scene.

This was not to mean the he could go to one of the sex movies and be stimulated, nor did it mean he could go to a swingers' society and watch the act and be stimulated. Johnny Torrance was a voyeur…. a peeping Tom. He had to spy on the sex act, on the girl undressing when she or they did not know he was watching. They had to be completely ignorant of his presence, otherwise he remained as cold as ice and physically unsatisfied.

It was a tough life on the poor fellow. More and more people were keeping their shades down. He even rented an apartment on the fifteenth floor of a very tall building, and purchased a telescope. The window in his bedroom had a commanding view of many miles of the city, and the tall buildings some distance away. He could set up his telescope and peer into any window he chose and never be caught. But the windows where anything interesting happened were few and far between.

Since his strange sex life commanded every moving, every waking hour of his life he wished he had stayed in the smaller towns. At least there he could go out and prowl the streets and there people still left their window shades up at night. He could search out a likely house and soon he would know if anything would be happening. It usually did in the small towns.

In the smaller towns there was much less outside entertainment for people. Therefore, they made up their own entertainment. The entertainment where the stage was the bedroom and the props were the bed… sometimes the chair… sometimes the floor. But there was always something going on.

Perhaps the first or second, or the third house didn't prove fruitful, but he always knew he didn't have to go very far until there would be another house, and about nine in the evening something would be happening.

Dinner would be finished and there would be that lack of entertainment, and the boredom would set in as it does in most small towns and the sex scenes would start. How many fools there still are in the world would leave their shades up.

Johnny Torrance would hop the fence and conceal himself in the brush very near the window, and he would unzip his trousers and lay his cock out in his hand. He would take the handkerchief from his pocket later, but that was only to clean off. He liked to orgasm in his hand, and he always timed his ejaculation to the exact instant with the man and the woman. He was watching their orgasm. He could tell just as if he were mounting the woman instead of the other man.

Sometimes, through some noise or other, he was nearly caught. At such times he couldn't masturbate there on the spot and he would have to carry the memory of what he had seen off with him. Sometimes, if the window wasn't too far away, he could make it all the way back to his apartment. But at other times he had to find some secluded spot where the memory could be replanted to his mind's eye, then he would masturbate… a sign board, another house, a yard, behind a barn.

But the one scene was only good for the one time of masturbation. The same scene replayed a second time did him no good, therefore he was always on the prowl every night, looking for a new scene of action. Of course he could return to the same house, the same window to find another show going on and that was alright. It was a new show. It was not a replay. After all, the same actors appear in many pictures and one goes to see them in the new role. Few want to see them in the same picture time and time again. But a new presentation is an entirely new entity. He didn't mind that at all.

He'd never been caught!

But as he grew into his thirties he knew the small towns would be the place he'd be caught if he were to be caught. And there are just so many places he could voyeur in the small town.

He moved quickly, on a Saturday, to the big city. He didn't take the apartment on the fifteenth floor right away. First there was a small place. He had to look around. The big city held many apartment buildings. But all the bottom floor apartments were like second stories. There was always that sheer wall up to the first set of windows. It was no good for his problem. And he couldn't go out into the suburbs every night. It took much too long by bus and he had never learned to drive a car. That however was high on the list of his things he must learn to do.

An apartment higher than all the others was the only thing to do. Thus, the fifteenth floor apartment.

His problem was still not solved.

He had a clear view of the city and the other apartments and the windows. But they were all too far away. Strain as he might his eyes could not make out the slightest figure in the windows. There were many many windows and all lighted at night, and most of them looked like they kept their shades up, but he could get no charge if he couldn't see the action. Imagining the action was no good. That would be like seeing a movie. He had to see the actual people in the act, then his imagination could take over and he could satisfy himself.

A telescope! A very powerful sea-going, Mars-sighting telescope was the answer. It had to be the answer.

On the first night he sighted in on no less than four dozen windows and people were watching television. But he realized that they would soon retire, so he watched one window steady for three hours, until the set was turned off and a light came on in the bedroom.

"Hell's fire," he screamed in anger as he realized the man was going to sleep and the woman was about to join him… in sleep.

The same scene happened night after night for another two weeks. The big city certainly wasn't like the small town. The people in the big city had other modes of entertainment than the sex scene.

"But somebody behind all those windows must be doing it. How in hell do they propagate the race around here? They are always telling in the papers that the big city birthrates are higher than anywhere else in the world. Then how in hell do they make babies if they sit in front of their televisions all night?"

Johnny Torrance was undoubtedly the most frustrated man in the world, and that proved over into his work. He was fired from six very good jobs in as many weeks. And after the last one he decided to go on unemployment for the length of the run, or at least until the frustration left his soul alone.

Then the night vigils started in earnest... all night visual vigils on any lighted window. He was quick to learn how many people stayed up all night watching their television sets. He swore he would never own one... especially after seeing the kind of shows they were presenting. And since he couldn't hear the sound they appeared even worse.

Then there was another night when he decided to change his point of view. He had not looked out of the living room windows. There wasn't as much of a view in that direction and all the places were much further away, but after all he did have a powerful telescope and if the thing could register spots on Mars then it certainly would register the full scene of people doing things in the privacy of their apartments.

He turned out all the lights in the living room and made sure there was no light behind him which could silhouette his frame, and then settled down in a huge easy chair as he faced a great set of double door windows.

There were no lights. Not as many as on the other side of his building. But there were lights and there were shades up. But again, there were also television sets, and the booze guzzling, beer swilling people. Perhaps more so because he was looking downtown where the people were not as well off as on the uptown side of the building.

He lowered the telescope downwards toward the streets and the alleys on an off chance that somebody might be making it in the back seat of an automobile... or even an alley. He knew that winos often made out in alleys with their battered up broads. And he knew that kids often made it in the back seats of cars on side streets.

But even there he drew a blank.

The telescope leveled itself on the roof tops. It was hot... the middle of the summer. Surely some of the roof tops would present some unsuspecting subjects. He had heard talk about people doing it that way when the weather was hot and the heat chased them out of their bedrooms.

It was simply another blank.

"Son of a bitch!" he screamed at the top of his lungs. He wanted to pound his head against the wall. He tried to masturbate from memory again. But the limp organ simply lay in the palm of his hand like a dying worm or snake... and was just about as useless to him. "I've got to have some release," he screamed. "Somebody has got to do something that is going to help me before I go completely stark raving mad. I've got to have a release. I've got to have a release."

He went back to the telescope and scanned the whole area again... the alley... the cars... the roof tops. It was as if he were watching the repeat showing of a bland, but horrifying movie. And then there were the rows of windows again... the beer and the booze, and the frowzy housewives who went to bed with their horrible flannel robes on. "In the heat of the summer don't they ever take those steaming, stinking things off?" and he was screaming once more, but not taking his eyes from the telescope.

It was a fact that he wasn't going to see anything on that side of the house. At least the other side held many more windows, and he hadn't looked into the alleys and the cars there. The idea had only entered his mind the moment he did it. So he picked up the giant telescope and lugged it back into the bedroom where he made sure it was steady. Once more he focused downward to the alleys and the cars. There were much fewer alleys there and certainly fewer cars parked on the street of the residential section.

If he cursed at the other roof tops he outdid himself with these because many held outdoor swimming pools on the roof tops, and patios, and sunning chairs and couches, yet not one was in use. It was like a wind had come up and blown every living human off the parapets. There was nothing to see but the moon glowing on the pool waters.

He sighed. "I might just as well give up. I'm never going to see anything here. I'd better move on. Maybe to another section of town." Then he leaned on the window and far across the void he saw a light come on and there was a dark shadow behind a shade. He dove for the telescope, and in focusing it in he saw the definite silhouette of a girl behind a thin set of shades. Then the shades went up.

The girl had long blonde hair. She was wearing a tight sweater and a short skirt. He couldn't see below her knees because of the window sill. But he could clearly see the titties stretching the wool of the sweater to nearly a splitting point. And her face was one of the most beautiful he'd ever seen. Then she moved out of eyesight and he cursed her, but kept his eyes glued through the telescope. Then after he got done cursing her, he began to pray.

The only thing he could see in the room was a large, full length mirror and an enormous poster advertising the motion picture *Lawrence of Arabia*. He thought it strange, but then he knew movie buffs have strange mementos of their favorite films. That was probably her story. He wondered what her name was. Then he prayed some more…

His prayers were answered.

The girl returned into his vision. She stood for a long time admiring herself in front of the mirror. She turned first this way, then that, then she moved to the giant poster and kissed the picture of Lawrence. "So that was it, she's got a hang up for the poster," Johnny mumbled to himself, but he also unzipped his pants and put the limp dork in the palm of his hand. He was positive this night he was going to get his rocks off. That girl in the pretty sweater and skirt wasn't going to let him down. And moments later he could feel the dong hardening in the palm of his hand.

The girl slipped the sweater up over her head and neatly laid it across the back of a chair near the mirror. He could see her brassiere covered front on the mirror side and her lovely smooth back on his side. Then she reached backward and unzipped the skirt. It fell to her ankles. She wore no slip under the mini skirt and her pink panties came through very clearly to Johnny Torrance. The thrill was almost too much for him. He had waited so long. He knew the sacs behind his dork was as full as they had ever been. He knew the release was liable to blow him right into eternity… at least out of the chair. He grinned in delight as the girl's hand went up and down the back of the sheer nylon panties.

"Honey… honey, get with it. Take 'em off… Take 'em off. I'm going out of my mind." He masturbated harder and harder and his dong grew stiffer and started to throb in those pre-explosion stages.

Then the girl's hand went down into the front of the panties which he could see on the mirror side, and the hands played there. Johnny Torrance knew exactly what those hands were touching, and he could almost see their hair through the nylons, but the powerful telescope was not powerful enough to see through cloth, sheer or not, at that distance.

And the next moment she had reached up and un-snapped the back of the brassiere… but she didn't let it fall off her shoulders… Instead she took her hands from the front of the panties and viewed herself sexily in the mirror again… then Johnny Torrance was about to shoot his load. Over and over it throbbed, then suddenly went completely dead as he saw the girl pull a dork out through the leg of the panties… a dong as big as his own, and sacks that were just as full as his.

The man in the girl's clothes masturbated wildly… Johnny Torrance moaned… he couldn't finish… Then he jumped out of the fifteenth story window.

THE END

So Soon To Be an Angel

no author listed

in Garter Girls *Vol.5 no.2 June/July 1971 on Ed's resume 1971*

ANGEL FLOATED ACROSS the stage like an angel. And very soon she would be an angel. She didn't want to be an angel. At that time, in her twenty-second year, she would have believed she was too young to think about being an angel. Twenty-two was much too young to die. But she was going to die and she didn't know it. She hadn't even given it a thought. All she thought of was the tinny music, a beat to which her feet found a certain rhythm. She hated that cruddy music. She felt her legs were designed for dancing to better orchestrations… orchestrations, hell, that bunch didn't even have sheet music… They blew right off the top of their heads. Sometimes it sounded like they had taken the tops off their heads with the blow.

Angel's biggest problem was that it wouldn't matter what kind of music she had. She danced like she had two left feet… or right ones, as the case might be, and from whatever direction one might be looking. But on the ad boards outside of the bar it said in bold red letters, Angel's Fire Dance. So the unsuspecting patrons expected a dancer. Good, bad or indifferent, there was going to be a dancer.

What did stand up in Angel's favor was the beauty of her face and the elegance of her exquisite body. This of course took much of the curse away from what her well-turned ankles promoted across the age-scarred stage. The one time she did look good was when she tripped daintily across the stage in the finale with her sheer white veil floating out behind her entirely naked body. That's when no one was watching her feet. Only the pure grace of a tremendous body... of firm upturned mounds pointing straight ahead toward the wings... caught the attention of all. And Angel never returned for bows. When the dance was finished she was done until the next performance an hour and a half later. That was specified in her contract. The customers paid their cover charge to see her dance. They were not paying to see her bow and scrape in appreciation. Angel figured all the appreciation should be on the customer's side of the fence, after all, it was she who was giving her all. They should appreciate that fact.

"Get me a double Scotch, Perry," she snapped at her faggot masseur almost before she slammed the dressing room door behind her and certainly before she plocked herself down on a white fur-covered divan across the small room.

"You know you shouldn't drink that rot gut, Miss Angel. It's bad for your waistline." But he was flitting toward the door, knowing what her retort would be.

She reached over to grab up a heavy leather pillow, and threw it in his general direction. "Get the hell out of here and do what you're told, you

fairy bastard." Then she leaned her blonde head back into a pink fur-covered pillow and closed her eyes, letting the back of her left hand shade the light from her eyelids. "They're all against me," she mumbled. "Every one of them. It's me that pays their salary, keeps them in business... keeps this joint open, and all I get is lip. I'll quit this racket one of these days and see where that puts them. This scab joint will float down the river with the rest of the crap, and that faggot and all the others will be on the unemployment line... that's where they'll be." Then without opening her eyes she reached over and picked up another leather pillow which went in the direction of the other, only a little more to the left where it knocked over a tall vase full of roses which crashed to the floor. The noise didn't even disturb her. Her paranoia held her full attention... only the thoughts in her mind... outside elements didn't bother her.

Perry returned with the double shot of Scotch and crossed directly to her. She had heard the door close and her simple movement was to reach out with her right hand and capture the glass. She drank heavily from the contents. The liquor burned all the way down and she spluttered. "This damned stuff gets more rotten every time they pop the cork."

"What did you do, wash your undies in it, Percy?"

"Perry," he corrected as he moved to the wardrobe hanger and selected a white feathered dress for the opening of her next performance. "I've been with you more than a year now. That's long enough to know it… my name is Perry, not Percy…."

"Percy… Perry… Mary… Helen… it's all the same to me. All of you are the same to me. Your kind as well as the kind that sit out in front of that stage ogling at me all night and swilling their cheap liquor at a buck and a half a throw, plus cover charge. You're all a bunch of creeps. They should build a happy farm with a rubber room as big as the whole United States and put the entire population of males into it, then lock up and throw the key away." She finished off the drink and threw the empty glass across the room. There was never any way to tell when she might throw things.

Perry took the feather-covered white dress from the wardrobe hanger and shook it out. "I've selected the white feather dress for your next entrance. I didn't think you'd want anything too tight the way you're feeling."

She snapped up to a sitting position on the edge of the couch. "Then you wear it! Take it behind the curtains, put it on, and do what you do when I'm not around. Give me the tight red satin with the sequins. I feel like hell tonight so I might just as well dress in the devil's own colors." She stomped to her feet and reached behind her to tear the trailing, sheer white material from the choker around her neck. She let it fall to a soft heap at her feet and she was naked to Perry's eyes, but the little man could care less.

"Your belly button needs powdering," he remarked as he replaced the feathered dress and took down a red satin creation.

Angel stomped to the dressing table and pulled off a long-handled powder brush which she slapped into Perry's free hand. "Then powder it. That's what you're here for. Stop your faggot screaming and do these things."

Perry put the red dress on a clothes tree where it could easily be reached when the time came, then went about powdering the girl here and there on her lovely body. His pressure was as if he were dusting eggs. "You do have a lovely body," he mused. He also knew such words always calmed her when she was in one of her snits. It was about the only way she could be calmed. She liked to hear how beautiful she was. And as usual, as the compliments came, she slowly ambled into a more direct line with and closer to the full-length mirror. Then when he mentioned her hair, her hand always drifted up to it and the fingers drifted through the silken folds.

"You really do think I have a lovely body, don't you, Perry?" She viewed herself slowly from several different angles.

"There is none better. I've been around all kinds of show business for nearly twenty years, Miss Angel, and I can tell you in all frankness I've never seen finer."

"Even better than some of those movie actresses you used to dress?" She knew the answer, she'd heard it dozens of times but she never tired of hearing it again.

"Hell! You've got them all beat by a mile. What you've got is absolutely real. You start cutting through all that dress padding and foam rubber and take off the wigs and you can hardly tell them from the mop stick you find backstage where the cleanup lady left it." He took her hand and eased her across to the well-lighted makeup table and lowered her into a white fur-covered vanity chair.

"I really was made for better things, you know, Perry." She tilted her head slowly from side to side, getting the full impact of her own image.

"Of course you were. I am sure that other things are in store for you. Things more important than you've ever dreamed of. You were born for that."

"You always know when to say just the right thing. I think that's why I keep you around. Sometimes you make me so mad I want to kill you, but then I think how sweet you really are, and how tenderly you take care of my body... then I'm not angry anymore. You are a dear, Perry. Now be so kind as to get me another double Scotch."

"Do you really think you should?"

Her eyes suddenly glared, but they did not turn from the mirror to face him.

"There are still four more performances tonight."

Her eyes hardened even more. "A double shot and get it now and get the hell back here with it before I finish putting on fresh lipstick. That takes exactly three minutes."

Perry tripped to the door and was gone. But it was the ethereal reverberations of his voice which caused her eyes to soften again. "*I've never seen finer.*"

"Yes. Yes. He is right. I do have a luscious body. And I named it with the perfect name. Angel! Whoever heard of an angel with a name like Rebecca? Mother! Father! What stupid illiterate, unimaginative people you were. Rebecca Stunisky." She mused over that until Perry returned and handed her the glass of double Scotch. She took it in a tight fist but still did not turn away from the mirror. "Now isn't Angel Stunning a better name than Rebecca Stunisky?"

"Who is Rebecca Stunisky?" He knew, but it was the way he was supposed to answer. Perry was an excellent dresser, and he knew at all times what was expected of him. If that was the way Angel wanted it, then that was it.

Angel took another long gulp and let the ice tinkle in her glass as she lowered it from her lips. "It doesn't matter." She cupped her chin in the free hand but kept her eyes on the mirror. "Stunisky might be all right for a Russian ballerina, but not for an exotic dancer."

"Was that your name? Rebecca Stunisky?" Again, it was the way he was supposed to ask it.

"None of your business." She finished off the Scotch and tossed the glass back over her shoulder. It crashed just under the wardrobe of costumes. Perry sighed. It was another mess he would be expected to clean up. "Damned stuff tastes more bitter every night. I think I'll switch to bourbon."

"Changing off once in a while is said to be a good thing. Sometimes the system gets much too used to one thing, then it doesn't have the same effect anymore. Sometimes it even gets bitter." He kicked a larger portion of broken glass away from her chair where it had bounced back from the wall.

"When was the last time I fired you, Perry?"

"Two weeks ago."

"Why did I hire you back?" She took her hand away from her chin and turned sideways on the chair so that she could look directly at the little man. But she also did another apparent move. She opened her legs wide and the softness of her blonde pubic hairs winked at him.

"Because... because..." he stammered, "you demanded I make love to you... that way."

She laughed broadly and crossed her legs. "That way, is it?" Then she snapped her legs wide apart. "Want to do it again, like right now, Perry, little thing?"

Perry moved quickly to the door. "I'll get you another double Scotch. You've got to get ready for your next show. It's only a little while off." He went out through the door and closed it quickly.

"Make it a double bourbon this time," she screamed after him, then turned back to the mirror and nearly fell off the chair with her laughter. The dizziness she figured to be the effects of the whiskey. "Oooppps," she grinned and steadied herself. "Damned bitter Scotch. If that jerk of a bar-tender is sending me his damned cheap bar-booze I'll see that he gets a can tied to his tail before this night is over. Ed will do anything I want. He won't let the help treat me like some Main Street wino. He's hot for me, and he'll do just anything I tell him, and I'll tell him to tie a can to that ass's tail."

She forcibly pushed herself up from the makeup table with both hands and unsteadily made her way back to the couch where she laboriously stretched out, and made the same hand to eye move that she had produced earlier.

"Never affected me like this before. Not two little double shots." Then she reached her free hand across and outward toward the floor, to where the sheer white material of her veil lay. She captured it and rubbed the sudden wet sweat from her forehead. She opened her eyes and took the left hand down so that it could also capture the cloth. She looked to where the sweat had made a wet stain. "Good God, I hope I'm not catching something. That's all I need is to get laid up now. I got too many expenses to take care of. The new house! The new car! The new color set! My new mink and all those new clothes." She came to an unsteady sitting position just as Perry entered with the double bourbon in his hand.

He crossed to her and with one hand she took the glass and with the other she reached in and captured the ice which she transported to her forehead. The cool of it pressing against her skin gave a sudden shock, but a pleasing sensation to her senses. For a moment it relieved the dizziness.

"Is something wrong, Miss Angel? Can I get you something else? An aspirin… something?"

"I'll be all right. I think I must have danced too strenuously on that last run. I'll be all right." She held the ice to her forehead again, and drank the entire contents of the glass in one swift gulp. It caused her to choke more than she usually did from the sudden burning invasion. "My throat feels like it's on fire. Damn that bartender! If he's been putting that cheap crap he serves the customers in my glass I won't only see that he's fired, I'll see that he's murdered."

"It's the same bottle you always have, Miss Angel."

"That shows how much you know. How in hell could it be the same bottle when I always drink Scotch? This crap is bourbon and it's just as bitter, but it doesn't come from the same bottle I always drink out of when you know I drink Scotch."

Perry walked across the room to the wardrobe hangers and picked up the white feathered dress and put it on the ready hanger after taking the red creation and returning it to the wardrobe hangers. "My, you always did look so good in white." He fluffed out the feathers.

Angel looked across to him through blurred eyes. She spoke slowly, each word a difficulty of speech. "I said the red one. Tonight I want to dance with the devil."

Perry crossed back to her as she stiffened in front of him. He laid the dress out neatly on the upper pillows then leaned down and captured her legs. He lifted them up onto the couch and made sure they were straight. Then he took her arms and crossed them over her naked breasts.

"Your lovely body will look so good in the white feathers. Like an angel on a soft cloud. A body such as yours should always be preserved in white. White is for the angels, or so all the good words tell us."

He unzipped the back of the feathered dress and with little difficulty slipped it over her stiff body, then zipped it up again. Although she could move nothing else she still was conscious enough to understand what he was saying and she could see what was happening through the blurred eyes.

"White is for the angels and you are so soon to be an angel. You must go with the good before you make someone else like me make love to you like that. It just wasn't fair."

She closed her eyes and it was all over.

THE END

STARVE HELL

(provided by Greg Javer)

from Boy Play Annual *1973*

RONNIE LOOKED OUT of his window into the bleak, cold night. California wasn't supposed to be that cold. But it was cold as the Arctic. And it wasn't supposed to be as cold as it was in his room either. But when he ran out of money the manager had told him to get out. He hadn't gotten out. There was no place else for him to go. However, he also knew that if he'd gone out of that door he'd never have gotten back in. The manager would have blocked up the keyhole. He had to stay in that room. At least until his food supply had gone… two cans of beans, a can of Spam and a can of corn. The bread had been gone for two days and the coffee that morning… and the heat had been turned off by the manager early that afternoon. It was the manager's greeting to Ronnie's attempt at barricading himself in the room. He turned his eyes from the window and looked around the room which was nearly as bleak as the outside… the window faced upon a littered, filthy alley. The room held a small table and one torn, overstuffed chair and a pull-down bed which never went up into the wall. The hinges had long years ago rusted away… the bed clothes smelled of silverfish and mold. But the place had only cost five dollars a week. It was easy to pay while he washed dishes at the hash joint. He didn't know how to do anything else. He'd dropped out of school as soon as his age permitted.

"Shit," he mumbled, then got up from the chair and crossed the room to the table where the opened can of Spam rested. He cut off a large chunk and popped it into his mouth. Then another, and another until it was gone. He might have opened the beans or the corn but the operation seemed too much of an exertion for him.

"What the hell am I doing here?" he rambled on as his mind raced back to two weeks before, the night he had lost his job for putting the make on one of the waitresses in the back storeroom of the hash joint and the owner had come in and caught them. He'd barely gotten his cock out of his pants, and the girl had stepped out of her panties when the jerk came in and raised the roof.

Ronnie honestly hadn't known that the girl was the favorite of the boss and she wouldn't put out for him. They were both fired on the spot. He picked up his ten dollars and was gone.

But he was angry. He was as angry as hell. A lot of the girls, most of them that he'd ever met, fell head over heels for him. He never had any trouble in getting them to lay down and spread their legs for him. They liked what he had between his legs, and they all wanted to try him on for size. Most of them couldn't take his entire shaft. He was built much too big for most of the girls…. But he kept trying. In fact, if he didn't ask the girls outright, they were all set to rape him and take what they wanted. They simply had to try him on for size. He never attempted to hide his ample attributes on that section of his anatomy. In fact, he emphasized it by pulling it up, straight along the fly of his very tight Levis. He was "like advertising" he always said to those who asked what he thought he was doing.

He was still advertising when he entered the gay bar on West Third… only he didn't know it was a gay bar. It seemed to be like any of the other beer bars that he'd ever been in, and he'd been in a lot of them and some damned tough ones in his travels across the country.

He didn't get the implication of what was happening until his second beer, that night when he'd gotten fired, and gotten angry, and decided to get drunk. It was during his second beer that the well-dressed young man moved up softly and took the seat next to him.

"Would you drink with me?" inquired the young man.

"I can buy my own." He didn't want to be bothered by anybody. He wanted to take his vengeance out on the beer in front of him, and he figured there would be a lot more beers before the night was over.

"I'm sure you can…. But it's such a cold night and you looked like you might need a friend." The young man looked away, but there was a queer twinge in his tone. "I need a friend. I've been looking for a friend all evening. None of these characters in here appeals to me."

Ronnie still didn't get the point that he was being propositioned. He'd never been with the queers before, as how would he know the difference… although he had read about that deviation in life. It was simply that he didn't know any of their approaches.

For a moment he felt sorry for the young fellow who seemed lonely like he said. "Alright! I guess you could buy me a beer. I'll buy you one next. Like I said. I got money to pay for what I want."

The young man turned to him and there was a warm, pleasant smile on his face. "I do thank you for that."

And the beers were ordered and there was a lot of small talk and Ronnie soon found himself pouring his heart out about the recent injury to his conscience and pride.

"Women are like that," grimaced the young man. "They get a guy into all kinds of compromising situations then turn their back on the guy."

"She got fired too."

"Serves her right."

"But look! I wanted to lay her as much as she wanted to lay me. I mean, man, she was a good looking chick, I can sure as hell tell you that."

"There are more things, more important things in this world than good looking chicks… that I can tell you."

"Like?"

"Supposing we start with eating. You lost your job. You've got room rent to pay and you have to eat and you seem to like your beer. Have another."

"I will." Ronnie found himself slowly disliking the young man even though he didn't know why. But there was such a hatred coming from his mouth when he referred to pretty girls. "They're always just around the corner to lead some really good guy astray. And Ronnie, you most certainly do look like a good guy."

"I ain't had no complaints."

"I'm sure you wouldn't have any from me either." Ronnie didn't get that remark either, so he sipped of the fresh beer which had been put in front of him. "I've got some very good whiskey in my apartment. They don't serve any of the hard stuff in here, you know."

"How do you know I ain't got any up in my room?" Ronnie didn't look to the young man, but the dislike grew.

"Well… your job for one thing. But I bet you would like to have some of the good stuff. And perhaps I could feed you something else you might enjoy."

Ronnie began to feel the beers. He really would like to have some whiskey. The beer always went to his head fast, and it went to his kidney's even faster. And when the liquid filled the pint or more of his bladder he excused himself and went to the men's room.

It was a strange sight in there. There were four cubicles with toilets and there were two men standing over one of the toilets in the same booth. They closed the door when he entered. And there were four urinals. Two of them were occupied, but the men weren't looking at their own peckers when he took his out of his fly and flashed the golden stream into the proper place. They were staring at his. He felt embarrassed. But then he'd been looked at by men before.

"Damn… maybe they're some of them queers," he muttered, then wagged the dew from the end and was sure he heard a catch of breath to his left. Thus quickly he zipped up and went back to the bar where the young man waited.

"I don't like being stared at when I take a piss," he grumbled.

"Maybe you have something worth looking at…" Then he caught himself. "I mean for certain types of people."

"The girls sure like to look at it. I don't mind that… the girls looking at my thing."

"How about that whiskey?"

"Yeah! Why not? I don't want to have to go back to the shit house again and get stared at. You got a private bathroom, don't you?"

"Two of them. You can take your choice." And they left the bar. The young man even had a car. Ronnie liked that because he felt he could get a ride home to his room after they had had enough to drink. Then too maybe he could just pass out in the young man's apartment. He still wanted to get drunk and forget all his troubles. The only way to forget all his troubles was to get roaring drunk.

"You mind if I get real drunk?" asked Ronnie when he looked at the well-stocked bar in the lavishly decorated apartment.

"Drink all you want, my boy." And Ronnie thought that was a strange way to say something to him. "My boy." Why, the young fellow was no older than himself. "My boy… shit." He moved to the bar, then looked back to the young fellow.

"Help yourself." And Ronnie did. He took up a thick glass and poured it nearly half full, then downed it.

"You have no reason to be without money," said the young man.

"I ain't got no job. Then when I run out of the money I got, I won't have no money. And I don't know where I can get another job."

"A good looking… well-built guy like you doesn't always have to have a job to have money in your pants… not a good-looking guy like you… if you know what the score is."

"I don't know what you mean by score?"

"Why starve when you can be eating regular!"

"Damn it! I told you I ain't got no job and I ain't got much money left." He downed the whiskey and poured another. He was getting to dislike this young fellow more and more with every passing drink.

"You're built good. I'd like to see you naked."

Ronnie laughed. It must have been some sort of a joke. Why in the world would this guy want to see him nude?

"Sure! I'll show you me." But he only stripped off his pants and his dong hung low and long. Ronnie knew what it would look like when it got hard…. But it only got hard with the girls. "And I know why you want me naked now. You're one of them queers. You want to put your lips around that thing. Is that it? You want to turn me around and put it up my bung. I know about guys like you, that's for damned sure."

"You know about guys like me, like hell. Sure, I'd take you on. You're my type. But only one time. I like to break my clients in. But then I act as sort of a… sort of a manager for them. I could get higher than going rates for you, my friend." He reached out and touched the shaft and Ronnie felt a twinge similar to that which he got when the girls touched him… but not as thorough. "I could really sell you on the street, big boy. But I'd like to find out just how good you are first."

Ronnie slammed out his fist and knocked the guy back against the wall. He thought momentarily about throwing his glass of whiskey into his face. But why waste good whiskey? He picked up the bottle and left the place.

However, there in the bleak cold room, he knew what he had to do. He looked at the whiskey bottle which had been empty for several days. There was an apartment across town… he'd have to walk… but there was that apartment and a young man and there would be a lot of whiskey….

"And I guess I could use a manager… at least for a while," he thought… then as a last gesture to the bleak room he threw both the beans and the corn out through the window to the bleak alley beyond.

"Starve hell," he said and slammed the door behind him.

THE END

CAPTAIN FELLATIO HORNBLOWER

from The Boyfriends *Vol.3 no.3 on Ed's resume 1971*

AN ATTORNEY JUST doesn't seem to make it unless he specializes in one particular vein of law. Anyway, that's the way Captain Ralph Henry Hornblower (late of the U.S. Navy and far from being a Captain—more like an Ensign) thought. And there was no one to argue with him, certainly not his landlord who rented him the entire penthouse suite of a tall office building.

Of course, Captain Hornblower (and his magical title) wasn't always the success he presently claimed. There were the lean years right after World War II in which he served. There was the struggling through law school, and the time he was caught having a fruity session with one of his classmates, at the all-male school. But it was better that the incident be kept quiet than to have him expelled and with all the notoriety that might accompany such a scandal. Besides, it was thought, boys will be boys, and being such they are always investigating things... even their bodies... or the body of the boy in the next bunk to him. It was one of the hazards of a one-sex school.

And if we pinpoint it right down to the nitty gritty, the one time he was caught wasn't the first time he'd done such a thing and it certainly wasn't the last. Captain Ralph Henry Hornblower was quite the rounder, and if the nickname started anywhere, it started in those law school days. And the name stuck with him throughout his own circles and cliques.

Captain Fellatio Hornblower!

And to the Captain it was a badge of acceptance, a badge of honor. But the badge did little for his general law practices when he went out into the make a buck world. There was too much general for the Captain and very few clients. Thus he hit upon the one program which turned out right for him. There had been a time that he, starving, and an author, starving, sat down to bite a crust of bread over a bottle of cheap wine and eat a few other physical morsels that the author decided he should quit writing about the world and places he'd never been. He should write only about the things he knew and start selling for money instead of rejection slips.

This hit home for the Captain also. After all, what did he know about general law except what he learned from law books? And there was a general law practitioner on every street corner and hundreds more in every tall office building. He had to specialize, and like his writer friend, he had to specialize in what he knew.

Thus back to the law libraries and to the musty books dealing with all the sexual deviations known to mankind, but especially to homosexual relationships where it concerned the law. And it would appear homosexuality of any kind had a hell of a lot of relationships with the law, when discovered. Yet he couldn't find one attorney who specialized in that one phase of crime in the entire town. There was a built-in market for him. *It takes one to know one.* It certainly takes one to understand one. And Captain Fellatio Hornblower was the *ONE*.

He didn't have to advertise even if advertising was permissible in his profession. One case, selected because he was on the right spot at the right time when an arrest was made put his name up high. He simply presented the boy with his card which simply read HORNBLOWER, then an address and phone number. It might have smelled a bit of the old ambulance chaser, but it was only a one-time operation and the word got around like wildfire and was accepted just as the wheat accepted quickly the wildfire.

Hornblower moved up quickly in the legal world, once he had made the change over, and continued to climb the ladder of success until he reached the penthouse offices, with an apartment and bar attached for special occasions. And there were many special occasions, and the more financially secure he became, the more lavish were his special occasions.

However, the one thing for sure: if a client got Fellatio to blow his horn the courts stood up and took notice.

A successful lawyer first charges a lot of money, and second wins a lot of cases. But then a lawyer doesn't become successful and make a lot of money if he doesn't win cases. Fellatio Hornblower seldom lost a case, that's how good he was. He had a good voice, a resounding one when he wanted, but most of all he had convincing tones which could sway the hardest of jurors. And strange as it may seem, it appeared most of the time that the jurors were waiting to be swayed and enjoyed the process. He was a showman from the word go, and along with the medical terms for the things his deviate clients might have perpetrated, he sparsed his words with the hardcore terms which shocked, but enlightened the listeners.

There were none, even the most ignorant, who didn't know exactly what he was talking about. And there were none that didn't hang onto each word he spoke and dangle expectantly for the next one.

But it wasn't only the jurors... the judge and the clients themselves were just as enthralled. His court appearances also assured a packed court-room. The showman of the attorney's circle. The director of thoughts and curver of minds. The twister of fiction which always came out fact.

"But then, who really wants to put these poor homos behind bars anyway? The greatest number don't even need a doctor. They don't go around molesting children. They are in the greater part consenting adults doing their thing."

It always worked!

"Besides! You the taxpayer must pay for every inmate the prisons house. Leave those expenditures for the real criminals who are out to do harm to society. There is no harm in the makeup of the homo. Leave him alone and he is bound to leave society alone. Why, ladies and gentlemen of the jury, there is a place in this world for each and every one of us... and we must understand that all of us have our own little problems. You! You! You! You and you! Do you think your problems rate that you be put away behind prison bars? And perhaps one or more of you may have the same problem as my client. Perhaps it might be one of your closest relatives or friends. Think about that! Would you care to be, or have your relatives or friends in the same situation as my client?"

It always worked!

Then there was the ceremony of paying Fellatio or the devil, his dues. And it always took place in the penthouse, starting with the desk where the check was presented, then to a congratulatory drink, then on into the bedroom where any other little gratuity might be in order. Gratuities were always in order, and the pleasure of being on the outside looking in caused those gratuities to be considerable in a tremendous amount of the incidents.

"What do you do when you find out a client is really guilty?" questioned a friend.

Fellatio could only laugh. "Good friend! All of my clients are guilty, or they wouldn't have been picked up and charged in the first place. The only problem is what is the extent of their guilt. And is it worth making a big deal out of? Most of the cases are dropped because of insufficient evidence. Witnesses don't like to appear in such cases… all the embarrassment and that sort of thing. In the beginning, the excitement of the moment, they will swear they have seen everything, but when it comes time to get them on the stand their memory has an immediate blackout, a failure which can't be redeemed. The more vile the deed, the less available the witnesses.

"In the kind of cases I handle it is seldom the arresting officer is on the scene during the commission of the act. He is the second party brought in and therefore must take the word of those who have been the informants. Very poor witnesses for the state. After all, what can they say except to repeat what they have heard secondhand? A complaint is made and they must act upon it. That's where I come in! A complaint is only a complaint until the facts are proven. Law is a very strange and intricate entity. But one by which we must all live and be governed.

"The law is the law. But there are thousands of ways of interpreting the law. And that's the key to the entire operation. Interpretation!"

Fellatio Hornblower knew whether or not he was going to win a case even before he entered the courtroom. In fact, his brain was so attuned to what the eventualities would be that he knew how a case would run even before he took it. Fellatio liked to win. He didn't take cases he knew he'd lose. There were a few losses however, but it was through tricks he had not expected. There were not many.

Then there was one Paul Mestroni who was picked up on the beach in an automobile. He was naked and the young sailor with him in the back seat had the thirteen buttons of his front flap open and his manhood was rigid and being serviced by Paul. The boys in blue surprised the action with a double flashlight blast. There was no dressing or zipping up of trousers. They went to the station in the black and white as they were. The arresting officers were first hand observers.

Fellatio Hornblower was contacted by Paul when he used his one phone call, and bail was set quickly by a desk sergeant. But the arraignment was delayed until the next morning.

Fellatio had to know the story. "You know what this is going to do to you in the navy?" he asked of the young, frightened sailor who shook his head. "Well, the one thing for sure is you'd better unpack your civilian clothes."

The shore patrol came into the station waiting room and took him from the police. He was not to be Fellatio's client.

"Poor kid," muttered Paul as he got dressed from the bundle the police had tied his clothing into. "But if they stand around on street corners looking for some action they gotta expect to be busted. After all, I didn't rape the punk... and he wanted five dollars. You know what that makes him! You should, you've handled enough of their kind."

"You know, you guys never cease to amaze me. You go out looking for a score on any street corner. You pick up bums, tramps, bumboys, anything to get your jollies. You speak all kinds of words of love to them in preparation for getting his pants and drawers off, then when you get it, or get busted, the love words cease to exist and he becomes what you went to pick up in the first place: bums, tramps, bumboys!" Fellatio Hornblower frowned deeply, the same frown he had used on tough witnesses or an obstinate juror. "Whore! I wonder which is the worst whore?"

"Well," grinned Paul fixing his tie. "That's the name of the game, I guess. You win some and you lose some. The street corner whores are always the losers. You know that!"

"You keep saying, I know that. Listen, mister. I don't know anything about your kind of life, physically that is. I look a case right up the ass and see where the dirt is. Then like a dutiful mother I wipe it clean. Then you go right back on the street the next weekend and the whole process starts all over again."

"That's what keeps you in business, barrister."

"True, so true. Sadly true, but true. There are times I look forward to my retirement."

Paul grinned again and slipped into his violet, velvet jacket. "You'd die within a year. Lawyer, you couldn't last a month without the entanglement of cases like mine. You going to get me off?"

"I haven't heard all the facts yet."

"That will come later. You going to get me off?" He opened the packet containing his wallet, watch and diamond ring. He selected five one-hundred dollar bills and handed them to Fellatio Hornblower. "Just a retainer as usual."

"Want to visit a psychiatrist for another six months?" Fellatio pocketed the money after folding it.

"Hell, why not! Especially if the next one is as cute as the last one."

"Okay! You'll get off with a slap on the wrist as usual. I'll see what I can do about the condition of the psychiatrist's appearance."

A jury loves to think they have saved some poor boy from a life of torture in some prison when they feel he has a slight mental problem. It is easy to sway them into recommending the criminal proceedings be dropped and the poor lad have a few psychiatric treatments. No one wants to confine a sick person to a cell, unless he's dangerous or has committed some heinous crime. A poor homo getting mixed up with strange boys who lead them on... Paul would never see a second appearance in court... on that particular charge. There would be others. Of that Fellatio Hornblower could be positive. They always came back... most of them. But generally, the crime was no more than the first time. The only difference was that the charge was a second or third or whatever. None of them ever changed. They could take psychiatric treatment from now until hell freezes over and they would come out with the same ideas as when they first went in.

None of them wanted to change!

That was the entire point. In order for any psychiatrist to help a person, that person has got to want to be helped. Like the alcoholic. He can't even start for a cure until he admits he is an alcoholic, then wants the cure himself. The homosexual male or the female, or any of the other deviates... they simply do not want any kind of a cure. They like life the way it is. Any change would take away from their personality. They want to retain that personality.

"Like many of them want to be picked right out of the crowd," tells Fellatio Hornblower. "Not all of them, of course. Some would rather stay in the background and not be discovered. But many want to be recognized. It does something for their ego. That particular difference takes them out of the realm of the common ordinary status and puts them in the different limelight. That's the way they must have it for a comfortable life.

"At first when they're caught they are scared out of their wits. The cops and the booking and all the other processes that go with being arrested. But by the time they get to court there is the feeling that they have suddenly begun to enjoy their position in the unusual. Actually, when the trial is over and they are once more on the street, there is the feeling also of reluctance on their part that it's all over. Now they must return to their regular life and all the spectacle is gone.

"Naturally I make it more of a spectacle, in the courtroom, than it really needs. But that's what wins cases. I blow my horn a lot. Fellatio Hornblower, the hornblower. That's me, and I guess I get a lot of my kicks being in the limelight, too. Right out there in the courtroom. And I'm always out to win. I hate to lose. That's why I don't lose very often. I can out-shout any other attorney in the country. I can out-shout just about anybody in the country. And as I learned a long time ago, the guy who shouts the loudest is the one who is listened to and heard the longest.

"Hitler was a master of shouting. And he will go down in history for all time. Perhaps I won't go down in history, but you can bet your ass I'll be heard as long as I'm around."

Fellatio Hornblower then ushered Paul Mestroni to the door. "Don't you want a little something extra... like in the bar and the bedroom?" questioned the startled man as he was shown to the door.

"You're not my type. I'm not one who goes around street corners for my character analysis. That's where you belong. See you in court... next time."

THE END

UNFRIENDLY PERSUASION

Boyfriends Vol.3 No.2 May/June 1971, no author listed on Ed's resume.

MARTIN HAD ALREADY AFFIXED the pink bikini panties, panty hose, brassiere, slip and skirt into place. All that remained was to slide into high heeled shoes and put on the new pink angora cardigan, then he would be ready for the street. He was young and extremely good looking with tender features that took little more makeup than lipstick, mascara and eyeshadow to transform him into one of the sexiest dolls on the street.

There was no need for a wig since his own hair was shoulder length, a style of the present, and it was pin curled every night to keep it well-shaped.

Strange as it may seem, Martin wasn't a full-time "drag queen." He actually didn't prefer women's clothing to his male attire. But dressing so was the easiest way to pick up other males, therefore he had perfected his womanly arts. And when some straight got his hands too close to the golden fur box, Martin simply told him it was that time of the month, "she'd" have to take care of him orally, take it into her mouth. And if his hands went to "her" titties… that part was alright. There was enough fatty tissues around the boyish nipples to make fair-sized mounds when formed with a tight brassiere. The "trade" or "trick" could play with them all night, through and underneath the brassiere and never get wise… just as long as the brassiere stayed in place. Martin never undressed further than the slip when confronting "her" customers. She didn't have to once they learned about her discomforts during that time of the month. Usually she didn't even have to go so far as her slip. All the guy was interested in were her ruby red lips, and what they could do for him. Some did insist that she take off her sweater or blouse, or whatever so they could see her youthful titties, but if they insisted too hard when she rejected the plan, she simply got angry and told them it would be her way or none at all. They always came around to her way of thinking.

Then she was ready. She thought a moment longer about taking along a light coat, but decided against it. At that point she was an all sweater girl, and there was nothing like a sweater front to catch the eye of an ever-ready male. In so thinking, Marion (as close as she could come to Martin) raised both of her hands to lightly push up her dainty boobie front through the sweater. It chilled her deep to her groin and her penis strained at the panties in anticipation. It was a tremendously exciting feeling but Marion detested masturbation except as a last resort…. She grinned back at her reflection, knowing full well she'd had few last resorts since becoming Marion full-time on her nightly and weekend prowls.

She checked her dainty wristwatch and found it to be just before ten in the evening. Just about the right time for the bars to have enough variety of patrons where a pretty girl like Marion could more or less pick and choose the companion she wanted. It was pretty piss-poor when she had to take on just anybody. That wasn't really the name of her game. But then that didn't happen anymore… then she had to jerk-off. There had been so many times she'd wished she were twins. Too many beautiful tricks had slipped between her fingers due to the fact that she had to make a choice. Some which looked like the best bet had turned out to be the most tremendous of duds, and the rejected one had to have been better. Of course, that was something she couldn't really be sure of, but the dud… anything would have been better. She liked the way her high heels clicked on the cement sidewalk, and she liked the way her tight skirt pulled rhythmically at the calves of her legs with each step. And with each pull she knew it was that much closer to the time when the ache in her groin would be satisfied. Soon her lips would press over a lob, then there would be no stopping the surging fire which would spread through her entire body. She wished she had a hole instead of a pole… after all, she was a whore and she knew it… a male whore in female dress, but a whore nevertheless… women whores could do so much more with their clients.

No matter how many times Martin had looked into his mirror and found Marion there he always got the same reaction. "What a beautiful girl I would have made… what a shame I am lost to so many men who'd give their eyeteeth for half an hour with me."

The bars were no more or less crowded than they generally were at ten-thirty of a Friday night. And as usual there were other faces than the regulars…. The brutes… the straights… the trade… the curious and the vice. The vice, that's the one she dreaded without reservation. Of course, she didn't feel that it was pure luck she hadn't been busted before… so many of the other drag hustlers had… she felt it was because of the perfect makeup, and because of the discretion with which she picked her tricks. There was no law against Martin dressing as he was, but picking up her trade for illicit reasons always beckoned the long arm of the law.

Marion was a perfectionist in dress and makeup. Undoubtedly, she'd never been tagged as anything but a female who minded her own business… talked with many interested males… then left the bar by herself. It was only known to those who went with her that a prearranged meeting was designated before she ankled out of the establishment.

Then too the city is big and there are plenty of bars. If she traveled to them every night for a lifetime she would not have to set foot in the same bar twice. Safety has always favored numbers… and variety was her spice in life. She did, however, make repeat performances once in a while, but with some period of time in between. There was good reasoning in that procedure also. Some of the places she liked, and did return to, had to permit her an absence period so she wouldn't run into the same trick again. It didn't always work out that way, but the bets were better than even… well worth the chance. She just didn't approve of taking on the same customer twice… besides… she couldn't use the "HOLY WEEK" dodge a second time. Twice burned makes for a hot situation. It was better to slough them off with a curt, "Hello…. How are you?" and "Ohhhh, I'm sorry. I really am! I have a previous engagement." Her musical voice always carried the words off with the ring of excusable truth.

Marion looked back across the cement parking lot to where she had parked her convertible and those blue eyes roved over the several dozen parked cars. The cocktail lounge which she had picked was jumping with customers… there would be no failure in making a quick conquest. Again, the numbers value struck her mind. The more men there were, the better her chances for picking just the right type of companion she'd like for a couple of private hours.

Of course it didn't always work out the way she planned, but even before leaving her apartment, Martin discussed, with Marion through his mirror reflection, the exact type of male fruit he'd like to digest on that particular occasion. A selection which the vehicles in that parking lot presented told her she might have to change her plans. After all, pre-selection might turn up the right one... but more than the right one had to come from sight selection.

Marion's high heels sunk deeply into the thick pile carpet of the cocktail lounge, and daintily she walked across to the bar. Ladylike, she might have otherwise seated herself in one of the booths, but the gigantic mirror behind the bar afforded her a sweeping view of the entire interior of the establishment without anyone catching her roving eye... at least until she wanted them to. After all, eye-catching was the final come-on before capture... the big lure when a selection has been made. After that there was little work left for her to do. A bit of conversation over a cocktail or two, then the meeting arrangements and nature took over from there. She knew her business well and once she had made her choice the guy didn't have a chance.

The room was crowded as Marion had expected... and her face lighted up with delight as she viewed the admiring men as she passed them, then perched daintily on the stool. A uniformed bartender took her order, a martini, then moved off, leaving the sparkling mirror clear for her scrutiny. It didn't take Marion long to spy her intended conquest. And even though he sat at a table with two other girls Marion had little trouble capturing and holding his eyes.

He appeared to be tall and well-built with a full chest under the straight cut suit, and his wavy dark hair framed a ruggedly handsome face... and after a few moments of the eye catching, it became apparent the two girls at the table with him knew what was transpiring, but other than slightly furtive looks they made no other outward sign of being annoyed. Marion figured that the guy was a real stud and if the girls ever wanted him again, they just better not attempt stopping him from any amours to which he might want to direct his attention.

It must have been that way because only a few more moments passed as he killed off his drink, then stood up and crossed the plush carpet to straddle the stool next to Marion. Without a word he indicated to the bartender that Marion's glass was to be filled and that he was in need of another himself. There were still no words until after the bartender had brought the drinks then walked off to service another customer.

"Tommy Cassidy," he said, then cocked a questioning eye.

"Marion... Marion Fox!" Marion felt the sweat rivering down through the pubic hairs under her panties and panty hose. Briefly she wished she had worn a panty-girdle... it always sopped up most of the sweat moisture when her hot sexual body fires started.

"Nice young ladies don't usually come to a plush bar like this alone."

"What makes you think I'm alone?" It was a silly question, but the only thing which came to mind at the moment. However, she quickly added, "I like to start the evening out alone. I don't generally end up that way."

Tommy looked Marion up and down approvingly. "That's easy to see. Are you on the town or on the make?"

The dialogue was extremely abrupt, but there was little which could shock Marion into a startled facial expression any longer. She let a light grin pass the corners of her lips. "I suppose you might say, a little of each." She finished the martini.

"It's a long night, and if we don't make the scene, then that could leave me all hot and bothered… and maybe you can see, I don't have to take that kind of crap." He indicated the girls back at the table he'd just left. "You interest me, so if I'm going to lay out for a good time, I expect one in return." Then he looked deeply and directly into the blue pools of Marion's eyes and was strictly blunt with his question. "Your apartment, or mine?"

"Whoa, you do come on strong, don't you?"

"Life was made to be played to the hilt, not screwed around with. I get to the point! Win, lose or draw, there's always somebody just around the corner… or I go back to the broads over there at the table."

"Perhaps you'd better go back to your girlfriends. Maybe they like your attitude. I don't!" It was a lie, but once started, Marion had to keep up with the pretense if she was to win the man. The only problem was, Tommy hadn't been bluffing. He got to his feet, leaving behind the untouched glass of Scotch and water and was about to return to the table. Frantically Marion grabbed his arm. "Where are you going?"

"Maybe you've had a lot of guys kidding you before, sister, but I'm not one of them. I speak my mind and it comes out clear, even if it's not always clean. I put in the pitch and you rejected… that seems to be about all there is to it."

Marion spoke slowly, the heat increasing throughout her entire loins. She had to have this rough, tough one. "That isn't all there is to it!" She dug into her shoulder purse and took out a calling card which she stuck into his hand. "My place! I have everything there we'll need for a nice… time."

Tommy looked at the card and grinned. "You coy broads are all the same, aren't you? Make like you're going to fall apart then come on strong because you can't see yourself losing." He looked at the card again. "Okay… your place! How about half an hour?"

"That will be just fine." Then she turned to watch as Tommy returned to the table and picked up one of the girls' drinks. She couldn't hear what they were saying but Marion knew the talk was all about her because the girls gave quick glances in her direction. Of course that kind of thing she didn't like very much because it could take some of the protection away from an illicit affair. But then Tommy hadn't appeared as any conventional type right from the beginning, and she did want him.

Marion didn't leave the cocktail lounge immediately. She played it in her usual manner, so that it didn't look like a pick-up. She waited a full ten minutes, then moved slowly to the door, but once outside her steps quickened. The cool air going up her miniskirt did much to ease the heat, but the longing remained, and she knew it would until Tommy had dropped his pants in front of her. It was the only way the hot rocks would cool.

Tommy's knock on the door was loud and clear. Marion had wanted to change into a sexy negligee and nightie over the undies, but there hadn't been time; then, too, Tommy's kind might be the physical type and it was much more probable that he wouldn't attempt tearing off a sweater and skirt… whereas the flimsy negligee might fall too easily under any grip.

Marion opened the door. "Come in," she directed, then stepped back a few steps. Tommy moved in quickly and there was a tremendous leer on his face as he closed the door behind him. He then took her hand and led her across to a couch. "You sure got a hell of a body. Let's see it!"

Marion feigned the blush she could always bring on. "I know you'll be angry. I should have told you before. But this is my time of the month…. Please don't be angry with me. I won't let you go away 'hot and bothered' like you mentioned…. I'll take care of you… the other way. Honest, I want to see you again when I'm alright… that's why I didn't brush you off in the bar. I wanted you so bad I could taste it. Now, at least, maybe I can do that. You aren't mad… if we do it that way, just this once, are you, honey?"

"Hell no," replied Tommy with a broad grin, then took off his jacket and unbuckled the thick belt from around his waist. "I don't know what other way you had in mind, but I'm not one for playing games when sex is involved. You just have at it, and mind you do a good job or we just don't ever get together again." The trousers dropped, then the undershorts, and the BULL DYKE spread her legs far apart…

THE END

LIKE A HOLE IN THE HEAD

as "Dick Trent"

on Ed's resume in Pendulum *vol.3 no 1 Pendulum Publishing Nov./Dec. 1971*

TERRI WAS NEARLY FIVE years older than her sister Barbara but both of them lacked nothing for the beauty of face and lusciousness of figure. They were born of the same mother but different fathers. Yet this never made much of a difference in their personal relationship. They loved each other as sisters should. But they were as different as day and night when it came to the kind of careers they would follow.

Terri had had it in her mind ever since the earliest days of her memory that she was going to become a movie star. Barbara had no such intentions. Right after Barbara graduated high school she took a job as cashier in a supermarket and there she felt she might spend that portion of her life until someday when she married. It was a comfortable job, right in the neighborhood where she still lived with her mother. And the pay was right. She also had read something on dental assistants and had been considering that as some future adventure. But it wasn't really that solid in her mind. There was still a lot of time. She was only twenty.

Terri, on the other hand was twenty-five but looked a bit older. Not that this took away any of her beauty, because she was a beautiful doll and her mirror always told her that. But there were some minute lines which could be seen when she took the light make-up off each night before retiring. But then it might have been worse. She had been, for some time, living a tiring life.

She found out early in pursuing her movie career that it wasn't always what you knew, but it always was who you knew. She knew that an agent would be the most valued friend she could ever have on her side. But then how was that arranged? Girls in Hollywood were a dime a dozen and most of them as beautiful as she, and nearly all of them certainly more experienced.

Her first meeting, however, with anybody from the motion picture empire was with a bit player. He'd done little work, but every once in a while his face did crop up in some television production or some extremely bit part with the cheap independent productions. Therefore he could classify himself as an actor. And since Terri had seen his face on the screen she was all aglow in meeting him.

She went to bed with him the first night of their meeting. She knew what she would have to do if she were ever to work her way up the ladder.

Then there was the independent producer who captured her from the bit actor, and the failing star who captured her from the independent producer and then there was the agent who spilled cigar ashes all over his vest which covered his obese belly. She never could figure out how she made it with him. But it was through him she got the first part of her career. Everything about her was delicious on the screen until she opened her mouth… the words came out like the sounds made when one squeezes a wet dishrag.

There were a couple of other bits, but most of the time they were what was classified in the industry as silent bits. She was putting out for the guys in command and all of them wanted her again and again and they knew they would have to give her what she wanted… pictures… but they couldn't take a chance on giving her any lines.

Even dramatic school hadn't helped any. She sounded beautiful in her normal voice. But it just wouldn't record. There are many people so inflicted. They just won't record. But Terri still found this hard to believe… in fact, she wasn't going to believe it. But deep in her subconscious she wanted someone who would be of a lesser entity in the business she could lord it over.

Barbara was the likely choice.

Barbara wanted no part of the business. Therefore, if Terri could change her mind there was no doubt she could have someone just a little bit under her. She didn't hate her sister. But in attempting to bring her along the movie path, Terri would be like the teacher. The one with the experience and the one who could stretch out that helping hand of superiority.

"But I've got two left feet," grinned Barbara when Terri approached her with the entire subject and that at least she could take some dancing lessons.

"And I can't dance at all," informed Terri. "But it's too late in my career to start now. I'm a dramatic actress and that's where I head up best. Now you've always been light on your feet. I bet I could have you dancing within a month or two. You don't want to stay behind that cashier's counter all your life."

"I like it! I like my boss! I'm close to home!"

"Which brings up another thing that's noteworthy," cut in Terri. "Living at home! You've been living with mother so long everything you seem to do depends on her advice. You've got to get out on your own sometime. I mean really on your own where you have to make all the decisions."

"I know… but…"

"You can move right into my apartment in Hollywood until we get you all straightened out. Maybe you can't act or anything like that. But when you learn to dance you'll make more money in one day than you do in a month at that grocery store…"

"Supermarket."

"They're all the same to me."

"But I've heard all the stories about guys telling girls all sorts of things about movies and clubs and it turns out they are recruiting for white slave markets."

Terri laughed. "Do you think I'd ever let you get mixed up with anything like that? Besides! Those kinds of affairs went out with the high button shoes. The laws are very strict about any kind of work. They've got to have licenses. But you'll be with my agency. They handle dancers as well as other talents."

"You really think I could make it, Terri?"

Terri patted her younger sister lovingly on the shoulder. "I wouldn't be talking to you now if I didn't. You're as good as being cast for your first picture right now."

And some days later Terri turned over in bed and faced her naked companion of the night. His name was Ted and he was another of the actors of little renown she'd been meeting on the sets. She wanted to meet and gather with the stars. But when a bit player steps above her ranks she is generally looked down upon. There is such a class situation in the film industry.

They had talked and Ted leaned over to capture a half cigarette which he snubbed out the night before. "I think you're crazy," he said.

"Because I want my little sister to get ahead?"

"Because you ain't got nothing to offer her. You want her to walk down the same office rugs you did? You even said she hasn't got any talent."

"I can get her in! Besides, maybe I can make something out of her. And she is learning to dance real good. I saw that myself."

"Learning to dance is a long way from being Ginger Rogers." He rolled over to face her again. "Look, why don't you face facts. All you want is a whipping boy... in this case, girl."

"How do you mean?"

"You ain't making it in the business, and you want her to get in and flop on her ass also. In that way you have somebody close to you that you can look down on."

"Who put you in the psychiatrist chair?"

"It's as plain as the nose on your face."

"Well if that's the way you feel about it, get your filthy shorts on and get your filthy ass out of my apartment."

"Look. The kid was perfectly happy out there in the world of squares. Why don't you leave her be? She doesn't want this kind of life. You want it for her! You're going to ruin that kid if you persist in this attempt."

"Get the hell out of my apartment." She cracked him with a stinging blow across the cheek and he doubled up his fist. It was only pure self-control which kept Ted from jamming his fist into her mouth. "Well, go ahead, hit me and see where you land, buster."

He got out of bed and dressed quickly. "It's not worth the trouble or the effort. I was going anyway! I've got a six o'clock call this morning." He moved to the door, but softened as he opened it and turned once more to her. "I'll call you when I get off this afternoon."

Her eyes blazed in anger. "You'll call me shit!"

"Okay. I'll call you SHIT." He slammed the door.

Barbara had proved to be an excellent student and she really did come across as a dancer. Terri was proud of the results, but she knew that deep down she wished her sister hadn't been so damned good. But there was no turning back at that point except to say...

"Yeah! You looked real good up there, kid. But you know, I've been thinking. Maybe I have made a mistake. Being a dancer is one thing. But there is still all the acting and the speaking of lines that goes along with being a dancer. I don't want you to get hurt or to fail..."

"I won't fail." She reached over and hugged Terri tightly. "Oh, sis. I can't tell you how much I appreciate what you've done for me."

Terri sighed. "And just what have I done for you? Probably spoiled your whole life, that's what. There you were perfectly happy being a cashier, having your boyfriends. No complications. Yeah… just what have I done for you?"

"Made me see the daylight for what it is. I'm going to make you proud of me."

"That's what I'm afraid of," Terri wanted to say, but it was only her silent thoughts and she was embarrassed even at that. "I guess you'll be good at anything you try."

"Well, dancing seems to be much like running your fingers over a typewriter or an adding machine or a cash register, only you're doing it with your feet."

"I still wish you'd reconsider. There's still plenty of time for turning back."

"That's something I'm never going to do. You've given me a taste of what it's like to be graceful and to want to get ahead. I've met some people already… real glamourous people who think I'm really good."

"People? Who?"

"Oh, just people! Nice people! We have parties, you know."

"I don't want you running around with strange people."

"Hold on, sis. You're not my mother. And even if you were, it's too late to tell I can do this, or I can't do that or who my friends are going to be. I've been with those tacky little boys around the store so long I thought they were the only kind of people in the whole world. Now I know what real people are and I mean people who can really do something good for me."

"You'll get laid and you'll be on your way back to the fish market where you came from."

"I've been laid before."

Terri knew she had but it was unpleasant hearing it from the girl's own lips. One doesn't really look upon her little sister in such a light. Even with the passing of a thought it would be dismissed. But how can one dismiss the spoken words… spoken with all the frankness of a young girl who knew what she was saying and apparently proud of it.

"You don't care to tell me who these people are?"

"It really doesn't matter who they are. But they are all interested in the dance and dancers. We have had several talks… several of the other girls and myself and Mr. Dodson."

"The name rings a bell. I've heard it before."

"It's possible. He's an older man. He and his wife and Mr. Fifer. They've been putting troupes together for years. You should see some of the brochures for their dance lines." She hugged her arms around the front of her tight sweater, and her arm position just below her breasts made her youthful breasts stand out with the perfect contour of a girl who wore no brassiere and didn't need one. "It's all very thrilling."

"What do you think of it, Ted?" Terri questioned that night when he came to her apartment.

He laughed. "Shall I say I told you so?"

"But it worries me. Do you know anything about those people?"

"I'm with the movies, not the world of the dance. It should be easy enough to check them out. Hey, girl! It looks like you might have created a Frankenstein monster for yourself."

"You're a big help."

"Look, I'm not working tomorrow. We'll both go have a talk with your sister. But I don't see anything so horrible in the whole affair except your suddenly suspicious mind. Perhaps she is as good as they say. You said she's good. Come on, if the horrors come from that old monster, jealousy, knock it off and let the girl live her own life."

"I'm resigned to that fact now. But after all, I did bring her into the world of the tinsel and the glamour and I feel responsible for her. I don't want to see her get hurt. And I'm afraid if they ask her to join their traveling company she's going to hop right on the train with them."

"That's the only way to get breaks. Hop right on the train the minute you sign the contract."

"You will go with me tomorrow?"

"I said I would! Now slip on that black nightie with the black marabou fur. Get me all sexy! It's been a long day and I need your hot body next to me."

"I'm afraid I won't be very good tonight."

"I'll get your mind off things… Other than the things I want you to be thinking about."

Barbara was gone when they arrived at her apartment the following day. She had gone and signed out of the apartment house. She hadn't taken all of her clothes with her but she had sold everything to several of her neighbors.

"It must have been what she was driving at yesterday when I saw her, Ted. It must have been, only I came on so strong she was frightened to tell me anything more about her leaving than she did hint at."

"She'll be alright."

"If they're bad people we'll never find them. They can always change their name."

"You got her in the business, Terri, that's for sure, but you can't take all the blame. After all, she did want in, or she'd still be in the meat market."

"Maybe she's in a worse meat market now than she was before."

They were not to know how much of a meat market the former cashier really had gotten herself into... not until it came out in the papers how the beautiful young dancer had been shot in the head by persons unknown in some far away country... and as the article read: "probably another hapless American victim who had been lured into the slave market and killed when she found out what it was all about and wanted out..."

Terri would never forgive herself.

THE END

THE RESPONSIBILITY GAME

by "Dick Trent"

from Savage Sex *Vol.4 no 2. Apr./May 1972 on Ed's resume.*

DAVE CAUFIELD PULLED his head slowly away from the gilded, silken crotch of his secretary and wiped his chin in the crook of his arm. It had been a long affair. They had both climaxed twice during the previous hour but there was a tremendous reluctance between them both to stop their actions. However, there was simply a limit to both their capabilities. Enough was enough… for the time being.

"Drink, Tina?"

"I need one," replied the luscious blonde naked as she came to a sitting position on the leather couch with her legs hanging over the edge. The words had come slowly, softly, almost a whisper, but through a rush of hot breath. "You take all the hell right out of a girl."

"Isn't that the way it's supposed to be?" And he was also naked. He crossed his plush office and pressed the switch which moved a false wall and the well-stocked bar was revealed. "As I remember, you take Scotch?"

"You know I do!" She pulled her pink satin mini slip to her and draped it across her exposed pubic region. "I think I could use a strong one… even if it is during working hours."

Dave started pouring the stiff jolts into the two chubby Scotch glasses. "You don't have to worry about working hours as long as you're with the boss." His grin was tired, but honest. Then when he had finished pouring, he lifted the glasses and carried them across the room. He gave one to the girl and noticed where she was looking… and that there was the same glint in her eyes which had been there every time she had looked at that thing.

"Don't you ever get enough of that?"

"Is there enough?"

"I do believe you're insatiable."

"I hope so."

"Maybe you'd better join a group club."

"Show me the way."

Dave picked up his tie from the back of the leather chair and draped it over his almost limp manhood. "There, that better?"

"Looks a little bit like a gift-wrapped sausage now," she laughed then took a long swig of her Scotch. "There. That does feel better." Then she sighed broadly. "I've thought about swinging clubs. But I've also thought about the trouble I might get into. I think you're man enough to handle me. You have been for the last three months. Say, you know! I'm glad you hired me."

"That goes double right back at you." Naked, he moved to sit behind his massive desk, and put his feet up on the polished mahogany. "I've got big plans for you."

"I'd say you've already given me something big."

"With the business I mean."

"Honey," she furthered. "You've been giving me the business."

"Ahh, now cut it out. I mean I've really been thinking about you. About us! I'd like to keep you with me."

"Lord, I'd rather have it no other way."

"You really like it here, don't you?"

"The pay isn't that much," and she grinned and flipped the mini slip on her lap. "But the fringe benefits are something else."

"How'd you like to be a vice president?"

"I love anything to do with vice."

Dave took his feet down from the desk and the grin left his face. He formed the most official look he could muster. "You've got to take this seriously or we might just as well forget what I'm about to say."

The grin also faded from Tina's face. "Sorry, Dave. I thought we were still kidding around."

"I never kid when business is concerned."

"I'll listen quietly."

"You haven't answered me."

"About what?"

"How would you like to be vice president here in my firm? I think you'd find quite a jump in your salary."

"Such a promotion and after only three months."

"The time is unimportant. It has been the way you handle things, of course there are many of my employees who have been with me for years. But there isn't one of them that I could honestly say is right for the position I'm offering."

"I'm flattered."

"Of course, you should be," he replied matter of factly. "But you must realize you've more than earned it."

And her mind was laughing at the big jerk. Earned it! He could bet his sweet ass she'd earned it. How many times had she lied to him, to herself, to the silent world around them about what a great stud he was and how long she could stay with him… and how much torture she had put herself through to stay in the saddle with him so that he could have a double blow-off when he really wasn't even good for one.

A young man, a good looking man, a well-built man and a jerk. You bet she earned it! She'd like to have narrowed her eyes and told him so. She would've liked to have thrown the Scotch into his face then spit on him. But that had not been the plan, even from the start.

Of course he had hired her on the spot. It was all a part of her master plan… there had been the club he generally frequented about cocktail time… she knew he had a wife somewhere… she knew he had a big bank account… a big firm… she couldn't get to the bank account because of the wife… but the firm was wide open… it was a corporation with dummy officers. He ran the whole thing. All she had to do was get in with him. That had been easy… a green mini cocktail dress of slipper satin… shoes and mini purse to match… her blonde hair streaming down her back… those luscious red lips… she really didn't like to paint them at the bar… but it was an attraction getter… there was no doubt about that… and Dave Caufield always had a couple of drinks at the bar before he went to the table which also was always reserved for him.

She marked her time until his arrival. Then when he took a stool at the bar she moved from her chair at a table and took the second stool from him.

That's when she ordered a Scotch and water and did the lipstick bit. Naturally it looked like a pickup bit and naturally Dave was a guy who had been around. He couldn't have missed a come on.

"Finish that one and there'll be a second one waiting for you right in front of the stool next time," he had said.

"Why wait for the delivery?" she had grinned and moved over to the stool.

Then there were the introductions and there were several more Scotch drinks, then there was his car and then there was his apartment… the one he kept as a home away from home… and there was his bedroom.

Did she ever give him a ride that night. She rode him to a complete standstill. He thought he was something else… and she proved to him that she was something else… she was the best bronco on the range and she made him believe he was the best broncobuster in the world… and he should believe it… she told him enough times that night.

Then the following morning she discovered a closet full of nighties and negligees where she selected a sexy pink set with marabou trim, and went about making coffee for them both before he woke up. But they were not to drink their coffee the moment she brought it to him.

His eyes had opened only slightly… too much of the night before… but all that dropped away when he caught sight of the vision of loveliness, the sex goddess which stood before him. To hell with the coffee! He jumped, naked, out of bed and took her in his arms. Their tongues had met and twisted and turned as they had the night before. His legs went around her so that she fit down his "V" and his hands pawed at her back, then into the front of the negligee and nightgown… then when the hand was free again it went up under the nightgown and negligee and played with the golden pubic region…

He was steaming all over again and Tina knew she was not going to have the coffee she so much desired at that moment. She would have to go into her act once more. But there was going to be much more in the act.

His hands flew from her all over again and he backed up a step and his eyes narrowed. Suddenly his hands lashed out and tore the flimsy nightgown and negligee until there was nothing left to hold it together and the material fell in soft cloud-like folds at her feet. Then he knelt before her and took her as he had not taken her the night before.

Later when they both sat on the edge of the bed with the coffee in their hands and they were sipping of the hot brew he looked at her with his boyish grin. "My wife never let me do that to her."

"She doesn't know what she's missing."

"I've wanted to do that with a lot of the girls. I… I… I just never had the nerve."

Tina had grinned, "I'm glad I turned you on like that. I liked it."

"When I saw you standing there all pink and blonde and I thought about last night, I simply couldn't keep my hands off you. I've always wanted to rip the clothes from a girl and do that other thing. I'm not sorry I did."

"I'm not sorry you did either." He was falling into her plot… how well she knew the symptoms.

"Now what can I do for you?" He was serious.

That had all been three months before and during the three months they made it every afternoon in his office and at least twice a week when he had to remain in town *on business*. And then the moment came which she had been waiting for…

"You really do mean you'd like me to be a vice president?"

"There are a lot of responsibilities connected with the job. But as I said. The money will be well worth your acceptance, and you're very well qualified for the position."

"Do I also get a silver key to the executive washroom?" The tension was broken and they both laughed.

Tina slipped into her short brown mini skirt and white angora cardigan after she had straightened the slip down over her exotic body.

"You'll even have your name on your office door."

"I guess it pays to be a vice president."

"Almost as much as it would to be president."

"I think I'll let you keep that position." She grinned. "You fit the chair better."

"There will be a lot of papers to sign." He pulled on his trousers and shirt, then started fixing his tie.

"I write a good signature… took a penmanship award in school."

"Miners have been known to transfer millions with a simple 'X.'"

"Well, I guess I've gone beyond that stage. I'll make sure anybody who reads the message over my signature knows who it came from."

"Always efficient, aren't you!"

"If I weren't you wouldn't be asking me to take over as vice president."

"Well, we might say I feel that running this corporation with a dummy board of directors is for the birds. It was alright in the beginning, but now with the firm as large as it is I'd like to have some decision responsibilities taken off my hands. I'm just tired of the full responsibility. A couple of minds put together are always better than one."

"I only hope I can live up to your estimation." She didn't give a damn about his estimation… the only estimation she had in mind was just how big is the company. That was going to be one of her first investigations. Then she would make further plans from there.

Dave, fully dressed and once more the business executive, puled open the top drawer of his desk and took out the official document. "Come over here, Tina"

Tina adjusted a tiny brown nylon scarf around her neck to top off the angora sweater, then moved across the desk. He handed her the paper… the very official looking document.

"It's all ready for you… witnessed and all." He pointed to one of the lower dotted lines. "Just sign there."

"Shouldn't I read it?"

"Sure, if you want to. But it's a waste of your time." He stuck out the pen.

She shrugged. After all, it was the paper she wanted. She signed. "I'll have your copy notarized while I'm out this afternoon. By the way, your office is right next to mine… right through that door. It will make it even more easy for our get-togethers than before."

"That's what I call real cozy."

"Another drink? To celebrate our sort of partnership." He walked to the bar and poured. She didn't have to answer him. Then he walked back with the fresh glasses and they clicked glasses and drank. "I guess that makes it official."

She thought it was wise. She put the glass down and locked her arms around his neck and their lips and tongues met for a long moment. "What was that for?" he asked, grinning.

"Just for being you."

"Okay. More of that later. Go on into your new office and sign the papers on your desk. There's a lot of them. And I'll be out of town for a couple of days. So hold down the fort and keep those lazy characters outside busy. And when you get those papers signed have them mailed out right away. And you're nuts if you try and read all of them. I don't."

"You're the boss."

"No, you are," he grinned, then moved to his door and went out.

The papers were signed. They were mailed. And the company books were brought to her upon request. And over the following week she realized what had happened… she knew or almost knew when she found the reservation note on Dave's pad. A reservation for Argentina.

She had played him for a sucker and he had played her for the dummy she was. And when the auditors came it was only a short while until the officers came with the warrant for her arrest… The vice president had become the important one. After all, the president was in Argentina and there was no extradition proceedings possible. And after all… she had signed all those papers which directed the banks to shell out the money to the bearer of the copy… Dave's copy…

Dave had had all those other people's money in the bank… and he really had become tired of the responsibility. The only responsibility he wanted was the money in his own name.

In time Tina might be able to play the responsibility game again… maybe!

THE END

WHERE DID CHARLIE GET ON THE TRAIN

SWAP Vol.5 No3 July/Aug. 1971, no author listed, on Ed's resume 1971

A GREAT MANY PEOPLE would like to know where Charlie got on the train. There were the cops, and there was the insurance company, and there was his studio and there were a hell of a lot of girls and there was the track-crew who scrapped up his tattered remains from the rails and ties. About the only one who apparently didn't seem to care much was his wife, Sheila, who stood to be a hundred thousand dollars (double indemnity if it was a case of accidental death) richer from an extremely concerned insurance company. She had cried momentarily, if half an hour in all of eternity might be considered momentarily. Even then she didn't know if she was crying for him, or just what the tears were really for. Charlie had been a rounder and a bounder... the vows of marriage were something the studio felt should be done when the young starlet, Sheila, turned up pregnant by him.

But there was never to be any thought of settling down to any home life where Charlie was concerned. His dialogue was always – "Why should I settle down and make one woman miserable when there are so many I can make happy?" A corny line which was far from original, but it served the purpose.

All those concerned were positive where he got off the train. He might have been dragged a few hundred yards along the tracks, but the blood splotch at the moment of impact was quite clearly visible in all its tell-tale vividness. In fact it appeared that most of the life giving blood rushed out of him in one great gushing explosion as the first set of wheels cut him clean in two. Hamburger would be a mild explanation of his final condition when the last set of wheels completed their task.

A ticket had been issued in his name at the main depot in Los Angeles, a drawing room for two. The train had pulled out of the station and the same porter carried his duties through to Las Vegas and the next porter took over from there would hold so through to Salt Lake City. No one had entered that locked compartment. The porters and the conductor had the only keys. The keys were not used. Yet it was apparent Charlie was on the train. His remains were found just under a hundred miles west of Salt Lake City, on one of the long, seemingly endless desert treks.

"Sure there's a highway along most of that right of way, but not at that spot," observed a police official who had been assigned to the case and was making direct reports to the Insurance Investigators. "But not at that spot. The rails are more than a mile and a half back across the desert. There isn't even a wagon road back that far. And there are no wheel tracks. Of course there is always the possibility that sand may have blotted out wheel marks, but that is extremely farfetched. It would take a dune buggy to get in there and they dig in heavy. And would have taken one hell of a sand blow. There is wind on the desert most of the time, but there's been nothing heavy for more than a month, and for the amount of sand to cover any wheel tracks it would also have nearly covered the body. Sand cover I rule out completely… there was little or no sand around the body."

Then came the all-important question which the Insurance Agent Investigator had to ask himself. "So the first line of thought has to be directed at who will benefit by Charlie's death, and it comes out the wife. And because it was, or let's consider it to be, an accident there is the double indemnity clause. A hundred grand is quite an incentive when there is no love lost between them. A hundred grand is quite an incentive, love or no love."

Thus arose another question. How could anyone be sure that particular train was the one which tore Charlie apart? Simply because there was a drawing room in his name, didn't mean he hadn't taken a later train. He wouldn't have had to register his name as a simple Joe passenger. And it was an official from the train company who forwarded his official report. They knew it was that particular train because parts of Charlie's body were scrapped off the under carriage of the last six cars. The first of the six cars being that which housed the drawing room he should have occupied.

"Certainly I knew he was going on that train," told the wife. "He was always going somewhere. He rated pretty high with his studio and whenever there was to be some kind of a location shooting he went, on his own, to look it over, then give his approval or disapproval. His words held great weight at where the pictures would be shot. Sure, I knew he took chippies along with him, he always did! He never tried to hide the fact, and I could care less… and of course I wouldn't divorce him for his discrepancies. He made too much money. He was a big time director… He was also a big time bastard. You know what a bastard is, don't you? Well he was a *big time* bastard."

Which brought a noted Beverly Hills Banker into the controversy. A rotund man, a very rich man, but a man who smoked Mexican rope cigars because they were long enough to cut in half, and in that way he got two for the price of one. Although other than that he always picked up the check, especially if there was a pretty, young girl in attendance. She might be choking to death on the smoke from the rope, but he was still making with the silent pointed passes.

"There had been times Charlie had considerable funds in my bank… considerable I say. He has an alive account, but no sir, nowhere the kind of money the fair lady expects. He'd put quite some funds into a couple of motion pictures which weren't exactly box offices smashes. In fact they went right down the drain and television hasn't bothered to pick them up. I'd say he rather took a hard beating. I must say, in defending myself, I advised him against the venture. But he said the studio needed the money. He even tried to get me to put up a pile from the bank's motion picture funds. I wouldn't even bother to investigate the possibilities after I read the scripts. I guess, from the look of things, he must have nearly financed both shows by himself. You know the saying… a fool and his money are soon parted. The only trouble with that remark: Charlie never appeared to be that kind of fool."

Joe Henderson, head of publicity for Acme Studios poured several double shots of Scotch as he talked in his usual very casual voice. Every word he spoke always seemed to come out in a matter-of-fact statement with emphasis upon nothing, except for a pointed and very definite move when he shot down the Scotch. "Now I don't know anything about the studio being in financial difficulties, I rather think it's quite sound. All six of the films he pushed out this year have been great money makers. The stock holders are happy for a change. But those two bombs Charlie financed and directed… I don't know why he insisted on putting up his own cash. Maybe he wanted the bigger part of the action. You could never figure Charlie. His pictures didn't always make a lot of money but the studio figures on some losses during any year. I guess he did have his share of rough ones the last year or two, but we put on a good publicity campaign and pulled them out. We just couldn't do anything with those last two. He didn't give us anything to work with. We can scream sex all day long, but how many ways can you spell it. And no matter what the advertisements say or the photos depict, if the patron goes into the theatre and the picture leaves them cold, they are going to demand their money back and tell their friends to stay away. They stayed away in droves from Charlie's attempt at being his own boss. Anything more than this will have to come from the front office… the big man himself. Only Tom is out of town for another week. Tom Corona, he's the president of Acme you know."

Carry Nation, that wasn't her real name, but once long ago she had played the part in a top movie and she did such a convincing job the name stuck with her. Carry was in charge of the publicity photograph files. There were a lot of early photos of Charlie around, but he had been reluctant in later years to have the newer pictures shown around. But Carry had a goodly amount and she supplied the latest for identification purposes. They could be circulated around for the news media and for whatever other identification purposes they might be helpful in.

"He seemed like a nice enough fellow. Of course being stuck here in the file room so many hours a day I don't get to walk the lot much except for my lunch hour. I get to say hello in the commissary once in awhile. He was a pretty fair hand with the ladies and Scotch. He was quite a Scotch drinker he was. But he could sure hold it when he was younger. Course lots of things in a body changes when you get a little older. He'd get unsteady on his legs sometimes over at the Brown Derby. I don't get over there as much as I used to either, but there are times I like to meet some of my old friends and we get over there. Charlie was generally there if he wasn't on a picture. Last time I saw him… let's see… that was two weeks ago Friday over there and the parking lot boy had to help him to his car. The boy tried to get him to take a taxi but he wouldn't hear of it… kept cursing all the time… mainly kept cursing the studio."

Helen Talbert had been Charlie's secretary for more than five years and it was apparent why. She was a luscious dish and she wore the pink angora sweater and brown miniskirt with the ease of any starlet on the lot. She could have easily made it to the starlet ranks, but she long ago decided on a career where she knew she was going to eat every day, have a few cocktails when she wanted and have a roof over her head.

When interviewed she held down what had been Charlie's desk in the big deep-pile rug covered office which was lined with books and the leather-bound manuscripts of all the films Charlie had ever done. And behind a secret wall, opened immediately by Helen when she entered, was a well-stocked bar. There were more than a dozen bottles of Charlie's favorite Scotch.

"He liked Teachers, I don't think it's the best for my tastes, but he liked it and he was the one who had to drink it… and he was the one paying for it. I don't like drinking on the job, I guess mainly because I can't hold my liquor very well, but Charlie always insisted I join him. I didn't take much, but there were a few times I had to take a cab home. Originally I was strictly a martini drinker, but Charlie touted me off on Scotch and I got to like it.

"I've never seen him fall down, but Carry Nation, the old biddy was right about his feet getting unsteady lately. Not that he was one of those falling down drunks because half the time it was hard to tell if he'd been drinking or not. But he was getting unsteady during the last couple of months. Maybe he had too much on his mind. He didn't do too good with those last couple of pictures he made. You know he financed them well, that's a lot of money to spend on a couple of box office busts. He desired to boil himself once in a while. If something like that happened to me I think I'd find some harder stuff to get smashed on.

"And I have no idea why the studio didn't finance the pictures. They always did before! But not this time! That you'll have to get from Tom Corona. He'll be back in the morning. Being the studio head executive I guess he's the only one who can give you any straight answers. All I can say is I'm sorry he's gone. He was a good boss. Sure, I dated him a few times and we made the bedroom scene, I'll admit that to anybody. But now what worries me is we might get in one of those baldheaded, stinking cigar smokers like certain bankers I know who try to put the make on any girl in the studio just because they put their money up. Lots of girls don't play it that way. Now Charlie… he was the dream boss for any girl."

Helen Talbert crossed her legs tightly and shivered at some hidden thought and reached for a fresh Scotch and water.

The pleasant voice of Tom Corona belied the hardness of his business judgment. But reading behind the lines saw him to be an executive who knew his job. "It's a simple story, why he had to finance his own pictures… those last two. First of all I was going to cancel his contract. The last three he made financed by the studio were only saved by the publicity department. Even the big names I had in it couldn't have saved the budget if the publicity department hadn't come through for us. Charlie simply lost his touch. He couldn't tell a good script from a bad one and he couldn't work with his people any longer. A lot of directors, with as much time on the stage as he had, go like that. But in Charlie's case I think the booze had a lot to do with it. I gave him three chances and that was to be it. But I let him use the studio for those last two bombs. He financed them and I said I'd put them into release simply as a favor to him, and even knowing how bad the scripts were. I almost begged him not to put the dough into them, but he did and I guess he took a hell of a beating. I know I did! I laid out the dough for publicity and advertising. When the publicity department hasn't got anything to work with... that's it... The good Lord himself couldn't have saved those two belly aches."

The two negro train barmen had both been out of town when Charlie's pictures were published in the newspapers and shown on television. But Rusty had held down the lounge bar from Los Angeles through to Las Vegas and he was relieved for the rest of the run by Henry. Rusty was a tall man and owned a deep voice. "He didn't get on in Los Angeles, but he got on at a special stop in San Fernando. He didn't give a name I guess, or somebody else would have come up with it, like the conductor or even his porter. He just got on and came right to the bar and there he sat all the time drinking down straight scotch with water backs."

Henry voiced up, "Then when I took over in Las Vegas he never got off the train during the layover. He just kept looking bleary-eyed into his glass and when it was empty he always shoved it right out for a refill. I never did see no man who could put down that much Scotch... any whiskey for that matter, in such a short time as he did. But he was a sad man.

"Now when we came cross the line into Utah there's ain't no more drinks served, so I do a lot of other things around the bar. Most always the passengers leave the bar, but not Charlie. He just sat there with a fresh glass of water every so often. And I know he was drinking from a bottle he hid under his coat, and I was supposed to stop anybody from doing that. But when you don't actually see something... well, you can't do nothing about it. And the only thing I ever did hear him say was over and over again that he'd been shot into oblivion and that's where he was heading... only he'd go into oblivion in his own way. Broke man had a right to choose his own way. That's what he said. And the reason I know about the bottle under his coat is 'cause I found the empty under his chair after he left… That was about a hundred miles this side of Salt Lake City…."

CONCLUSION: Charlie got on the train in the city of San Fernando, just outside of Los Angeles. He drank continually for the entire period to the spot outside of Salt Lake City.

There he either fell or jumped from the train platform which fronted his drawing room car. He had never entered the drawing room. Charlie had been a powerful man. He couldn't accept defeat gracefully, proof being what it was, the file was closed as accidental death. The platform had a faulty catch on the door.

THE END

TANK TOWN CHIPPIE

by "Ann Gora"

in Gallery vol.2 no.2 Apr./May 1973 on Ed's resume 1973

SHE HAD ALWAYS STATIONED herself near the edge of the tank bat-talions. She could easily have set up business in the more enjoyable sec-tions around the regular bases, even the airstrip, but that wasn't where the big money was. The base held a lot of dog faces who got little or no money, and those at the airfield were always on the go someplace so they could get girls wherever they wanted. They didn't have to depend upon the Vietnamese girls... no matter how pretty they were.

But the tank corps. That was different. They were locked into their saddle for months at a time. They came in from battle in their iron and steel monsters for a few days rest and for their equipment to be revamped then they were off again. And they always had bonus money to spend.

If they wanted a girl, they had to take what was immediately pre-sented to them. None of them seemed to complain... especially when they were with Cobra... that's what they called her... she didn't know any other name.

And she liked that name which was given to her by that first tank bat-talion who had returned to the back lines for their week rest period... and the name was passed on down to the next; and the next, and all the future companies which would reside in Cobra's presence. They told her she got the name because of her quick lips... her sparking eyes, her sharp teeth, her rhythmic body and her long fingered, graceful hands.

She liked the attention the men gave her. She liked the presents they gave her... and later when she learned what it was all about, she liked the money they gave her for her services... the pay she received for what she gave almost free previously. The Americans were indeed generous.

She could live far above the standards of any other Vietnamese girl, other than those who were in the same business as she... and indeed there were hundreds. But Cobra was one of the prettiest around and she was never without company when she wanted it... and she learned quickly that because of her beauty she could pick and choose her men, and she could command nearly as much money as she wanted.

If the soldier balked at her price, she would simply turn away saying that she could go elsewhere for her night... they always changed their mind. One look at Cobra and they always changed their mind if she was about to walk out on them. Then, as only the underground grapevine knows, she learned about the coming pullout of all American soldiers from the battle zones, most of them being returned to their own country, she could see the handwriting on the wall. Her days of wealth were coming to an end. The Vietnamese soldiers would take over all the bases, those which would be kept in operation... and the Vietnamese soldiers had no money... they might barter with bananas. Cobra would have nothing to do with that. She had learned a new kind of life, and that was the life she was going to keep.

Tony Armando was in the last group... a very young fellow, just over twenty, a devoted Catholic, wide-eyed with the adventure he was witnessing, but very tired from the weeks of battle.

If he knew what Cobra's profession was, he did not show it. He never would show it, nor would he believe it if he heard such from his buddies. In fact, if any of them were to mention what they thought in his presence he probably would have split their lip and flattened their nose. But it was never mentioned... not even at those times he spoke her name over and over to the others and they full well knew who he was talking about.

He met her the first night he arrived at the back area. He hadn't planned on going anywhere; the cot on his tent looked like the most inviting place he'd ever seen... and he knew that once he got into it he wouldn't be disturbed by anything for three days... even meals were at a special time and if you weren't there... you just weren't there... this was complete rest...

But he lay on the cot for just under three hours and sleep eluded him. He looked to his watch and it wasn't yet nine o'clock. So he sat up and swung his legs over the edge of the cot and lit a cigarette. He puffed at it a few times then got up and walked out of the tent. He wasn't going anyplace special. Just outside. He wanted a change of air for the moment, which he thought might give him the powers of sleep. He was still too keyed up with all the weeks of action. He knew it would take him some time to come down... even though he knew there would be no more battles for him to return to.

Standing in the flap opening of the tent and looking out across the field toward the high chain link, barbed wire topped fence and to the small campfires beyond he found himself wondering who the people were and why they resided so close to a military institution?

But then he knew these people were hungry and perhaps they felt if they were closer to the camps they could grab off some of the leavings, perhaps steal it directly.

He didn't know if it were permissible to leave the compound, but he'd never know if he didn't try. And there was a tremendous curiosity about who those people were.

There were a couple of guards at the gate, but all they did was take a brief look at his I.D., and told him to watch out for the snakes along the road... and that's all there was to it... and little did he know he was destined to meet Cobra.

Cobra saw him before he saw her. She watched him look at each of the small tents, and the sleeping bag arrangements and the bonfires. She couldn't have realized his thoughts however, even though those thoughts were about the lack of male Vietnamese... but there were many soldiers in various stages of lovemaking.

Tony was not some backward jerk. He knew what was happening, and what the soldiers were doing. But he was naive enough not to realize the complete prostitution arrangement into which he had entered.

Cobra had only met two other Americans who were so young when it came to understanding anything real about sex, therefore she could spot the symptoms in Tony while he was still some distance away from her.

She had thought of what she must do for some time. Her only problem was how to go about it. But she did know she would need someone like the boy who approached her. She was the professional. He was the amateur. Under such circumstances the professional had to win.

Tony had always been embarrassed when meeting a girl for the first time... especially if she was a pretty one, more so if she were a beautiful girl… he was frozen, looking down to where Cobra sat… their eyes had met. The Cobra had hypnotized her victim. But they would not speak for several moments and all that Tony could find to do with his tongue was to lick at his dry lips.

"You would like some tea, American soldier?" Cobra broke the silence.

He still couldn't find any words, but he felt his legs sagging. The music of her voice had sent both sounds of music and senses of shivers through his body. He had suddenly felt weak all over, and he knew he'd better sit down before he fell down.

Cobra already had the tea poured into one of her fancy, hand painted cups as he sank crosslegged to the ground next to her. She handed it to him and he took it with unsteady hands and so that he still wouldn't have to talk for the moment he began sipping of it, keeping his lips on the rim.

"You are lonely American soldier?"

He gulped. He knew he'd have to speak. "I… I… I been in battle. You don't get too lonely when you're in battle. Too much to do to worry about anything except getting out of there alive."

"It is terrible… war," she sighed. "But you will go to your America now… very soon… you will not be in war anymore."

"You know about that."

"Everyone knows about that." And they talked until there was nothing else to talk about. Tony felt he should get back to his tent, but something kept him there facing the girl… it was as if he was trapped and loving every moment of it.

"You would like to make with me?"

He thought he understood her right. And he thought he understood what she meant. "Did you say… ?"

She stretched back on her blanket with her legs close to the small fire so that the light would fully expose her attributes as she pulled up her skirt. She wore no panties. The pink lips nearly hidden in her love nest seemed to be winking at him; urging him to come closer, to permit them to give the love kiss they promised.

Cobra reached over and took his hand. She laid it fully across her pubic mound and Tony began to sweat as he felt the erection starting between his legs. Her inner thighs began to quiver, and the vagina lips smacked against the palm of his hand. He had never experienced intercourse before. He'd never even gone that far with a girl. Once in the back seat of a car he had gotten up under a girl's sweater and felt her titties through a brassiere… but that was as far as she permitted him to go.

Anything else he learned from pictures and books and listening to the other guys around the barracks talk. Naturally he had never let them know he was a virgin. He always had a few stories he could tell… thanks to the cheap novels he had picked up along the way. It's just a good thing the guys he told his stories to hadn't read the same novels.

No matter. He had enough knowledge stored up, in his studied mind to know what the girl was doing to him, and what was happening to him. He reddened but it couldn't be seen by the faint light of the small fire, and he permitted himself to be pulled down beside her… he didn't want the lovely girl to know he was a virgin either. He'd do everything he learned from the books and hope that he could put it over; get away with it… only he also hoped that they could hide somewhere. He didn't like the idea of doing it right out there in the open like so many of the others were doing…. He didn't like it that way at all.

She anticipated his thoughts as she pulled another blanket seemingly from out of nowhere and put it up over them. And the next moment she had his fly open and his penis deep within her.

He exploded almost immediately. He felt that she was the most exciting woman that the world could ever produce, and he told her so… he did not tell her she was the only woman he had ever had. And even though there was no one else to base his findings on, he was positive she was the most exciting woman on earth, and the only one for him. No other woman would ever be able to satisfy him like that. Indeed, he would never think of another woman ever again… no one but the lady Cobra.

Thus he told her so.

"It is good I hear such words from you, Tony," she said on their third visit, and just after he had taken himself out of her and they lay back resting.

"I knew you wasn't one of them prostitutes right from the start. And you never did ask me for no money that first time. That's how I knew you really liked me… that you didn't pick me up just because I would have some money in my pocket like the other girls I heard about. I knew you stopped me with your eyes because I was something extra special. I guess you was a virgin… huh?"

She blinked, but he couldn't see her. "I liked it very much being with you," she answered him indirectly.

"I sure don't want to think about leaving you."

"I would not like you to leave, Tony."

"Course I gotta leave this base soon. We're all going home."

"I will cry very hard."

"Maybe you won't have to."

"I should not like to have to cry."

"Well now I got an idea. But you gotta understand. When I'm out of the Army I don't make a lot of money. I work in a factory… piece work… you know what that means, piece work?"

She thought of the piece work she had been doing. "I know what it is, piece work."

"Well, I got to turn out a lot in order to even make a hundred bucks a week. But I live with my own family and it don't cost much to live… and maybe in a few years I can get at something better… after I do some more schooling… anyway… what I got in mind is if you'd take a chance with me?"

"In Vietnam one is most fortunate, very rich who makes a hundred dollars in a month. Are you asking me to marry with you, American soldier Tony?"

"If you think you could take up with an ugly, lead foot like me."

"You are not ugly and you are not lead foot. I would take up with you."

And they were married the day before he shipped out. She would follow as soon as all the paper work and the passport arrangements could be made. Red tape could take months at times… and as the time dragged on Cobra began to worry. She found little use for her trade any longer… and those who wanted it seldom could pay… she had dipped so far into her savings, she was sending more and more cries for help to Tony… and he was always right there with the money by return mail.

She began to think that perhaps she had misunderstood her husband. She knew that a hundred dollars never seemed to be very much to the Americans, but Tony had made it seem so high… yet that was all he made during a week and she asked him for four times that amount the last time she wrote and there it was.

Six months later she was with him… in the sleezy tenement type apartment with the yelling brats, the mice and the cockroaches at nights… the smells of all the neighbors' cookings and the rotting cellars, and the unclean clothing which had been hung out to dry… or hung in the halls…. It could only remind her of that time with her own parents before she became the professional she was… and when her husband took her with his sweaty body he smelled like the soldiers who had just come in from the field.

Lady Cobra would not remain in that situation very long. She knew she was not put upon this earth to be a piece of nothing… when all along the Tankers had proven to her that she was a real piece of something….

She put on one of the fine outfits she had persuaded her husband to get for her and she went out through the rotten street… and she walked until she found the better streets… and she went past the low-class hotels, then the better class hotels, then the high-class hotels… and finally there were the ritzy hotels… once more she had located her Tank Town.

THE END

Never Fall Backwards

as "Dick Trent"

in Fantastic *V1,N1,* Gallery Press *Jan./Feb. 1972, in the book*
Short Wood *on Ed's resume 1972*

Rick Perry leaned back in the booth... the darker booth at the back of the cocktail lounge and lifted his tall whiskey and water. He made the ice clink in the glass as he moved it in circles about eye level. He'd already had seven or eight, or nine. He'd lost count long ago. He did know he'd had four before Terri and Vance joined him in the booth. But the four didn't bother him any. He had a great capacity for liquor... even though he had only acquired a real taste for it during the past year... when things were getting tougher and tougher... the jobs were rough and more demanding... and when he came in off the set he felt like all he wanted to do was sit down and have a couple... then the couple went to a pint, then a fifth, then a quart... then there was a complete loss in the counting.

"You're working tomorrow?" Terri was deeply concerned.

"I'm always working tomorrow. And that goes for Saturdays and Sundays, too." Rick's voice was becoming thick. Perhaps he felt that the drinks were doing him no harm... that he didn't feel them... but his constitution always told the story when he started to speak.

Vance leaned over the table after he had gulped down the remainder of his Scotch. "What's the job?"

"High dive from the wing of an old bi-plane. The Johnny Walter's picture."

"I heard about that stunt. Two guys have already turned it down, Rick."

"Who the hell cares what others do, Vance. I'm the King of the stunt men. I don't turn anything down. I just get more money for doing what I can do."

Vance tapped his glass on the table and a topless waitress crossed to him and picked up his glass, then looked around at the others with her eyes questioning about their own levels. "Sure, I want another," piped up Rick, then downed his whiskey which encompassed three quarters of the glass. He shoved the empty to the girl, but Terri put her hand lightly across to his arm. She tried for a weak smile.

"Do you think you should?"

"If I didn't I wouldn't be ordering it."

"That's a long dive from the wing of the plane into that hard ocean."

"So I better be drunk when I do it." He snapped her hand from his arm then reached down to pat the topless waitress on the fanny. "Now you be off and you get little ole Rickie a good stiff double one this time." He turned back to his expectant friends. "You know the only thing I won't do when I'm drunk. You know what that is, gang?"

"You never drive a car when you've been drinking." Vance tapped his fingers on the table. He was nervous for his friend. And the nerves caused him to want also to double up on his drink order. He did so by snapping his fingers to get the girl's attention then holding up two fingers to form a "V" when she looked to him. She got the message.

"That's right. I don't drive. Now, not that I'm scared of anything. But the one thing you can't fight and that's the little boys in the blue uniform with the big gold badge and the big gun on his hip. And you can't fight that guy, later, the guy in the black robe that sends you to jail after he's cleaned out your bankroll. Now that's the only reason I don't drive a car when I've had more than a few shots… like right now." Rick had told the story over and over again… ever since he had been picked up for drunk driving back in 1965… seven years before. He didn't approve of the other side of the bars and he wasn't going to see them again… not for drunk driving.

"Anything else, like diving off the wing of a plane into the cold Pacific… Hell ma'an… I could do that with a blindfold over my eyes."

Vance chuckled. "Better not say that too loud around here. Johnny Walter might have spies and you'd find yourself doing just that when you get up on the wing tomorrow."

"It would cost him another grand."

"Is that what you're getting for the jump?"

"Dive, Terri… dive… not jump. Anybody can jump. Hardly anybody can dive. You see we get up there in that old two-seater and we have one hell of a fight with the plane being run by the ground radio equipment… and we fight all over that damned thing… up there about ten thousand feet… then we sky dive all the way down to five hundred feet and I get the lumps and go over the side… Bang… there I go down toward the water, flopping all the way… and bang… that's the end of the chapter… continued next week to see if our hero gets out of it alive…." Rick sighed. "And it doesn't matter if I get killed or not when I hit the water… because next week all we see is Rocky Cliff coming to the surface so he can continue on to another adventure." He sighed again then looked up as the topless waitress moved to the group and put the two glasses down on the table, then moved away back toward the bar. "What are you working on, Vance?"

"My thin little frame gets into a sweater and skirt for an automobile fall… I'm taking the lumps for Shirley Lane in her television special."

"Now that's what I call action," laughed Rick as he took a great gulp of the Scotch and water, then coughed. "I said a double but I think she forgot the water."

Terri started to turn toward the waitress across the room. "I'll call her back."

Rick stopped her movement. "The hell you will. This is the way I like my Scotch. All that water cuts the taste. This way I can feel it burning all the way down to my balls… That's the way I like things. All the way down to my balls. Hey, how about you and me going over to your apartment for a couple of hours, Terri?"

She grinned. "Even if I took you up on it, you couldn't do a thing about it. Ten seconds after I got you undressed you'd be asleep on my new fur blanket."

"Ahh, but in those few seconds 1 could look at your magnificent body. You know I always like to see my girls undress before I take my rags off."

"You wouldn't even be able to see my magnificent body."

"Then you could gaze with wonder at my magnificent body… that's what you could do. Besides, this Scotch costs ninety cents a shot. Over at your place I could drink all night for free."

"And get up at six for a plane ride and a cold bath in the Atlantic…"

"Or a cold dry period in a casket," ventured Vance.

"Sometimes, Vance, old buddy, I think you think I'm no good at my profession. Sometimes I think you think I should be knocking off a hundred and fifty bucks a day getting dressed like a fag and doing what you do. Ma'an, I get a grand before I even get out of bed… before I'll even get out of a bar... before I'll do any of their crap. Yeah, you stick to the frilly undies and let your old father do the tough stuff. Sometimes I think you just ain't got it in you to be a top stuntman."

Vance knew there was no answer to the remarks. He did get two hundred and fifty a day, not a hundred and fifty... but that was about the best he could command... and he wasn't big enough to double for the top stars... mostly the tough stunts the girls had to do... he didn't mind the fag tag, but he wished once he could get the big dough like Rick. But that took a lot more guts and skill than he had. It was one thing rolling out of a moving vehicle into a well-designed, and spotted sand pit... but going off a cliff into three feet of water... or riding a wing through a rain storm... or like Rick was to do the following day... take off a wing and go through five hundred feet of space to hit water which could be as solid as cement... that was something he couldn't fathom doing.

"Yeah, guess you're right, Rick. I just ain't got it in me for the big time."

Rick reached over and playfully clipped him on the jaw. "Don't let it throw you. You'll live longer than me."

Terri winced. She really did like Rick. She wished he would become completely serious about her. They had made it in the bedroom many times during the past four years of their close friendship. But there had never been anything permanent about the arrangements. And she had made it several times with Vance and he was a sweet guy also... but not one she could ever get serious about. She hated the thought that Rick would become seriously injured... killed. She loved him, the crazy nut. But he wasn't one who could return any kind of love. Friendship... yes. Sex... without a doubt, one of the best she had ever had in bed... she loved to wrap her legs around his hips... his neck... anywhere he put his body... but that was the total score. There was nothing that could be added to it.

And she had seen the change coming over him during the past year... about the time he started the heavy, hard, serious drinking. Before that he'd map out whatever stunt he was going to attempt... only there would be no attempting about it... He had it all mapped out and could tell exactly how many bruises, if any, he could come out of the stunt with. But when the booze became his steady companion it wasn't long before he no longer took up pencil and paper and figured things out for his own protection. Many were the times he didn't even bother to pick up the script and see what the stunt was all about. The director or the assistant hired him over the phone saying "a high dive" or "a cliff dive" or "an auto crash," or whatever, then he waited until he was on the set where it was explained to him what they wanted.

He simply did it... he took from the past and brought it to the present in his mind and, completely unprepared, he took off and did the work.

"He's been lucky," Terri had told her friends. "But luck has a way of running out. It all started when he took so heavy to the bottle... that was on his thirty-sixth birthday. He's thirty-seven now. How long can he put his body through this kind of torture? I haven't even seen him eat in the last month... not even the box lunches on the location. He's always got that bottle around him somewhere. Maybe he really does need to be boozed up before he goes up. Maybe he's losing his nerve. Something's got to be wrong."

"What time you hitting the air in the morning?"

"Just about the time the sun comes up over the yardarm. The director wants the sun at my back so that I don't look too much like a double for the great star Rocky."

Terri blinked. "At that time of the morning you're going to be diving into almost pure blackness. You won't know where the air ends and the water begins. That water will be as black as the ace of spades that time of the morning."

Rick grinned. "Now do you see why I don't want any more water in my booze today." He laughed loud and long. "Now wouldn't it be all easier if I took a dive into an ocean full of Scotch? Think I'll bring that up to the next director who wants me to make a high dive."

Vance finished off his drink and stood up.

"Where are you going, old buddie?"

"I've got a fitting. Got to fill out the sweater and skirt... and look over the fall area... take a couple of practice dives in the skirt. Can't catch my high heels in the hem. I got to practice. We're all not as talented as you, old buddy."

"Nobody is as talented as me, old buddy."

"Pay for my drinks. You're in the big dough."

"You got it. See you here tomorrow about this time... if you're finished."

"I'll be finished. Just about the same time you're hitting the cold black water I'll be hitting that soft sand pit and my day is over."

"And about the time I hit that cold black water, my day will be over."

"I only hope," whispered Terri almost to herself, "that it's only the day that will be over."

Rick looked away from Vance's retreating figure and looked to her. "You say something?"

"Nothing important."

"Honey, love, you should figure it that anything you say in this world is important, otherwise you shouldn't waste your breath saying it."

"Are you out to kill yourself?"

"Not lately."

"You're acting like it."

"I've done this kind of dive a dozen times."

"And you were sober and you plotted out the whole routine. You kid Vance about going out to practice. Well, I can tell you he's in as much danger as you are if those high heels did catch in the lining of that skirt. He's smart in getting out there and getting the lay of the land."

"That's what I'd like to do."

"What?"

"Get the lay of the land." And he laughed so hard much of his drink slopped out onto the table.

"You just can't be serious, can you?"

"I try not to. There's too little of life ahead of us to waste it all in serious crap. Take the knocks and take the good as it all comes. You get to like the old world when you look at it that way... Just let everything come and let nature take its course... Now what about you and me going over to your apartment and getting all cozy?"

"I suppose I'll never hear the end of it if I don't take you home with me." She was thinking more about getting him into her bed than anything else... with her or without her he would crap out almost as soon as he hit the bed... she knew that to be fact from the many past experiences. She wanted him sober for that ride... she didn't want that to be his last ride.

"You'll never hear the end of it," he muttered and got up, taking her arm at the same time... and she steadied him across the room toward the entrance to the cocktail bar.

And it was four o'clock the next afternoon that Rick and Terri sat across from each other in the same booth and they were totally silent as they held their glasses tightly in their hands. They had been silent, that way, since two in the afternoon when they had arrived, separately, but both with the same information.

The high heels had caught in the hem of the skirt. The funeral would be on Thursday…

Rick finally brushed his hand through his thick black hair which was still damp from its exposure to the black Atlantic that morning. He looked across to Terri's tear-stained eyes.

"I always told him he didn't have it in him… I always told him that a stuntman never falls backwards."

THE END

THE SAGA OF RANCE BALL

by "Dick Trent"

Roulette vol.6 no1 Jan./Feb. 1972 on Ed's resume (1971)

WORD GOT AROUND the industry fast that Rance Ball was in town. Some hated him and others just disliked him, but all agreed that he was a necessary entity in their business. After all, he did pay money for what he wanted. It was like trying to squeeze water from a rock. But when he dug down into the briefcase he always carried for his checks and contracts he didn't hesitate in signing his name. And his checks never bounced. That was about the only good thing anybody had to say for Rance Ball... his checks never bounced.

"You're a shit-head." It was always his first remark when he visited a client. "You've always been a shit-head and you will always be a shit-head."

"That's what I like about you, Rance. You're all one color. You never change," replied the Independent Producer, Harry Conners.

"That's why I'm a millionaire and you never know where your next buck is coming from."

"From you, Rance."

"Yeah, from me! I wonder what you shit-head producers would do without me around to bail you out. You couldn't even raise up a hardon with a naked broad playing with herself right in front of you and you with your zipper down."

"Try me some time."

"Tell me, Harry, you still ain't makin' it with the broads in your films?"

"That's my business."

"Tell me the gory, bloody details."

"You'd like that, wouldn't you?"

"It would be more fun than watching the crap you turn out you call movies."

"Sex movies."

"I see more sex on the street than I ever see in your pictures."

"But you still buy them."

"Because I got a lot of theatres to service... and them theatres got a lot of customers who want to jerk-off in the front row. Only I ain't doin much more business with you if you don't get some better stills than you been gettin'"

"What's wrong with my stills?"

"They don't sell the product. The product don't sell the product either. But at least the stills get the slobs in off the street and once they're in the theatre seat it's too late for them to back out."

"That's right. You don't give them their money back if they don't like the show."

"I don't give nobody any money unless they deliver something to me."

"My stills are the hottest around."

"Pussy... that's all they are. The guy and the broad makin' the scene on that crappy bed, on that crappy blanket you use in every slobbering picture you make. Well, once you seen pussy and once you seen that shitty bed you know what you're going to see on the inside. The same old shitty Harry Conner picture. The same ugly dames and the same pockmarked characters you call men, making it on that cruddy bed."

"Now you're telling me how to make pictures."

"Somebody should."

"I got a budget to keep. So I spend money and maybe get a new bed. Who pays me extra for more money in the budget... you?"

"I don't never pay no more money."

"Then you get the same cruddy bed."

"Shit!"

"And the same ugly broads and the same pockmarked guys and they keep doing the mouth and the pussy job like always."

"You want to know something, Harry?"

"Even if I didn't you'd tell me anyway."

"You're a small time shit-head and you always will be a small time shit-head. Say, where do you get the bread to pay the lawyers when you get busted?"

"I don't get busted."

"You mean you ain't never been busted! That's different from when maybe you might get busted. You know porno is still against the law."

"You threatening me?"

"Now why would I do a thing like that to my old friend Harry Conners?"

"If you thought you could make a buck out of getting me busted, you'd do it."

"Ahh, now, I ain't really that bad. Sure, I like a buck. But I make more bucks seeing that you stay out of the clink... not in it. You just keep making your shitty pictures and I'll keep buying them and that way we both stay in business."

"The kind of dough you pay it's lucky I stay in business." The producer frowned and lit a long black cigar.

"You could offer me one of those."

"Buy your own. I can't afford giving cigars away. I'm on a tight budget."

"You are friendly today, Harry."

"And I don't buy lunches either."

"I bet you brown-bag your lunch."

"Only if it comes in a bottle."

"The booze is getting to you, that's what makes you so mean and cheap, Harry."

"Mean and cheap! Why you old bastard..."

Rance interrupted the producer quickly. "Bastard... maybe... old...? I'm younger than you. But bastard I am. I admit to it with all the pride I can sum up." He grinned and took a cigarette from his pocket and fired it with a silver cigarette lighter taken from the same breast pocket of his jacket.

"I don't know why I sit here and listen to your fat mouth puking out words that should be flushed down the toilet."

"You listen because I only come out here to the coast twice a year, and every time I bring you a bundle of money." He laughed. "And from the way you so-called producers talk about me, and say things about me, I kinda figure I'm a legend in my own time."

"You can say that again."

"I'm a legend in my own time."

"How come you always must have the last word?"

"Because I'm the guy with the loot and the loot man always has the last word."

"Someday maybe that will change."

"Change? Balls! Money speaks louder than any actions. There ain't nothin' around like money. You got it, you're somebody. You ain't got it and you're a shit-head like you."

"I got money."

"Five bucks for another bottle."

"Christ man, I ain't got all day to sit around here yakking with a mug like you. Dig down in that briefcase and come up with the green backs."

"How many reels you got?"

"Five. Hour and ten minutes each!"

"You should have double that."

"I got a tight budget. I want two grand a print."

"How many prints?"

"Ten each"

"That's fifty prints. You're talking a hundred grand." His eyes narrowed.

Harry Conners nodded and puffed more heavily on his cigar. He knew he wasn't going to get any hundred grand. But he was going to give the fight of his life. Bullshit he was. It was all in his mind. He had the fight and the words of the fight all written out. They were in the top drawer of his desk. He had them memorized. At least he had had them memorized right up until that moment. Until the moment he said two grand a print. Then his mind went blank. There was no doubt he wasn't, never had been and never would be any match for Rance Ball.

"Sell then to somebody else."

Harry nearly dropped his cigar. "Make me an offer then."

The chunky man leaned back in his chair, narrowed his eyes and crossed his arms over his ample belly. "Two hundred and fifty dollars a piece."

"Hell man, that ain't even enough to pay the tab per print... a thousand."

Rance sighed. "You drive such a stupid bargain, Harry. It's no wonder you should be flushed down the toilet. My top offer. Three hundred and a quarter."

"Seven fifty, or I sell to somebody else."

"Five hundred... my top figure... or you do sell to somebody else."

Harry didn't have to think it over. He was afraid Rance would simply get up and walk out. He had done that very thing before. "I'll take it," he said quickly.

"I knew you would."

"How did you know?"

"You can't afford not to."

"You're pretty sure of yourself."

"You're hungry, Harry. When a man is hungry he will sell his soul for less than thirty pieces of silver. You see… it's like I said. You got money, you're king. You ain't got no money and you're shit. You see! You got money and you'd have stayed at the two grand figure and said take it or leave it. Only you don't say that to me. I tell you to sell it to somebody else. You ain't got somebody else. So you'll sell it to me at my price. You're a slob, Harry Conners."

Rance reached down to his battered briefcase and opened it. He took a long time taking out the check book, then unscrewing his fountain pen. It was sort of a ritual. He liked watching his clients squirm. It was as much fun as stealing the prints for short money.

"How many you going to have for me in six months?"

"Maybe none."

"You're the producer. You eat or you don't eat." Rance Ball had shrugged as he spoke and he didn't look up to Harry. He started filling in the blank spots on the check receipt pad.

"Five grand is all I have left out of the twenty-five grand. Five grand ain't much for six months work."

Rance laughed. "Trying to make me think you're making money. Five grand, ha! You're lucky if you pull five hundred out of this stack after you've paid your bills."

There was no use in Harry attempting to overshadow the money-hungry leach. He knew all the angles. He knew to the penny how much Harry could take for himself.

"You're penny ante, Harry. But I like doing business with you. Maybe I should come more often. So how many will you have for me in six months? I want double the order."

"So you ask me a question, then you tell me the answer. What kind of a mind do you have anyway?"

"A mind for good business." He tossed the check across to Harry while he signed some papers and pushed them across to Rance who put them in the briefcase and snapped it shut. "A mind that don't never let the other guy win. You like that kind of mind, Harry?"

"You stink like maggots."

"The maggots will be the last thing on earth."

"That's the only thing that makes me smile at you, Rance Ball. One day they'll get you too. Then where will all that money go?"

"I ain't leaving unless I take it with me." He laughed at his own joke.

"Deep down underneath, Harry, I think you like me."

"I don't even respect you… so how could I like you, Mr. money-bags. The film is in the vault… just show them the papers and they'll give it to you."

"You've got to give me instructions like I'm new in the business? You gotta be kidding." He stood up and shook some ashes from the front of his coat. "Make me some homo stuff with a drag queen. I got a whole chain of houses through the south that likes them kind of things. Make it in color."

"You sure know what you want, Rance."

"Like always! I tell you what to do and nobody puts anything over on me. Never nobody ever puts anything over on Rance Ball."

"Like you said. You're a legend in your own time, all the producers know that much."

Rance Ball swelled with pride. "I like that. A legend in my own time."

"As long as your checks are good."

"That's a cashier's registered check… like always."

"So how come you got so many blanks to fill in on the face of it."

"Look at it again. I fill in the blanks on the receipt side."

Harry looked at the twenty-five thousand dollar cashier's check and smiled. "So it is."

"Cash it anyplace," and he walked to the door and left without another word.

Harry reached into the drawer of his desk… a shabby scared desk in the twenty-five dollar a week rental office. He took out a bottle of whiskey which had perhaps four or five shots in it. He downed them quickly then crashed the empty bottle against the far wall.

Harry then stood up, stretched and put the check to the inside of his coat pocket. He walked across the office to a closet and took out his already packed suitcase. It would take Rance Ball more than an hour to get to the lab for his film, that is, if he even bothered about getting the stuff that day, sometimes he waited a week.

But it would only take Harry Conners ten minutes to get to the bank a few blocks away. He would cash the twenty-five thousand dollars and within the hour he would be on the plane for Mexico... the plane for which he already had tickets. There would be no one sharing any of that twenty-five thousand dollars. The creditors could go to hell.

Nobody could put anything over on Rance Ball... Nobody but the shit-head Harry Conners who could easily be in Mexico when Rance Ball found there was no film in the vaults.

No one could possibly put anything over on Rance Ball.

Harry Conners would laugh all the way to the bank.

THE END

THE FRIGHT WIGS

as "Donna D. Dildo"

from Wild Cats *Vol.5 No. 2 Pendulum. Not on Ed's resume but reads like Ed (in "Short Wood")*

TOMME WAS A PRIVATE eye… and Tomme was a hell of a good looking broad… and Tomme thought she was a hell of a good private eye. She didn't have a tremendous number of clientele, but there were only so many hours in a day, and they had to be divided around according to the importance of any particular case. Which meant, in most cases, which one was paying the highest fee for her services. Or on the other hand, who proved the most interesting to her in other aspects.

She did four years in the Marine Corps and directly out of boot camp she was assigned to the military police detachments and there remained for her entire enlistment, although she did pull time in Vietnam for six months. It was this period in her life when she decided some kind of police work was to be her vocation. But she didn't want to join a police force where she couldn't do what she wanted and would have to adhere to specific hours. Thus it was only natural she looked into the private-eye business.

During her years in the marines she learned much of judo, and once out she immediately took up karate. Also in the Marines she learned about guns and how to shoot them. She kept up the practice even upon leaving… during the period whereby she underwent intensive training with a private detective schooling organization. She was damned good at everything she did.

"You take to this work like a seasoned officer… a man," one of her instructors had told her upon presenting the diploma. And the words actually irked her no end. The one thing she didn't want to be was a man, and she didn't want to be referred to as being a man, or even being associated with men... unless as business demanded. That was always something she couldn't get away from. She had to associate with them. They were a part of the world around her. Yet the strangest part of her entire make-up happened to be that she was generally the aggressor in any love affairs... with women.

But also she was not any counterpart of the characterization usually afforded the lesbian *butch*. She didn't wear the hard tweeds, or the pulled down hat or even the flat shoes. Her clothing was always of excellent taste and ultra-feminine such as the fluff of their sisterhood wore. However, she could defend herself in just about any situation as good as any truck-driver-type bull-dyke. And in the same vein, if she picked a fight she had a damned good chance of coming out the victor.

Of her three cases presently in the works there was a divorce case in which the young wife declared the husband was blackmailing her, a skip-trace thing for a collection agency, which she didn't relish, but would get around to "one of these days," and finally a lost person's case... the one she liked the most.

The missing person was twenty-one, female, extremely attractive, 36-24-36, and with all the other attributes which went into making up a love-ly, desirable blonde. But of even more interest, the client had informed Tomme that the girl, Gloria Hartson, had no boyfriends who could be contacted. "She just never seemed to like boys much," said her father, a retired oil man from Texas.

"She'd just as soon stay home with a good book, or listen to fine mu-sic... or just saddle up one of her horses and ride out over the plains."

"What makes you think she came to Los Angeles?" asked Tomme as part of her interview.

"'Cause this is where she said she was coming... just for a visit, she said. And because we got two letters from her. Here's the address they came from. And they came more than six months ago."

Other than a photograph of the beautiful girl in a tight sweater and shorts, that was all the information Tomme was given. It was for damned certain she had precious little to go on. But from all her past experience, Gloria Hartson rang the lesbian bell a loud gong. And to make the as-signment even more tough, the hotel manager informed her the luggage left behind by Gloria had been held for the legal length of time, then sold for back hotel room rent. There were no phone calls registered from her room, but the night clerk did remember her. She went out for long walks at night, and never returned with a man. When he was asked if she ever returned with girls, he again shook his head and told her the girl always went out alone and returned alone. He'd never seen her so much as talk to anyone, except the desk clerk when she asked about mail. She'd only gotten one letter in the time she stayed there. Tomme reasoned it was the single letter the girl's father had said he'd written months before…all others had been returned to him and the girl's mother. The night clerk had no knowledge of those. They would have been returned before he came on duty.

If ever there was a dry trail, Tomme was on it. But the girl fascinated her to a point of tender, but demanding distraction. The picture of the girl preyed on her mind continually. She was going to do everything in her power to find that girl and make physical contact. The money was secondary. The girl was the thing which mattered above all. And the photograph was not enough. It turned her on. It had from the moment she received it, but pictures were only a flat introduction. An introduction, however, strong enough to make Tomme want the real thing.

But there was just nothing to go on. It was like being in a bare room and staring at the walls, where the mind's eye couldn't even frame a picture. It was all one big blank nothing. But Tomme was reasonable enough to realize people just don't disappear off the face of the earth… generally! The girl could be running scared in the big city…but that wasn't probable because all she had to do was wire Papa and she'd be in the lap of luxury back on the ranch.

Of course, there was the one standout of the girl's character. Apparently she wanted nothing to do with boys. The one way Tomme could go, for a start, was through her lesbian connections. It seemed the most logical way to proceed. There was simply something, perhaps in her sixth sense, which led her to that conclusion. She never went against her own first judgments. That was also part of the leftover of her Marine Corps training. Her judgments did prove to be successful when they were snapped by a well-adjusted mind. She'd always prided herself on that much of a fact. She had a sharp mind. And the kind which came across when necessity arose. If anyone could find Gloria Hartson, it would be Tomme.

"Butches" and "fluff" alike at the lesbian bars liked Tomme. There was no pulling back into their shells because she carried a gun and a police permit card. After all, she wasn't like being the real law. She was the private kind. She wasn't out to bust anybody unless she got paid for it. Then too, she was one of them. She could go either way, "butch" or "fluff," and she always sprang for a couple of beers when she talked to anybody. Tomme didn't like beer herself, she was the cocktail type. But most of the lesbian joints were simple beer bars so she always set a big one up in front of herself and let it sit there. Somebody would gobble it up after she had gone.

But that was all right. Anybody who wanted flat beer could have it… and she supposed it was better than letting it go to waste.

She noticed some of the recession had hit the bars like it had many other businesses. The patrons weren't in any great numbers, and those who had attended weren't buying the liquid refreshments as readily as days of old. The heavy lushes were down to mediocre drunks, and the mediocre drunks were mere tipplers.

Cruising the bars took just over a week before she hit the right one. It was far on the other side of town from the hotel where Gloria Hartson had stayed. The old Butch who recognized the photograph eyed it all the time she talked.

"Sure. That looks like her. Only that ain't the name she used. I don't remember the name. Real nice kid, but all mixed up inside of herself. Ain't no doubt she was going the lesbian route, but she was kicking at her insides all the time she was digging Dyke Anne's pitch. Imagine getting broke in by something like that old crone."

"You figure the kid was fresh stuff?"

"As fresh as any that ever come down the pike, and just as scared. She wanted to go all the way, that was for sure, but old Anne must have scared her off. She left here but fast," the hefty woman cackled over her beer. "That's one time that old bitch didn't score with a virgin. That's one she ain't never gonna brag about cherry-breaking. The old bitch got stood right back on her ass. The kid just tore out of here like the scared chicken she was."

"Silly to ask, but you don't have any idea where she went?"

"Hell no! She just took off on the run and crying like a school girl. My bet would be some hospital, that's how bad off I figured her to be. But what the hell, it wasn't any of my business. I don't get involved with people's unstable emotions."

There were a couple of dozen big hospitals, many more private ones and thousands of doctors. And if Gloria Hartson was using a different name, the task was going to be almost as impossible as it had been in the beginning. Each place and person would have to be contacted personally and shown the picture.

As it turned out the task was more easily accomplished than she could ever have figured. Gloria Hartson under a Jane Doe tag had been admitted to County General two days before. She had taken an overdose of sleeping pills. She was found curled up in the doorway of an office building when the early morning janitors had come to work. The police were called, and she was taken to the hospital.

"Is she booked for anything?" Tomme knew the head nurse and knew she'd get straight answers.

The head nurse, a lesbian of the first water herself, shook her head. "Not yet. If they want to be bust-happy they can probably throw a vag charge against her. The sleeping pills can be claimed to be accidental. But if she's who you say she is nobody's going to put any charges on her. You taking over?"

"I already have." Tomme winked, then made her way to the elevator which would take her up to the fourth floor and room 419 where Gloria Hartson stared at her through bleary eyes. "I guess you can consider me your mother superior for the time being," Tomme informed her before any formal introductions were offered.

"I'm not well. I don't want to see anybody. I don't want to talk to anybody."

"Well now, let's just say you don't. But let's say it's my job and I'm the one who will do most of the talking."

"You another cop? They've been all over me ever since I came to."

"I'm private. Your father hired me." Tomme was quick to catch the flicker of doubt which crossed her fogged eyes.

"I don't want my father to know anything about this."

"I won't be the one to tell him. But you can bet your sweet bippy he'd have heard about it if those pills had worked, or you weren't found in that doorway in time. What in hell gets into kids like you? You're just starting a life, and already you want to end it. You've got a beautiful ranch, money. You've got to be out of your beautiful mind."

She leaned back against the pillows and put her arm up over her eyes. "That's just it. I feel like I am out of my mind, or going out of it fast."

"Want to tell me all about it?"

"I don't even want to think about it anymore. I just want to go to sleep. Maybe I want to go to sleep and just never wake up. Why did it have to be me?" Then she suddenly looked up, directly at Tomme. "How did you find me?"

"You covered your trail very well. Except for your human nature which took you to the lesbian bar. It wasn't hard after that."

Her eyes narrowed again. "The…the…the lesbian bar…then you know?"

"That you're a lesbian? So what's the problem in being a lesbian? Lots of girls and women are lesbians. You must have seen a lot of them in the last few weeks. Did you know what you were before you left your home?"

She nodded slowly. "That's why I left. I thought I could lose myself in the big city. I thought here I'd meet other girls like me…other lesbians, and that I'd get lost in their world. But the other night when that… that Dyke Anne put her hands all over me and breathed on me with that breath which smelled like maggots, all I could do was run outside and puke. After that I went to a legitimate doctor and told him I was having trouble sleeping.

"After puking and crying and running like I did, the doctor had to think I was really run down and I got a prescription for the sleeping pills. I took them all, then I started back to the motel where I've been living. I didn't make it. I know I should have waited until I got to the motel and I can't explain why I didn't. It just seemed important that I got the pills inside of me and let them start working. I had a horror of being in that motel room waiting for them to work."

"So you wanted to kill yourself because you found out you were a lesbian, and from what you saw in those others, you hated the whole sphere of that kind of life?"

"I didn't hate being a lesbian so much. It was other facts. I was frightened to death that I'd turn out like that Dyke Anne and the other crones who were hanging around in that beer bar."

"Which was your problem from the start. You had money. You just went to a dive…the wrong place to start out. All lesbians don't hang out in the joints, you know. There are a lot of lesbians who wouldn't be caught dead in such a place. And all lesbians don't look like the witches you saw. Those are the bums of the society, the fright wigs of the sisters of Lesbos. You just didn't look in the right places.

"So when you get well, I'll take you to some of the places I know and you can bet you'll change your mind. Sleep-pills will never be needed again. Wow, girl did you get off to a rough start."

"But I've always read about lesbians and they were all that kind of people. I didn't want that to be it. I went looking to prove the stories were wrong, and all I saw was more facts establishing what I've read."

"My dear girl, horror stories have been with us for centuries. Beauty doesn't sell books or newspapers. People want to know the gruesome details, the gory details. That's what satisfies their own sadistic or masochistic tendencies. There are many lesbians who throw such trash in the ash can because they know different."

Gloria rose slowly up on one elbow and looked at Tomme curiously. "How do you know so much about the subject?"

Tomme hands on hips, made several graceful turns at the foot of the bed, and when she faced the girl a bright grin crossed her lovely features. "It's simple, honey. I'm one of the cocktail-type of lesbians. Now if you'll rest up tonight, I'll take you home with me tomorrow and I'll show you how the cocktail lesbians make love. Just call me Tomme."

THE END

OUT OF THE FOG

by "Joe Baga"

in Two Plus Two *vol.3 no.2 May/June 1971. on Ed's resume*

MARGIE PULLED THE THICK leather belt around her knee-length, white, fake fur coat three notches tighter than one might think her waist would permit. But that's the way she liked it. Her enormous boobies pressed the front far out and rounded her ample rump to what she felt was an attractive attraction.

Actually, she wasn't a bad looking girl… just a bit hard of features, but they all melted into the right places. Her nose was under her eyes and her mouth was justly situated beneath a straight nose. However it was her hair which shot down any girlish, facial features she might have presented. It was cut short in a boy's styling and plastered down like a turn of the century bartender's.

Perhaps that's what she'd like to have been… a bartender. She liked to drink, and she approved of and appreciated sex. In fact, the more she drank the more intense her sexual urges became. As a bartender she could keep up the "HOTS" and have an ever changing procession of lovers.

But Margie was not a bartender. She was a personnel manager for a large department store… and having held the same position for years her drinking and sex sprees were relegated to Friday and Saturday nights. Sunday was held in abeyance for sobering up and resting. But then she was lucky at that, having two days off in a row. Most of the girls rated split days. Her position and seniority, however, gave her the command of her days off. It was lucky she could play the game that way because it took most of Sunday to dry out and get her faculties back in shape. She was also thirty-two and found the coming-off period lasted longer than when she was twenty-two. However, age hadn't put the damper on her sexual prowess. If anything, the experience of age heightened the enjoyment, and most of her partners, especially the younger ones, went away more than satisfied. In fact, they might have taken some new teachings with them.

Actually, she hated being a teacher, but the punks who were coming along the life-cycle knew nothing about romance involving sex. If an affair gave them some sort of a climax, then that was all there was to it. It was as if all the niceties had been omitted from their early encounters. It wasn't so bad with the virgins. Inexperience in virgins was to be expected. But the others—the hop-on, hop-off artists—were "just too much." Margie wanted and needed a lot of love in her sessions. She demanded it of herself, and promoted it into the others… thus her feeling of having to teach a great many of them.

As she pulled the bottom of her fake fur coat down through the belt, giving the coat an even more full-skirted appearance, she made up her mind that any fluff she'd bring home that night wasn't going to be some spring chicken fresh from high school. She wasn't in the mood to be a teacher that weekend. Just for once she wanted to lay back and enjoy herself with somebody who had like talents. She wanted to feel talented hands and talented muscles… a soft tongue and sensuous lips. However, there was no thought in her mind that she was going to pick up some old bag, either. There were a lot of young ones around who had the kind of experience she wanted.

The night held more than a simple chill. It was downright cold and the fog was of the wet variety. Margie pulled her coat collar tightly around her neck and held it there as she made a dash across the community parking lot to where her late model sedan rested. She cursed the fact that it would take several moments before the heater could send off welcome heat waves from the warming motor. But that was to be expected, and she geared herself to the fact and after turning on the motor she sunk down deep into her coat and put her hands in the pocket. She wasn't going to move the car until the heater poured out the warmth. The chill had settled right down into her bones to a point even her thoughts of later settling down beside a warm body did no good to relieve the present chill.

It was a good car, and a damned good heater however, and once the elements were right the car became toasty warm and she straightened up in the seat again. This time she turned on the windshield wipers so that the grey, wet mist could be squeegeed away. There was a lot of good rubber on those wipers also which made for a clear glass.

Being as good a driver as she was, she really didn't mind the pea-soup fog, but it was annoying. Of course in the daytime it would have been much worse. At least during the dark hours the street lights were visible, where they didn't need searching out. February always held such dreary days in Southern California. One could count on seeing the sun quite seldom during that month, and sometimes right up until the first week or two of March. But the rest of the year made up for the few days of miserable weather.

She wanted a drink almost as much as she wanted the right girlfriend. There had been plenty back at the apartment, and although she didn't approve of carrying a bottle in the car, that was one night she wished she had. However, even as she thought those wave patterns, the green and red neon lights of a roadside cocktail lounge beckoned her through the mist. "What the hell," she thought silently. "A little fortification never hurt anyone."

The car moved easily off the highway and the wheels crunched onto the gravel parking area in front of the cocktail lounge. She parked as close to the front entrance as she could, then, once more preparing herself for the outside chill, she pushed up the coat collar, held it tightly around her neck, then walked quickly to the entrance and went inside.

She'd never been in that lounge before, but she ventured a guess that it would not be her last time. It was a most delightful place with a deep pile carpet, and red and purple velvet drapes lavishly spaced around the entire area. The red jacketed bartender grinned broadly and was still grinning when he returned with the tall scotch and water she'd ordered.

There was very little physical action in the bar… a couple in a booth at the darker corner of the room… two heavy set bowlers laughing into beers and a young street-walker type who was seated in a booth near the entrance… her eyes almost glued to the doors. Margie noted that she never moved those eyes even when she sipped from the double martini in front of her. However, Margie wasn't looking for any other action out of the place except as many scotch-and-sodas she felt she needed to fortify her for continuing the trip into town… fifteen miles by the surface streets she was driving… ten by the freeway which she detested. A tall scotch for each three miles ought to do the trick. She didn't want to pull off a drunk driving charge, but she knew she could handle three scotches without any trouble. The three came from the fact she was measuring the freeway mileage.

She was on the second tall one when she again looked across to the girl and saw her get up, go to the entrance door, look out, then return to the booth. The girl was obviously troubled and was doing little about hiding those facts. Margie could only think, however, that the girl was waiting for her pimp who was late, and the thought gave rise to a light grin at the corners of her lips. Actually, she didn't know why she thought the girl to be a street-walking whore… she was young and she was pretty… but there was something about her… perhaps in the makeup or the way she nuzzled into her cocktails. Three had been served her since Margie arrived on the scene, and it was also becoming obvious the girl was not a heavy drinker. Her eyes showed the effect of the strong concoction. But she didn't appear to be the kind who would make an alcoholic fool of herself.

Margie knew it was none of her business, but she couldn't help it. She was just naturally the curious type. Nothing ever went on at the store that she didn't know, or found a way of finding out the score. Secrets were not invented to be kept from her. But the cocktail lounge was not the store… and she knew nothing of the girl or her problems. Curiosity killed the cat and all that sort of thing… only she didn't feel that way.

She motioned for the bartender and when he confronted her, she ordered a double martini in a low voice, and told him to take it to the "lonely little girl over there." The man saluted her with a circle and three fingers and did as he was told. When presented with the drink the girl looked quickly in Margie's direction then back to the door… but she didn't refuse the drink. It was captured in her hand almost before she let go of the empty she was holding. The bartender shrugged knowingly as he passed Margie. She cocked her head around just enough so that if the girl should look up, she'd catch her eye. Possibly the girl knew that also, because she didn't look up, or in any other direction other than the door.

The mental strain of over-curiosity told more gravely on Margie about the time she saw the bottom of her third scotch and water. And there was only going to be one way to settle her inquisitive nature. She informed the bartender that she needed a refill and so did the girl at the table, and that he should serve both drinks there. Then she got up, crossed the room and locked herself down in the chair opposite the girl. They stared at each other until after the drinks were put in front of them.

Then the girl muttered a simple, "Thanks," and lifted the fresh drink.

"Thanks? That's all I get is thanks? I set you up two rounds and you spit a thanks in my face?" Margie tried to sound as unpleasant as possible, but without trying to make the girl angry.

"So what do you want, a medal? I didn't ask you for this lush. I've been getting my own all evening."

"No need to get on your high horse. I'm only trying to be friendly. This old world sure could use a lot more friendliness."

The girl gulped down the double martini, then shoved the empty glass to the edge of the table. "Okay, friendly... so buy me another and maybe I'll tell you my life story." She snapped her fingers as if to emphasize her words, then she grinned. "Sorry about that! I don't mean to sound rude. But I'm angry at someone else and I guess because you're the first one to come along, I had to take it out on you. No offense intended! It might have been the bartender or the waiter if they'd have said anything more than what'll you have. Get what I mean?"

Margie then tried for a pleasant smile, and in so doing captured the bartender's eye and indicated the empty martini glass. "I take it you're waiting for someone."

She nodded. "Two hours. And I don't wait any two hours for anybody. Only I'm doing it. Now what in hell for?"

"You're doing the waiting. But I don't mind doing the listening. I've been listening to stories all my life... and not all of them printable, if you know what I mean."

"I think you're trying to tell me something." She pulled the fresh martini in close to her as the bartender moved away.

Margie nodded slyly. "Only that I'm a good listener, and you looked like you might need a set of big ears. Then too you were alone and I was alone... and from what I've always learned, most people don't like sitting in bars alone. Isn't that why singles go to bars in the first place? Bars are the best place in the world for making contacts of one kind or another. Did you ever know that some of the most important deals, and the most lasting friendships have been made over the cocktail bars? It's a true statement."

"True... but I can't consider it profound. Do you have a name or do I make one up for you?"

"Margie. Last names don't matter... in the beginning anyway." Margie captured her drink again and gulped. "You want to tell me yours?"

She shrugged lightly. "Why not? Toni. Like you said… last names don't matter… in the beginning anyway." She eyed Margie carefully over the rim of her martini glass. "You selling or giving it away?"

There was no shock for Margie. "I haven't had to sell it for years. Are you a pro? Or out for the hell of it?"

Toni looked at her wrist watch. "More than two hours." She looked directly into Margie's eyes. "Right now it looks like I'm out for the hell of it… and out six bucks on cocktails. Men… they can never be trusted."

"An old friend?"

"Never saw him or heard of him before this afternoon. He makes the pitch, I accept and now it appears he rejects."

"Guy has to be a fool to turn a dish like you down. Now maybe I could suggest an alternate… and the booze will be for free. I have been known to whip up a pretty wild martini. I was heading into town but that fog out there is too much. We could cuddle up on a bear skin rug in front of my fireplace… if you have a mind for my type of company."

"I don't drink very much." She tingled the glass. "Only when I get angry. I'm not angry any longer. Disappointed, but no longer angry. I'm always disappointed when somebody hits my addition to the bank account."

"I haven't paid in years. I don't expect to start at this late space in life."
Margie spoke simply.

Toni gave one of her frequent shrugs, "Maybe I'm in the mood for a lot of martinis. Like maybe I won't have to be angry to get a little drunk, and you look like you know your way around. Let's get out of the male world for a while."

"I've been out of the male world all my life. I work in it all week, but I'm never really a part of it. I honestly don't despise the male issue. I just don't like it or approve of their attitude toward sex. I've got my own code and I live by it. Do you like to hear things like that?"

Toni turned a tipsy eye to her glass, then back to Margie. "Honey, I don't even know what you're talking about. But the words sound good to my rejected body. Your car or mine?"

"You'd have a hell of a time finding my place in this fog. I'll get you back when you're ready."

"I won't worry about it."

Margie took the initiative in paying off the bartender. Then, pulling up her collar and taking the girl by the arm, she led the way to the door and out into the fog, where Toni also adjusted the collar of her coat. However, she didn't seem displeased at the damp situation. She breathed heavily, sighed broadly and a light smile curled the edge of her lips.

"Strange excitement comes out of the fog sometimes." She looked directly into Margie's eyes. "You step into it and never know what might pass you by until you've reached the other side. I'm glad we didn't continue on to the other side. We probably never would have met."

Margie felt a deep warmth and she could wait no longer to feel the girl's lips on her own and each of their tongues searching out the mysteries of the other.

THE END

THAT DAMNED FACELESS FOG

by "Dick Trent"

in Young Beavers *Vol.6, no.1 Mar./Apr.1972 on Ed's resume 1971*

JOSH NEVER DID LIKE the fog and he liked it even less as he stood on the street corner in the big city, the first big city street corner he'd ever stood on… but the rundown street didn't look much different than the dive kind of town he came from… what he could see of it. He wondered why that was? Why that he had to leave one dump just to end up in another?

But that was the street that had the bus depot and he'd just gotten off the bus.

There were a lot of Honky-Tonk kind of places all around, on both sides of the street, but it was hard to read any of the names because of the thick fog. But he knew they were Honky-Tonk kind of places because of those bright lights and the blaring kind of music that shot out through the doors. He suspected that people were going in and out through the doors but he couldn't see any… except when he walked on and got close enough to the doors to see the dark shapes moving in and out.

He sure as hell didn't like the fog. It was bad enough back home where he'd come from… damn, how bad it was back there. But at least he knew his way back to the shack on the old farm where his father and mother and all them brothers and sisters were share croppers. At least he could always grope his way through the fog enough to find his way back there. But damned if he knew where he was going to go there in the big city where one street he was going to find out was just like another. Even up town he was going to find out they might be different than downtown but one street was going to look like another… and hell's fire where in hell was he going to go?

There wasn't any shack to make his way home to, and he didn't know just what he could do to get in out of the fog. He knew, one thing for sure, that he couldn't go into those Honky-Tonks because he wasn't quite seventeen and he sure as hell didn't look any twenty-one. The old sheriff back home made it so he could work as a swamper in one of them places back there. No sheriff in the big town, he was sure, would let him get a job like that because there was too many old men out of work that needed jobs like that. But when he did work in one back home he learned what the Honky-Tonkin' kind of business was all about… and the kind of girls with their rouged up faces and lips and the long black eyelashes they glued on their eyelids, and the red and the blue and the yellow satin kind of dresses they wore, way up around their asses where anybody could see if they had any panties on and what color they were and if they had any panties on at all. And those that didn't let that thick black brush wink the pink little lips right at some guy and they went off to one of the rooms upstairs, or the guy took the broad out someplace.

And he knew exactly what they did when they went to the rooms. He'd seen pictures, and he'd had the same thing done a few times by his cousin Brenda. Damn she was a good lay…. And damn she knew a lot of tricks that could turn a young boy's body on like it was fire, and when that final minute came she would spring up and hit that thing with all her might and would leave him all tied up in knots wondering when the next time would be. He never had to wait long when Brenda was around. She was damned hot for his young body.

And he wondered where in hell he was ever going to get some broad like his cousin Brenda there in that big town with the fog lying all over him like a grey, wet blanket… like the grey, wet blanket he slept under at home when it rained and the roof leaked. It was almost like there wasn't any roof at all the way the rain came in and it rained most of the summer, and in the winter when it didn't snow. It's a wonder any of his family ever lived as long as they did… and truth of the matter was none of them had colds much…

God took care of his own little children!

He'd forgotten that saying… something his old grandmother had taught him often when she was reading from her dog-eared Bible and was trying to ease the mind of the family when they were doused in troubles.

Then they'd all pray and things seemed to have a way of working out for them.

But that was in a place they all knew. The shack! And the town... the town and the farm where all of them had been born and grown up... even his grandma had been born and brought up on that land. A lot of her brothers and sisters had left the farm for what they said was better things, and they headed for the city the same as he did... and none of them had ever been heard of again.

He couldn't help but wonder if he would ever return to the farm... if they would ever hear of him again.

Then his cold hands dipped into his pocket. He didn't know how much money it would cost him to live in the big city until he could get a job. He knew he would have to get a job and that it would take money to live there. But just how much until he did get a job... that was the question... and when would the damned fog lift so he could tell one end of the street from the other.

How damned much money?

He wondered why he hadn't thought of that before he got on that bus at the crossroads? At that time it didn't seem to matter as long as he got away from the place. His old man had gotten mad at him because he kicked over a pail of milk which the old man would have to pay for. It wasn't Josh's fault, but Josh got the back of his father's hand and a split lip anyway and Josh ran back to the cabin and pried up the loose board under his bed and took out the handful of crumpled one dollar bills and jammed them into his pocket then headed out the four miles across country to the bus stop at the crossroads... there had been no fog there... and the bus cost ten dollars and he had counted out that much then jammed the rest of the dollar bills back into his pocket.

There were a few but he didn't know how many. He didn't count them on the bus. He had read some stories about what happens to folks when they take their money out of their pocket in front of strangers. He wasn't going to do that.

But what the hell... there in the fog!

He gripped his hand over the crumpled bills and drew them out. He stood under the bright lights of a honky-tonk, and leaned back against the brick wall. He looked to both sides of him and ahead, but the fog only permitted a few feet of penetration, but he saw nothing of human shapes. It was safe enough.

There were nine one-dollar bills. That was his entire bankroll and it would have to do. But then again, the thought came to him as to how much he would have to spend to find someplace to sleep. And sleep was something he sure had to have. It had been a long bus ride, and when they got in the fog the bus had to slow down and then it was even more of a boring time in that ride… especially at night when there was nothing he could see out of the windows. His first trip away from home and he couldn't tell one tree from another, or if there was a road, or if there was grass or houses… The last twenty-five miles had been one long, grey, wet blanket of nothingness.

He jammed the nine dollars back into his pocket but didn't take his ass away from the brick wall. He just leaned back there with his hands dug deeply into his pockets…

Now what the hell do I do?

The words fell as heavily on the fog as if he had said them aloud. It was a frightening aspect of his young life. Always before there had been something around that was friendly, something or someone to whom he could turn for protection. That was not so there in the fog as he leaned against the brick wall. Everything was unfriendly, almost unreal. It would have been completely unreal if there had not been the honky-tonks and the fog. They were not the same ones he had known back home, but they were the same kind of places and the fog was the same kind of thing, therefore they did give him some rise as to friendliness… loneliness, however, was more to his way of thinking.

He knew he couldn't just go up to somebody's door and ask to sleep there. He knew that much. He couldn't even do that back in his home town.

He knew what a hotel was and what kind of a service they were supposed to give to a guy, but he'd never been in one and he wasn't quite sure just how to approach that subject. Was he supposed to just go in, find a room and lay down? Or was he supposed to find some kind of an owner and get him to give him a room? It was a problem! And then it was kind of late at night and maybe the hotel owner would be mad if he was to walk in and wake him up.

But he couldn't stay out there on the street all night. He knew that none of them ever got colds, not much anyway, back home, but he knew sure as hell he'd catch his death if he stayed out there on the street in the fog all night… that fact was as plain as the nose on his face… He just couldn't stay there without any blanket to wrap around him... and he didn't have a coat... only the old sweatshirt he always wore when he went to town and he never had owned a coat of any kind. There was never enough money for anything like that. They always made do with what they got from the parson at the church. Every Christmas time that old parson came around with something... some old clothes of some kind and once and awhile a basket of food on other holidays... but never a warm coat.

Josh figured that was something he was going to get just as soon as he got a job in the big city. A coat sure would make him feel good. He would have something when he bought that coat... something nobody in his whole family ever had in all their lives... even his old grandmother.

But it didn't seem that he was going to get anywhere. It looked like he was going to spend all his life right there up against the brick of that building and looking out into the damned faceless fog that surrounded him and the whole street. That fog was creeping in on him and was going to strangle him right there on the street before he could even see what a big town looked like. And that was something he just didn't want to happen. He didn't want no old grey, wet fog strangling him before he could walk the streets on a clear day and see for himself what the big city was all about... like the pictures of the big towns he saw in the picture books. He could read some, but he sure liked the pictures better. The words of reading told him what they wanted him to know, but the pictures turned on his imagination to what he himself wanted to know... or to what illusions he wanted to conjure up... the pictures he sure liked, and he wanted to see the real thing... where the pictures came from... where the cameraman had stood and aimed his camera and snapped the picture that they printed in the book.

No damned fog was going to rob him of that!

He took his foot down from the wall and took but one step when he felt the light tug on his arm and he turned to face the woman in the red satin dress, the red satin dress that was up to her ass. Only the fog didn't let him see if she wore any panties or if she was showing her bush. Then he looked up to the overly painted face and the ratty fur cape which hugged her shoulders.

"What do you want?" he stuttered.

"Maybe you," she winked.

"You don't want me."

"Don't be too sure about that. And maybe you want me, boy."

"You're one of them painted up ladies, and I don't want none of you painted up ladies… and don't call me boy… I ain't gonna be called boy no more, no how."

"Now you don't have to get the hairs up on the back of your neck just because I speak to you… here on the street in the lonely fog."

He didn't know what getting the hairs up on the back of his neck meant… but she was talking in such a soft voice, and she sure didn't look like much trouble. But she was one of those painted ladies he had always found hanging around the Honky-Tonk when he had been a swamper and he knew they always took the men and they always wanted money, and his hand gripped the nine one-dollar bills and pushed them as deeply into his side pocket as he could.

"I don't mind talkin' to you. I just know what you painted ladies want from the guys, that's what I know."

"Well now ain't you the smart one."

He blushed. It couldn't be seen in the fog, but he blushed. "Ahhh, hell, I ain't so smart."

She knew that for sure. She let her hand go up and caress the side of his cheek. "My guess is you just got off the bus, and this is your first time away from home and you just got out of school work."

He blushed again. "I didn't go to school much. So 1 guess I ain't so smart much."

"Why you're just about as smart a young fella as I come across all week."

"I did just get off the bus. I guess I did just get here and this is my first time away from home and I'm in the big city… I guess."

"You sure are, honey."

"Well I gotta be goin' now."

"You got someplace to go?"

"Well. I gotta' be on my way to look for someplace. I guess I can't stay out here in this damned fog all night. I'd catch my death. That's the way my old granny used to say it. Stay out in the fog like this and you'll catch your death…"

"Me too! I don't like to stay out in the fog long."

"Then why don't you go on home? All city folks gotta have a place to stay. That's what I gotta have right now."

"I got business to take care of here on the street first… fog or no fog."

"You in business? You mean you ain't one of them painted up ladies like I know about from the Honky-Tonks back home? You really got a business here on the street in the fog? What kinda business?"

"Maybe you could be my business. You got any money?"

"Sure. I got nine dollars so's I can get me a room and then look for work when this damned fog goes back where it come from."

"Now ain't that nice! And maybe I can help you find a job."

"You could? You damned sure could, painted lady?"

She locked her arm through his and started him off through the fog. "Why now, I sure can. And first I guess maybe you and me should get out of the damned fog, huh?"

"That would be nice, I guess…"

"You just let me hold onto the nine dollars, and we'll take care of everything."

"Why sure, painted lady friend." He dug into his pocket and handed her the nine one dollar bills…. And then he was leaning up against the brick of another Honky Tonk…. After all, it would only be a matter of a few minutes before his new friend, the painted lady returned…. After all she was a friend, and she said she was going to get him that room so he could get out of that damned fog… that damned faceless fog….

THE END

ONCE UPON A GARGOYLE

originally published in Fantastic Annual, *Gallery Press, on Ed's resume 1973*

THE FIRST ONE to notice Johnny Limbo was a young woman secretary who had gone to the water cooler in her office and while drinking looked over to the next building just across the busy thoroughfare. Her office window was twenty floors above the street, almost even with the roof of the other building, the edge upon which Johnny Limbo was perched.

She didn't immediately cry out. She was much too dazed for that. But in her quick freeze she did drop the paper cup and contents and her wide eyes stared at the boy in as much of a trance as his eyes were as they gazed to the traffic far below.

It wasn't until one of the other secretaries noticed her frozen attitude and went to her that she screamed in the terror which was racing through her body. The touch of the other girl's hand on her angora sweater covered arm brought her back to her senses...and that scream brought every member of the staff to her side. She pointed to the roof across the street, but she hadn't needed to. Her transfixed stare gave intent of the direction... and the cause for her shock.

"He's going to jump," declared someone. Then another, "Get the police." "Somebody call the cops." "Damn fool will splatter all over Market Street." "Probably on dope, like most of them." "Maybe he wants to be seen on television." "Just another nut... let him jump if that's what he wants. World too full of nuts already."

Then the police came, and the fire department and the television camera crews. They stationed themselves on the street, in the office and on the roof behind the heavy frame of Johnny Limbo who had not turned to look back to the lip of the roof which was about two feet above his head. During the ensuing time it took the police and others to arrive on the scene after the notification he had climbed down from the roof to an ornamental gargoyle and was straddling it as if riding the back of a horse.

But his eyes remained on the street below. Uniformed officer, Parker Steele, was first on the scene. He didn't know much about such affairs, and he knew nothing of psychiatry, but he knew he had to be careful in his approach to his words as well as his actions. He figured forceful orders were the best start.

"Get your ass up out of there." Not a blink. "I'm a police officer and I'm telling you to get your ass up from there." The boy spit into the street below. "You got a name?" And still nothing.

Parker leaned over the low parapet and looked in both directions just below the roof. Twenty feet on either side of the boy was another gargoyle, but no ledge, nothing to aid him in getting any closer. Of course he could have reached down and grabbed the boy by the hair, but there would be no way of hauling him back to safety that way. Even if he could have held onto the boy's hair for any length of time there was no way he could be helped by anyone else.

"What the hell am I doing out here thinking about risking my life to pull a jerk-off like you back to the roof?" he sneered aloud. "I say, go ahead and jump. You'd save the taxpayers a lot of money. All they'd need down there is a janitor, or a street cleaner to sweep you into a bucket."

The boy only spit again and his eyes seemed to watch the spit travel downward until he couldn't see it any longer. But still he had moved no other muscle. It was as if he were hypnotized by the sights below.

Then the other police arrived, and far below there was the screaming of sirens from both the police units and the fire wagons. Windows in other office buildings opened, and the long snout of a television camera became evident directly across from him… and there was the noise of other camera equipment being set up on the roof in positions where the lenses could be focused on the boy.

"If he drops," the director was heard to say, "we'll have him covered from the high angle down, and from the street level as he goes down… and from across the way. They'll get it in their homes live first, then with all that material, what a tape we'll have to cut." No one on the roof paid much attention to him other than the camera crew.

Two of the detectives closed in on either side of Parker. The senior leaned over. He looked around much as Parker had, then his eyes focused on the back of the boy's head. He didn't look at Parker as he spoke. "You first on the scene?"

Parker nodded. "Parker... 52nd Division."

"Lewis." Then he was silent for a long moment as he lit a cigarette. "He say anything?"

"Nothing, sir."

"Hey, kid," shouted Lewis, overly loud. "Smile... you're on camera. That's what you want, isn't it?"

It worked. The kid snapped his face upward to face the men, of which there were more than a dozen suddenly looking down at him. The boy gripped the iron neck feathers of the gargoyle more tightly. There was anger steaming in his dark, youthful eyes. "That ain't what I want at all."

"Well, what you want and what you get is two different things." Lewis flipped his cigarette out over the parapet, letting it fly so that it barely missed the boy's ear. The boy didn't flinch... but he turned to look back down to the street.

"Why don't you all go and leave me alone?"

"If you wanted to be alone you should have gone off in the woods someplace. How in hell did you expect to be alone when you put yourself center stage like this? Boy, you're all alone out on a gargoyle with a million people watching you. Is that the kind of alone you wanted?"

Suddenly he let go of the iron feathers of the gargoyle with one hand and momentarily it looked like he would be flying into midair with the birds that flew dangerously close to him... he was much too close to their nest. But he didn't topple and the cops let their sudden intake of air ease through their lips.

Johnny Limbo had another use for the free hand. "A million people, huh?" It was a deep question.

"If that's the kind of alone you want, you got it, sonny boy." Suddenly Johnny's hand moved and in the flickering of an eye he had unzipped his trousers and taken out his cock. He began to masturbate it furiously. "This is what I think of them. Let them watch. Let them all see it. Let them know what I think of them." And his dick steadily grew into his full erection. It wasn't very long or very wide... but what he had was doing the trick. His hand action lasted a full two minutes until it ejaculated and the sperm shot out over the grotesque face of the gargoyle and went its way down to the streets below.

"That make you happy?" Lewis finally muttered.

Johnny Limbo wasn't a very good-looking boy. He was much too overweight. His black wavy hair was sparse giving the sign he would be bald by the time he reached twenty. His arms appeared too long to match the rest of his body, and his legs too short and stubby to give him any great stride. But he did appear healthy in every other aspect... only his mind wouldn't have been classified as very healthy at that moment.

"How long have you been planning this?" The boy didn't answer. "Okay... so if you're going over the side, you want to give us a name? We're going to find it later... when we go through your pockets or check your fingerprints."

The TV director called over to the cop. "His name is Johnny Limbo and he's just turned fourteen. His aunt, a woman named Cora Williams called the station and they relayed it here."

Lewis looked down to the boy again. "Just a snotty-nosed brat of a kid... and you're causing all this commotion."

Johnny snaked a look back to the officers and his lips curled back in a wild sneer. "Why couldn't that fuckin' old bat leave me alone?"

Parker tapped Lewis on the shoulder and they moved back a few feet from the parapet. "Young kid like that isn't like the older ones. He's just liable to go over. The older ones can be talked out of it most of the time... they only think they want to die. The young ones... I've seen them go before. They just don't care."

Lewis frowned. "We'll get a net stretched a couple of floors below him. But that's going to take time. We've got to stall the bastard."

"You have an approach? I tried the hard line... so have you."

"Let's see if we can come up with the whys and wherefores of his climbing up here in the first place. I won't play the *go ahead and jump bit*, or the *come on back up here bit*. We'll just see if we can't talk him into his story."

"Sounds good."

Then the two men moved back to the edge of the parapet and leaned their elbows on it. "You don't like your aunt, huh?" Lewis had changed the tone of his voice to one of sympathy.

Johnny kept his eyes to the street. "She's alright, I guess... only I wish she'd leave me alone."

The television microphone was brought in closer so that each word could be heard. It was news. The people had a right to see and hear all the action... no one pushed it away.

"She the reason you're up here?"

"She couldn't be no reason for nothing."

"Are you bad in school?"

"I don't know."

"You got a girlfriend?"

The question seemed to hit a mark deep within his being. He suddenly shuddered and froze. His hands gripped the iron feathers of the gargoyle. Then he began to rock from side to side on the ornament... he permitted his body to sway farther and farther over each side. "You want to shake that thing loose, stop it," commanded Parker. But the boy continued... the daze-like trance coming back to his eyes. The two policemen again stepped back from the parapet.

"I think you hit something with that girlfriend bit," said Parker.

"Yeah! He tightened up pretty good. But look what it caused him to do." Then Lewis shrugged. "But I gotta keep on with it." Lewis looked up as a Priest moved in to them. "I don't know what his religion is, Father..."

"I'll do what I can," the Priest moved back to the parapet with them after he was brought up to date, and the fact that the officers believed a girlfriend had something to do with the present situation. "It's something about your girlfriend, isn't it, Johnny?" The Priest had proposed the question and the boy still swayed dangerously from side to side. "I'm Father O'Donnell. I'd like to help you. Is there anything I can do?"

"Go away, bastard," screamed the boy as he stopped his movements suddenly and gripped the iron feathers and froze again.

"Come now, son," reasoned the Priest. "Every word you're speaking is going out over the air. You don't want your friends and relatives, and your girlfriend to hear you talking like that in what may be the last moments of your life."

"Shit," screamed the boy and once more took his dick in hand and began to masturbate but it would not come to an erection. He slapped the muscle hard. "It's no good. I'm no good. Fuckin' girls are no good."

"Boy!" shouted the Priest. "If you've ever had any good in you..."

"Not that way, Father," whispered Lewis and put his hand lightly on the Priest's shoulder, then looked down to the boy again. "You want me to call your girlfriend?"

"I... I ain't got no girlfriend."

"Strong boy like you and no girlfriend?" Lewis tried for more of the answer. "A guy with a muscle like you have?"

"Never had none. Never had no girlfriend. I'm fat, and I'm ugly. I stand up and my arms hang like an ape. They always made fun of me. I ain't never had no girlfriend."

The officers and the Priest looked at each other and they knew the answer was near. They moved back from the parapet and huddled again.

"I'm no psychiatrist," informed Lewis. "But I'm sure we're on to the reason for his being out there. Now if only we could get him up here, or at least in a position where we can grab him. Guess the only thing we can do is keep pumping him about coming up and talking it over."

The boy was swaying back and forth and sideways on the iron ghoul when they returned. "How about coming up here on the roof and telling us all about it? I promise we won't take you anyplace until you're ready to go. Just come on up and talk it out with us."

"Nobody would ever talk to me about… it… they only laughed. The girls were the worst of all. They laughed the loudest. God damned girls… they think because you ain't pretty… handsome… then you ain't got no feelings… you don't need nothing like the other guys can get… whenever they want it… I can't never get any of it… I ain't got no girlfriends."

"Just what is it you're trying to tell us, lad?" questioned the Priest sympathetically and all those listening at their television receivers across the country strained their ears for his reply and the reason for his precarious position on the iron monster. "I'm sure you want to tell us the whole story. I'm sure we can help you. But please come up here where we can hear you better… where we can help you. All of us want to help you."

"I ain't got no girlfriend." He lifted his eyes and saw the girl in the angora sweater who had first saw him. She was looking across to him, her eyes frozen on him and he could hear an announcer's voice coming over the television in the background.

"No girls would have nothing to do with me because I'm ugly. They wouldn't even take me if I put a bag over my head. They only laughed." Then he took his eyes from the girl in the angora sweater and looked back to the men above him. "God damn it… I want a girl. I want to get fucked. I want to get laid. I want to get sucked. I ain't never had nothing but doing it with my hand. I want a real girl…" The tears welled up in his eyes. "Only no girl will ever fuck an ugly pig like me. No girl will ever suck me. No girl will ever go to bed with me… I'm going to die… I'm going to die right now because I'll never know what it's like to be a real man…"

And the girl in the angora sweater across the street screamed at him with all her might... "Don't jump... whatever you do, don't jump... I'll fuck you...." She threw up her skirt and pulled down her panties and spread her legs wide apart and her voice rose in hysteria... "I'll fuck you. Come off that thing. Come over here and I'll fuck you until it hurts. I'll love you. You're not ugly... I'll fuck you... Come over. Let them help you over here. I'll fuck you...."

And Johnny Limbo jerked upright. His ears strained and he felt the sincerity in the hysterical words. He quickly came to a standing position on the wide back of the gargoyle... and it would have made little difference if there had been a net under him or not... no net could have taken his weight and the weight of tons of iron as the gargoyle broke away from the building front and plunged downward... twenty stories... the girl in the angora sweater screamed... Johnny Limbo never heard it... but the television cameras covered every angle from their three positions.

THE END

MICE ON A COLD CELLAR FLOOR

from Fetish Annual *Pendulum Publishing, story on Ed's resume 1972.*

HARRY POOLE ROLLED over on his back and put his hands under his head but his eyes were turned enough to watch Edith Spectre as she reached down and pulled up her panties, they were soiled from both the floor and the action they had just gone through. Neither had bothered to undress. They had simply stretched out on the old mattress which had long ago been discarded to the cellar floor. Harry had unzipped his pants and Edith pulled down her panties until they were secured to her body by only one leg.

"It stinks down here. It stinks down here more every time we come down here," the boy muttered.

"Yeah." She sighed. "But where else could we go? There ain't no place."

"There's always got to be someplace else. Only we just ain't found it yet I mean... there's always got to be someplace else."

"Not my house... not yours... my ma'd kill me and your pa would take a hammer to your head."

"He wouldn't give a frig that I took you up there and laid you in that crummy bedroom... only... he's always got some of his stinking whores in there. Old bastard take a club to me. I'd bash his head in with the stove leg, that's what I'd do. I'd rip off the stove leg and take it right to his friggin' head."

"Then you'd go to jail. Then what would I do for some fun with you? There wouldn't be nothing I could do. I'd just dry up and blow away, that's how much I'd be needing you, and you know I wouldn't let no other boys touch me like that." She hugged the well-used green cardigan sweater around her ample breasts against a sudden chill which swept through the cellar.

"I better not catch you messing around with none of those other creeps on the street. You're my girl, and you better believe that, that's what you better believe."

"I believe it alright, Harry. I been your girl for ages… ever since I can remember… ain't I always come with you when you wanted me? An', ain't I always stood outside the stores when you went in to take something? I've always been your lookout."

"I ain't never said you wasn't a good girl. But you don't go off with none of them other creeps. You know they screw anything that will lay out for them. You know the whole mess of them gets the diseases more than you can shake a stick at. An' I don't go with none of them street cunts either, cause I ain't gonna catch none of their diseases and get myself laid out in no graveyard just for a piece of ass from one of them."

"You always got me." She reached over and took a handful of his crotch. He didn't brush the hand away nor did he encourage any further stimulation.

"I ain't gonna bash the old bastard. Ain't no real reason. I just keep out of his way. I sleep up there in that friggin' room when he's busy in the bedroom, and that's most of the time… then I listen to them snore… and I want to go in and piss all over them. But I don't. I just stay away and mind my own business and think about the next time I can come down here with you… that's what I think about."

"I like it when you tell me you think about me."

"I think about you and that sweet thing between your legs and those beautiful titties up under your sweater, more than you could ever think I could think."

"You won't never leave me, will you, Harry?" *

"Sometime I gotta go… sometime I got to leave this friggin' street. That's gotta be. I ain't gonna stay here and rot like the old man… and your mother."

"But you'll take me with you. Won't you, Harry?"

"I don't know where I'll be going."

"I'd go anywhere with you… just as long as I'm with you."

"I ain't got no education. I'm nearly seventeen and I ain't got no education. I never could learn anything in that friggin' school, that's why I quit. Only nobody wants a guy my age… not even to be a box boy. They hire those creeps from the school for after school and weekends… and here I can give them full time and they don't want no dropouts…that's what they said… they don't want no dropouts. An' I'll be frigged if I'll go back to school. No, I just got to get away from here. An', if you went with me, how do you know I could even get a job where I could make enough money to keep a pretty girl like you happy?"

"I ain't so pretty."

"Don't never say that. An' I find somebody who says that about you I'll knock their friggin' teeth in. Don't never say you ain't pretty. Harry Poole don't never go with nobody that ain't pretty. You get what I mean?"

"I'm pretty? You really mean that?"

"You bet your sweet tits I do."

Then they were silent for a long moment… the sounds of the outside world drifted in and they listened… the buses, the cars, the horns… and the scratching of the mice in the darker corners of the cellar.

"What do you think it's like when you die, Harry? I mean… we wouldn't hear no more voices and there wouldn't be any touching anything… I mean maybe somebody can touch us but we couldn't touch back no more…"

"Well for one friggin' for damned sure thing I ain't gonna be no old creep… I figure I'm going out while I still look good. I seen some of them old folks that died over at Delancy's dead house. They looked horrible. I don't never want to look like that."

"Me neither."

"I'll make a deal with you. If… and I said *IF*, I take you with me when I leave the street we'll make a pact that we go out together and while we're still young."

"That's the only way I figure to go, I'd get sure scared if you weren't around when my time comes."

"You got a long way to go before you come to that place. You may look beautiful like a woman and your tits built up early, but you're still just past fourteen. Ma'an, have you got a lot of life to live."

"So have you."

"Not as much as you. I'm older."

"Seventeen ain't very old."

"It's old enough. I been around, you know. That makes people older. I heard my old man say that. And he's been around, too."

"Sometimes my ma can't hardy ever get out of bed in the morning to go to work. She looks old. I guess she's been around, too."

"Sure, anybody that looks old has been around. That's how you can tell who's been around."

"You sure don't look old…"

"Maybe I ain't been around enough yet… give me time… but I never want to look as old as my old man…"

"Or my ma…" Her hand had been absently working on his shaft and it stood erect once more. "Want me to do some more?"

His hand reached over and caressed the back of her hair. "I ain't had time enough to get ready yet."

She giggled. "You look like you're ready."

"I'll be the one to tell you when I'm ready."

She let the fingers of her free hand reach down and rub the crotch of her panties. "I'm hottern' hell again."

"Then take your hand away from my prick and you won't get to thinking things that gets you all excited. I'll tell you when I'm ready again." And she removed the hand, but kept her other hand busy with the front of her pubic region through the sheer nylon panty material.

"I like the way you make me feel. You get me so hot and juicy like. I like the way you make me feel. I can't even smell this old cellar smells when you get me all worked up like this."

"Nothin' can take this old cellar smells out of my head. I could blow it up… if we had someplace else to go. Only we ain't got someplace else to go… not till I get ready to leave this friggin' street… only I ain't got no money to leave this friggin' street and I ain't got no place to get some."

"I'm always afraid when you go out into one of them stores at night and I do your lookout."

"You just do a good job being a lookout… only I can't carry enough to make it even worth my time. Little crap! But it's the only way I can get a buck when I need it. But there ain't enough bucks to see me on my way. Then what if I get to another town and I'm broke… I don't know the backdoors there like I do around here. Sure as friggin' I'd get caught the first time out. I got to get me a pile right around here where I know where I'm at, that's what I got to do."

"I sure like to help you."

"You're just a damned friggin' good kid. Sometime, maybe I'm going to do something real good for you."

"You always do something real good for me, Harry."

"I mean something real great… spectacular… yeah, that's the word…

spectacular..." He rolled the word over his tongue as if it tasted good. "I like big words like that. Maybe when I leave the street, if I learn some big words, I can use them and make everybody think I'm really smart."

"I think you're really smart."

"That's because you're real dumb. Anybody that knows more than you do would look real smart."

She pouted. "I ain't so dumb"

"All broads are dumb. If they didn't have that thing between their legs they wouldn't even be worth having around. That's all you broads have got... that thing between your legs, and them things up under your sweater, and they ain't any good except for looking at."

"You'll make me cry."

"Then go ahead and cry... see if I care if you cry. I don't care if you cry."

But she didn't. She knew when Harry was depressed, even if she didn't know the word. "Don't make me mad, Harry."

"Ahh, frig it." He muttered. "I ain't mad at you. I'm just mad at the street." He reached over and took her hand and formed it around his tool. "Go ahead. You can do it now. Maybe that's what we both could use." The mice in the dark corners began to scratch at the rotted bricks and cement again. "Maybe it can take our minds out of this hole for a little while again."

She continued the slight masturbation movement but raised her head and went very close to the shaft. "It always have before, Harry. When we do things to each other there ain't nothing else we can think about. You always said you liked me best of all, that's what you always said."

"You are the best." His hand dropped to one of her breasts as it dipped up under the bottom of her sweater.

She looked to his shaft and let the end of her pink tongue wet her lips.

"Would you... would you like it this way this time?"

"You are the best, the very best," he sighed.

Her lips dropped down over the shaft and her hot tongue began to do its work. She made all the proper sounds and Harry began to twitch in reaction from the very first hot connection...

But as he drifted off into the solitary, exotic trance the sound of the mice became overpowering to his other senses and he heard himself say, "We're nothing but mice... just like them mice in the corner... we're all mice on a cold cellar floor."

THE END

THE DEVIL & THE DEEP BLUE-EYED BLONDE

not credited, but on Ed's resume 1971 in Switch Hitter *Vol.2 no.2, June/July 1971*

THE REVOLUTION WAS in full swing. It had been for some time. The streets ran red with the blood of both sides, and the broken dead bodies clogged the gutters where they had been kicked or shoved in order to keep the streets open for the easy passage of military vehicles of which there were few. Neither side were the bad guys or the good guys, and neither had a workable army. They were simply men hastened into weak formation so they could fight one another. There was one small faction in control of the small government, and there was another faction, the revolutionaries, which apparently didn't like the government the way it existed. Since elections were thought to be rigged, the revolutionaries felt there was only one way of putting their cause across. Bloodshed!

Bloodshed was easily come by. Neither side liked the other under any circumstances, therefore it took little convincing for any of them to take up arms and slaughter each other.

Strict gun laws had kept the revolutionaries underground for a long time. But the night sneak raids had netted them a fair arsenal of small calibre rifles and hand guns along with some sticks of dynamite and hand grenades... but they knew the night and secret raids would have to continue all through any war they brought about. Of course, there would be some daytime skirmishes which would net them further supplies, and no wounded or dead man was left to rot with his equipment intact.

As with all revolutionaries, the men believed their cause to be just and they were going all out to prove their point even if it meant leaving

189

not one man in the federal forces alive. Extinction would keep them out of power forever.

Victoria Karzon stepped briskly across the body of a man on the sidewalk. His stomach had been slashed open and the flies, depositing their maggots, had already begun to gather. The smell of death was all around her and it bothered her nose, but she didn't wear a handkerchief over the area as so many others did. She felt that the handkerchief might be like the bull's eye of a target, and a bullet in the head was something she could do without.

Such a lovely head! Blonde! Deep blue eyes captured a dainty oval face which held a determined chin and full red lips. At any other time she would have been dressed in the torn shorts and tie around blouse and would have been carrying a rifle or the tommy-gun she preferred. But her mission there in the late dusk of the day was not to hunt down the enemy and riddle him or her with bullets. She had a much more important assignment. She was to track down and capture the hearts of more important leaders of the revolutionary movement. They were becoming stronger in manpower and fire power every day and it gave the government authorities reason for deep concern. What had at first appeared to be a simple uprising, of which there had been many over the years, was working itself into a fullscale blood bath. The revolutionaries were getting their information somewhere because they had been much too successful in discovering supply depots that were held in the top secret classifications.

Victoria hadn't always been a blonde, as several of the government officials could testify to, but it was thought that her assignment called for the hair color change. Most of the women around the revolutionaries were the dark haired, olive skinned variety and her beauty and pink skin, virgin appearance would stand her in excellent stead. Her tight sweater and hip revealing mini-skirt would do the rest. All she had to do was pass through the unseen lines and she was bound to make a connection with the male population who were sex starved for her kind of woman. And she was all woman!

"How far do I go?" she had asked of her superiors when the subject was first approached as being her assignment.

"As far as you have to!" The simple answer rang in her ears and she knew what was expected of her. She would be a sex supply source, until she found the information which was required. At least she knew she was healthy and could last a long time. But with her interrogation aids she felt it wouldn't take long to find out all which was required. She also realized, and was fully informed, that there was the possibility she would die. One slip and she was gone as if she never existed. There were no trials on either side, especially where a spy was concerned. And the death didn't always come by a quick bullet in the head. The revolutionaries were very inventive in their means of execution. It was never quick, and it was never clean... and sometimes many questions were answered. But in the end there could only be expected the same black oblivion which a hangman might produce. It was not a pleasant thought. But Victoria felt she was more than well-endowed to handle the illiterates she would be dealing with.

She hadn't counted on Mario Cantrell, the ruggedly handsome Field Marshal of tactical operations. He was more than six feet and there wasn't an ounce of fat on him. His muscles rippled even as he talked, let alone when he walked. His voice when at any pitch, an ordering pitch or a low command, held the same power of authority. And when an order was given there was no argument from his men. They hopped to it and got the job done. Many died through those orders, but there wasn't one who returned that wouldn't immediately go out on another mission if they were so ordered.

Victoria had been approached by two cruising revolutionaries and asked about her identification papers, and they were informed by her that she was not a resident of their country and was simply looking for a way to get off the island. Her papers had been lost in the hotel fire two nights before. There had been a hotel fire and it was completely gutted, so there was no way of checking that out. Then, too, Victoria didn't look like the inhabitants of the country, she was pink all over and the dark olive skin of the others proved a striking difference.

She was not immediately released and sent on her way. This was a happening she counted on. She was taken immediately to the field headquarters and put in a large room with several other "political prisoners," and during the four hours she was held in that detention room she saw several others taken out by three or four guards. Then when she heard several shots fired after each of those incidents, she ventured to look through a small smoke stained, wire covered window and she knew then, for fact, what her imagination told her. The prisoners were being executed.

She had not yet begun to fight. When the next set of executioners entered for a new victim she collared one around the neck and screamed blasphemy into their ears followed with, "I'm not one of your God-damned political prisoners, buster. You'd better get somebody of authority in here damned quick!" There was much more which spewed viciously through her luscious lips before she was pushed aside and the soldiers captured their next victim and left with the screaming man having been dragged all the way.

However, her tirade had worked. Within a few moments two side-arm bearing soldiers came into the room and told her to come with them. Again she started to scream her resistance, but the soldiers only laughed and grabbed her by each arm and she was forced from the room. She was not headed for the courtyard and the political prisoners' firing squad.

The office she was headed into appeared to be the basement of another much larger building. And it must have originally been a wine cellar because the large wine kegs lined the walls and some of the soldiers which lounged around were tapping the spigots to fill their cups.

The immediately impressive Mario Cantrell sat at a paper littered desk with his back to the far wall. He never once took his eyes from her the moment she entered to the point where she stood in front of his desk. He smiled broadly and waved the two soldiers away. Victoria watched them move to the wine kegs.

"Anyone as lovely as you that could be a politico would have to be lacking in the sexual education which can only be attributed to some mere baby."

"I'll take that as a compliment," replied Victoria, attempting to keep a straight, solid face.

Mario nodded. "It was meant to be." Then there was small talk and chit-chat and a chair was produced for her to sit on and both finally held tall mugs of the bitter wine in their hands. "At another time, perhaps I might have had champagne to offer you." He shrugged. "But these are trying days." He sipped silently from the wine mug, then didn't look at her as he spoke. "What is your purpose in this country?"

"I was vacationing, and I would have been long gone if you'd have left the airliner intact and not blown up the main rail line and put holes in the bottom of the small boats which would have gotten me someplace."

He shrugged broadly again. "Ah yes. War does strange things to what otherwise might have been a simple outing. But I do believe we might be able to help you. We do not wage war upon women, children or foreigners,... unless they get in our way or are in the pay of the enemy."

"Hell, ma-an," she laughed. "If you were to charge me for this mug of wine I couldn't pay for it... so that lets in the pay of the enemy out, doesn't it?"

He joined her laughter. "There are many ways of paying for wine. I shall perhaps suggest one or two for your approval." He waved the remark away before she could come up with an answer. She full well knew his meaning. "But let us not talk of payment for anything so cheap as wine. You are in need of transportation to a more friendly atmosphere and I am in a position to offer you such transportation."

"For a price!"

"Of course," he winked.

She knew the price but then all along she knew there was to be a bedroom scene in her future. It was the only way she was going to find out the necessary information. The largest rifles and ammunition had to be coming from governmental sources, that was well known. But how did Mario's revolutionaries know the exact locations, or where a convoy would take to the roads, or when the few remaining ships would cross to and return from the coastal countries? That was the much needed knowledge.

"How will you get me out?"

"By boat! We have a few! It is the only way off the island presently. We will be leaving on a special mission very early in the morning. I can see you safely away from the island and deposited in a place where you will be easily picked up."

Victoria didn't answer him for a long time; she couldn't appear too anxious. However, when she finally did answer she said simply, "I'm willing to pay the price."

Mario took her by the hand and led her to a small bedroom behind the wine cellar and she knew each of the men in the command area knew what was about to happen. Their chiding remarks followed them even after the door was closed.

Sometime later as they lay naked, side by side on the soiled cot, she wished Mario wasn't one of the enemy. He had been a tremendous lover. He was tender, not rough like so many of the governmental higher ups she had serviced during the past few months. He knew what he was doing with his tongue and his hands were as tender as his endearing words. He took a long, long time in his foreplay and every move rose up body heats and soft moans of true feeling from deep within her being. She had performed a military duty, but she had enjoyed herself throughout the entire affair, and when it was over and they were both exhausted she wished the morning was a long way off. She wanted to try the man on for size again, and again and again. But it was not to be.

Still later they had another mug of wine delivered to them by the ugliest soldier she had ever seen, and that was the last thing she remembered until the cold sea breeze awoke her and she was securely tied to the bow of a small wooden, coastal patrol boat. There were two weary soldiers in the stern and Mario stood at the wheel near her. She struggled at the ropes, but whoever had tied her knew his business.

"This is one hell of a way to treat a passenger," she finally said with the cold wind attempting to push the words back down into her throat from where they originated.

"Ahhh," sighed Mario, "war makes such strange bed fellows. Why could not you have been what you looked like. The sweet innocent little piece of rag and hank of hair. You were such a delightful bed companion. You could have been so useful to me in my insatiable sexual desires. You are so different from most of the woman around here. Now I must tell you I know exactly why it is you were sent into my ranks. But I am a dangerous fellow, and I am a bit of a sadist. I want to hear your mission directly from your own lips. And believe me when I say I am a bit of a sadist." He leered. "Perhaps I am really the devil."

Victoria remained silent. She continued in silence as the two men moved forward and tied her ankles to a long, stout rope, then when her arms were freed, they did the same to her wrists. "I am sure you have never been keel-hauled, dear young lady, so I shall explain it to you. The ropes around your ankles and around your wrists are a continuous length which stretches from the port side of this craft, down under the keel and comes up on the starboard." He laughed sadistically. "You will not have to go down eighteen feet, then be pulled under the twenty-eight foot beam very often before you talk to me."

Victoria shuddered at the thought, but she had been commissioned by the heads of state and the Governor himself had been informed. She could not go back on her orders. Besides, how did she know Mario knew all he professed to know? Perhaps she had let something slip in her own dialogue which made him suspicious and he was tempting her into telling all she knew. The enemy always worked that way.

The men lowered her over the side in the roughest manner possible and a long tearing splinter from the side of the ship cut her naked middle and up across her breasts and played with the underside of her chin as, upside down, her hair touched the water where her arms were already immersed. She was held there for a moment with the blood rushing from the minor, but painful wound.

"So that you will know when you come up on the other side that I speak the truth," informed Mario, "my information comes directly from the top man of your government… The Governor himself. He wants the revolution to succeed so that he can run things as he wishes. Those he has put so solidly in command have red-taped him so badly it is impossible to dip into the treasures any longer. We are his new forces. He couldn't let his lieutenants find out any information you might gather… now could he?"

She was pulled into the water head first, the salt biting her cuts viciously. She held her breath and hoped it would last… perhaps she would live. She would tell and Mario would take her back to bed with him. All of a sudden she wanted to live so badly. To hell with revolutions…! Her eyes saw the keel pass above her and she only felt the first sharp sting as the sharks, brought on by the fresh blood, left only empty ropes dangling in the water.

THE END

WANTED: BELLE STARR

originally published in Woman's World *V2.N2 Gallery Press Mar./Apr. 1973 from Short Wood, on Ed's resume 1972*

SAM BASS ROLLED his hairy legs over the edge of the bed, but he also turned his head to look at the lovely redhead who was still stretched out on the bed. She was just lighting up a black Mexican cigar.

"Belle," he said. "If you ain't the damndest piece of woman I ever did meet."

"That's what keeps you coming back for more, Sam Bass, my old stud." She flopped the cigar to the other side of her mouth and puffed the end into a bright red tip.

"You didn't need to take the chance of coming back here. You could have sent me a message with one of the boys... there's always somebody passing through that could have told me where you were. There ain't no wanted notices out on me, like there is on you. You take the damndest chances for no reason at all. There's lawmen and bounty hunters all over the countryside that would like to get your pussy in their sights. They'd send a bullet up your ass just as quick as they would any man... quicker I suspect because you strike like a rattlesnake... and there ain't a cowboy in the world that will cotton up to a rattlesnake."

"When I need a lay, I need a good one... and you're the only guy I ever knowed that could satisfy me... so I come on over to you." She grinned and knocked the cigar ash to the floor beside the bed. "They couldn't see me if I was to walk right in front of their eyes... only I don't do that. I ain't interested in one of them getting lucky. I got a lot of pussy left that I figure to use before somebody cashes in my chips."

Sam Bass pushed up the window and urinated through the opening then returned to sit on the edge of the bed where he also lighted up a black

Mexican cigar. "An' don't you go trying to make me believe that I'm the only guy you laid up with. You been gone most a year, and I know that hot little box of yours. You got to have it when you got to have it."

"I didn't say nothing about not having any, Sam. I just said when I needed a good one, you're the only one that fits into that purpose."

"You sure know what to say to a guy to make his head all swell up."

"That's all according to what head is swelling up," she laughed and he slapped her a friendly, but resounding crack across her buttocks which she had turned up to him as she knocked the ash from her cigar again. Then she sunk into deep thought. "Sam?"

Sam stretched out on the bed, on his back. He wanted more of the girl, but he also knew he would have to rest for a spell longer.

"What's troubling you?"

"Nothing really troubling me."

"You ain't letting those wanted posters and all that reward money bother you, are you?"

"Naw, Sam. They seem to bother you more than they do me."

"Then what you got in your craw?"

"You know what a lesbian is?"

"Lesbian…? What's that? Some kind of new animal I never heard of?"

"It's a woman. Well, kind of."

"Well… she's either a woman or she ain't a woman. There ain't no some kind of…"

"There sure is. You go to the whorehouses when you're up in Frisco and the other places."

"All men goes to whorehouses."

"And you ain't never heard of a lesbian?"

"I sure ain't." He got up on his elbow. "So, what's this some kind of woman that's a lesbian?"

"She don't like men."

"Lots of women don't like men."

"This is a special breed that don't like men. I mean they don't like to go to bed and get laid by a man."

"Now what in hell kind of woman would that be? Women was made with pussies and men with dicks and they was meant to get together. That's only natural. Damn! A woman that don't like sexing it up with a guy… she don't know what she's missing, I can tell you that. Where did you come by some woman like that? I never heard tell of such a thing."

"First one I met, I met down Arizona way. And from then on I kept looking to see if they was any more than just that one I met in the saloon… old Hose Nose Kate's place."

"That old whore still running a place?"

"Bigger than ever. But anyway, you know she's going to make a buck any way she can. She's got all them girls to service the men. But she done found out that there are some women who want to be taken care of too…"

"Like I said… all women like to be taken care of by a good man."

"No, these women want to be taken care of by other women."

"Now how in hell they do that?"

"They lick 'em."

"To hell you say."

"They sure do… with their tongue. They do with their tongue just like what a guy does with his pecker."

"To hell you say."

"I sure do."

"Must be some kind of a freak lady."

"But that's the whole point. There wasn't just that one. They's a whole school full of them… when I started looking around I found them all over the place. Some of them will go get laid by a man, but they also like to get laid by the other ladies."

"Now what do you suppose this country is coming to… To hell you say… what did you call them?"

"Lesbians."

"That don't sound like no friendly kind of name."

"All them broads that are that way like the sound of the name lesbian."

"I sure wouldn't."

"Well, you ain't one of them broads. You're a stud… the best in the country."

"Tell that to the other broads around here next time you decide to move around the country for a year and leave me cold, naked and unsatisfied. So, what happens with those broads?"

"I guess they just keep right on living… they seem to be happy. They get along. And they get as many girls under them as a stud like you gets."

"Now that sure is hard to believe."

"Sure it is until you see it right up close with your own eyes."

"You saw it up close, with your own eyes?"

"You damn well right. I wasn't going to let an opportunity like that get away from me. I like to learn everything there is to learn when it comes to bedroom action."

He swung his feet over the edge of the bed again but braced his hands, palm down on the bed. He eyed her questioningly. "You let one of them lesbians, lesbian you?"

She nodded… "And I lesbianed her right back. I got a longer tongue than I ever knew I had."

"To hell you say… you did that… You put your…?"

She cut him off. "Don't knock it until you've tried it, old friend."

"Well I ain't going to do no such thing. I ain't going to be one of your lesbians."

"You wouldn't be a lesbian. A man can't be a lesbian. Only another woman can be a lesbian."

"I got a tongue. I sure as hell could do the same damned thing if I wanted to… but where in hell would I get any of the feeling of shooting my gun off if I only use my tongue. Hell! Take your lesbians and toss them over a bronc." He chewed on the end of his cigar a moment. "Why, things like that could put a man right out of business. What would happen to all the men if the women only wanted to shack up with women? That sure don't seem right to me… and I stopped beating my meat when I was a kid. I got to have a woman. Now what would I do without no woman? You liked being a lesbian?"

"I liked what I did."

"You did, huh?"

She nodded. "All the times."

"All the times? More than once?"

"It got like cigar smoke with me. I had to have it, that's what happened to me right from the first time I lesbianed."

"To hell you say."

She hugged her own breasts momentarily, then let one hand drop down to her crotch where she let the fingers drift over the soft pubic region. "I tell you. There wasn't nothing I ever did before that was like it. I shot right up to the clouds, and when I fell back to earth it was like falling right onto a feather bed, all soft and comfortable like."

"You said I always did that to you."

"Oh you did, Sam… all the time… only different. It ain't like being shot up there by another woman."

"I should hope not."

"Ahhh… Sam, you'll never understand."

"I ain't sure I want to."

"There's just something different about a woman."

"I've knowed that for years."

"She smells all pretty like, and she's got such a soft body, and her tongue is so soft and her hands are so soft and gentle. Getting it on with a man and he's hard and hairy, and he smells like… like… well, like a man."

"So now you're getting it on with women and you don't like men no more?"

"I didn't say that."

"You just about did."

"All I said is from that first time I lesbianed I got hooked on them. 'Course you've always been the greatest when you're between my legs. But I got some fun out of other guys before. Only once I let a girl tongue me, and I tongued them back it wasn't the same with other men anymore. It was like they just couldn't send me the way they used to."

"Girl, you've been lesbianed right out of the human race if you ask me."

"Or into the human race."

"Girl, you should never have taken up in my path. You should never have taken up bank robbing, and stage robbing and cattle stealing. It's taken you to the worst places on earth. It's spoiled my little sex broad. You should have stayed right here and let me do all them other kind of things. Now you got wanted posters all over the place and a price on your head and you've been lesbianed."

"That's why I had to come back to see you, Sam."

"To show me you've been lesbianed?"

"More than that."

"I've lost you."

"No, you haven't."

"You gonna give up being lesbianed?"

"I didn't say that either. I came back to see if you would be like all the other guys I've had in the past year… duds… that's why I came all this way. I had to let you poke me with your pecker between my legs… I had to feel you sex me again."

"And…?"

"You're still the greatest and you sent me…"

"Then you'll give that other up?"

"Nope... I've got to have you both... I guess you'll just have to realize I'm bi-sexual..."

"Bi-sexual... now what in hell kind of animal is that?"

And she started to explain... there would be plenty of time... the posse never did know in what direction she ever traveled.

THE END

THE DEVIL COLLECTS HIS DUES

Illustrated Case Histories A Study Of Lesbian Practices Vol.2 No.2 Calga Publishing Aug./Sept. 1971 (no author credited, is on Ed's resume for 1971)

SHELIA AWOKE WITH a start. Her whole dream had been unreal, a terror of modern torture. The sweat poured down the front of her badly torn blouse top and dropped into the center of what was left of her brassiere. The brassiere also had been ruptured where only one strap held it into place. She would learn the rest of her pants suit were as equally destroyed, when the drug-enacted cobwebs were dragged from her brain. But the full realization of her waking moment would take more than an hour before the entire scene was clear to her. Before that moment when she shot back into a conscious state, she wasn't quite sure what had happened.

There had been Liza's party with a lot of booze, a lot of noise and a lot of people. A lot of people she had never seen before. But Shelia Allen had never been averse to meeting new people, even the hippie-types which Liza had suddenly presented onto the scene. Not so much suddenly and not so much presented. They were just there when the party got started. It was the first one of Liza's parties which Shelia had ever attended to which slob types were invited. Liza had always stocked her gatherings with the elite, or at least those with some influence, because the pretty blue-eyed Amazon was always looking to further her career. She was an exotic dancer of some renown and didn't plan on stepping down the ladder when it was just as easy to promote her way upward.

Liza was a lesbian, but she was a pseudo-bisexual because she'd go in either direction if the process made it worth her while. Otherwise she was strictly a one-sided lesbian and Sheila had been her running-mate more than any of the others who had come along during the previous three years of their relationship.

Which was another thing that made the whole affair seem weird. There hadn't been the slightest hint that Liza had taken up friendship with any of the hippie tribes. They had talked on the phone and had seen each other as regularly as before. But right up until the moment she entered Liza's big house for the gala social, "hippie" had never been mentioned. She tried not to appear shocked, but that was a difficult task because she *was* shocked. And she was irritated. And the other more conventionally dressed individuals were ill at ease. The creatures didn't even bother to set themselves, filthy clothes and all, on the furniture. They huddled in several corners of the rooms… cross -legged on the floor.

From all that Shelia could remember she didn't even see them move except to visit the banquet table and the champagne punch bowl. Those trips were made quite frequently. And when several times one or more of them arose, loaded up at the banquet table and disappeared outside to the lawn area, Shelia was sure they were storing up for the winter at Liza's expense. But Liza could afford it. Liza could, but she wouldn't. The bill would befall whichever of her amours was presently in favor, be he man or be he she-woman. But the whole things was most irritating to her. Not only because she hadn't been let in the know by Liza, but also by the sight itself.

She watched the tallest, bearded one cross in her direction and she knew he was heading for her, but wished to hell she was wrong. She wasn't!

"You a dyke, straight or just plain queer? I'm Coronet!" The words were fast and pointed.

So were Shelia's. "You're Coronet, so get lost and play with yourself. As for the rest it's none of your damned business. So go drown your snot filled beak in the punch bowl."

"How come a broad like you can be so soft and pretty and have such a filthy mouth?" He grinned broadly behind the beard and his body odor swooned Shelia's senses even from the ten paces to where he stood. "Shit, Pussy," he continued. "You could really be a soft-roller if you gave yourself a chance!"

Sheila turned from him and made her way to the punch bowl. His breath smelled like the words he was using. But Shelia found out quickly she wasn't going to get rid of him so easily. She hadn't witnessed his new approach, but there was no missing the sell as he sidled up beside her and dipped his used cup into the bowl and slurped from it when it was full. "Ain't many, Pussy, that get away with turning their backs on the Coronet."

Shelia looked down her nose at the individual and gave the most distasteful glare she could muster. "I doubt if there are many *girls* who would dare turn their back on you… especially in the dark." She ducked her eyes in order to miss his stare. "Now why don't you get lost!"

Coronet hadn't lost his grin though it was nearly hidden behind the straggly, dirt encrusted beard. "Give me half a chance and I could show you how easy it would be for you and me to get lost in a place you could really get rid of all of those hang-ups you got, Pussy."

"Stop calling me Pussy." No one in the room could possibly have missed the shouted demand and none of them could miss her move as she tossed the champagne punch from her glass into his face. Then she stormed away as the character stood with the liquid dripping from his beard.

Probably the first bath he's had since the doctor dipped him the day he was born, someone was heard to say, and another offered, "What makes you think something like that was born? To be born one has to have a mother."

Shelia didn't hear any more at that time. She felt she needed some fresh air and the only place to get that was out in the spacious flower garden which Liza was so proud of. It was an area which held an upkeep expense which was nearly as much as the rest of the house itself. But the fragrance of the flowers almost immediately cleared her head and took away much of the anger which had been built up by Coronet. She felt the anger had built swiftly, therefore it left just as quickly. She couldn't see spending the rest of the night, which could be very enjoyable, thinking about creeps. She would simply ignore him and the rest of his bunch. But she did wish Liza would come into the garden so they could have some small amount of talk. She would like to know what it was all about. Why in the world were there such creeps? There had to be some kind of an explanation. Some kind of logical explanation.

"You don't like me, do you?"

Shelia turned to face the creep who had come up behind her. Even the fragrance of the garden flowers couldn't fully cover the atmosphere which surrounded him.

"I think you stink." Then she spun to face Coronet directly. "Think hell! I damned well know you stink." She put her hands defiantly on her hips. "Now why don't you do something about that you bastard?"

He held up his hands lightly in feigned protest. "Ahhh, little pussies should be petted not spanked."

"If you were any kind of a man you'd take a swing at me and I'd knock you right on your ass. You understand that? Just take one swing at me so I have a right to put you down on your ass where you belong. You might think you're looking at fluff, buster, but this fluff's got a blockbuster that never fails."

Coronet grinned but that time his eyes held no humor. "Pussy… I'm all for peace… I'm one of the flower children, just as tame as those petals growing all around us here in the garden. None of us are ever looking for trouble, only peace and serenity. Live and let live. All the world should know how we feel and how we live."

"If the world knew about that and came to accept it, the soap factories would be put out of business." Then she became completely frustrated. "Now why in hell am I standing here talking to you? I've got better things to do with my time."

"Like going to visit your girlfriend in there?"

"Go to hell!"

"Ahhh, come on. You don't have to be coy with me. I know the score. I always know the score. That's why I'm sort of a leader to my flock."

"You said it… *your flock.* I'm not one of your flock." She started back toward the French doors which led back into the main room of the house, but Coronet captured her arm lightly and just as lightly turned her around.

"I told you I don't like people turning their back on me, Pussy."

"And I told you where you could get off this train." She shrugged off his arm. "I thought you didn't get physical… it was against your religion or something? Okay, you get physical, Charlie. You know that's just what I'd like to see you do, Charlie… just get a little more physical. Just call me match box because you just strike, man and we'll see where you light."

"Ahhhh, brave, brave Pussy. Just what in the world am I going to do with you? Here I am, a handsome…" Shelia cut him off momentarily with a short curt laugh, then he continued. "A handsome bachelor making a simple pass, directed to a luscious creature and the luscious pussy-cat is all hung up on pseudo-Tom. Now ain't that enough to frost your balls??? Seems like a hell of a waste to me. Now if you were to goof-off with me for an hour I'd show you something that sure ain't got no psedo ahead of the name."

"You're a dirty, filthy beast. How dare you invade the homes of decent people spewing this rot out of your mouth?"

Coronet suddenly laughed loudly. It was completely a sardonic gesture. "Pussy, whatever you think is all in your mind. I ain't said one thing out of line. You're the one putting the *pretty* pictures in your own mind. And they are pretty, aren't they?" His eyes rolled up and down the front of her then came to a full stop on the crotch of her red, velvet pant suit. "I know the pictures in my mind are pretty."

"The only pictures you know are pornography. I'd give ten years of my life to close off your camera for good."

"Don't ever bet any part of your life, Pussy. Don't ever offer any part of it. You never know how much is left. Then sometimes, if you've bet or offered in his way, the Devil steps in to collect. You know the Devil always collects evil debts. Haven't you heard? Sex is *evil... evil* spelled in another way is *live*. But in order to *live* there must be sex and that is *evil...* therefore the whole world is *evil* and one day the Devil will demand his dues. You said pornography. That deals with sex... that *evil* sex. Now you must put such *evil* thoughts out of your mind." His eyes suddenly were burning coals which held her captive... against her will.

She hated his guts. Yet suddenly there was a strange fascination about him. She couldn't take her eyes from him... from his eyes...especially she couldn't dismiss his eyes. They were like bottomless pits of deep blue water where she couldn't see anything but her own reflection. She knew she was being hypnotized, but the reflections she saw in those deep pools made her believe she was hypnotizing herself. She knew she was being hypnotized but she no longer cared. Everything was suddenly pleasant and serene.

She couldn't have found any *hatred* even if she understood the meaning of the word.... which she suddenly didn't. She thought her mind fought for the right to remember things but the calmness which had overtaken her only told her "What does it matter?" She was being led. There was no need of any other reasoning. All her thoughts were being directed for her.

She was told to drink and she did. She couldn't see the hand to mouth process but she knew she drank. She knew she drank several times but she would have a hard time proving that to herself. Her thought patterns were all mixed up. Nothing focused behind her eyes until some kind of eternity had passed. It must have been a long eternity... it was a long time and it was all black everywhere. She knew she caught a glimpse of the Devil several times and he was always disguised behind a thick red beard and there was a leering grin behind the beard. An *evil...* where had she heard that word before? *EVIL....*what a silly word. It was almost funny. But it wasn't funny, was it?

The kaleidoscope of colors suddenly burst her into another kind of eternity. With a melting pot of sounds and vibrations she realized there was nothing she couldn't accomplish. The Universe was hers to conquer. But she need not conquer. She had already mastered it, and had done so without half trying.

When the light blue, like the blue of the sky, visited her unconsciousness she knew she could fly and that knowledge was accompanied by the sound of flapping wings. Red brought the sound of flames and a searing pain which centered mainly around her groin and inner thighs, but flared out in all directions at the same time. There was a violation which pained not only her body but what little senses she had left. Something was wrong. For a long time, something was wrong. She began to hurt all over. Even the flashing colors were no longer a release or a relief.

Suddenly she exploded. Her soul spent rapidly out of her body. Quickly she realized the eternal blackness was overtaking her again and she fought with it with all her might. She didn't want to go there again. But fight as she could, she knew there was no stopping the progression. And just as she sunk into complete oblivion, she heard the words chanted over and over again... *"EVIL-LIVE-EVIL-LIVE,"* then suddenly *"DEVIL-LIVED-DEVIL-LIVED!"*

The room came down to a slow spin and once Shelia's eyes could focus she knew her surroundings to be the bedroom in which she and Liza had been together intimately so many times in the past. But getting off the bed and steadying herself in order to move to the bathroom was as difficult as had been the opening of her eyes. She felt there had been a shock to her whole system and indeed she knew it, and what that shock had been once she straddled the toilet seat. The bathroom mirror gave her all else she needed to know. The glazed red eyes. She'd seen those symptoms often with the LSD users. The reoccurring sharp pains deep within her lower quarters... she hadn't started life as a lesbian... there had once been men.

Shelia couldn't blame Liza. Undoubtedly her friend, through hypnosis and drugs, had also been forced into the same type of situation. But Liza, Shelia thought, must be considered the weaker. She would give in more easily because she could already be judged bisexual. Another man would make little difference and a post-hypnotic trance is easily set.

Shelia looked deeply into the mirror. She stared hard and determinedly. She would find the depth of her own soul through her own eyes. There would be no post-hypnotic suggestions in her case. And she would be ready for *him,* the next time the *Devil came to collect his dues.*

THE END

THE EXTERMINATOR

by "Ann Gora" on the page and "Dick Trent" on the table of contents Pendulum *vol 4 no 1, Apr./May 1972 on Ed's resume*

I DON'T KNOW when I first thought about it… Then again I guess I do. I know I was quite young… younger than I am now… I guess that goes back to just before the turn of the century… that's twenty-three hundred and seven… I mean now it is… Of course the turn of the century couldn't have a seven after it… could it?

But we were in trouble. I remember reading in the history books about the twentieth century when the world started thinking about the food supply and what was going to happen when the food supply went out and the population kept going on and on and they weren't going to get anything to eat. In the same century they went to the bottom of the ocean and got food… how long can the bottom of the ocean last? The *MASTERS* of today's world know… it just can't last forever… and the crops can't grow as quickly as needed… and there has to be somebody who doesn't eat.

There are no longer any backward nations as there were in the twentieth century… but there is still that same sex hang-up with the populace. They simply have to make the sex thing and every time they make it there's those bunch of damned brats who come through the same hole the joy stick went into for the pleasure of the flesh.

As long as there is sex there is bound to be offsprings and that is the entire problem… those damned brats who come through all those good times. And they have to be fed… that is, if they are going to continue their existence. Naturally there are the preventatives. The pill and abortions have long since disappeared as becoming among the unnecessary. It is only a simple trip to one of the Professors and without even taking their clothes off the girls are shot through with the electrical decompossessor and the abortion is completed.

But there is still that one thing which women can't seem to hold with. There are still the great many who want those brats, and they will have as many of them as they can, and since there is no longer any pain to child-birth they are having them like they are going out of style. The governments of the world have offered sums of money to women who do not have kids… but even that hasn't worked.

That's the way it has been since the beginning of time, and that's probably the way it would have gone throughout the remainder of eternity.

However at the beginning of time there was the necessity for all those kids. There was a world to be made. And because all kids were not born of the same tribes or nations, there was fighting and there had to be a lot of human cannon fodder.

It is said that all down through the ages they have enacted much like the insect species and the animal species of the world… they kill each other off in order to keep their own population down. Thus we might look to wars in the same light. But a few hundred thousands of lives is only a meager handful when the entire population of the earth is taken into consideration. That many can be produced during any one night the remaining armies are on leave and cavort with their girlfriends or wives.

I've also read in the history books about some world leader named Hitler in the twentieth century who exterminated millions during his reign… think of that… millions…that's a great number of anything. But that dealt with humans. He knocked off millions and it still did no good. Millions more grew up to take their place and the world was off and running again… all downhill where the bread line was concerned.

But then not only the bread line… the living line also came under observation. The deserts were full and the mountain ranges housed more humans than there was room for… and the amounts of living quarters floating on the oceans and lakes left little room to put down pipelines for necessary drinking water… even the surface of the moon had been taken over by the more brave and adventurous of the human elements. But the only real danger was getting to the moon. There have been many space-ships which have blasted off from earth and were never heard from again. Once they got to the moon they've got a full measure of safety because of the artificial oxygen which was invented about a hundred years ago.

But that is in the saving of lives!

Yet even the synthetic foods which are space lifted to those on the moon can't last forever at the rate it is being processed. Nothing grows on the moon and the moon gardens which have been built under glass, oxygen, atmospheric controlled super-domes have a long way to go before they are completely perfected... and even then it will take centuries before any sufficient amounts of provisions can be produced.

The moon migrations still aren't in any real danger, because the population is low enough to permit existence. It is only as time progresses and the population progresses that they will begin to realize the threat to their world. Then they will also be forced to do something about the population. Soon they will have armies defending the landing stations. They will be forced to repel new landings of other earth people. They will be forced into a process and annihilation... the same as we on earth have already begun.

For centuries scientists have sought ways of prolonging life. One hundred years was finally established... give or take a couple years.

Of course the population explosion had started long before the elongation of life, but when man started living to the ripe old age of one hundred, and in all too many cases, more than a hundred, earth found itself being cluttered up with a bunch of elderly people who could no longer produce any important activity... they were simply taking up space which rightfully belonged to the young... the strong youth who could perhaps devise ways of making the world over. Those who were not set in their ways. Those whose minds could be changed... for the better.

And it was also found that although these oldsters couldn't physically work for the betterment of the world, they could very well, physically add to the propagation of the races. With the coming of longevity so came the elongating of their sex life. They could produce and fertilize almost to the moment of their demise.

Since time lay heavily on the hands of the older ones, sex became the most enjoyable pastime. And the men of letters soon learned that their lifelong gains had turned into horrible, devouring monsters.

Moon migrations were the first advent of the governments in order to dispense with some of the population... not enough.

Then all the powers of the governments got together and put a ten-year ban on all sexual activities which would produce children. Fellatio and cunnilingus and other forms of non-child producing sexual activities were lauded by every high authority in the world.

The intercourse situations which would produce children were forbidden under threat of immediate execution. It was thought to be the only way out. The authorities had to step in and do something or in a matter of the following twenty years people would be eating each other... those who remained strong enough to eat. The world would die. Man could not survive under the circumstances of failing attitudes.

However even the threat of death did not extinguish the *missionary position*... although it did nearly extinguish the institution of marriage, as we have known it. Some did marry! But not many, and those who did marry were watched more closely than anyone else. This, of course, was the reason for marriages to be few and far between.

But there seemed to be just as many babies brought into the world. They were simply born behind closed doors, then deposited during the dark of night to places where they would be found and then delivered to the government hospitals and receiving centers.

People were still investigating the *missionary position*. Many of the offbeat sexual acts had been outlawed for years... as something which was looked down upon with disgust and contempt. Then when these positions were lauded and the *missionary position* became outlawed, it was the source of more intense investigation... that type of investigation was disastrous to the growing population... more so because the offsprings were necessarily taken over by the government... another responsibility... because they had no admitted parents.

Some were executed... both men and women... but the punishment, again, did nothing to halt the population rise, it was all sort of a dangerous adventure and the human being has always been interested in adventure... the dangers... the unknown... something different from their normal advances in life.

Something more had to be done.

Life was not going to continue into the next century if such a propagation pace continued.

But it had to be something which each individual in the world could relate to... could understand and know the conclusion.

Armies simply couldn't go out into the field with machine guns, tanks and cannons and shoot down entire villages... although this did occur in many of the more direct countries.

There were no warlike attitudes with the countries who took on that mode of extermination. They were simply lowering the population in the best way they knew. But troubles were heading their way also. Many of the soldiers had families and friend and relations in the villages which were being destroyed. They balked finally and turned on the government... then settled back with a new government and proceeded to repopulate the destroyed villages.

There was no answer in that method.

Wise men all over the globe were called into consultation.

Poison the water!

But then they themselves might drink it!

Poison the food!

But then they themselves might eat it!

Sterilize every male in the world!

But then what would happen when the race was about to disappear? There would be no one left to bring the world strength back. There could never be anymore humans born into the universe... and the universe would die... cease to exist as so many exploding stars have ceased to exist since the beginning of time. Earth would be a lifeless planet doomed to circle the sun for all eternity with the rain falling on no human and the snow never feeling a human footprint.

The animals might take over for a time, but it would be the insect that would eventually inherit the earth.

The earth must not die and every government in the world knew it. There could never be any help from those on the moon because they depended upon their very existence from those on the earth. If the earth died, so did the moon go back to its original state of death.

Blow up the moon and a few million would be taken care of in that way. It was a stupid thought.

The answer had to take in mind every male and female on the face of the earth. The concern must be with each individual as an individual.

If all the oldsters were to be eliminated, more than a third of the population would cease to exist. And if the age group were lowered to those about to enter the oldster category, more than half the population would disappear.

If this were carried out the population would return to less than normal and the whole process could start all over again, with the earth bearing the fruits necessary to keep the humans alive and to power the universe.

But what of those who would soon be an oldster... like the younger generation?

I had the answer to that.

And it has become the law of the land for the past ten years. The law became mandatory that no human being will live beyond the age of forty-seven. Upon that birthday the individual must enter into a contract with death... in any way he so chooses... but he must die on that birthday... and there was no getting around it.

All birth certificates and births from the moment the law was enacted were filed into the giant computers around the world. And when that person's time came he was notified in advance so that he could put all things of his previous life in order... then he must take his own life.

Should he not do so... the following morning after his birthday he would fall into my department. Because I am the executioner. It is my job and the job of my organization to see that no individual feels he is more important than any other. Each must suffer the same fate.

Presidents and Kings, the rich and the poor.

Each have their date with destiny... through their own devices, or through the device of the exterminatory.

It may seem hateful to those of you who will read this in the future, but watch news media, and see what happens again in the future when the population once more reaches overpowering aspects.

Mars may hold a few... in time... but the world at no time in any future history can keep doubling itself if it is to keep in existence... this plan will again, without a doubt, be taken into consideration at that future date.

It only takes those short ten years of such a plan to put the population back into a sensible state of affairs.

Only ten years...

Our ten years ends in two days. Something I had neglected to figure out because I was so thoroughly involved in helping to save the entire human race from extinction. Only two more days and the whole experiment is over and the governments will be much as they had been before... striving to keep above it all... and there will be armies again... and there is already enough food for everybody... until the next crisis in a couple of hundred years... and there will be the sexual enjoyments that all on earth may enjoy... and there will be the dogs and the cats and the other cattle who will feed freely once more... and... all will be quite normal.

And I have been no different than any other human. I have loved life and I have attempted to save the world. And in saving the world, I have neglected to save myself.

Two more days and the experiment is over and all those reaching forty-seven will no longer have to take their own lives or be visited by the exterminator.

Because today is my birthday...

I am forty-seven.

In two days there will no longer be any need for the exterminator.

But... after midnight... there won't be any exterminator anyway.

THE END

Time, Space and the Ship

as "Dick Trent"

(provided by Steve Paul) From Swap *vol. 6. No.2 on Ed's resume 1972*

DAWSON, A RED, RUBBERY-FACED man leaned back in his large desk chair and gazed out into the dark void of space through the gigantic window behind his desk. He puffed on the cigar for a long moment, letting his eyes glitter as brightly as the stars he was watching. "Ahh, yes," he sighed. "The Russians. They've been in our hair for centuries." He turned back to face the big uniformed general who sat across from him. "But this is the twenty-fifth century. They've been on our tail for five hundred years blustering this and blustering that and they still sit back and make with the scare noises."

"They haven't sat back with their space probes."

"And really, General Wheeler. What have they got to prove for it?"

"Mars, Jupiter, Pluto, and I wouldn't doubt but what they've got Mercury even though they said the ship burned up in the approach."

"Rather hot on Mercury, I'd say. But I agree with you. They could be lying through their teeth again. After all, we do have a metal which will withstand that kind of heat... and space suits for our people."

"But the Russians have been on all the planets before us. We've come along right behind them like some kind of an unwanted visitor. I tell you it is getting to be very disheartening for the taxpayers. They want to be first in something. If we are going to keep funding the space programs, then we've got to do something and we've got to do it fast."

"Just what would you have me do, General Wheeler?" Mr. Dawson was once more looking out of the large plate glass window and had his back to the General who stood up and crossed the room to pour himself his sixth shot of straight whiskey.

"How in hell should I know? You're the head of the space authority. I'm only an underling. I take orders."

"I take them too."

"Yes… but only directly from the President."

"Perhaps even he doesn't know what I have in mind, General." Dawson swung back to face the General again. He also indicated the wall bar. "Fix me a Scotch and soda, will you?"

The General did so. "You do have something in mind then?"

"I do!"

"Top secret?" Dawson nodded. "Everything I do is top secret."

General Wheeler returned to the desk. He put the Scotch and soda down in front of Dawson, then resumed his own seat. "I'm cleared."

"Of course you are."

"Then you could let me in on it."

"I could." He nodded, but there was that twinkle of secrecy behind his grin, even though his eyes sparkled.

"But you won't… is that it?"

"I didn't say that…. Not quite that."

"You are a confounding man, Dawson."

"That's why I'm in this position, General."

"Yes, I suppose it is." He sipped of the whiskey instead of taking it down in one large gulp as he had done before… many times before. "But it's big, huh?"

"The largest undertaking in our history. Perhaps in all history itself… and a history which will be made that we will never read about."

"Now you are being confounding."

"Not at all."

"By God, if I were going to sit down and make history I'd sure as hell find some way of reading about it even if I was deaf and blind."

"You won't read about it, General, and neither will I because we'd be long dead before the end had even begun to get started."

"Circles, man…. You're talking in circles."

"Well, I suppose I could send you down to the mortuary and have your body packed in ice, then when the time comes where we have advanced enough to know how to turn the dead back to life, you might come out of your ice package and read about what you did before you died."

"I say, old man, you're enough to put a man in his grave long before his time. I have no intentions of being packed in ice… at least not yet."

Dawson grinned. "I dare say you aren't. Oh, you'll be around for the start of the adventure, but neither you nor I nor anyone who is on this earth at this moment will be around for the eventual end. Nor will the crew who goes into space."

"I suspected that at least it had to have something to do with space. After all this is the space authority. But with our new space technology and speed it only takes a year to get to the furthest of planets… we've been there before… and I certainly have no plans of being laid away during the coming year. What in hell do you have on your mind anyway?"

"Perhaps the farthest reaches of space. Do you really know what infinity might feel like, General?"

"Well…. Well," he blustered and made fruitless circles with his hands.

"It's a long way out." Once more Dawson turned to look out into the blackness and to the stars beyond. "Out there are many galaxies. We all know that."

"Hell yes, we do. Billions of light years off."

"Billions of light years… like infinity… like eternity… to our small minds. But not so to the computers which have designed for this department the speed and the ship which could reach the nearest galaxy within twenty or thirty lifetimes."

"Man, have you taken leave of your senses? Why, you're talking about two or three thousand years."

"I said none of us would be around to read the history about that first landing."

"Now I know you've gone mad."

"Not really mad. But then isn't always someone declared mad when they have come up with something no one else can conceive?"

"You're serious… you're dead serious."

"As serious as I can ever be in this world."

"The taxpayers would never stand for it. The President wouldn't stand for it. You'd be laughed right into the rubber room at the happy farm."

"I have already perfected the computer and it has told me the direction… the scope and the atmospheric conditions on the nearest galaxy which is not unlike our own, but does have a few more planets and a few more suns… but planets with the possibility of life…. The computer has also perfected the space vehicle which would transport the crew there."

"Yes..." laughed the General... "and there I have you but good, dear fellow. What about the crew? I think they'd be rather old by the time they got there." He laughed broadly again. "Or are you going to throw them into suspended animation and let them also thaw out when they make the landing? Who would be around to feed their lifeless bodies... keep them going for two or three thousand years... your damned computer?" He laughed even louder.

"Oh, there are ways of overcoming everything."

"Why, the ship would have to be the tonnage of the tallest, largest building in the world. Even if it did get off the ground.... Man, do you know what kind of a crew a ship like that would need... and with all the supplies on board which would be needed, you couldn't possibly get enough humans on board to fill half the crew you need. Good Lord, I'm jibbering on about this thing like I thought it could be done. I'm talking just as insane as you are."

"But it can be done, General. And I am planning on doing it."

"You're planning on landing yourself in a strait jacket, that's what you're planning on."

"Within one year's time I will have my space ship, and the supplies and the rocket launcher and the crew."

"Good Lord, I'm listening again."

"You will be listening much more before I'm finished."

"I wish you'd simply have decided not to tell me anything about this affair."

"Have another whiskey."

"That I'll do."

"And bring me back another Scotch... make it a double one this time."

"That I'll do also... and maybe you'll drink some sense back into your mind. Dawson, once you were a very brilliant man."

"I still am a very brilliant man."

"Tomorrow I do believe I'll arrange for a psycho examination for you."

"You do that, General, but in the meantime, tonight, you'll drink my booze and listen."

"I'll drink your booze."

"And you'll listen."

The General picked up the larger glasses, filled them and returned to the desk once more.

"I honestly think," started the General, "that you think you mean what you're saying."

"I do mean what I'm saying."

"You would attempt sending a ship larger than anything in the world, off into space. The explosion of the rockets alone would shake up an entire state."

Dawson nodded. "Perhaps two states. But what are a few broken dishes or even rooftops, compared to an expedition like this."

"I'd like to be around to see the end of any experiment I get involved with."

"You can believe me in the fact that it will be a success. And perhaps from the after world we can look down on the success."

"Look down? You mean look up.... That's where you'll be looking from. People as crazy as you don't ever go up... they always go down... down... down... and the farther into Hades a guy like you goes the better."

Dawson's grin turned into a broad laugh. "The ship will get off the ground... and there will be a full crew, and that crew will be the ancestors of the crew which will finally land on a planet in that galaxy."

"You're talking about an entire civilization traveling through space for two or three thousand years.... Generation after generation with only that one purpose in mind. What would happen if there was a mutiny? The ship came back?"

"The ship could never come back. It must go ever forward to its goal. And there would be no crew mutiny, because the crew will be programmed into that one thought and every offspring of a child they would have would be programmed to that one thought. They would never know anything of earth.... Only the last of the generation... the generation which will land on that far-off planet will know what their ancestors had left back here. Only then will the library storehouses be opened for their knowledge... and we can only hope they use the information on the new planet for something more than we did."

"I tell you you're off your rocker, Dawson."

"I have already started the wheels into motion. Remember, I said I will be ready in one year's time. I certainly couldn't put this whole show on the road in a year if I hadn't already made a good start."

"Good Lord."

"Much of the ground work, the preparations have already been completed."

"The crew? What about the crew?"

"I don't have all of them yet. But I will find the others who will be quite willing to undertake this brilliant adventure... those who would like to go down in history with us."

"I can't conceive of it."

"You can't conceive of infinity... eternity either, General?... but they are both bound to come. You've got to realize that, General."

"Infinity... eternity... that I realize.... But this crazy plan of yours....I mentioned it before. How can you get a crew large enough into that ship to run it and still... propagate the race? You're going to have all those men working around the clock, eight hours a day, every day of every week of every year. And you're going to have the women there as dead weight, simply for bearing their children... dead weight where the equipment will be needed... and still you've got to have the women." The General shook his head in disbelief that Dawson hadn't taken that into consideration. The dead weight of the women passengers who were simply there for the ride so to speak... to bear the children who would keep the whole thing going.

But Dawson only grinned again and downed a great portion of his Scotch, then puffed on his big black cigar again.

"I have taken everything into consideration, General Wheeler. Everything which will make this whole experiment a complete success... and that goes for the dead weight. There will be no dead weight."

"If you mean half-and-half, like the women will work the hard work of the men. You'd need a race of superwomen for a task like that. And they can't be superwomen and have children, too."

"There will be no men on board."

The General's mouth gaped open and he spilled a portion of his whiskey down over his coat. "No men?"

Dawson shook his head and folded his hands over his ample girth. "No men."

"Only women?"

"Only women!"

"To run the ship?"

"To run the ship!"

"And have babies without men?"

"And have babies without men!" The General reached for the telephone.

"What are you doing?"

"I'm going to have you committed before you become dangerous."

Dawson laughed and patted the man's tough hand. "Women without men. But why is that so inconceivable to you... ? What would take up little or no space... where men would take up great quantities of space?"

The General blinked.

Dawson grinned. "Semen, my dear fellow. A very small quantity of semen, to be artificially inseminated at some prescribed intervals.... Of course some children will be born male... and they will have to be disposed of... but that will not be difficult for the ladies I have planned for the expedition... and the young girl babies will never know what a man looks like... except for that last generation before the landing. They will know all. The others will know nothing but what the instruction books inform them."

"And your crew of ladies, Dawson?"

"The strongest of the lot of the female breed, General... Butch LESBIANS!"

THE END

DIAL-A-VISION

by "Dick Trent"

in Black And White *Vol.2,no.2 June/July 1972 on Ed's resume 1972*

HARRY TOMAS WALKED out of prison. It had been fifteen years since he'd breathed the air of the so-called freedom on the outside. But he did what was expected of him… the thing all the prisoners had told him they would do the moment they got on the outside… and what all the others told him they had done when they got out and then had done again the moment before the great iron doors opened to readmit them on their further conviction and return.

That was to take a deep breath!

He had never felt that he was a member of that half, or that dark world of the prison. He hadn't killed those broads on purpose. He'd been drunk and the car he was driving went out of control on the rain-drenched street, and after the crash when he woke up in the prison hospital he found that all three of them, Shirley, Laura and Penny were in the morgue.

Conviction… then prison….

But he knew he should have only served seven years of that twenty-five year sentence. It was the thing which was usually done in that state. Serve seven years for that kind of a manslaughter conviction. But that was not to be so for Harry.

They had it against him. The whole world was against him. The authorities wanted him out of the way. They had tried over and over before the night of that crash to have him put away. They wanted him and his business off the streets.

Hell, what was a little bookmaking? That's how he started. Then during his trips around the street collecting, he found the girls of the street…

227

the girls for a night… the street-walking whores who weren't making out so good on their own, so he organized them and became their pimp.

But they were out there waiting!

Their eyes never left him. Somewhere off in the darkness, or with their back to the sun they were ever present waiting for him to make that one slip. And that slip came on a rainy, slippery street, and with a throat which still burned from the expensive booze he kept lushing up even behind the wheel.

They wanted him out of the way!

He never knew why he got interested in the modes for inventions by others. But he did! It was fun to see how a cannon was made, or how radio and television found their way from one place to another. And it was most interesting to learn the workings of a telephone. The telephone! That was the most intriguing of all. All those wires and those cables… and then there were the articles on phonovision where soon one might see the person being talked with on a small screen there over the phone.

Many visions had conjured up before his searching eyes when he thought of stepping over there to the wall phone which connected his cell block with the warden's office and to the switchboard which could transfer the call to the outside.

He wondered what would happen if he got over there and dialed a number and looked to a screen *(which was there only in his mind),* and he had dialed some broad who had just gotten out of the shower.

Thoughts of the nakedness he might see always caused an erection from which he demanded release. It was much easier to get that release in solitary confinement because nobody ever looked in to check up on him. All he had to do was look out through the peephole to the corridor and there was always a phone. He found many ways of getting into solitary confinement. There was no trick to that. Step on a guard's toe… spill the food in the mess hall… talk back to authority. There were never any problems of getting into solitary confinement.

And in the darkness he could dial and there would be some guy and girl going at it on a fur-covered bed and they didn't even stop when his call came through… the girl simply extended her arm and captured the phone and moaned and groaned into it. The girls never said anything. They always picked up the phone so he could see them and they would moan and groan and just go on doing what they were doing and Harry Tomas did what he had to do and was relieved until the next time his mind became on fire and he had to mentally dial the number… and it was always the same number. The number never changed. Only the girls who answered that number changed.

The girls changed… never the number!

He took that deep breath of fresh, free air!

He had to get out of that town. Out of that area… even though he couldn't leave the state… just yet. But he had to go where he wasn't known… or more to the point, where his physical condition wasn't known.

Forty-eight dollars wasn't going to get him far!

Ten dollars went for bus fare to a town nearly a hundred miles away. It wasn't one of the big cross-country lines but one of those small intercity busses which still remain in business even though the company is taking a daily loss.

Then there was seven dollars for the hotel room… a flophouse affair with beds for fifty cents and a cruddy room for a dollar. But there was a hot plate in it and he could cook what little he needed to eat. He'd learn to eat very little in the prison. Most times he was completely satisfied with the watered-down soup they'd shelled out. During the year to come he knew that at least the soup he could buy in a can was thick and full of nourishment. He could have hamburgers once in a while, and perhaps a chicken, but the soup must necessarily remain his more steady diet. No matter how much money he could make he would need it for other things.

There was a business to be started!

There were whores to be laid. There were whores to be organized. In all of those terrifying, confining fifteen years there wasn't one time when he hadn't thought about the whores he had once organized and handled. And every time he'd mentally dialed that telephone and watched the screen it was one of the girls he had known who was performing the action for him.

They would not be the girls that he would ever take in a car with him again, drunk or sober. But from that point on they would be transported in a much different way. He would never let himself in for that kind of trouble ever again. They would pay him, he'd see to that. But he would have nothing physically to do with the whores… other than relieve himself once and a while but he wouldn't even pick them up at those times, nor would he take them home when the session was over. If they were to lay with him, he knew how they would arrive and he knew how they would take off when it was all over.

Then he started to build that thing in the cellar of the flophouse. The manager let him have the never-used room in the cellar at the far end of the building for an additional five dollars a month, and two dollars for the electricity. It was a landfall for the manager, and no one would bother him. He could even put a lock on the door… a heavy one… as long as he paid for the damned thing. Harry Tomas certainly wanted a lock. He didn't want any prying eyes looking over his shoulder… no vandals breaking in and stealing the expensive parts. The creeps who laid out for fifty-cent beds would steal anything. It mattered little what they stole as long as they could get a few pennies for it. They would steal the shoes from another down-and-outer just as quickly as they would look at him. They most certainly would take all the wires and the tubes and the sheet glass and the other things he brought in there by the back way after dark when his movements wouldn't be so noticeable.

As long as the creeps on the floors above didn't know what was down there, there would be no trouble, and if they didn't see anything being brought in, then they wouldn't know that anything was there.

No one really knew what was going on in that cellar, or that anything was going on in the cellar until those nights when a sudden drain of power flickered the lights… sometimes blacked them out completely for a moment or two. But even then the incidents were not connected with the cellar… and if the flophouse manager thought about it he would have said nothing… after all there was seven dollars a month which he could put in his own pocket… hiding it from the owners. He didn't have to report anything about the cellar. The owners would never check on that. And if they did the manager would dip into his pocket and lay out the seven dollars, saying the man only just took it over. But that was not likely to happen… and the manager wasn't going to open his mouth about it to anyone…. Let the damned lights flicker. Let them die altogether for all he cared. The creeps that came there were dunderheads who didn't need any light anyway. And if any of them complained he could tell them to get their ass out if they didn't like the way he ran the place. After all the man in the cellar had been there nearly a year and he was always good for his dough… even when he raised the rent for the cellar space to fifteen dollars a month and no extra for the electric.

The man in the cellar was the KING PIN!

Harry Tomas was an inventor, inventing. He didn't need books any longer. He had learned all there was to know about the tubes and the wires and the transformers and the transmitters and all else that was needed to know about putting his machine together. It would be the most spectacular machine of its kind ever built.

The machine was the entire clue!

And the machine progressed and Harry Tomas's hair became more and more grey and the sleepless nights took their toll in the luster of his eyes and the wrinkles beneath them and the lines which streaked his face, and the coarseness of his hands from the changing climate in the cellar... cold... hot... dry... damp... he felt all the elements and he worked through them... and the machine grew in stature.... Harry Tomas viewed it as the most beautiful thing ever invented, and there were times as it progressed that he would stand far back from it and grin with admiration for his work, and there were times it seemed that the machine grinned back at him. He liked that also, because he knew it had to be a friendly grin.... Not like some monster with its mad scientist attempting to rule the world.

The one thing Harry Tomas didn't want was to rule the world. If anything, he wanted to get out of it. He wanted to be left alone. Something like when he was in prison and in solitary confinement... but not with guards on the other side of the door and not with mental pictures that weren't real, only figments of his imagination.

He would succeed!

There had never been any doubt in his mind about that... and it was no fantasy.... There had been no doubt since the first day he had picked up the first science book the first time he had entered the prison library.

Then it was the last day of the year. Perhaps not December 31st, but the last day of the year he had given himself and he was ready and his machine was ready.

It didn't look much different than a regular dial phone, except tremendously larger... he would have to use both hands to dial the number... and the television screen on top of the phone was little different than that which one might have in their home... it would give color pictures... and it was as large as a motion picture screen when completely unfolded....

But the glass of the television set would appear like water when the numbers were dialed... or perhaps jello which could be parted, then it would all flow back together again... or like the oil that Harry had spilled so often into the motors of the vehicles he had serviced on the job in the gas station that past year.

It was the machine of the future.

And it was all his.

He could dial any number and not only could he see she who answered, but he could step into the picture and visit with her and they could do all sorts of things… and the people he called could step right out of the picture and visit with him.

Harry Tomas could have his stable of girls, and he would have places where his phone could have small extensions and anyone who knew the right number could call his master transmitter and order any girl they wanted and she would appear right there in the apartment, and when the session was over she would step right back into the ooze and she would be gone until she or another was summoned. Harry Tomas was beside himself with glee as he dialed the number… the same number he had so often dialed from his prison solitary confinement cell. But this time when the bell stopped ringing and the color would come to the screen he would not be imagining anything. The creatures would be right there, and perhaps he would watch them as they had their affair for a while before he got into the action…. He didn't care what kind of an affair he dialed in on. As long as there were pretty girls, that was all that mattered.

It had been sixteen years since he had been with the soft fluff of the girl… felt her loving touch… felt her lips on his and her tongue sucking at his… or her lips sucking all over his body. But that soon would all end. But he would watch for a while to see if anything had changed during those years in prison.

But as he stepped back from the giant dial the screen was blurred beyond belief. He knew he had made no mistake. He knew everything was working properly. There was no chance that the set was out of focus. It was his eyes. He would then liked to have settled back a moment and cup his hands over his eyes and put them into total darkness and then, as in solitary confinement in prison, they would return to normal. He would see the luscious shapes and he could feast his eyes upon them for as long as he wanted.

His mind's eyes!

And at that point he realized the entire problem he sat there facing. Of course his mind's eyes could see everything clearly. They were pictures… moving perhaps, but only pictures painted there through fantasy and illusion.

He stuck his hand out and it went through the jelly, toward the three colorful shapes that were doing things to themselves. The hand through the jelly felt warm on the other side of the screen. He stuck his whole arm in, and then he bent his head forward and looked into the clarity of the bedroom beyond. It looked like a bedroom. There were three satin-lined beds and all the walls were satin-lined, but the three girls, he thought they were girls, were gone. But so was the blurred effect to his eyes gone. He could see as clearly as when he was a young man.

There was a strange odor... an almost sickly sweet smell, but that didn't matter. He could see, so he stepped into the room, through the jelly and when he stood in the center of the room he breathed deeply....

They always breathe deeply, even when going back!

Then Harry Tomas moved forward to the three beds stretched out side by side and as he got closer his clear eyes looked down and the beds were sunken... and they were not beds at all. He turned back to face the jelly through which he had entered. The thought of turning back froze him in his tracks and the clear eyes saw that there was no turning back. There was nowhere else to go. The jelly was gone. The entire room was one solid steel box... and when he turned back it was as he had begun to realize. The beds were not beds at all. They were ruffled satin lined, and they were three caskets....

And each was occupied by one of the girls he had seen on the slab in the morgue sixteen years before... and they had their eyes open... and they weren't doing anything to each other... and Harry Tomas knew he had returned to solitary confinement... for all of eternity...

THE END

THE MOVIE QUEEN

by "Ann Gora"

in One Plus One *vol.4 no.2 Pendulum Publishing Apr./May 1972 on Ed's resume 1971*

IT HAD NOT BEEN DIFFICULT.

She simply stated, "I'd sell my soul to the Devil for that chance!"

And the Devil came out of the dark in a puff of sulphur smoke. He was grinning and long white fangs snaked over the corners of his lips. She didn't have to say any more. She didn't have to make any explanations. The Devil had heard what he needed to hear and all which was left to do became for the creature of darkness to touch her lovely golden head with the tip of his forked tail.

There would be fresh human male parts, and he would supply them... and he would look across to the operating table where the dying girl struggled against her gag and the straps which bound her to the table, and he would look at the lifeless arm he had already nearly severed and he would feel that strange urge in his groin... and he would strip as naked as the girl and he would mount her, take her violently as the life blood drained from the deep wound... and he would feel a climax more powerful than the last time, or even the time with the whore on her bed or the other one in the car in her own garage....

He liked to watch them die. He liked to be making love to them while they died and he liked to send them off into eternity with that very last thrust... then there was his human parts bank to be filled...

Then the tail became a caressing fire. It slid between her naked breasts, fondled the pink, ripe nipples, then returned to her lips to melt inside her mouth and match heated moments with her tongue.

The forked tail would travel along, and entwine about her luscious naked body until it found the brushy cleft of her love nest… and it would enter… and there would be no feeling of pain… only a sense of well-being. There was nothing she could no longer acquire, and she knew it in that instant.

Then the Devil was gone and the smoke went with him, but there was still the stale odor of sulphur which would stay with her from that moment on… but a smell that only she would witness. There would be times when it was stronger than at other times. But it was such a small price to pay for all the benefits that were to befall her.

Immediate fame was hers. From the moment of that very first interview there came a screen test… a tremendously successful screen test which put her in the ranks of the immortals. She was the sex symbol of all moviedom from the first frame of film which shot across the giant silver screen. Time and talent would never run out for her.

Not until her time came.

It came swiftly. It came just as the seconds ticked past the hour of midnight. It came through the same grey-green smoke and heavy smell of sulphur as before. But the Devil wasn't smiling upon this visit. The white fangs seemed to drip blood. They were dripping blood. And he still didn't speak. Instead he lifted the forked tail and seared his message on the wall behind her bed. It would smoke for some time and the movie star would roll and toss in her bed throughout the night. And the message would still be burning, smoking, stinking when she awoke in the morning.

She knew the entire meaning. And she knew there was no denying its meaning, and no denying the Devil his dues.

It was easy for her to recruit the converts the Devil needed. She was a star. Everyone knew what she looked like. All the lovely young hopefuls looked up to her, accepted her advice, accepted her direction for them. And there were more and more of those hopefuls coming around the corner on any street, on any day during any hour… all moving into an infinity they thought to be of their own making.

The movie queen knew better!

They would visit her fur-draped bedroom, and she would take them with her tongue and she would fondle their breasts with her hands and her tongue, and when there was the male stud she would show him the path to riches he had never dreamed of… and she was the movie queen being directed by the Devil… and once the young hopefuls found the lust of her body they themselves had become pawns of the Devil.

To live is to have performed evil…. And to have lived one must have been in link with the Devil. The movie star was living… she was high upon the world and she would do anything to keep that distinction. She would *live evil* and she would have *lived* with the Devil if she were but asked.

The Devil took no individual mistresses. All were the same and all would do his bidding, and when they were demanded to perform oral intercourse upon his person… they would do so… and they would be damned… damned to the everlasting darkness of the caves beneath all eternity… for all eternity.

And the movie queen couldn't help but remember back when she had cursed herself, condemned herself and she knew there had been much more than the Devil putting his forked tail atop her golden head. There had been her lips and her tongue and she knew what he had forced her to do. She knew that he had put her immediately into the bonds of servitude. She would do his bidding for as long as he required… that would be for all time… all of her time on this earth and perhaps thereafter in *HIS* afterworld.

But there was still a lot of time, she figured, that she would be walking the face of this earth, breathing in the fresh air and glaring into the sunlight, and feeling the rain on her face. It would be a long time before she would have to face *HIS* blackness… there would be many more cameras to face, and many more autograph hounds to be serviced.

It was these, the autograph hounds, where her work would start. *HE* had decreed it so. He had come to her as he had so often before… in the night… when she was asleep… when she had no resistance… not that she would have had much resistance anyway. He held her mind with those terrifying red eyes.

The Devil has an insatiable appetite for souls… for the young… those who have turned into their teens and were budding out in all the youthful directions. Then was the time for the complete capture of their souls… at that point when they are looking forward to a lifetime which is still ahead of them… and they aren't quite sure what they want to do. But they know they want something better, more profitable than their mothers and fathers perhaps had… or didn't have as the case may be.

They would gather around her and they would listen… listen to the glories that the riches of the world could bring them. They would remain as if hypnotized, and they would hang onto each of her words. She could show them all they had ever dreamed of and perhaps more than they had ever dreamed.

She would hold them close in her arms and her tongue held a fire which nearly belied the fires of hell… but fires of delight and promise. And when she wrapped her legs tightly around the love partner her eyes became as red and as full of lust as the master himself.

And the movie queen would be out early each morning, and out late each evening with the words of glory and riches for all. There were so many young minds to be reached. And each of those captured felt securely that they had reached their own decision… unaided.

And the girls were taught quickly to lay naked upon satin covered beds with legs spread wide for the acceptance of a lover who would be going off to fight the battles… and all battles are not fought on the fields of blood designated for wars.

There were the meeting rooms and the campus grounds and there were the streets and the temples. All must be invaded. And to the male ego, the female with legs spread apart was a calling he could not deny himself. And the movie star was right there always prodding, always gesting, always imploring and enticing.

The Devil is continually in need of worldly representatives. His kingdom of the darkness is vast and ever in need of souls to kindle the flames… keep them hot for the tortures of the more damned.

There are those he must necessarily *LOAN* the riches and the prestige for a time. But it is only a LOAN and it is only for a TIME!

Then one day it must all be returned.

Youth remains with only the young. And when the skin begins to wither and the eyes lose their luster there is little use for the individual. And the Devil will not permit that individual to keep what really has not been his or hers all along. He will take it all back. He will demand everything… and the Devil is never denied.

The movie queen will awaken one morning in her satin nightgown and roll across the satin sheets and once more she will see the burning writing on the wall behind her bed and she will rise up and she will stretch and as she will let the satin nightgown drop around her ankles, she will move across the fur covered floors to the bathroom where she will look into the mirror and she will become frightened.

There will be the sharp lines at the corners of her eyes. She knows she will have to use a heavier makeup and the worm-like creases crisscrossing her lips will need a deeper shade of lipstick.

But little will help retard the aging process. The years were catching up with her. And the major parts in films decrease and soon she will be playing the minor roles, and then there will not be the satin covered bed, the expensive satin nightgowns and the fur rugs in the luxurious home.

Then she will turn, naked from the mirror, and return to the bedroom and look to the smoking letters on the wall. And once more she will read the legend.

"TO WHOMEVER I GIVITH, THERE WILL BECOME THE TIME WHEN I WILL TAKE AWAY."

She knew in the beginning that the Devil would one day demand her soul. She had sold it to him for all the riches which had been gained. But she had not bought youth with her soul... only riches and all that went with it.

She spread out across the satin sheets and cried. She cried for more than an hour. But crying would do no good... it would only tend to exhaust her and make her more depressed. Then once more she would return to the mirror and fight all the pressures which were building up inside of her. And she would put the makeup on more heavily. And she would wear a tighter brassiere and waist cinch. She would dress in her best and she would ride to the studio where there were still all the friendly greetings... but that was all there was... *friendly greetings*. The greetings given to old friends.

There would be no glamorous parts. There would be no renewing of the lucrative contract.

The house would go first. Then the car. And then the bank account. Soon unemployment would run out. It would be difficult to capture a card from the Extra's Guild, but she did have a friend or two there. They were those she had not sold in slavery to the Devil. They were those who were of sound conscience and doing the job the way they saw it... in the light of respectability and thought to their fellow man. They were those who had not been captured in her glory and sold over to the Devil for his fires of hell.

And she would work. A day here. A day there. And there would be the little, dumpy apartment she found she could afford. Then there would be no brassiere... no waist cinch strong enough, tight enough to hold back the folds of aging flesh which threatened to explode any dress she might wear.

She would ride the busses, and she would walk a certain amount of blocks in order to save pennies when the ride threatened to exceed her budget.

She would cry often and she would collect all the old newspaper clippings and pictures of herself which had adorned so many places in the homes of her former fans… her former recruits. She would find them discarded in trash cans. She would find them in the desk drawers and closets of abandoned offices on some of the movie lots.

They were the only proof that she had ever been there… that she had ever existed… that she had ever graced the big silver screen… that she had ever been enjoyed by the masses… that she could have ever convinced anyone of anything. She would collect them all, and she would clean them up and she would take them back to the one room flat and she would paste them into a large scrapbook which she kept beneath the pull-down bed which she never bothered to shove back into the wall. There it would rest until she found more memorabilia and once more it would come into the light of day where she would study it and she would remember and she would get up and look into the cracked mirror over the scarred dresser and she would let her hand run over the lined, withered face.

It would not change back.

It would remain, old and wrinkled from then on and into eternity.

She had fought the Devil… fought the Devil and he had won. The Devil always wins.

Then she would replace the scrapbook to its final resting place under the filthy bed and she would walk out onto the black street and she would find some deserted spot where she would take the sharp butcher knife from her wrinkled cotton stockings and she would stab it deep into her heart.

And when she lay on the street with a light rain starting to fall… coolly wetting her ancient nearly mummified face she would look off into the darkness for one last, long agonizing moment.

HE was there. His eyes as red as ever. His forked tail flashing behind him and the smell of sulphur so heavily over the entire area. And he was grinning again. Grinning as he had been that first time so long ago… so long ago when she sold her soul to him.

HE had come to collect his dues.

The Devil always came to collect his dues in time. The writing on the wall had told that legend. He had taken everything and then it was time for him to take the very last possession of the movie queen. Her soul…

The body will get old and wrinkled and withered, but the *SOUL* remained eternally young and it was only the SOUL with which the Devil had any use.

HE demanded her soul in that instant and he took it… took it back into the ebony of that which was behind him.

The worthless old body would remain behind for burial in a potter's grave. But the soul would find all the tortures of hell.

The Devil is accepted by the *very* young. It is only the aged who find there is little time to deny him. But then it is too late.

The grave is only for the aged and the withered. The Devil is only interested in the *SOUL*.

The youth find *HIM* attractive.

The old find him for what he is… the obnoxiously ominous creature of the darkness… the figure of death!

THE END

Invasion Of the Sleeping Flesh

by "Ann Gora"

in Orgy Vol.4 no.1 Apr./May 1972 on Ed's resume 1971

Professor Julian Smotherland held the distinction of being a brilliant man... a brilliant scientist... a brilliant scholar... a brilliant doctor of medicine and psychiatry... and if there were more years to a man's life he would have been the most brilliant of all men in all phases of the professions. But there are not that many years to a man's life... not presently in this the twenty-first century anyway.

Men of letters ever since the nineteenth century have been searching for ways to prolong man's life span and during the twentieth century some progress was made. The life span of man in the nineteeth century found humans living to the ripe old age of fifty. Naturally some went on further. But the general run of man found his demise coming during the years of his fifties and he looked eighty.

The middle of the twentieth century man found it not uncommon that he shouldn't contact his local undertaker before his late sixties or early seventies.

The twenty-first century has man considering a visit to the mortuary only after he has passed one hundred years. But it was still not enough time for even the greater of the great minds to absorb all the knowledge they wanted... and certainly not enough time to learn everything and still have time left over to practice, or teach, what they had learned.

This was a shocking revelation to Professor Julian Smotherland who hadn't thought much about death during the ninety-nine years he had lived to that point. He had been much too busy with his studies which had started at the age of five… a brilliant child of turn of the century parents… school teachers.

He had done much to elongate the life span of man during his years. Along with other studies he was able to find some time to write papers, and others who had practiced only one profession took heed to his words and progressed the work. But that morning of his ninety-ninth birthday he woke up and looked out across the cemetery which sprawled over several hundred acres just north of his window.

He couldn't help but think of what a waste the whole thing was… life… the elements… all those corpses out there in the cemetery.

Since they were in boxes, most of them airtight, the carcasses weren't even good for fertilizer.

Then he looked up to the sun. It was a cold sun on that clear December day, and he thought about what a waste the sun also was… all that energy going to waste when there was really no need for it.

And he looked into his mirror and saw the old man staring back at him and he couldn't help but think what a waste he had become. An old, withered, year-torn man with the most brilliant brain in the world and it wouldn't be long before he also was out there in the cemetery, a waste of all that he had gathered over those very many years… a fruitless trip through a lifetime and about to enter a thankless eternity. What in hell was it all for? He figured he didn't even have time to write a portion of his findings… certainly not all of them… and certainly not even one of them in depth.

What a waste!

Human resources be damned!

Cannon fodder was more like it. Everyone should be brought up to be cannon fodder. Why should anyone spend their life learning when it would all be taken to the grave with them? One should only have fun out of life. Do what one wants. But Professor Julian Smotherland had done all his life what he wanted… studied… and then it was too late.

Man had reached Mars!

So, what the hell?

Reaching Mars certainly didn't supply the answer for man's living forever. In fact many men had died in the attempt before a successful landing was reached.

Man should fight the battles and get himself killed when his youth begins to fade. He should not go on day after day watching his frame become weaker and his skin more creased and lined, knowing all the time that he is on borrowed time. He should venture into eternity and see what eternity is all about before he becomes so accustomed to the everyday life on earth that he becomes reluctant to leave it.

He should not shed tears as Professor Julian Smotherland did as he looked out over the vast, lonely, foreboding cemetery. He should not shed the tears in self-pity at the loss of a lifetime. When man has gained all the knowledge there is to be gained, then he should have an ever increasing lifetime in which to explore what he has learned, and to gain more into the insight of everything and have the time to impart his knowledge to others.

Then there came the dark clouds and the threat of snow. But first there was one small incision in the dark cloud which permitted a single ray of light to fall on one of the large grave markers.

It was a curious sight, and Professor Julian Smotherland watched that strange glow until the incision filled in and it was gone and the snowflakes began to drift downward. The power of the sun... that single ray... had tried to tell him something... he knew that much about the sight. And he knew if he concentrated heavily enough he would know the meaning.

It would not be found there in his bedroom on the second floor of the old house... perhaps in the vast library on the first floor. All that was known, and many unknown, unproven events were all put down on paper... and Professor Julian Smotherland remained in the library all the rest of that day and throughout the night and into the next day reading, searching, making notes and all the time the snow piled up on the outside. He would not be bothered by outsiders while the storm lasted. He was always bothered by outsiders and their questions... but he would answer the questions with the knowledge of fact. But the only question he wanted answered was that of the ray of sunlight and the grave which was lit by it.

He knew some of those answers by noon of that day and there was only the matter of stepping into his well-equipped laboratory and fit the pieces together. There was much which was not written... not known. But that which was written started the wheels in his mind turning and all the ninety- nine years of his life and the studies stored in his mind would find the connecting points.

After all it was the twenty-first century and soon would be the twenty-second. He wasn't sure he would live through that new year. But he wasn't feeling physically ill... only mentally disturbed at age. And perhaps there still was something he could do about continuing on. The sun was energy.

Most of that energy was wasted because it was not directed, channeled to a single point, where all the energy could be smashed to that one object....

Lightning was a force of energy, and when it was directed at any one point it could destroy, crumble an object into complete oblivion. The sun, harnessed in the same way, could be even more of a powerful instrument... for bad... or for the good. Wasn't life all energy? Wasn't it a fact that life necessarily needs the sun to exist? Then the more powerful the directed energy of the sun, the more possibility there was of expanding man's lifespan... as long as that sun energy was directed to the proper spot....

Professor Julian Smotherland knew from his many experiences over a cadaver in the laboratory that if he were to snap electrodes to the pituitary gland of that dead carcass, the body would jump around the table as if suddenly having become afflicted with St. Vitus dance. The body would then rest again when the electrodes were removed or the electrical current turned off. Sometimes the eyelids would flash open and closed. The lips would move as if the body were trying to say something... something from the deep, dark depths of the dead. The tongue at those times would protrude and the arms would reach out as if wanting to return, and the legs would jerk spasmodically in a dance of the doomed... the dance macabre.

The electricity had given some measure of life back into the corpse even though it had been dead and isolated in the refrigerator for weeks. Without refrigeration, however, the pituitary gland would most certainly be destroyed in a few days.

Did not then the pituitary gland have some control over the locomotion of the body? Wasn't it possible that the electricity flowing through the electrodes acting something like the commands of the brain waves when the body was living? And wasn't the energy of the sun more powerful than all the electrical forces in the world?

If a continuous source of energy could be designed into the pituitary gland, the locomotion of the body most certainly could be returned... and there was no reason not to believe that the patient could be returned to life, and when the energy source became more powerful the dead cells of the brain could be restored and the reborn body could go on in life much as it had before. It was more than a theory. The electrodes had worked on the pituitary glands in the laboratories. Little other thought than for the amusement of those who witnessed the reactions was ever realized. Even Professor Julian Smotherland in all his brilliance had neglected to give the performance much thought at those times.

But as he stood in his laboratory that cold December afternoon he gave it much thought. And he gave much thought to the harnessing of the sun for his purpose.

There was no reasoning for the fact that he should die and with him all the knowledge of all the previous ages, and then, perhaps what might come about in the future. If he could harness the sun for such a purpose he would be the future. He would have conquered death.

He would design the solaranite gun which would harness the sun energy and he would have it directed to his own pituitary gland. The energy would be so powerful, and with an endless supply of sun, the instrument would keep him alive for all of eternity.

Professor Julian Smotherland would like to have kept the knowledge to himself, but he knew that would be impossible because death never gave an appointment. One day it would just happen and he might be anywhere. He would have to be in his own laboratory in order to have the solaranite gun in working condition at that time. He would need colleagues to carry his body to the operating table and make all the adjustments his own dead body could not make.

And the colleagues, he knew, would be most willing to aid him. After all, each knew their own time would come and if the instrument worked they would gain as much as Professor Julian Smotherland. They too would be able to come under the perfection of the solaranite gun. None of them had anything to lose, and it wasn't as if Professor Julian Smotherland was killing somebody and hoping to bring them back to life. The solaranite gun would not be used until after his death....

But there were experiments to be accomplished first, before he told a single person, professional or otherwise as to what he had in mind.

There was the building of the gun itself… and the magnetic, pure silver, scope antenna which had to be fashioned and attached to the roof. It was designed on a swivel so that it could collect and reflect the sun in its travel across the sky, and it was designed to focus on the moon at night so that the reflected rays of the sun from the moon could also be captured. The solaranite, in order to be complete, had to be a twenty-four-hour treatment to the patient.

From the lofty window of his bedroom he watched the funeral procession enter the cemetery, and it was a long, crying burial service, but he watched the entire proceedings and sighed with relief when they left. But then his muscles tightened again when the gravediggers came into view and filled the hole in so carefully… so tightly packed. He did curse them for that job… but it was their job so he couldn't hate them too much. He was only angry because it would take so much digging to get at the body… and it was cold… and at night it would be even colder. But at least the ground around the grave would not be frozen since it had been cut through for the funeral.

And when the dark of night came he found himself nearly out of breath as he stood beside the grave with the heavy shovel in his hand. And when the task was finished he felt he would surely have a heart attack. But he didn't. Nor did he have one when he carried the recently dead young girl across an acre or more of the cemetery to his own laboratory.

He didn't strap the lovely thing to the table after he had stripped her naked. He wanted to see the body jump and come to life when the solaranite gun had done its job.

And as he looked at the lovely, naked dead body he realized urges he hadn't felt since he was a young man. He was much too old to get a physical erection, but the thought was there in his mind, and his eyes sparkled in a way they hadn't done in years. For a long time he let his hands run over the smooth flesh, into the brush between her legs, and over the mounds of the still very full breasts. He felt an urge to kiss her all over. But he pushed that out of his mind. The flesh was cold… the cold of the grave… not cold of that time of the year. The lifeless cold which only the dead knew, and Professor Julian Smotherland didn't care to ever know.

If he had such ideas as to what he might attempt with the girl it would have to wait until she was once more a living breathing entity in a world where sex predominated…. He didn't know what he could do for his own sex-minded releases, but he knew he wanted to hug that young, beautiful living thing… when she lived again.

But it was morning before he came out of his sex induced trance, and he shook his head to clear the cobwebs… and he downed a measure of pure, bitter whiskey, something he had prescribed for all his colleagues when they became frustrated or tired, or disappointed. Professor Julian Smotherland was only tired, but he had so much more to do.

The solaranite gun burst into a red glow when the thin line of the powerful sun ray, the energy directly from the sun itself smashed through the cold flesh just at the base of the girl's skull. There was a bit of smoking of the hairs around that area of the girl's neck and Professor Julian Smotherland made a quick mental note that the hair must be shaved from the spot before another attempt was made. But the burning hair did nothing to stop the reaction of the girl who sat up, mechanically, on the edge of the table and her eyes opened.

She looked curiously around the room and slowly her lips formed a word. It took a moment more for her throat to respond… and it took her another moment to realize she was naked and girlishly she tried to hide the beaver between her legs. But the Professor was no longer sex starved. He was the professional man… the professor and the doctor and the girl realized she was the patient… she did not know she had been dead… and the professor saved her that horror. He simply told her she had been ill and unconscious, then had her lay back down on the table again.

He removed the pressure of the solaranite beam and the girl immediately became one of the dead again. He brought the girl back three more times, and each time she was born anew and had no knowledge of the previous times, nor the previous death.

She would be returned to the graveyard later the following night, and there she would be found by the anxious relatives who thought some ghoul had taken her up and desecrated the body. But the body was untouched and none of them ever noticed the small patch of burned hair just at the bottom of her skull. She was buried again, and she would no longer return from the grave. The professor had won. And he knew there was nothing to stop him or any of his brilliant colleagues from continuing on in this life as long as they wished…. The burning solaranite gun would keep the brilliant minds alive and healthy for more advancements in their chosen lines.

Professor Julian Smotherland wished with all his heart that he could bring all those in the cemetery back to life and make productive robots out of them again. But it was impossible. The pituitary gland dies when it is not attended after a few days. Only those freshly dead might be restored… and the sooner the dead could reach his solaranite gun the more chance they had of survival.

Professor Julian Smotherland was no longer to leave his home. And there was standing orders at the college that someone was to contact him every hour on the hour, day and night… and if he didn't answer they were to rush to his place… and through the instructions they would know what to do… and his five colleagues in whom he trusted completely were ever ready… they also knew the old man didn't have much time left… but then when it was over he would be returned and he would never have to worry again.

Thus it was one month later... the sun burning high in the heavens that Professor Julian Smotherland felt the sudden slam of a freight train in the region of his heart and he slumped over his desk dead.... His last writings were of the sun's energies which was even powerful enough for the solaranite gun when reflected from the stars, those nights when the moon was not available... and his colleagues raced from the college.

His nude body was placed on the table and the solaranite gun was aimed to the base of his own skull at the spot where the hair had been shaved away.

The beam of light seared through the skin and into the base of the skull and the old body jerked and seemed to be pulling apart for a long time before finally Professor Julian Smotherland quite easily sat up on the edge of the metal operating table and looked at his smiling friends.

The heat of the ray gun felt good. It would always keep him alive. From that point on he could handle the equipment himself. He didn't always need his back to the ray, it would work through the front as well... and from great distances.

Thus he asked for the notes he had been preparing those moments before his demise and when one of his colleagues returned with it the clouds suddenly filled the sky and it turned completely black... the solaranite ray died slowly over the matter of a few seconds... but from the moment it began to weaken Professor Julian Smotherland lost the power of speech. He crumpled to the floor, and when the ray was completely gone he was once more dead... and he would be permanently dead.

And in those last few seconds of speechlessness, before his mind went dead, the brilliant mind realized he had not told his colleagues that all they had to do was turn on the solaranite gun again as soon as the sun returned, or the moon, or the stars which reflected the sunlight... but, as it was, it would be only a matter of days until the pituitary gland could never again be restored.

The colleagues of Professor Julian Smotherland realized in that instant when the gun collapsed that the experiment was a failure...and their good friend... the brilliant mind... was buried in a spot where his lofty window looked out upon him.

THE END

Exotic Loves Of The Vampire

(aka The Exotic Loves Of Dracula)

by "Ann Gora"

in Ecstasy *Vol.4 no 2 July/Aug. 1972 on Ed's resume 1972*

IT HAS BEEN so many months since Jonathan left for that far away place Transylvania. Such a very long time. Oh, how I desire him more and more with each frightening darkness... and when it is as dark and stormy, as terrifying a night as this I long for his strong arms gripping me tightly and his hands soothing my shaking body.

Only he can make me forget the storm and the horrible darkness and the violent thunder and lightning. It must not be much longer before our lips are sealed tightly together and our tongues can travel... circle... entwine... and our breaths will come hot and sear our very throats. The heat will travel steadily, rapidly downward until our stomachs boil and our groins are on fire.

His lips would then leave my own and his tongue would make a tiny rivulet down to that spot between my breasts. His tongue then would circle first under my right breast and then travel across to do the same under my left breast. It had always been the same way... first the right breast then the left. He never varied. And I came to desire it that way. I can only now smile with the pleasure of those days which seem so far off.

He would take each nipple for a long time. His tongue made slashing sounds and when his lips tightened, hot and wet around each there would be little sucking sounds that nearly drove me out of my mind. But I knew what to expect next... and I would not permit myself to go out of my mind until that time. I could never permit myself to lose one fantastic moment of what Jonathan could do with his tongue. If ever there was a sex expert in this world it was my Jonathan. And I, his Mina, tried to always reciprocate. Over and over again he told me that I was the best girl in bed he'd ever met. Jonathan taught me many things he had learned during his days at school.

I have very long auburn hair and it is a wonder that many times I did not strangle myself as my head thrashed from side to side and my hair cascaded all around like a waterfall gone mad. But to strangle myself would have sent me into oblivion and that was something which was not going to happen.

I can only write these lines now and hope and pray that soon I no longer will have to dream of the past and the enjoyment Jonathan and I have had. I no longer will have to only remember the thrilling climax of his lips and his tongue that sent such sparks through me, threatening to send me into the oblivion I knew I had to fight against. I must always remain fully conscious. To remain fully conscious is the only way to capture every second of such an exciting romantic adventure.

Jonathan was such an expert in the bedroom. He knew everything a girl wanted and needed for full satisfaction.

The body heats melted us into each other, his movements would become more and more rapid… then actually violent until he was groaning and grunting like a wild animal… and I, too, made the screams and yells of the damned right up until that final moment of climax when once again our lips were tight together and I screamed down into his throat… and the sounds would travel into his mouth, down his throat, echo throughout his stomach and spurt through him and back into his own body.

And I could feel those same sounds vibrating up through my stomach and back into my throat where I could send them back down again, over and over again until we both lay, perspiring, weak, panting on the wet sheets.

However, that is all in remembering. But in so doing I had made myself physically weak…. Then the horror came.

There was a sudden flapping at the window… a sound so striking, so weird, so terrifying as to capture above all the other sounds of the violent storm.

I quickly snapped down my silk nightgown. I suddenly had the fears that some voyeur had been lurking at the window and was watching my every move. But how could that be? I was on the third floor of that old mansion…. My cousin Lucy's mansion. It would be impossible for anyone to climb up to that window… even with a ladder on such a fierce night….

But for the longest moment I looked to the window without moving from my position on the bed. I was terrified at the sound of something I couldn't fathom. Most of us, when alone, and the night is dark and the storm violent, have felt this way. But I was terrified almost beyond my wits. There was nothing to see but the blackness and the flashing lightning on that most vile of nights.

I wanted to scream out for Lucy, who I believed to be in the next bedroom, but my throat had gone dry. I thought it must be from the terrible sexual heats I had experienced moments before combined with the terror of that startling sound.

My storm lamp flickered. It was on the other side of the bed… away from the window and this caused me to swing my head in that direction. There were no windows open. There could be none open on such a night. But the flame was flickering as if some breeze caused the action.

Then the sound at the window came again and this time it was followed by a shriek which couldn't have been human… yet it couldn't have been entirely animal… it was horrible… almost a terrifying sound from the grave…. My head snapped again in that direction.

But alas… nothing… only the black window and the lightning flashes, and the sound of a branch which had been partially dislodged from the giant tree outside my window… it was scraping across the glass… the sound of fingernails across plate glass which as you know, Jonathan, has always made me shiver.

I walked to the window, taking such a long time… precious time, in arriving at that position which was only a few feet from my bed. My eyes were glued on the blackness… the imperceptible darkness… the ebony darkness… the foreboding unknown beyond… the look of the inside of the tomb when it is closed.

I looked out through the window and into the storm. And I lowered my eyes to the left where I could see the front door of our mansion. There was a small light in the hall which shined through the barred window. A very faint light, but not so faint in that I couldn't see the two figures standing there.

One was a very tall man dressed all in black. I could not see his face. But he was bareheaded in all that rain, and he wore a long black cape. It appeared to be tied around his neck but the collar went far up around his ears and the hem fell nearly to his ankles. And it was very strange. Even though I couldn't see his face I felt as if he had eyes in the back of his head and those eyes were drawing me to him. It was the most hypnotic feeling I have ever had in my life.

And the second person. My eyes must have been playing tricks on me. I know they must have because Lucy later told me she had been with no one. But then in the beginning she also denied being out at all. Because when I looked to the second person it was Lucy... dear Lucy. I'd know her red coat and rain hat and boots anywhere. Of course, as I have said, the light was very faint and although she was facing me her features were in the shadows and I couldn't see her plainly at all. But I knew it was Lucy.

They seemed to be talking for a time, then Lucy turned and entered the house. The man remained there for a long moment, perhaps longer, then he turned and drifted into the shadows. I stayed at the window for just as long a time before I went back to sit on the edge of the bed. I was not to remain in that position long.

That horrible shriek filled the room again and the snapping at the window was more impatient than before. I snapped up and my eyes darted in that direction.

And there at the window was the most ghastly sight I have ever seen. Without a doubt the body was that of a black, gigantic bat with a tremendous wing span. The wings stretched further than both sides of the window and the upright part of the body went from the top to far below the bottom frame. And the face was chalk white... almost human... but again that must have been my imagination... the horror of the situation. But I could not have imagined the blood-red lips and the teeth which were still dripping blood.

I screamed! God how I screamed! With all that was in my tortured soul I screamed. I screamed with all the horrors and terror which must exist in hell.

Lucy wearing her pink satin wrapper raced to me and took me into her arms.... Frantically I told her of the horror I had witnessed through the window. She tried desperately to comfort my fears. "There are many bats around these lands and many of them are giants. That is why most of the peasants never go out of their homes after dark. What you have seen is one of them which has probably just slain a cow, thus what you suspect as blood dripping from the lips and the teeth."

"Or perhaps your gentleman friend who left a few moments ago when you came into the house…. It could have been he that was killed."

"What gentleman friend?"

"Why, the one I witnessed through the window… you both were standing at the front door… just moments ago."

"Why my dear Mina…. You are imagining things. I haven't been out of the house all evening. I've been with no man. I've been in my room or in the living room all evening."

I looked to her hair. It was ringing wet. I let my hand run through her hair. I didn't have to question her further.

"Oh, my goodness… how could I forget? While I was downstairs one of the shutters began banging against the window…. It was a disgusting sound and I thought it might awaken you. I couldn't get the window open so I necessarily had to go outside and make the quick adjustments. My hair isn't dry yet…. Now how could I be so forgetful as to not remember that small episode?"

She was lying to me. I knew she was! Or I felt she was! But what happened in the next few moments made me forget the incident… at least for a time.

The belt, tied loosely around her waist fell and the heavy satin robe came open. Her entire front was exposed to my eyes. Oh, what a luscious body dear Lucy has. I know my eyes must have given a sudden sparkle. I know I felt a heat wave pass through me like an electrical shock… it was the same feeling as when I saw you, dear Jonathan, all naked, for the first time.

Lucy must have suspected what I felt right there on the spot, because the next thing I knew she was taking me by the hands and gently standing me up. "Would you like me to stay with you tonight?"

I didn't have to be asked a second time. But sex, at that moment wasn't on my mind, although my body was giving me some indications that I would be receptive. "My God, yes. Please do! I doubt if I could bear another attack at the window tonight… alone."

"No one will bother you while I am here. Now get undressed and we will snuggle in close together." Whereby I untied the bow at my neck and at the same time Lucy took off her satin negligee and she was completely naked. I let my own negligee fall to the foot of the bed with hers and started to get into bed. She stopped me again. "Take off your nightie also and we will sleep naked… and very close… and nothing will come between our body heats as they melt together."

It all sounded so logical… she made it sound logical and I permitted her to take the hem of my nightie and slowly pull it up over my head. She let the nightie drift down to the negligees but that did not end it. I mean we didn't simply lay down on the bed and snuggle up like I thought we might. Instead her hands came to both my shoulders and her lips found mine. For the briefest moment I thought it was to be a goodnight kiss such as we girls have done often before. But it wasn't to be that way. Her tongue forced its way between my lips the same as you, Jonathan, have done that first time when you were teaching me that kind of heated kiss.

Oh, Jonathan, forgive me for what I am about to tell you. But it did happen and I cannot say that I am very much ashamed of myself. I couldn't help myself any longer. But I did enjoy what was to follow. I had been so overly heated where my body was about to explode before all that business at the window and when I was thinking of what you had done with my body… when her tongue pressed between my lips it was the hottest but softest instrument I have ever felt. I accepted it immediately. It was like a man entering me… only softer… only there was also the smell of delicious perfume…. I couldn't hold myself back. The heats hit me with all the force I've ever felt.

My arms went around her and I crushed her to me. I crushed her so hard to me that we both fell naked to the bed and we were tightly clasped to each other. Her legs wrapped around my body as I used to do with my legs around you and her pubic region matched mine. She started a circular motion that drove me up the walls. There was no longer any turning back.

For a long time she worked on my breasts… so tenderly she worked on them and after a time she turned so that my hungry lips could go to her own nipples. It was the first time I have ever done such a thing in my life but I enjoyed it…. God how I enjoyed it…. I have heard of girls doing such things with each other and I never thought in all my life that I would do such a thing. I had always felt it was perverted… degrading…. I must admit to my complete change of mind since this happening. Oh, this is not to say that I shall ever cut you out of my life dear, Jonathan… have not the least doubt about that. I believe it was so tantalizing because I longed for you so badly. My body was on fire for satisfaction. I had been using masturbation as a way out for so long. I could no longer do that. I needed a hot body next to mine… and all the terror which had gone on before made me perhaps more receptive than I might have been in another situation.

Lucy did to me what you have often done with your lips and your tongue only hers is so much softer than yours. Not that the enjoyment was any more intense, but it was a different type of enjoyment. It's like when I stroke the soft hairs of a pussycat or a small pup. Lucy is so soft and so demanding at the same time. It seems that her tongue never ceases in its movement… searching… ever searching… and her hands are here, there and everywhere at the same time.

Then it happened. The clouds opened up and the thunder crashed and the lightning electrified both of us and there was such a trembling which finally exploded into violent climax after climax.

I tell you I have never climaxed so much and so many times at once in my entire life. It seemed like the mounting pleasure would never stop… and I know that neither of us wanted them to stop… those delightful climaxes.

We will do it again tomorrow night… we have promised each other.

Lucy is asleep now as I write this… and as I looked down at her naked body I couldn't help but notice the small red marks on her neck… such as they might be pin marks… or punctures of some fanged serpent. I have reminded myself to ask her about those tomorrow. I will not worry myself any longer tonight… she doesn't seem to be troubled by them… she is sleeping soundly.

I cannot bring myself to fall into the darkness of sleep. Perhaps I will sleep in the morning when it is daylight… but no longer this night.

When Lucy and I had finished our first relationship together of this kind and she slept I once more went to the window and looked downward. There below a great tree I thought I saw the same man all in black with the long cape… but I'm sure this time I must have been mistaken because the wings flapped and the bat flew off into the storm and was lost into the darkness.

THE END

HOWL OF THE WEREWOLF

on Ed's resume as "Lust of the Werewolf" 1972, from
Deuce Vol.2 No.3

IT WAS THE CONSTANT howling which unnerved Rita. It hadn't ceased since the moon became full. She rolled over on her bed and looked to the bright moonlit window… then she cringed again as the eerie howl seemed to fill the entire night. There emitted no other sound… and it seemed closer… almost as if it were right outside the window.

For a brief moment, she thought about closing the window. But that would have made the room impossible. It was stifling even with the window open, it would have been a complete furnace closed.

But she got out of the bed and crossed to the window. She tested the screen. It was secure. Then she went back to the bed and took up a sheer negligee which she slipped into. She hugged her arms around her breasts as the howl came again and a sudden chill shook her entire being. A chill where there wasn't even the slightest breeze.

Once more she crossed to the window and looked out into the deep shadows. The moon made the countryside almost as light as day, but where the trees and brush cast their shadows it was pitch black.

And it was from the pitch blackness that the howls originated.

"And when the moon is full," she whispered to herself, "the werewolf prowls." Then she grinned. "Bullshit!" She turned her back to the window, but still hugged her arms around her front. "Now I'm talking to myself… and talking like a fool to boot." She began to pace the floor. "Got to get my mind off such thoughts. Damned nonsense coming out here in the woods by myself in the first place. What in hell is a city girl doing in the wilds… got to be out of my mind."

The howl came on strong, sharp, then trailed off in a long wail.

Slowly she walked back to the bed and laid down. There was one thing she could think about which might take her mind off of the present situation. SEX was a powerful mind exploder. If anything could dismiss those howls, the thoughts of sex would be that entity.

When was the last time? It seemed like a month but in reality it had only been three nights before. The night before her vacation was to start. It had been Willie. Good old Willie… the office manager. She'd had him several times before, but that last time stuck strongly in her mind. He came at her like a tiger. It appeared almost as if he'd been sex starved for months. But that wasn't so.

"It's just something I feel about you leaving for these two weeks. It seems like such a long time," he had said.

"It will go by faster than you think."

"I hope so. But why stake yourself way out in the woods like that? Going back to nature might be alright for some people, but good lord, Rita. You're city born and bred. Take a cocktail lounge and a television set away from you and you'll go ape."

"I'm taking a cocktail lounge with me."

"It won't be the same."

"So maybe I'll become a lone, silent drinker."

"You'll be back in two days."

"Not on your life. I'm determined to stick it out. I've never been in the woods before. It's something I've dreamed of for years. Who knows! Maybe I'll like it."

"Honey, you'll go ape-shit without a guy between your legs for two weeks. Look! You might kid somebody else, but I know you. You got to have a guy and his rod. You can't go two weeks without it."

"I'll take a dildo with me."

"Oh, be serious."

"What makes you think I'm not serious?"

"Snakes, wolves, bears… you'll piss in your panties every night."

"Maybe I won't wear any." Then she had reached over and pulled his head down to her pubic region. "Kiss me… kiss me there."

He buried his nose and his tongue deep into her muff and her eyes closed and her hands went to her own breasts which she rubbed rhythmically. Her head suddenly began to toss from side to side and her buttocks rose and fell to meet his every action.

The explosion, when it finally came felt as if it were going to tear her insides out. She liked that and she screamed at the height of the sensual heats.

A quick series of howls, one after another brought her back to the present... howls which seemed to be just outside the window. She came to a sitting position on the edge of the bed. Horror, terror is a thing that comes out of the night... an entity that does exist, a something that no one sees, but all can feel, realize. Rita was realizing that terror more and more with each passing second. She would have screamed if it would have done any good. But what good could a scream be? There was not another house or cabin within ten miles. That was the reason she rented that particular cabin in the first place. It was far away from anybody else and it was close enough to a quiet lake... she'd seen many pictures of the moonlight reflecting across a quiet lake. She wanted to see the real thing.

But it wasn't turning out quite the way she had thought it would. The days were fine. But the nights... that was something else. The night before had been bad enough, but that second night of the full moon... the howling outside had grown in intensity. She clasped her hands tightly over her ears but the sounds were not shut out... stuffing cotton in her ears also made no difference, she found that out the night before.

Where were the cricket sounds and the other night noises? There was nothing but that wolf howl... even more horrible when a cloud traveled across the face of the moon... the sound was a cry for release from the grave... a lost soul screaming from the depths of hell. She knew the sound was that of a wolf cry even though she'd never heard one before, except in the movies. And the wolf was outside, not there in the room. It couldn't come tearing through that tough screen on her bedroom window and all the other doors of the cabin were locked.

Rita had never been one to frighten easily. But she'd also never been alone in the woods, far from civilization before. The woods had their own sounds... sounds that would take a lifetime of living with them to fully understand.

She walked back to the bed and laid down. She locked her wide eyes on the ceiling where they would remain until the sun came up and the sounds of the woods came back to a more normal atmosphere. She hadn't closed her eyes all night... and even more so it was a long time after sun-up before she unfroze her body and stood up. All night she swore she was going to get out of that cabin as soon as the day was upon her once more.

But something about the sun, the daylight seemed to make everything alright again.

In the bathroom she stripped off her negligee and nightgown then lifted her breasts with each hand. They were firm and young and inviting... even to herself they were inviting. At times she would raise them high enough so that she might kiss each nipple. The thought raced through her mind even at that moment, but she didn't. Instead she got into a luke-warm shower which she later turned into a cold one. The sparkling clear water quickly snapped all the cobwebs out of her brain, and she began to feel alive again.

"Now why in the world would a howling dog or wolf or whatever it was give me such a sleepless night?" she said aloud to her towel while she went through the drying off process. "I've waited a lifetime for a vacation alone in the woods. I sure as hell would be a creep if I turned heels and ran. Silly!" Once more she turned and viewed herself in the full-length mirror. She turned slightly from side to side so that she could take in all the delights of her luscious body. "After all, I'm no child. I'm a grown woman." She winked at herself.

She put on a thin nylon blouse over a matching skirt. She hated sneakers but they were comfortable for the long walks in the woods she planned. But there was something more important than a walk that she had to do first.

The village was some twenty-five miles away, but she wanted a pistol and in order to get one she had to make the drive. She hadn't really noticed the place when she drove through it on the way to the cabin. But that had been at night and she was tired. She hadn't missed much. Except for a couple of cabins, there was a gas station, a beer bar and the general store. She went immediately to the general store.

"Oh no, ma'am," replied the ancient storekeeper as he looked over his steel rimmed glasses. "You can't take a pistol with you just like that. Takes three days. Got to put the order through the police and get their okay and that takes three days... Way out here... maybe five or six. But three days is the shortest time."

"But I need it right away. There's a wolf prowling around my cabin. I need the protection."

The old man winked, perhaps remembering incidents in his own youth. "I sure bet there's a lot of wolves prowling around your door..." Then he changed the subject back to the gun again. "Ain't nothin' I can do about the pistol. But if you really got to have a gun." He turned to a gun case which he unlocked and took down a twenty-two. "Now this here's a new light weight twenty-two. Holds twelve shots, long rifle. This you can take right with you."

"Will a twenty-two kill a wolf'?"

"If you hit him in the right place. You a good shot?"

"I don't know. I've never fired a gun before."

"Then you better stay in the cabin at night and keep the door locked… You don't need no gun."

"Show me how to use it."

She reached the cabin just as the sun was sinking over the distant mountain and the rays had turned to a fire red. She watched the shadows deepen for a long moment then she picked up the rifle and then entered the cabin. She put the rifle and an extra box of ammunition on the kitchen table, then went into the living room area where she sunk into a deep fur-covered chair and kicked off her sneakers.

The drive had been tiring. She had taken her time on the mountain roads, but still it had been tiring. She closed her eyes, and when she opened them again it was nearly dark and the man in the white shirt and denim slacks stood looking down at her.

Rita snapped forward in her chair, startled.

The man grinned but made no move toward her.

"I have a gun in the house," she said for lack of anything else to say.

"I know. I saw it on the kitchen table." Then he waved his hand slightly. "There is nothing to be frightened of. I knocked several times and when there was no answer I tried the door. It was unlocked, so I came in. It was easy to see why my knocking went unanswered. You were really asleep."

"I had a sleepless night and a very long drive today." She felt no fear of the man. She stood up. "Are you lost?"

"Something like that. I've taken a cabin in the higher mountains for the summer. I started for the village and only got this far along the road. Seems that a boulder cut loose from the high ground and fell to the road. I didn't see it until it was too late. Broke an axle I suppose. Yours was the closest cabin. Thought you might have a telephone."

"I don't."

"I guess most of the cabins up here in these mountains lack the modern means of communications. I suppose I'll have to put up a smoke signal like the Indians."

Rita laughed. "I certainly can't send you out at this time of night to roam through the fierce jungle. You know there are wolves out there."

"I've heard them." He lowered his eyes momentarily then raised them again. "A body'd have to be dead not to hear them."

"You're welcome to stay here tonight." She indicated the living room couch. "You can stay on the couch then in the morning I'll drive you into the village."

"Now that's what I call hospitality."

"Like a drink? Whiskey is all I have."

"Now that's what I call double hospitality."

She got up and went to the kitchen cabinet. The drinks were mixed with water and when the man had captured his he sank down on the couch while Rita went back to her chair.

"I'm Rita Raleigh... secretary... on a mountain vacation for two weeks."

"Kent Tenstyle... rich... young... and willing."

Rita liked that part of it. It had only been a few nights, but she felt the crotch of her panties getting damp. "And good looking," she ventured.

"You're not something a guy could turn away from either, Miss Raleigh."

"Miss Raleigh makes me sound positively ancient. Let's make it Rita."

He nodded and took a large gulp of his drink.

"I had my dinner in the village before I left. But I can get you something."

"Don't bother. I'm not hungry... for food that is." His eyes twinkled, and Rita had been around men long enough to know what that twinkle really meant. She could almost picture his thoughts as his eyes roved over her lovely body, and she wondered if he could figure her thoughts.

He moved to stand very close to her when she went to make a refill of their drinks. She didn't turn to face him at that precise moment but she could smell this man smell behind her and again his thoughts seemed to be pressing themselves into the back of her head.

She liked what she was feeling and the closer he came to her the more that feeling was intensified. She found herself wanting to feel his arms around her... it seemed an eternity since she had a tongue sticking into her mouth... the male sex organ parting her pubic hairs. Her thighs trembled at the thought... the expectancy. And when his hands came down lightly on the back of her shoulders she turned slowly. He took the glasses from her hands and put them on the kitchen table near the rifle and ammunition. They looked at each other for a long time, their eyes locked in the heat of the moment.

His arms went around her and her lips raised to his and then she was feeling his tongue slashing within her mouth. And with their lips locked together he used his right hand to unbutton her blouse and when it opened her naked breasts popped into sight. "The bedroom," she mumbled through the tight lips....

"Yes," he sighed, but didn't release the pressure of his lips. His hand found one of her lovely globes and he placed the nipple between two fingers. "The bedroom."

The movement of light in the sky out through the open kitchen door caught his eyes. He focused them on that growing light.

Rita's eyes were closed and she clung to the man desperately, as one who is starved for all the experiences she craved.

At first it was only a crescent, but the yellow glow was quickly forming into the perfect ball it would soon be. The moon was following the sun around the earth. Soon it would be full, and clear in the deep black velvet of the night.

Kent stared at the coming event, and the corners of his eyes began to twitch. At the same moment Rita felt the change in her lover. She pulled away slightly and looked at him, but his eyes were fastened to that void out beyond the door.

"What is it, Kent?"

He did not answer her. In reality, he had not even heard her words. His hands dropped to his sides as he turned full to face the open door. Momentarily Rita stepped around in front of him, but he didn't seem to realize her presence. She moved back more to the center of the room. Her eyes dropped to the rifle then once more raised up to the back of Kent's head.

Something strange was happening to the man. The hair, damp hair, at the nape of his neck was growing by the second. She looked down to his hands and the hair was growing rapidly there. His shoulders seemed to broaden and become slightly hunched forward giving his back a rounded appearance.

"What is it, Kent? What's happening?"

Still there were no words from the man, but she could hear his sudden heavy breathing and a slight gurgling sound which drifted up through his throat. His back was to her and it heaved heavily. He began to pant like a dog in heat.

Fright built itself quickly in Rita's heart. She snapped up the rifle and aimed it at his back, but she did not fire. "Kent. I want to know what is happening!"

Her breasts popped in and out of her open blouse front with every panicky breath she took. She bit at her trembling lip. One hand left the rifle to brush the hair out of her eyes, then went immediately back to steady the weapon.

Kent threw his head far back and the howl of the wolf filled the entire room and it was only topped by the piercing scream which issued from Rita's throat.... Then she fired shot after shot from the rifle. She saw each of the bullets strike their mark in the creature's back. The rifle then locked in silence when the last shot was fired. She screamed again and the rifle fell from her hands. Her eyes went wide in terror as the creature turned to face her.... The lips parted to reveal the flesh tearing fangs and the drooling saliva which flowed over the corners of his lips. His face was completely covered in hair... the gray-brown hair of the wolf... of the werewolf.

He snarled, then wailed again. His hands went up high as he started in for the kill.

"None but the silver bullet can kill a werewolf," she heard herself say, realizing as the claws tore her clothing from her body. She tried to turn and run but the claws dug into her flesh in long jagged, blood-letting cuts. Then she was on the floor and he was on top of her. She felt his muscle enter her and he pumped explosively at her over and over again until that final moment of climax... and at that moment of climax his fangs tore into her throat....

She died with the scream and the blood gurgling in her throat, and her thighs quivering from the effects of that last climactic explosion.

THE END

WITCHES OF AMAU RA

by "Dick Trent"

in Horror Sex Tales. *The Jumbo Book 1972 story on Ed's resume titled "Witches Tale of Horror"*

THE CONCLAVE STARTED precisely at midnight on October 31st. It would last the full ten days. And there would be murder and most of all there would be lust… debauchery.

Karen was tall… a long legged, five foot ten. She had a luscious body. She had breasts which nearly defied imagination. And dropping the eyes downward, her legs were a perfection of mold and design. She had it made and she knew it… and she was going to use everything about that body in order to promote her own ends.

She was a witch and a God-damned good one…. God-damned is the right word because all the witches believed they were God damned from conception. And they further believed that there was no *BIG BLACK* before conception. They were selected from elements of the darkness who must do the bidding of the Prince of Darkness… his every bidding.

Thus is the belief of the witch.

Thus is the demand of the Devil.

Karen found a belief in the material things. Karen found herself smashed with colors and men, and the long green, and men, and the feeling of youth and men… men… men….

But Karen was a witch!

Nothing was going to change that!

Her every move in life was to progress the conclave to which she belonged. It was a life to which there was no turning back… the black book of Satan had written it so. The red mark of lightning on her left hip designed it so.

But she was not happy being simply one of the masses… one of the followers. She wanted with all her heart to be the witch princess and she knew what she would have to do to gain that distinction. But only with that distinction would come the wealth she knew and felt she deserved. Only with the acceptance of Amau Ra, the all high Amau Ra„ could she attain such a high place in the order. Amau Ra, full of lust… insatiable in his demands upon the women who surrounded him… but women who disappeared when he was through with them or when they displeased him, or when they became old and ugly or ill from some malady or other.

She knew the chances were dangerous for her but she also knew the stakes were high and worthy of any chance she would have to take. She knew what she would have to do to gain his favor… and that October 31st midnight black mass was her best opportunity.

Karen felt she would have to be completely out of her mind to permit such a chance escaping her. She felt Amau Ra would be drunk as he languished back upon the black silk and satin pillows in his throne room behind the opening of the Cave of Hates. He would be half crazed through wine and in the lust for sexual encounters. New sexual encounters. She felt this but had never seen him.

Karen was not on the list for his favors. But she would find a way. The demands she made upon herself were more powerful than any moral issues which might have been brought out. Therefore when she entered the bed chambers of Toni, who was to have the honor, she felt no compunction as she began her play with the girl.

There would be soft lights and there would be a congratulatory drink of wine and Karen would cement her lips to those of the girl and their tongues would meet, and Karen would tell Toni all the delicious things she would like to hear. And Karen would capture that tongue over and over again, and her hand would run down the front of Toni's sheer negligee much as the hands of a man might. And Karen's soft pressure would capture each globe in turn and silently caress them while her eyes held the others transfixed.

Then Karen's lips, blood red lips, would encircle the entire right breast and slowly pull forward until only the soft, pink nipple would remain captured between those luscious lips. She would repeat the loving movement over and over again until Toni sighed, then cried out in the ecstasy of what was happening to her.

But there was no more thinking of what might happen. Karen was in the room with Toni and she transferred her lips and her hot tongue over to the left breast and the sucking, the caressing actions of her lips and the inside of her mouth blazed a new path of erotic pleasures through the girl's breasts and down into the pit of her stomach and centered in the region of her vagina. Her legs began to twitch and her pink buttocks could hardly remain solid on the fur-covered couch where she had lain back.

Toni knew she should not be so excited before she was called into the chambers of Amau Ra. She would be spent and she would cause displeasure from the exalted high one. But she also knew she didn't want those lips, that tongue and those hands of Karen's to stop. She wanted Karen's tongue to river between the breasts and stream down over her flat, hard middle and to encircle her navel, then move further to investigate what was behind the brush in the "V" of her pubic region.

Karen's hand had already drifted to that region and probed and petted and slipped across the little man in the boat... and Toni could no longer contain herself as she reached down and grasped Karen's head and pulled it back up to her. Their mouths crushed together and their tongues entwined in a dance of pure delight and Toni's body moved furiously but rhythmically on the bed... inviting Karen's body to come on top of her.

But Karen was not ready for that at the moment. She held their lips cemented together, their saliva mixing as joy juices will mix and her hand captured the globes, transferring over and over again from the left to the right. Then the probing finger and the tickling of the pubic hairs. Karen wanted the girl weak, willing and ready when she decided it was time to put all of her pressure into the place of delight.

Karen's lips were driving the girl mad and she wanted to cry out in lust. But it was impossible. Her sounds only traveled down the throat of Karen and were lost... but the rumble were tones of beauty to the witch. With every effort the girl made it would make her that much more weak when the time came.

The time came as Karen rolled over on top of the now naked girl and captured the same rhythm... then she added a sliding to and fro motion which drove the girl into deeper exotic fits.... She was about to climax wildly when Karen took that advantage for her entire purpose in the affair. She shoved her own pubic region hard against that of Toni and as the girl screamed in her climax, Karen jammed her tongue deep into the girl's mouth and closed her lips airtight across those of the girl and at the same time shut off her complete air supply by clasping the nose tightly with her hand.

It was a long moment before the choking girl realized what was happening. Then her eyes opened in terror. She struggled to free her body from beneath Karen's. But Karen was much more the stronger of the two and she had a living purpose which gave added strength.

Toni's hands clawed at Karen's back. But the clawing grew weaker and the breathing grew more shallow under Karen's own breasts... the breathing ceased all together. There was no more movement except that Toni's hands fell limply to her sides on the bed. But Karen didn't immediately remove her body or her hand or her lips. She had to be sure that there was no longer any spark of life.

She held the position for a full five minutes... but a five minutes which seemed an eternity. Then she stood up and looked down at the lifeless girl... white in the pallor of death.

Karen permitted a self-satisfied smirk to cross her features. There would not be a mark of violence on the lovely girl's body. She simply stopped breathing.

"This will make Amau Ra very displeased," remarked one of the two High Priests who entered to escort Toni to Amau Ra's bed chamber. "Could she have taken her own life? There is a wine glass on the stand beside her."

"It was mine," replied Karen as she picked up the glass. "She didn't want to drink before she visited the bed chambers of Amau Ra." Then she took down the remainder of the warm wine and replaced the glass. "She was sitting there talking with me of the delights she felt she would enjoy tonight when she lay with Amau Ra, then suddenly reached for her middle and sunk back to the couch and assumed the condition you now see her in."

The second High Priest frowned deeply. "There is no time to select another for Amau Ra's pleasure. Pleasure hell. Amau Ra will be a raving tyrant. He hasn't had any in more than a week and his frustrations are going to tell on every member of the conclave."

Karen assumed her most sexy pose. "Would I not do? Am I not more beautiful? I have often found it strange that Amau Ra has not noticed me in the past. I am quite sure that I would more than please the master. I am well schooled in all that can be done in the bed chambers. True, I have not been exalted to the post of High Priestess. But under such circumstances as this, it might be accomplished here and now. It is in your power to perform the ceremony which would make me worthy of Amau Ra's bed chamber."

The two High Priests looked to each other, then back to the girl.

"You are sure you know what you are doing?" asked one of them.

"I am ready to do the bidding of Amau Ra at all times. It is my only wish in life... and after death."

Again they looked to each other.

"Other than we High Priests of the order, only a sworn High Priestess may gaze upon the person of Amau Ra."

Karen grew impatient. She knew that all her hopes of the easy and wealthy life would go out the window if these two men of high place would not select her at that precise time which she had designed.

"It would seem to me that most of the witches you have selected to become High Priestesses must have been lacking in something which could please Amau Ra.... He certainly has to select enough to satisfy him. I know I am the best of them all. I've talked with many and they know nothing of what I know. I could teach them all tricks which would stand any man on his ear.... I mean that literally."

"She is so eager," replied one.

"Yes.... So eager," said the other, then turned to Karen. "Your wish shall be granted."

Karen took a deep sigh of relief.

"There is not time for the ceremonial robes and all of the readings. But there is time for the most important rite of all. Kneel!"

She knelt before them.

"The snake is the God of all the darkness. It is the snake who has enhanced life... who might bring into the world all the wickedness we worship... and it is to the snake you must extend your soul. You will sip of his venom so that a part of the snake will always be within you and therefore making you a blood sister to the snake and a High Priestess of the snake. Are you prepared to do all this?"

"I am."

"Then all is well. And you will be ready to enter the bed chambers of Amau Ra at the scheduled time."

"I am more than looking forward to that pleasure." And her heart jumped, skipping a beat as she thought of all the riches, all the wealth she would soon have. And to be the exalted High Priestess to Amau Ra meant she would have control over the entire conclave, including the two High

Priests who stood there before her so pompous, so high on themselves. But she would have the last laugh. She would be Queen of all the witches the world over.

"Prepare your lips. Prepare your tongue."

Karen licked her reddened lips with the end of her tongue so that the moistness made them sparkle even there in the half light.

Both men raised their hands high over their heads. "Receive this woman into the realm of the dark world where she will reside as Priestess of all high. She will receive the snake of the living." And he raised his long robe and shoved his snake close to her lips.

At first she was startled. Her eyes went wide.

"Fellatio is the final step in taking the venom."

She knew what they wanted and she was prepared to give it to them. She was prepared to drive them up the walls if necessary. There was nothing she wouldn't do to get into that bed chamber where Amau Ra waited… probably not so patiently.

She took the rod into her hands then buried it deep into her mouth, letting her lips curl around the tender parts, and travel up and down the shaft until the first High Priest was beside himself with the ecstasy of the moment… and when finally he exploded he had to retire to the couch beside the dead Toni and pour himself a large goblet of wine. He didn't look up as the second High Priest mirrored his earlier movements and Karen showed her skill again. But this time she took longer. She wanted to show the man that there was such a fine line between pain and pleasure.

She proved her point during the next fifteen minutes of her attack. Then she too drank of the wine and stood waiting the next command.

"Did I not tell you I was superior to all the others you have selected?"

"You are truly the more superior. It will be so sad losing you to the higher echelon. But there is no time for changing our minds now. Amau Ra awaits. It would be crushing if his hungers were to go unheeded."

"I need no rest. I am prepared to accept him in all he wishes of me."

"Then, High Priestess Karen… we will go through the caves and into the bed chamber behind the throne of Amau Ra."

And they moved through the caverns, creepy, damp, ancient caverns hollowed out of the sheer mountain by nature and the elements… and when they came to the darkest of the compartments, the High Priests suddenly grabbed her arms and with all the force they could muster, they tossed her forward.…

She fell to the ground but she turned in time to see the gigantic door close behind her and she heard a bolt thrown into place. Slowly she stood up and looked around the room which was lighted by only one oil torch…. There was a deathly silence which prevailed….

Then a hissing sound.

There were no satin pillows… no silk pillows for the throne of Amau Ra… only wet straw and mildewed rocks… where the gigantic BOA CONSTRICTOR resided….

She became immediately transfixed by the horrible length, the hypnotizing green eyes which were surrounded by blood red… the fantastic teeth and the forked red tongue which flashed in and out of the saliva-dripping mouth.

It waited… impatiently… but waited. Karen knew what she must do. There was no turning back. The hissing called her. She was a witch and her master demanded her. The dreams of wealth died quickly… her mind became a confusion of demands… demands sent upon the thought waves from the gigantic snake….

She crossed the room and her hands cupped the head of the snake lovingly. She bent her moist red lips down to the head and her tongue ran lovingly over the unblinking eyes… down the monstrous snout… then she lay back upon the damp straw and opened her legs wide… her vagina winked at the creature and it snaked forward. The forked tongue snatched at the clit and an intense reaction swelled inside the girl. The head entered… her legs stretched apart to their fullest… the head disappeared and it was followed by moving lengths of the body….

The reptile was killing her. The pain increased to where she could only open her lungs and cry out with the screams of the damned, and still the great length continued to enter… more and more of the slick body… the massive roundness….

Karen thrashed about. Her hands clawed at the slippery body. Her nails dug into the skin but was only greeted by a rubbery-like substance which could not be torn….

The sudden deep faint came as the only release for the pain she was enduring… until at last she would die from the torturous body which was curling up inside of her….

Indeed Karen was a tremendous delight for the hungry Amau Ra.

THE END

THEN CAME THUNDER

no author listed, from Two Plus Two *vol.3 no3 Sept./Oct. 1971*
on Ed's resume

THAT WAS HER NAME, Thunder. And that's the way she came on…
like thunder… like thunder that slammed to the earth, raced across the
fields and bounced against the distant mountains only to re-echo as it
slammed back and forth from precipice to precipice. And once she got
started she was just like the thunder also… it was hard to stop… if not
impossible.

Strange thing about the girl… her voice didn't match her looks. She
was blonde; the hair falling below her shoulders; she had a lovely face with
big blue eyes and her figure matched that of any high-priced sex model.
But she was neither. She wasn't high priced nor was she a model. She was,
however, a topless waitress in one of the middle-of-the-road clubs where
the salary matched the atmosphere and the tips never over-shadowed the
atmosphere either. But the job didn't pressure her too much and she enjoyed people as long as they remained simply that… people. When they
started with the passes (the men) or thought she was their ass-slave she
turned them off like a cold water tap. She could also invoke the meaning
of the sign which hung on the foyer wall… *WE RESERVE THE RIGHT
TO REFUSE SERVICE TO ANYONE.*

She'd never had to resort to such drastic measures, but she threatened
it a few times and that was enough to change the rudest of any lot. Her
thundering voice, that thundering voice which came from such a
shapely body was over-powering enough. But she only had to use it once
on any single unruly character. And most of them came back again and
again, but completely changed in their attitude.

These were the men customers, of course.

Thunder had a different approach for the girls... the ones she liked. Even the resounding thunder drifted off to other ports of call. Thunder could be the most tender of the tender when she wanted to be... wanted to promote her point and have a good acceptance of any situation. But there was no mistaking the fact that Thunder was the aggressor and any fluff she came in contact with knew that fact right from the start.

Thunder was also known to have turned on a great number of virgins in her time. Virgins which might have gone on into what might be considered a normal sex life. But Thunder considered her sex life as normal as anybody else's. She preferred it lesbian style and that's the way she was going to continue for the rest of her life. And there was a lot of that life left. A lot of that beautiful life left. She was beautiful and life was beautiful, but she was no *fluff* in the arrangements even though she preferred to dress in *fluff* clothing instead of the man type like most of the other *butches* she knew around the stem.

Because of her apparent beauty, even without makeup, she had little trouble enticing some newcomer to "at least give it a try."

After that it was up to the *"new-born fluff"* as to whether or not she would continue along in the same vein. The selected girls were few and far between who didn't come back for at least seconds. Thunder has that effect on people... on girls she had a tremendous feeling for. She'd bat those big blue eyes, shake the lovely, long blonde hair and at the same time make sure her firm, well molded, pink tipped breasts shook with the same rhythm and any red-blooded female, so inclined, would melt under the sudden spell. She produced a hypnotic trance as few others in her class could accomplish.

Sylvia was very much like Thunder, except where Thunder thundered, Sylvia purred. None of Sylvia's friends could ever swear they'd ever heard her speak loudly in any way, shape or form. But her voice held a command that had the same authority as Thunder's.

Both of them knew of that fact and both hated the other with the purple passion of jealousy. Friends of both had expected the battle of the century for a long time... a battle which would leave both with hands full of hair gone, black eyes and bloody lips, and perhaps a broken bone or two. But the steaming in each was held to verbal insults which were not followed up, except with backstabbing words to friends... threats of what each would do when the time was right. The time never seemed to be right, however.

There was no doubt in anybody's mind that the time had to be right sooner or later or both the girls would lose their leadership and points of honor with the other girls who had always respected and feared them for those particular attributes. But any leader holding the respect of their underlings had to accomplish certain things from time to time. That's only good business, and good business is qualified by how much publicity can be arranged to keep that particular leader in the limelight.

There was no doubt but what both the girls had enough publicity on their own… separately. But that was the entire problem. Each was a publicity-hungry giant as to her own command of the situation. But the publicity simply outshone any reported action. But then again, there was little action to be reported.

"Christ, why should I get in a hassle with the bitch?" thundered Thunder. "She's liable to get in a lucky punch or two. I like my nose where it is."

"A beast of burden, that's what that lesbian whore is," came Sylvia's sweet tones on the other side of town. "She's got a kick like a mule, I'm told and I don't kick. She's liable to damage my ass, then where'd I be?"

Thus, the stalemate continued and no amount of coaxing could change either of their minds. But they would lay a heavy hand upon one of their followers if they persisted in too much of a difficult measure. At least they kept some measure of leadership over them in this way. But the descent was becoming more noticeable every day and both Thunder and Sylvia knew that they were not going to be able to keep them under their thumb much longer. There had to be some kind of a blow-by-blow arrangement.

Which is exactly the format they finally came up with and accepted one to the other. A blow by blow affair! But not in the general sense of the word. Of course hands, feet, heads, teeth, anything pertaining to their body could be used to render the opponent helpless and spent. But there would be no punches, kicks, fisticuffs involved at all.

The ring would be a bed, and since both preferred the softer things in life, the bed would be covered with a pink nylon fur, something easily washable because there was bound to be a lot of sweating during the encounter, and possibly spots of other natures. The pillows were of nylon satin and were expendable… to be used in any way possible. But these were not all the elements which could be brought into value.

Hell… not by a long shot they weren't.

Each of the girls could bring her own implements which she selected. Instruments they figured might be used to wear down the strength of the other. Size, length, material, or usage was of little matter. It is a well known fact that dildos come in a tremendous amount of variations, each different kind designed to bring on a different reaction. Lesbians above all know of their value and they are always on the lookout for something different. Both Thunder and Sylvia set their girls about looking for anything different.

Because this blow-by-blow match was going to be a lesbian affair to which only one of the girls would be strong enough to raise herself up from the bed when the marathon affair came to a conclusion. And there would be no technical knock-outs permitted. The loser had to be completely finished, spent, weakened to a point where she would not rise up from the fur coverlet without a long period of unconsciousness. There would be no giving up… no crying *"Uncle"*… there would be only a total blackout whereby no decisions had to be made as to who might have won *"had something else happened."* There would be no rematch. One would be the supreme ruler over the entire clan for both ends of town.

No one expected the affair to last less than one twenty-four hour period. But there were heavy bets on the fact that a week would be more like the minimum encounter. From that point on the real odds started. Some for the contestants and some for the time expansion while the majority laid their bets on both contestants and time. And to all there was the deep-set admiration and jealousy in that they were not also participants.

For hours on end, starting two days before the scheduled start of the match the bedroom, the future scene of the encounter, was visited by scores of anxious visitors. The bed area was roped off, but the dildos and other implements were set out, but guarded by a security force of six tough bull dykes, so that they could be felt, examined and admired.

However, the greatest innovation was the one-way glass which had been installed over one entire wall through which the entire action, at five dollars a head, could be witnessed and the participants could not be bothered or hindered in their planned, or unplanned actions. And the sound proofing would keep the cheers or the boos away from Thunder and Sylvia's ears. After all, each had their own cheering section so the outbursts really would mean very little.

The expected gate was of great value to the girls because there was a two-hour limit for any viewer. Of course they could remain as long as they wanted as long as the five bucks came across every two hours. And the same six security dykes would be handling the audience so there wasn't going to be anyone who could lie about their time expiration.

Unlike most fights of the century there were no handbills or newspaper or radio or television advertising for the event. That simply wouldn't be kosher. Besides, that particular type of encounter was looked rather down upon by the mass public, so the entire affair had to be shifted about, advertised strictly by word of mouth. But it is sometimes said that word of mouth is the best form of advertising the world has ever known. And it became true for Thunder and Sylvia's fight of the century. The word went out far and wide, and by that second day before the encounter when the doors were open for inspection, the lesbians had begun to flock in from several neighboring states. The word might have gone out worldwide and visitors from all over might have come, but the date for the blow by blow battle had been set too close to the date the acceptance for the battle was taken. There just wasn't enough time for the word of mouth campaign to reach much further than the few neighboring states and the major cities. The smaller towns would have to be satisfied, as well as the rest of the world, with films and other types of reports which would be issued later, when it was all over. The secret films were easily another source of revenue… a very likely sum. Even though the winner would come out of the encounter with the lion's share of the profits, it would still be worth it for the loser who would retain twenty-five percent. The winner, of course, the other seventy-five per-cent, less the small amount of expenses for the bed, the mirror and the things to be used on each other, as well as the fur-covered pillows and the clean-up materials. Food and drink could be had at any time as long as the action was not halted. Sleep was not to be permitted under any circumstances.

The first glimpse the thirty-odd girls and women saw through the one-way glass was of two immaculate, pink bodies with the shapes of goddesses. And at that same instance when Thunder and Sylvia saw each other naked for the first time in their lives, they both knew the entire session wasn't going to be so bad after all. The excitement of the moment caused their full, round breasts to heave up and down, forward and back, an added excitement to their eyes, their emotions and the heat which was building deep under their silk-haired muffs… beavers to the enlightened.

The clock struck midnight and the battle of the century was on. They started with their arms tight about each other and their lips cemented together, their tongues searching out the secrets of their mouths. It had been prearranged that the match would start that way. It had been previously a reluctant way to start, but they had agreed. But as their lips met and their tongues searched and their hands investigated, there was no longer any reluctance... They were immediately into it. The sweat appeared on their foreheads almost from the outset, and both knew that little rivulets of body juices ran down the inside of their naked legs. Their feet moved slowly, rhythmically through unrestrained desires. Then they fell to the bed, still locked together.

When the second hour arrived, they had already gone through every available implement which had been selected and accepted. They were useless in bringing on any more power to their affair, any more sexual heats, any more erotic pleasures than their own bodies, their own hands and lips could muster. They were on their own with themselves, and all the pushing, gouging, inserting, feeling, loving, moaning, crying, cooing, love-talk only made their bodies writhe in ever increasing desires.

Thunder and Sylvia were a match for each other. First, one was the aggressor, then the other. The hatred between them melted swiftly. All that was left was the desire for each other and after the sixteenth hour, after climax after erotic climax had passed, they refused to permit any rest to capture their sweating bodies. The sweat poured from them like the steam from an overheated radiator on an automobile. In a way there were times they were like automobiles... strictly mechanical, but soon one would touch the other in just the right place and the automation stopped and the love of life and what they were doing took over completely. Thirty-two hours later the two spent girls had investigated every crease, every line of the other's body. They had investigated with hands, with noses, with feet and with soft tongues. There was nothing else new to them, yet they wanted to find more and more. They were two mechanical girls who had the determination suddenly again to win. Tired, hopeless, exhausted to a point where their minds no longer reacted like human beings they began to claw and to dig and then...

THEN CAME THUNDER... It wasn't Thunder's body which won. It wasn't her overpowering lovemaking, because she was as exhausted as Sylvia. It wasn't that she found yet another place for investigation and for turning on a renewed heat. *It was that voice of thunder which suddenly screamed up the canyon and the sound was so terrifying that Sylvia simply fainted from the vibrating sounds inside her!*

There may have been many amazed reactions, but for one thing there was dead silence in that amazement behind the one-way mirror.

Thunder came on like thunder and there was no doubt but that she had won. She might have done so sooner, but she had her own words about that.

"Sure, I could have done it sooner. But I was having a ball... Sylvia was one fine opponent. You know... I think I'll make her my lieutenant."

THE END

THE RUE MORGUE REVISITED

by "Dick Trent"

in Horror Sex Tales, *The Jumbo Book-Pendulum 1972 on Ed's resume 1972*

PARIS, FRANCE RESIDENTS were shocked as they opened their morning papers to read of the gruesome murders which had occurred during the night in the Rue Morgue.

"EXTRAORDINARY MURDERS : —This morning, about three o'clock, the inhabitants of the Quartier St. Roch were roused from sleeping by a succession of terrific shrieks, issuing from the fourth floor of a house in the Rue Morgue, known to be owned and lived in by one Madame L'Espanaye, and her daughter Mademoiselle Camille L'Espanaye. Both extremely lovely looking women.

"After some delay, caused by the almost impossible task of gaining entry, the gateway was broken in with a crowbar and eight or ten of the neighbors entered, accompanied by two Gendarmes. By this time the screams had ceased, but as the party rushed up the first flight of stairs, two or more voices were heard arguing and seemed to come from the upper part of the house. As the second landing was reached, these sounds had stopped and everything became deathly quiet. The neighbors spread themselves about and hurriedly ran from one room to the next. Upon entering a large back chamber, on the fourth floor (the door of which was discovered locked, with the key inside) was forced open... a spectacle of horror presented itself and immediately made the neighbors gasp with terror.

"The apartment was in the wildest disorder... furniture was broken and thrown about in all directions. There was only one bedframe and from this, the bed had been removed and thrown in the middle of the floor. On a chair lay a razor blade besmeared with blood. On the hearth several thick chunks of gray human hair lay… also dabbed with blood and seeming to have been pulled out by the roots. Upon the floor, amidst a pool of blood, were found two topaz earrings, three silver spoons and two bags containing nearly four thousand francs. A small iron safe was discovered beneath the blood-soaked mattress. It was opened but nothing appeared to be taken.

"Of Madam L'Espanaye, no traces were to be found, but an unusual amount of soot, observed in the fireplace, caused the Gendarmes to search the chimney. The corpse of the daughter had been forced up the small opening for quite a distance and was crammed in head downward. The body was still warm. Upon examination it was discovered that the body had been disfigured and mutilated. The details are inhuman in nature and the editors wish to advise its readership to conclude their reading if they are in the least squeamish about such matters.

"The girl's left breast had been severed from her body. Her nipple was later discovered beneath a chair in the corner of the chamber. Dark bruises and deep indentations of fingernails were found about the throat and it appeared as if the victim had been throttled to death.

"After a thorough investigation of the house, the party made its way to the small paved yard near the rear of the building, where they discovered the corpse of Madame L'Espanaye, with her throat so entirely cut that, upon attempting to raise her, her head fell off. The body, as well as the head, was fearfully mutilated… the former so much so as to scarcely retain any semblance of humanity. Further, a broken broom handle was shoved deep into her vagina." The following morning the newspapers had little or nothing to report. "THE TRAGEDY IN THE RUE MORGUE:—Many individuals have been examined in relation to this most extraordinary and frightful affair but nothing whatsoever has transpired to throw light upon the murders."

I became involved quite by accident. I had been visiting my old friend Monsieur C. Auguste Dupin, a man of many literary works; an expert in crime and its causes, more than once the Gendarmes had called him in for explanations on their most difficult cases. This was to be no exception, and because I too am a writer of mystery and the macabre, my friend invited me along for his investigations.

The room was as the papers had described it as Dupin took a long time in surveying every corner… every square inch of the blood-soaked room before he finally turned to me.

"You see," he uttered. "I have shifted the question from mode of departure to that of entrance. It is my idea to state that both are one and the same. Let us now revert to the interior of the room. Let us survey the appearances here. The drawers of the bureau have been rifled, although many articles of the apparel still remain within them. The two bags of gold lay open and upon audit it contains nearly the total… four thousand francs. It is obvious that robbery was not the intent. Certainly her small though not inexpensive amount of jewelry has been found intact. Most definitely robbery was not the reason behind these murders.

"Keeping in mind the peculiar voice, the unusual agility needed and startling absence of motive, let us look at the butchery itself. Here is a woman strangled to death by manual strength, and thrust up a chimney head downward. Ordinary assassins employ no such mode of murder as this. Now you may suggest that Madame and Mademoiselle had very peculiar visitors into their rooms, or were at least reported to have had… well, to this I say their childlike games were for mutual satisfaction… the visitors and their own. Certainly their actions, the simple dischargement of semen indicates these men to be without a violent and aggressive nature. All seemed perfectly content to do without physical contact. In fact, they showed a decided preference for this kind of sexual fulfillment. In the manner of thrusting the corpse up the chimney, you will admit that there is something positively irreconcilable with our common notions of human actions, even when we suspect the persons of being the most depraved of men. Think, too, how great must have been the strength required to thrust a body up such a narrow aperture.

"Turn now, to other indications of strength employed. On the hearth were thick gray tresses of human hair. You are aware of the great force necessary in tearing from the head even twenty or thirty hairs together. You saw the roots in question, clotted with fragments of fresh scalp, a sure token of the abnormal power which had to have been exerted in uprooting perhaps a half million hairs at a time. The throat of Madame L'Espanaye was not merely cut, but absolutely severed from the body… the instrument, merely a razor. As for the broom handle brutally thrust into the woman, it is clear this was snapped in half, then inserted without forethought. The girl's left breast, hideously severed from her chest, I believe, to also be a mere addition to the grotesque crime. It is of my opinion that these additional acts of violence were without forethought of intention. As to the girl being criminally raped… that being the natural response of any male animal toward the female of the species, no matter which species.

"If now you have properly reflected upon the odd disorder of the chamber, the super-human strength, a ferocity of brutality, a butchery without motive, a grotesque horror absolutely alien from humanity, a voice foreign in tone to all witnesses and a required amount of astounding agility, what results then can we conclude? What impression have I made upon your imagination?"

I felt a sensation upon my flesh as Dupin asked me that question. "A madman," I said, "has done this horrible deed. Some raving lunatic, a sadistic sex crazed lunatic, most probably had escaped from the nearby sanitorium."

"In some respects, you are correct. But a madman's hair is not like the kind I hold in my hand. I disentangled this little turf from the rigidly clutched fingers of Madam L. Tell me what you can make of it?"

I was completely unnerved. "This hair is most unusual! This is no human hair."

He nodded and the veins in his neck seemed to bulge the tautness of his flesh.

"I have not stated this, but before I agree or dispute your observation, let us look at the little sketch I have prepared. It is a facsimile of the fingernail imprints found on the Mademoiselle's throat. You will take notice that the drawing gives the impression of the assassin's ability to maintain a firm hold on the victim's neck until death. Attempt to span this graph."

I made that attempt. "This is no human hand print."

"Read this passage from Cuvier."

It was a minute anatomical and general description of the large and fulvous orangutan of the East Indian Islands. The gigantic stature, the prodigious strength and activity, the wild ferocity and the imitative propensities of these mamilia are sufficiently well-known to all. I understood the full meaning of what Dupin was suggesting.

"The description of the digits is in exact accordance with this drawing. I see that no animal, but only an orangutan could have made the impressions as you have traced them. This tuff of hair, too, is identical in character with that of the beast. But still I cannot understand the particulars of this frightful mystery."

"Nor do I, but I suspect the animal escaped from his owner and found his way into the house quite unintentionally. We shall soon learn if my suspicions are correct, for last night I placed this advertisement in the newspaper upon our way home."

I studied the advertisement carefully. "CAUGHT... in the Boise de Boulogne, early in the morning last, a very large, tawny orangutan of the species Bornese. The owner (who is suggested to be a sailor, belonging to a Maltese vessel) may have the animal again, upon identifying it satisfactorily, and paying a few charges arising from its capture and keeping." Then there was a telephone number.

"How is it possible that you should know the man to be a sailor and belonging to a Maltese vessel?" I questioned.

"I do not. But, I discovered this piece of ribbon on the premises and it may belong either to the deceased or a sailor flying the Maltese colors."

And at that moment there was the sound of steps on the stairs outside of the door.

Dupin cautioned. "Be ready with your pistol, but neither use it nor show it until I signal you." The front door of the house had been left open, and the visitor had entered without ringing and started up the steps. Now, however, he seemed to hesitate. Shortly we heard him coming up again and upon reaching our chamber, rapped upon the door.

Dupin was cheerful and hearty of tone in his greeting. "Come in."

He was a sailor, a tall, stout, muscular-looking person, with a certain daredevil expression of countenance. His face, greatly sunburnt, was more than half hidden by whiskers and mustache. With him he had a huge oak cudgel, but appeared otherwise unarmed. "Good evening," he said.

Dupin eyed him cautiously. "I suppose you have called about the orangutan. Upon my word, I almost envy you... the possession of him. A remarkably fine and no doubt, a very valuable animal. How old is he?"

The sailor drew a long breath, with the air of a man relieved of some intolerable burden. "I have no way of knowing... he can't be more than four or five years old. You have him here?"

"We had no conveniences for that. He is at the livery in the Rue Dubourg. You can have him in the morning. Of course, you are prepared to identify him?"

"To be sure."

"I shall be sorry to part with the beast."

"I don't feel you should have gone to all this trouble for nothing, sir. I am quite willing to pay a reward for the finding of the animal... that is to say... anything within reason."

"That is all fair, to be sure." Then his eyes narrowed even more and his eyebrow cocked. "My price is that you shall give me all the information in your power about the murders in the Rue Morgue." And in so saying

he quickly walked to the door and locked it. He put the key into his pocket and at the same time drew his pistol and placed it without the least flurry, upon the table.

The sailor's face flushed… he trembled violently… but was silent.

Dupin calmed the man. "You are alarming yourself needlessly. We mean you no harm. We do not accuse you of the crimes, merely of knowing who committed them."

The sailor slowly recovered his composure, but the boldness was gone from him. "So help me, God. I will tell you all I know, but I do not expect you to believe what I say. But I am innocent… I will tell all."

In substance, he told that he had recently made a voyage to Indian Archipelago and upon arriving in Borneo, he and a companion had captured an orangutan. This companion died and the animal became his exclusive possession. Upon his return to Paris, he lodged it safely in his residence in town, keeping it carefully secluded from neighbors, and in a room of its own under lock and key. It was his intention to sell the beast.

Upon returning home from some party on the night of the murders, he found the beast in his own bedroom… the animal having broken down the door of his room. With razor in hand, he was standing before the mirror attempting to mimic the antics of his master. Terrified at the sight of such a dangerous weapon in the hands of such an animal, he grabbed for his whip. Upon the sight of it, the orangutan sprang through the door of the chamber, down the steps, and through a window, into the street. Immediately he followed the ape, razor still in hand, down the street.

Fortunately, the streets were deserted as it was near three in the morning. Passing down an alley in the rear of the Rue Morgue, the beast's attention was caught by a gleaming light from the open window of Madam L'Espanaye's chamber, in the fourth story of her house. Rushing to the building, it clambered up the lightning rod with inconceivable agility, grasped the shutter, which was thrown open and by means, swung itself directly upon the headboard of the bed. The entire feat did not take more than a minute. The shutter was kicked open again by the orangutan as it entered the room.

Pleased at seeing the animal enter a confined area, the sailor, with great difficulty, decided to go after him. A sudden chill of horror crossed his brow, for he was seized with great fear as to what the animal might do with the razor he possessed. With desperation and strained energy, he climbed the lightning rod after the ape. Upon reaching the window he glimpsed inside and nearly fell from the sight that greeted his eyes. The daughter lay sprawled upon the bed. The lower portion of her gown was soaked in blood and her thighs were spread wide apart. Obviously, the animal had indulged himself in a fit of sexual frenzy, for the girl's canal looked as if it had been pulverized by a thick hard pole. The beast was then holding Madam by the hair and was flourishing the razor about her face in imitation of the motions of a barber. The screams and struggles of the lady (during which time the hair was torn from her head) changed the ape's mood from lightness to wrath. With one sweep of his muscular arm, he nearly severed her head from her body. The sight of the new blood inflamed his anger into frenzy. Gnashing his teeth and flashing fire from his eyes, he flew upon the girl and imbedded his nails into her throat, retaining its grasp until she expired. Slicing wildly and without aim, he severed the girl's breast from her chest. It fell slightly to the side. Another slice severed the nipple, which flew across the room. (The sailor didn't know quite where.) The beast, in savage fury lunged across the room and quite suddenly looked toward the window where his master stood, rigid with horror. The animal's anger suddenly changed to fear and he skipped about the chamber in agony of nervous confusion; throwing and breaking furniture as he moved, dragging the bed from the bedframe. In desperation, as if to hide something, he seized the corpse of the daughter and thrust it up the chimney where it was later to be found.

Returning to the mother, he mindlessly took the broom, snapped it in two, three, then four parts and solidly smacked a section up her vagina. Half crazy with fear of the whip, the ape picked the woman up. Her head hung nervelessly loose… then he hurled her through the open window.

As the ape approached the casement, he straightened out Madame L'Espanaye's mutilated body. The sailor ran in terror toward his house, dreading the consequences of the butchery and gladly abandoning the orangutan. The words heard by the witnesses were the sailor's exclamations of horror, co-mingled with the fiendish jabbering of the brute.

Having heard the entire story, we insisted the sailor accompany us to the police station. Here, my friend could not help but indulge in a sarcasm or two about the inability of the law enforcement to see beyond the obvious.

"You see, my friend," he stated to me in front of the Prefect of Police, "when reason and analysis is applied, the most astounding results will occur. I should be invited to lecture at this establishment. I should, but would decline, for to have words of wisdom fall upon the ears of the deaf is a most frustrating experience, one of which I can live joyfully without."

THE END

TRY, TRY AGAIN

by "Ann Gora"

Suck 'Em Up *Vol.4, No. 2 Oct./Nov. 1971*
(not on Ed's resume, but his)

TONY WAS REALLY WORRIED. Worried sick! He'd report to his desk job at the office and it was apparent there had been another series of sleepless nights. His eyes were beginning to sink deep into his skull and tremendous dark circles had given an empty socket, skull-like appearance and there was no color to the visible skin. His well-tailored suits began to hang around his shoulders like those on a scarecrow… and above all he had missed another two days work that week. That was six days in three weeks. The company wasn't going to put up with such things much longer.

Already there had been remarks about seeing a doctor, and when those became dull requests they were changed to read the legends of vitamins and perhaps a psychiatrist. That was the worst dig of all because Tony knew exactly what was wrong with himself. He simply wasn't getting any. He couldn't hold an erection in the past three months. Sex had flown out the window where he was concerned. And it wasn't because he couldn't get a girl. There were plenty of them around, and most found him quite attractive. But suddenly the girls left him cold. There they would be, naked and inviting on the bed… their legs spread wide apart and their breasts, firm young mounds, pink tipped orbs stretching for the ceiling… lips as red as the deepest sunsets… moist, luscious tongues which flicked across the lips… everything the setting required for the right atmosphere. Everything! Everything but his erection. As soon as the girls had taken their clothes off, discarded them to a chair beside the bed and stretched out naked on the bed, the feeling of sexual fires died like so much cold water had been poured upon them.

And he knew it would be like that way again as he ushered the girl, her name was Jeanie, into his lush apartment. It would happen all over again, but he couldn't give up trying. And Jeanie, whom he'd just met in his favorite cocktail lounge, was one of the prettiest he'd ever captured. She hadn't been an easy capture, but once she made up her mind she wanted him, she was ready and willing to go wherever he wanted her to go.

He locked the door behind them and gazed at the gorgeous creature dressed in the furry pink angora sweater and matching pink miniskirt. Her legs, encased in sheer nylons ended in shoes which curved to the curve of her dainty feet. She was all woman and there was no doubt about that. When he kissed her the erection was there and when he clung to her he jammed the bulging front of his trousers tightly into her crotch through the skirt. His hands drifted longingly through the fur of the sweater and down over the soft material at her rump, taking each cheek in turn... caressing... squeezing... Everything felt so good to him then.

Jeanie was only another in the long line of girls who had given him such an erection... such a feeling of delight, of longing, of pure anticipation. But as with all the others, she removed her clothes, putting the angora sweater over a chair and the skirt next to it. Then her sheer nylon panties and matching brassiere joined the other articles and she was naked and alluring on the white sheets of his bed and the bulge in his trousers fell to nothingness.

He took off his own clothes and laid down beside her. All the world became a bore. She worked on him for more than an hour. She used every trick in her womanly book and still his maleness refused to present itself. He was as flaccid as a limp worm held by one end. He slapped it several times and cursed it with all the vile names he could muster and Jeanie spread herself wider until she fingered herself for release. It was the only thing she could do! She had become worked up through the expectation of what this handsome man could do for her. Then nothing! And she was left high and dry. It was the only thing she could do!

Then Jeanie got out of the bed and crossed to his well-stocked bar where she poured a double shot of scotch. She wasn't ready to leave, to give up yet. She would give him another chance. But she had to fortify herself first. Scotch was a good fortifier she had found out over the years and through many sessions with the opposite sex.

But when she looked back across the room to the bed she felt the hope of that kind of a climax leaving her. He wasn't looking at her. He seemed to be looking through the chair where her clothing was. A vacant stare, and still his manhood lay limp and unused. She could only sigh and take another double shot. Then some of the hope came back. It wasn't the sight of his nakedness, but the force of the alcohol as it once more heated up her insides, alcohol had that effect on her! A false sense of security! A false sense of daring!

She knew there was something in that man, and she wanted that something in her. The third double shot of scotch and the clicking of the glass forced Tony's eyes to her direction.

"I'm sorry," he said slowly.

"How long has this been going on?"

"Three months."

"You must be starved."

"I've lost thirty pounds." He sat on the edge of the bed and looked to her. "You're one of the most beautiful girls I've ever met. If anybody could have done something with me, it would have been you. I guess that makes you my last chance. I might just as well go over to that window and jump out."

"The only thing that would prove is that you have guts. They'd be spread all over the sidewalk down there."

"I just don't know what to do. I get all worked up in the beginning... then... well you saw what happened. Just as soon as we're naked in bed I go soft all over and there isn't anything anybody can do for me."

"We'll try again," she said simply and finished off the rest of her drink. She then moved across to the bed and laid down beside him again.

He felt her hands, her lips, her tongue doing all the things they were supposed to do. All the things which had turned him on so furiously only three short months ago... three short months ago when Paula had been there. They'd come in and she was wearing only that white fox fur coat. She had nothing on underneath... and the weather had turned cold and she was still wearing the coat when he took her because the apartment heating had gone bad. It had been a tremendous affair. Then the heating was restored and Paula had removed the coat. That's when he felt the pangs deep in his chest and they were like a real hurt.

His manhood fell and with it all the powers he ever had for committing the act of sexual intercourse.

Jeanie tried for another half hour with the same results as the previous attempt. And this time she knew if she drank the entire bottle of scotch it would do no good even for her own prowess. Therefore she fingered herself once more for gratification and swung her legs over the edge of the bed. She sat there for a long moment, then after giving a great sigh she stood up, stretched and walked into the shower.

She took her time in the shower even though she wanted out of that apartment. She wanted out where she could find a man who would be addicted to her charms and she could be completely satisfied in the only way that kind of satisfaction could come. But she took her time letting the warm water sooth her aching body, then she took equally long in drying off and used some perfumed powder she found in the toilet closet.

She inched her steps across the bedroom, taunting the man with the move, but the same sigh escaped her lips as she sat down on the edge of the bed and drew her nylon panty hose over the nylon panties. She adjusted her brassiere, and she could feel Tony's eyes boring into her back. She stood up without looking at him and slipped into her shoes then skirt. She took a long time in letting the soft pink angora sweater drift down over her head and over the rest of her body.

Then she turned for one last look at Tony's limp member. She would have sighed again. But instead her eyes went wide. He was as stiff as any male she'd ever seen. Once more he was ready. And his body throbbed noticeably. His eyes were glassy and his tongue flicked across his dry lips. He couldn't take his eyes from her clothed body.

And Jeanie realized the score!

Quickly she removed the clothes and watched his stiff member shrink back to a limp worm. But she knew then the cause and she gathered up the clothing and tossed them on his stomach. The first touch brought his member erect.

"Put them on," she demanded…

Ready for anything, Tony rose up! First, he put on the pantyhose over the pink panties, then the brassiere. Slowly the skirt was fastened into place with Jeanie's help and she made him take a long time slipping the angora sweater down over his head. The front of his skirt stood out some distance in front. She laid him down and put her body beside his. Now they could make it and Tony knew he might have to spell his name "*Toni*" from then on.

THE END

THE LOSER

by "Shirlee Lane"

Not on Ed's resume, but an article in the magazine which is credited to "Ann Gora" reads like Ed. In Girl Mates *Vol.1 No.1 Gallery Press Sept./Oct. 1975*

MISS RILEY WAS THE ONE who caught them. She didn't make her presence known at that point, but she listened at the cubicle door. She was fifty and starting to shrivel up, but she still wanted some and none of the other girls in the office wanted anything to do with her. She never tried a sex promotion on them because their attitude had always proved they accepted her only as head of the department and not in any personal or friendly way. She hated them for that.

She hated the two girls behind the locked cubicle door. She could have turned right around and left the restroom as soon as she realized what was going on, but she didn't. She listened with hatred at first, then the hatred turned to interest, then to sexual fantasies. She might very well have stuck her finger into the leg of her own panties and brought on a relief of her own. But she didn't. She stood there and quivered, shook all over until she had to douse her face with cold water. The splashing told the girls within the cubicle that they had been discovered.

It wasn't until punch-in time the next morning that Terry Abernathy was summoned into Mr. Willowby's office. He had always been a kindly man, a delightful boss. He wasn't kindly that morning. His face was stern. He chewed on the end of his cigar. He didn't look up into the lovely girl's face for a long moment after she entered and had said, "You wanted to see me, Mr. Willowby?"

His red face turned into the grey of embarrassment.

"Errr, yes. I did, Miss Abernathy." He still didn't look up. "I do believe we have a rather difficult situation here."

"We do?"

"Yes… yes… yes… quite so! I'm given to understand a rather strange occurrence took place in the ladies restroom yesterday during the lunch period."

"Can I deny it?"

"There wouldn't be much point in doing that," he looked up. "Would there?"

"It wasn't Dena's fault. I sexed her into it."

"It makes little difference whose fault it was. Happenings such as that simply cannot be tolerated. I have no other choice but to terminate your employment immediately."

"I suppose it would be proper for me to say I understand. But I don't feel in a proper mood. If it had been some guy and a broad it would have been different."

"That isn't the question here. Two girls doing… what you were doing. Miss Abernathy, it's unthinkable."

"If it's so unthinkable, it would never have happened. Lesbian love is very 'thinkable'… quite the rage in some circles."

"Those circles do not include this office. Your check has already been prepared. You may pick it up from Miss Riley."

"Ahh, yes… Miss Riley… the dear old soul… perhaps you'd better get her retirement check ready. I wouldn't bet on how long it is before she takes on some new chick in the toilet… some little bitch who feels strongly for advancement, and doesn't mind the smell of an ancient crotch to get it."

"That will be enough of that."

"It sure will."

Terry turned sharply on her high heels and left the office. She stopped long enough to clean out her desk, slip into her long sleeved, white angora cardigan, sneer at Miss Riley as she picked up her check, then was gone. The local cocktail lounge was in the same building so she didn't have far to go before attempting to drown her emotions and to brood over losing Dena her job. She hadn't seen Dena that morning so she could only surmise that she had been the first one fired. The kid couldn't afford to have something like that done to her.

But screw it. They were both over twenty-one, not much over that age, but over it just the same, and they both knew what they were doing and what would happen if they were caught... they were caught and the consequences were paid.

"So what do you do now, Terry?" asked the bartender. She had told him she got fired but not the reason.

"Get drunk," she told him.

He grinned. "I mean after that."

"Suffer a hangover, then see what the world out there has to offer me."

"Good-looking broad like you shouldn't have much trouble in finding what you want."

"Don't kid yourself, Henry. It took me nearly a year the last time, even though I am an excellent secretary."

"Ever think about modeling? It's a good career and I hear they pay through the nose for girls that have a shape like you have," he winked then added... "and with a face to match."

"I don't like taking my clothes off."

"Never?"

"Well... hardly ever," she matched his grin, then giggled when she thought of those same words being sung in a Gilbert and Sullivan opera. Then she clouded over and lifted her martini. "Oh, I don't think I'll have too much trouble, Henry." She knew he wouldn't fully understand what she was going to say, but she said it anyway. Perhaps only for her own enjoyment in saying her own thoughts. After all, she understood, and that's all that was important to her. "I'm just a victim of social circumstances where that company is concerned. Someplace in this town there is a place for me... I mean a place which can understand what a girl must do sometimes. I don't mean simply *want* to do... *must* do."

It was true. Henry didn't understand. But then he didn't understand many of the things spoken by his clientele. He always kept his nose clean with, "Yeah... I guess you have a point there. We all go misunderstood sometimes." He filled her glass, watched her drink, then further watched her as she left the cocktail lounge.

Terry felt a little fuzzy from the martinis, not drunk or anything like that, but just fuzzy enough to know she didn't want to take the bus. She took a taxi. To hell with the cost. Taxi drivers had to make a living also. This driver put the make on her and she wanted to slap his face, but she didn't. She didn't tip him either when she got out in front of her apartment building. He went off angry, but that was his problem.

A long, hot bath followed her entrance into the apartment, then a telephone call to her friend Doris Lyles. "What happened this time?"

"The same old thing. I got caught."

They continued their conversation when Doris entered Terry's apartment a half an hour later and poured herself a drink. "When are you going to learn to keep that cunt in your panties when you're on the job?"

"Dena made me so hot I couldn't help myself."

"How many jobs is this now?"

"Five! But this one lasted a year."

"That doesn't pay the rent when it comes due on the first, sweet thing."

"I won't be hurting for a while. This job wasn't the greatest, you can bet on that. There's always another just around the corner."

"That is, if you know which corner to look around. Hey girl, have you looked at the state of the economy lately?"

"That doesn't bother me. What does, is what do I want to do? I don't want to take just another job. I've got to be where I have some freedom of action. Look, Doris! I've got a right to be happy too, and when I spend eight or nine hours on some job, I want to get some enjoyment out of that too. That's a lot of life you spend at an office."

Doris deliberately moved to the couch and sat very close to the lovely, blonde Terry and just as deliberately she let her hand brush aside the sheer negligee which had been snuggled across her legs. "Sure it is, but you're not going to find any office that gives you blowjob time in the restroom... even if it is your lunch hour. That kind of lunch you'd better confine right here to your own apartment... or mine." Her hand moved to the golden mound of pubic hair and caressed the soft strands with delicate fingers. Terry slowly lay back and opened her legs.

"I like that," she cooed.

"I know you do." She pulled the negligee away from Terry's luscious breasts with her free hand. Her lips went to each of the nipples and her tongue flipped over them with talented swipes. Her searching fingers found the clit and she took it between her middle and index fingers. She worked on it expertly. She began to tremble when she felt Terry's body first go limp then tighten.

Terry was breathing hard when she crossed her legs tightly so as to increase the pressure of Doris' fingers. If she could live that moment forever it would be all she could ask from life. Nothing held so much enjoyment for her than to have the delicate hand of another woman caressing her, to have the soft, velvet tongue of another woman on her breasts, her lips, her vagina.

She knew it wouldn't last. She knew that within moments, extremely short moments, her legs would stiffen out in front of her and she would bite into her lower lip until it almost bled and she would scream the screams of ultimate pleasure and she would shoot her load until Doris' hand was sticky and wet. Then she would relax, but only for a moment. Doris would be ready. Doris always came last. She wanted it that way. Doris wanted to bring her lover to a full, blown climax before having herself taken care of. The excitement of listening to her lover breathing hard, giving little sounds of sexual throes, then the final scream and the blasting off was the big turn on for the pretty brunette. It had always been that way, even before Terry came into her life.

"Want to stay the night?" asked Terry as they later showered together.

"I'd like to, but I can't tonight. My father's coming into town. And as always he's only going to stay a couple of hours and has to see me… and I have to see him. He pays the bills, you know. So when daddy calls… dutiful daughter heeds the call. Rain check?"

"Always!"

They dried each other off and Terry helped her beautiful friend dress. Terry was nearly turned on again as her hands brushed Doris' breasts and especially as her fingers drifted through the mound of hair as she slipped on the girl's panties. "Ohhhh, you do have something about you!"

Doris blinked and grinned. "Drives you up the walls, does it, sweetie?"

"More than I care to think about right at this minute, you bitch!" And they kissed each other with their tongues lashing back and forth.

"You're no slouch at this business either, lover." Doris backed off. "And I'd better be going before I change my mind and take you up on the night's lodging."

"When do I see you again?"

"Tomorrow, unless daddy decides to stay over, which he never does."

"I'll count the hours."

"That sounds like a bad movie script."

"I mean it."

"I know you do." Doris leaned in so that their lips met again, and they held for a long time, with each stretching out a hand to grope the other—tenderly—sexually—a promise of things to come.

Neither had to say another word. Doris turned from Terry and the door closed behind her.

Terry did not look forward to the rest of the day or the coming night. It would be long hours before she was being held tightly by the velvet-like arms of Doris, having her body explored over and over again by the soft fingers. There was even the deep thrill in just thinking about what had happened and what would happen again the next day, and many successive days in the future.

She laid back on the couch and explored her own love tunnel—but it was not enough. She drifted off to sleep and when once more she awoke it was night and her doorbell was ringing. She tied the negligee around her with a fluffy belt, pushed the long hair back out of her eyes and nearly went into shock when she opened the door.

"What are you doing here?" she asked Miss Riley.

"I've come to see you."

"I can see that... so what the hell do you want? Haven't you caused me enough trouble?"

"I like lesbians. I thrive on lesbians."

"Well you're damned well not going to have me, you stinking old bitch."

"I don't want you for myself. Can you ever fathom why I told on you... why I had you fired?"

"Because you're a damned old faggot, that's why."

"I have a very profitable business on the side. You might say I recruit right there in the office... lovely young girls... girls who love girls. I watch, and I choose... and I don't mind using a little blackmail to see that they do things my way. I have many ladies who love young beauties like yourself. You see, I'm going to make you happy. You'll be able to work the way you always wanted to. Think of it! Sex every day... all day. You're hired, my dear... and I know you won't deny my offer."

THE END

HOOKER BY CHOICE

by "Ann Gora"

in Goddess *Vol.1 No. 2 Nov./Dec. 1972*

FRIDAY NIGHT. It was always a good night on the street. Saturday night was just as good. But Stella liked Friday night the best of all. That's the night the factory paid their workers and they all went to the check cashing stands and certain bars to get their paper changed into the coin of the realm... that spending money which was so important for the sustaining of life... the stuff they worked all week to acquire.

Stella knew every place in the small town where those checks could be cashed. And she got to know a lot of the workers which were interested in what she had to sell.... Yet the best part was the great turnover of workers.

Except for the real old-timers who had moved to the factory when it first opened right after World War II, there was a great change over in the personnel. They were easy to pick from the others. Most had no family. They moved into the one room cabins and the hotels when there were rooms for them. They liked the hotel better than the cabins because there was the telephone and the hot and cold running water and the electricity and the heat which was all taken care of in the rent. The cabins were different. Everything was separate and had to be registered for by the renter... and there was always the huge deposit. The utility people weren't dumb. They knew well the turnover and they could easily look back into their books and see how many thousands of dollars were still owed by those who had skipped.

The newcomers were always reluctant to put up those huge deposits... most of them didn't have it in the first place. They were lucky to have gotten as far as the town and the factory in the first place... there would be two weeks from the time they started until their first paycheck… that was cause enough for many to sleep in the park on the outskirts of town and in the railroad yard… and even the dump… wherever they could find a box or something to cover them and somewhat protect them from the elements.

And there they would stay until some cash was in their pocket and they could make the move to a place with a real roof over their head. During that first two-week period the only real horror to those living outside in the elements was when it rained… and it rained a lot in Willowsport.

Stella, although an old hand at her profession, hardly looked her thirty-two years. She dressed the part… never too daring… but always in clothing designed for the girl in her early twenties, and she was an artist when it came to makeup. She had once been a hairdresser and that was an easy job every Wednesday afternoon for her… that's the day, the entire day she put aside for doing her hair and making all the tinting and curling which was necessary.

She would remain twenty-five for the next ten years. She was positive of that… that is, if she didn't take on too many customers in any too short a period of time.

Hairdressing had been a lot of bullshit. But she had leaned in that direction during her high school years and it was only natural that she went into it when she graduated.

Hell's fire! She could make more in three hours on a Friday or a Saturday night doing what she liked than she could by working at the beauty parlor all week… and she didn't appreciate working on the ratty heads of those old bitches anyway. It seemed to her that every one of those broads married to the steady factory workers were old before their time. They all had a house full of kids… house apes all of them…. Perhaps some of that would change when the cable came through and the television reception was improved.

But until that time the old man would come home, eat his supper and hop into the sack with the old woman. They might be Stella's age, but they sure as hell looked like the old woman who lived in the shoe… and she wouldn't blame their condition on the hard winters and the wet summers. There was only one thing which brought on age like that and that was night after night in the sack getting pumped and then letting the stuff lay in there until another brat was born.

With the amount of kids each family had in that town, Stella figured if anything ever happened to the factory and they were forced to go on relief the country would soon be broke. God forbid such a happening. Relief would also be disastrous for her business. They wouldn't be able to afford her services any longer.

God, what in the hell would she do in such an event? But that was a thought she seldom ever permitted to enter her mind. That was a something which couldn't happen. But she saved a great portion of her money anyway.

It wasn't only the transients that she catered to. There were a lot of the regulars around the town which looked her up. Once they had their pile of kids they got bored with the whole affair.

"Every time I stick it into her, out pops another kid." That was a line she'd heard over and over again. And she would girlfriend them and pat their head and be most tender. And she would say all the words they wanted to hear. And when they left her small cabin which was directly on the end of the bus line, they felt they had been well serviced and went home much happier for the session. How they accounted for the money they had spent she never knew... and couldn't give a damn.

She had something to sell, and if they wanted to buy it then they damned well were going to pay for it.

Stella sold love. She sold feigned understanding. She sold her breasts and she sold her mouth and her pussy. She sold her body to whoever could pay for it. And she sold them any particular type of service they wanted. She had never been with a woman for sex. But if there was a woman who wanted her and had the price, Stella wouldn't turn her out into the cold. Not by a long shot. She'd take her into the warm bed and the fires would be turned on the same as she would turn up the sex furnaces for any man.

However, her eyes were always on those newcomers. She'd watch them come into town. She'd watch them go to the employment office. And she always knew when they were hired. She didn't have to make any contacts on the inside, in the employment office to find out. She could tell by the expressions on their faces when they came out. Most of the time they carried the little yellow paper in their hand, the slip telling them to report the following Monday. They always began on Monday... the closest one to the first and the fifteenth of every month.

Those hired on the first found their paycheck waiting for them on the fifteenth, and those hired on the fifteenth found their paychecks waiting on the first... on the closest Friday... and they also found Stella waiting for them on both dates.

Stella felt sorry for many of those who found they were not suited for the job and were turned away… but only those she wanted to take into her bed. The others, the tramps, they could all go to hell. She was particular in who she took among those newcomers. Some of them could be mighty mean… especially if they got a lot of liquor in them.

Which was another entity she watched carefully. She never took a guy who was overly drunk… and she never allowed more than three drinks during any one session. She'd kept her good looks all those years and she wasn't about to let some pig of a drunk knock her around. Her teeth were excellent and all in their proper place, and that's where she was going to keep them come hell or high water. Money couldn't replace what God had taken such care in giving her.

"I could get three broads for the price you charge, girl!" That was another statement she'd heard over and over again. There was a simple stock answer. "Then get them." She knew it was all a pile of crap. Perhaps they could get a bunch of tramps for some cheap price where they came from. But Stella was one of four girls handling all the trade in the town. She felt the other three weren't as good, as pretty, as perfect at their trade as she, but they were all good girls and they worked together as far as keeping the price at the same level. They all charged the same amount for the same amount of time given. Ten dollars a half hour… and the money was regulated up or down according to the time limit. However, they figured fifty dollars was enough to charge the characters if they wanted to go the whole night.

Stella liked the whole night routines because most of them could only get it up twice, then they would fall asleep and she could either sneak out for a while and get a quickie on the side, or if she felt she wanted to rest, she too could lay back, sleep and feel secure in the fact that she had made a good nights wages and didn't have to work very hard for it.

"What's a good lookin' girl like you doin' in a ratty business like this?"

"Making money, buster, making money. Now, do you want to make the scene, or do you want me to lay here all night and listen to the words coming out of your mouth?"

"For ten bucks a half hour, I got a lot of things I want you to do with your mouth."

"Then let's get at it, buster… let's get at it. Time goes mighty swift when you're enjoying yourself."

Then there would always be the very young ones, generally the offsprings of the fathers she had taken on over the years. Papa had sent them to her for their training. After all, she was a professional and they would learn quickly what it was all about… and it would save Papa all the embarrassment of attempting to spell it out himself.

"Pa sent me."

"Yeah, he told me last week you might be dropping by. You got the money with you?"

"Sure."

And the bashful youth would reach down deep into his pocket… much deeper than the pocket could ever stretch, and his hand would come up with the five or ten. She had never gotten more than a ten from any one of those kids. She had to work fast to give them a lifetime of training in such a short period of time. But she was good at it… yet she always felt that if one of them would come up with a twenty or a fifty she'd send the newly elated boy out into the world much better equipped.

"Okay, boy," she'd order. "Drop your pants and let's see what in hell your dad's so proud of."

"Drop my pants?"

"That's the way it's done, buster."

"Do I have to?"

"You might just as well get used to it here and now… because when you leave this room you'll be craving to take them pants off in front of every girl you meet."

"I never."

"Of course not, you never…. But you will."

And then she was at the buckle of the belt or the strap of the overalls and before the kid knew it, he was standing there stark naked in front of a naked woman for the first time in his life and it would never be the same from that time forward. The female body would be his entire lure in life. He would work, he would slave, he might even go hungry just to please the woman or women of his choice… he would have a lust that would last to nearly the day he died… most of them.

Strange as it may seem, most of the fifty dollar sessions came from older men… those in their sixties and early seventies… few survived the cold winters after they reached the age of seventy. But then it wasn't strange really that the older men wanted the all-night treatment. It took them all night to do what they used to do all night.

Stella didn't mind the older trade even if they did smell of old age. They never knew why she did what she did but she always made them take a long shower or bath and then she sprinkled them with perfume. She had all the excuses which were necessary and none of them ever balked at the treatment.

"I like sweet smelling people."

"Just as long as you get this stuff off me before I go home again. Somebody along the way might think I'm some kind of a sissy… then too, Ma sure as hell would know I was playing with you or one of them other three."

"What you ought to do is gather Ma up out of her wheelchair and drag her over here to watch, give her some new ideas… bet it would give her a whole new lease on life."

"It would put her in the cemetery."

"You mean to tell me you think she don't know that you're out sowing some ancient wild oats?"

That was another question she had put to them from time to time and they never had a straight answer.

Every woman in the town knew their men went to see one or more of those four hookers. Perhaps there was some jealousy involved, but it never came to light. There was never a beating because of it… no murders… perhaps it was because when the men were away it gave the wives a bit more chance for some honest rest… and they weren't being pronged and they stood no chance of getting knocked up all over again. In fact, if one were to stand close to many of the bedroom windows around the town they might well have heard great sighs of relief on those special nights.

"You doing any good tonight, Stella?"

"Three in the sack so far, Doris, and the night is still young…. How about you?"

"Guess they're going for pink tonight. I wear my new knitted pink pants suit and they have been dragging me off for half a dozen fifteen minuters. By this time Sunday night I'll be rich. Maybe I'll even go up to Freemont and see what the big trade is all about."

"You've been going up to Freemont ever since I've known you. How come you just never get on the train and go?"

"Oh, I got the cash alright. You know that. We all get good cash on the weekends and I sure could go if I could."

"You could if you could? Now what kind of talk is that, Doris?"

"I mean I work so hard that by Sunday night all I want to do is curl up in my bed and go to sleep and by the time I wake up Monday night I guess I just don't feel up to no long trips. Besides, there's a lot of servicing to be done here."

"You can say that again."

Then Stella would spy the curly blond headed youth she'd been trailing since he arrived on the first and she knew his hot little hands held that white pay envelope and she waited until he cashed the check and stuffed the hundred and sixty-eight dollars into the pocket of his jeans before she made her approach. There was nothing in making a success of the approach. Stella was a professional all the way. She never lost a trick when she set her mind to it.

After all, what kind of entertainment was there in such a small factory town? There was a show that changed pictures once a week, and a bottle shop and two beer bars. Stella felt it was so much better giving those boys something that was pure human nature… and didn't all the books and papers say that doing what you do in bed was really very healthy?

Stella wanted to keep that town a very healthy place in which to live and work.

THE END

Filth Is the Name For a Tramp

by "Ann Gora"

on Ed's resume originally published in Body & Soul *Vol.6 #1
Feb/Mar. 1972*

MALA DIDN'T LIKE that end of town. It was much too dark. Of course the darkness should have been her friend. It hid a multitude of sins… her sins. But she was frightened of the dark. She had been ever since she was a small child and had accidentally been locked in a closet for several hours… the several hours her mother had been out of the house and until her return. But she needed the darkness now… she needed it as a cover for her professional advancements.

The bright lights of Barkley Avenue were only half a mile behind her and to the left. But she was going another half mile ahead of her and to the right of Armount Street where there would be more bright lights… and another section of theatres and bars showing topless and bottomless performances and *skin flicks*.

Going the short mile through the warehouse district alley would save her cab fare and if she had to walk the connecting brighter streets she would be walking more than five miles. Time was money to Mala. The more time she spent on her feet the less time she would have on her back… making money.

At least her mind told her these things.

There had been no action on Barkley Avenue at all that night and she had been hustling since just before dark… seven o'clock. There had been a couple of bum passes in her direction, but no one she thought could pay her tab. After all she wasn't any three buck hustler. She hadn't earned less than thirty bucks a trick in the two years she'd been on the stem… and in most cases her price hit fifty to seventy-five bucks. She could easily spot the John who had enough in his wallet to pay to score with her.

How her mind loved to live in the past.

Beautiful! Blonde! A divine figure in the tight red satin cocktail dress… her ankles so well turned over the plastic high heeled shoes. A white angora stole draped carefully over one shoulder. Mala was a beauty! To the guy who could afford her one might feel also went the luck of the Gods. He was going to have a rare treat. She didn't allow much rough stuff. But the John's seldom ever wanted to play rough with her. Those that did found themselves going out the door quicker than they had entered it.

She often did walk the lighted streets.

The clicking of her high heels on the empty street made a hollow echoing sound which bounced against factory walls on one side of the alley then traveled across the space again and repeated over and over until the sound died out in the distance. Only the sound didn't die. Only each individual sound died, because there was a continuous motion to putting her feet down and the heels rekindled the ether waves.

A slight shiver raced through her body. It wasn't cold and her angora stole was sufficient against any summer chill. But the shiver came twice more. She stopped suddenly. She cocked her ear first one way, then another. She didn't know in the least what she might be listening for… but listen she did. There was no sound except very distant automobiles, almost completely muffled by the distance.

There had been more than some kind of feeling that she had heard sound. One can feel sound as well as hear it…she'd always believed that. The same way with sight. Many optical illusions could play tricks on the sight patterns. But there was nothing strange to be seen any more than there were any strange sound. All the shadows appeared to be in the right places. All the sounds of which there were none, were in the proper perspective.

She moved forward a few more steps, then stopped again. She realized in that moment what the whole problem was. There was no sound. Not even the distant automobiles. At least there should have been a car or a rat racing about, causing some sort of sound or some sort of movement to the shadows. But the shadows were silent… as silent as sound itself. It was as if the world had suddenly stopped and she was captured in some vacuum.

She forced herself on for several steps more just to make sure that she could still hear. Her heels made the same hollow clicking sounds on the cement and she was satisfied. She stopped again. This time she made a full turn... very slowly so that she looked all around her.

The beautiful girl thought about screaming. But what in hell would she be screaming about? She shook her head against the silly panic, then screwed her face up in a grotesque mask which she forced her thoughts to believe was a smile. The grotesque smile made her face hurt. As is if the creases were being formed through completely dry skin. She let the grin fade. It was no grinning matter.

It never was anything but a serious matter.

Then she didn't even want to hear the click of her own heels on the cement. She started believing that the panic introduced might go away. If she could sneak through the deserted street unheard. She attempted not to make a sound. But in so doing she could hear her own intake of breath. She tried holding her breath, but she had never been one much for doing that. She couldn't even stay under water more than a second or two. She had tried it over and over again, but once she had submerged she'd pop almost immediately to the top again.

She let the air rush up in a gush, then breathed a bit more easily as she slowed her silent footsteps. After all it had not been the first time she had walked through the deserted streets... or alleys, or warehouse districts.

The first time had been a warehouse district. She'd taken a John in the back seat of his car. She gave him a complete round the world trips for a stinking twenty bucks. Then when he had her do everything to him and he was satisfied, he zipped up his pants and kicked her out of the car and drove off, leaving her in the deserted (*or so she thought*) warehouse district. She had worn no brassiere, and the cardigan sweater was open down the front when she was forced out of the car. But worse than that, her skirt and panties were in the car. She was naked from the waist down.

But there had been nothing she could do about it at that moment except button the sweater and pull it down and attempt to make it appear more like a very short mini dress. She wished she had a belt and her eyes kept looking down to the dark street in front of her where she might find, perhaps, a length of rope, or something she could tie the sweater down with.

That's when the attack came.

The stinking wino jumped out of a tight section between two buildings. He had a knife. Silently, and with his stinking breath assailing her nose he buried his scabbed lips over hers and forced his thick maggot-like tongue into her mouth.

He took her violently.

She didn't faint from the violence of his attack, but she did have to pass out from the smell of the creature, and it was daylight when she came to again. She was a complete mess from the street dirt, and the smell of the creep had remained with her. She ached all over and it took her some time, and with the help of a wall to pull herself to her feet. She knew she was still naked but she could care less... and it would seem the taxi driver she hailed cared even less. All he wanted to know was if she had the fare or not. He would get it at her apartment. He had other ideas about his tip and perhaps at another time she might have given it to him. She had given it to taxi drivers in the past who had gone along with her. But she was hurting too much that morning.

She had gone through the alleys many times before. She had suffered the cold. And she had suffered the rain. There were other attacks. She'd lived through them. There would be others and she'd live through them. She had what every one of those creeps wanted.

But each time she felt the same feeling of eyes watching her. Eyes staring from the blackness. Each time she felt that silence and she felt the panic. But what was there really to worry about? She had what she wanted. And she'd lived through it. She always did.

The voice came from the darkened corner of one of the buildings.

"Maybe I could find five dollars!" It was a very deep... very husky voice.

Mala slowly turned in the direction of the voice. Generally she could distinguish the darker shadow of the human form even in the black shadows cast by the building. This time she couldn't.

"What makes you think I'm some kind of a five dollar whore?"

"You was some kind of a high priced whore you wouldn't be working this shitty warehouse alley."

"Maybe I'm only out getting some fresh air."

"Maybe you'd shit if you eat regular."

"Shut your filthy mouth."

"No shit talks to me like that."

Mala squeezed her legs tightly together. She felt the safety and the security of the four-inch blade she had strapped to the inside of her leg.

She started to move on slowly, but her eyes remained on the dark shadows where she felt the voice had come from. She walked ever so slowly.

"Five dollars," the voice taunted.

"Wipe your ass with it." She did not stop her forward movement.

"I'd like to wipe your pussy with it."

"I wouldn't waste my time."

"Five bucks buys a lot of wine."

"Not the kind I drink."

"Alley sluts can't be choosers."

"Slap your balls a couple of times and maybe you can skin your own banana."

"Hey, you got a real mouth, ain't you! Maybe I'd like to try that on for size too."

Mala stopped and with defiant hands on her hips she turned to face the deep black which was some distance behind her by that time. But still the human shadow hadn't presented itself.

"How to hell black are you?"

"What's that to a street tramp?"

"I just wonder which is blacker. You or the shadows you're hiding in. Or are you some kind of grotesque monster that's afraid to show himself?"

"You sure do have the big words. Maybe you got other things just as big. Maybe you got big things I'd like to see! I'd like to play with!"

"You ain't got the guts. All you got is a black space to hide in. You're the kind that goes around writing on shithouse walls then going off and jerking off."

"I could slit your throat for saying things like that."

Mala rubbered her legs together again. She felt much like a cricket might when it is making the sounds of the night. Only her sounds were silent and comfortable over the blade. "Not from that distance you can't."

"Why don't you come over here?"

"Now I know you must be endowed with the looks of a beast. Would I be repulsed at the sight of you?"

"Five dollars will give you a look."

"Now I should pay you five dollars?"

"Maybe I'm such a monster you'd enjoy giving me five dollars for a look… and another ten to take me on."

Mala turned and started along the street again. She felt the sweat going down the back of her neck having originated in the roots of her neck hairs. Only it was no longer the fear of panic or fright. She was angry. She liked the creeps to jump out of the dark at her. Then she knew what to do with them. But when they stood in the darkness and voiced their heads off. That made her angry. There had been a few like that. Only a few. She became violent at such creatures. They should all jump out of the darkness at her. She always knew what to do to them.

She then felt the presence behind her… getting closer. But there was still no sound of other footsteps. But she knew he was coming up behind her.

It was simple for her to reach down and capture the blade in her hand. But the time was not ripe as yet. Such moves had to be sudden… deliberate… unsuspecting. It was the only way to take such creatures, always much stronger than her. But it was like the old saying. The bigger they come, the harder they fall.

"You play it right, bitch whore, and maybe I'll let you walk out of this alley in one piece."

Mala kept walking, but at a slower pace. She kept her eyes straight ahead, as if she was searching for that bright spot a half a mile ahead.

"You ain't so smart… so brave when I'm so close… are you?" The voice was directly behind her and Mala could feel the hot breath on her neck. He was very close indeed.

"Now maybe I'm really going to try you on for size… just see how you and me fit together." Mala was still silent. "From the looks of the back of you… maybe I'll even take a trip around your back door. You'd look so good in a bed. But I like the dirt. I like alley floors. I like you under me. I take you on top of me. I like you on the alley floor. That's where I like you best. That's where I've liked all of them… On the alley floor… all that white skin and those fancy clothes getting all torn and dirty and shitty from the crap and the crud on the alley floor. It's all best when everything is so dirty."

Mala did everything she knew she must. The same thing she had done so many times before. She knew what the creep held in his hand… ready for instant action when he would push her to the ground. Only Mala knew all those actions.

She suddenly doubled over and the blade was in her hands instantly and in the same instant she turned and what he was holding in his hands detached itself from his lower quarters and it lay there like a dead, bleeding worm in his grip.

His wide eyes didn't see much more because the blade slit deep into his throat and cut from ear to ear.

Mala didn't bother for the creep to drop. She turned and slowly made her way along the nearly silent alley. Some of the sound had returned. There had been the dull plop of the body falling behind her. But that was all. Her heels soon picked up the rhythm they had once before, and they continued on to the end of the alley without faltering. There had been no others ahead of her otherwise she would have felt the silent eyes upon her and she would have listened to the silence of the sound.

Then at the end of the alley, just before it met the bright lights of Armount Street she turned and looked back along the darkness behind her. She reached down into the rubble and took up a discarded cloth which she wiped the blade clean with, then fastened it once more to her leg. Then slowly she made her way back into the alley. After all. It was a long time until dawn. The creep's body wouldn't be found before then. She had plenty of time to see if she couldn't attract another customer.

THE END

CLOSET QUEEN

no author listed

in Male Lovers *Vol.3 no. 2 June/July 1971 on Ed's resume 1971*

CARTER WINSTON HATED the name Closet Queen, but that's exactly what he was. He'd always felt that the powers that be who had gone up the toilet trail before him certainly could have had more of an imagination when labeling people's actions. He knew he could have thought up a better name. Of course he'd tried, at times, but mind weary he'd always put it aside to another day, and when that day came, there was always a future day to advance the procedure.

Closet Queen indeed!

Carter Winston simply knew where the goodies could be located. Besides, he wasn't the only one who frequented the toilet areas for his dessert. He knew many others like himself. But he sure as hell hoped that the others wouldn't find out too quickly about the new source. He'd been lucky three times already that week. Even the fuzz hadn't caught onto the new base of operation. A really nice, clean place. A janitor came in twice a day to clean up and put the perfumed disinfectant cakes in the urinals. There had been a lot of other places which he had frequented over the years where the urine and fart smells almost took his mind off the business at hand... or was it in hand?

But not the men's room at the Le Grande Theatre. It was always *spit and polish* clean and perfumed. It hadn't always been that way. Only for the past three weeks, since the new owners took over and apparently were doing their best to make the theatre a *Le Grande place* to come. Not only was the place clean and smelling delicious, but the lights were subdued. None of the ordinary glaring white globes. Purple brilliance shrouded the room in the most restful illumination any person could want. Especially a homosexual person like himself.

There were three toilet stalls with doors which locked on the inside, and there were three urinals against the far wall. That, of course, was the pick-up area. Generally, it was the pick-up area. But someone, before his finding the place, had a bit more imagination. A hole, just the right size for a rather large penis, had been bored through the shielding between the first and second stalls. The edges of the hole were sandpapered smooth for easy sliding, and a neat sign in perfect plastic painted letters told the legend… "TRY ME."

The first time he'd seen it, almost three weeks before, he did just that. And there was no hesitation from the other stall. However, it wasn't all quite that simple. No one simply shoved their dick into a hole because a sign said to. At least not Carter Winston. He liked what he had too much. There had been lots of fun between him and his manhood for a lot of years and he hoped to keep it in the same healthy condition for a lot more years to come. Once he'd heard about a guy doing something like that, and the creep on the other side stuck a hat pin through the head and there the poor guy hung screaming until an attendant came and unpinned him. Undoubtedly the poor fellow was never the same again. Carter Winston wasn't about to let something like that happen to him. It was a horrible thought. A hat pin stuck straight through it on one side of the wall and he on the other, and no way of getting at that pin or pulling his john through.

That first time he'd shuddered with that horrible thought until he felt the warm caresses of lips and tongue. But there had been some preliminaries involved. He'd followed a young fruit, at least he was quite sure the fellow was a fruit, into the restroom. Then he stood back as the young man unzipped his fly and did his business at the urinal. But when he was through he didn't zip up his pants. Out of the corner of his eye the man cased Carter, and while Carter watched from the first urinal, the boy's erection seemed to be created from out of sheer magic.

Carter suddenly matched him in size, and silently they went each into a booth and that's when Carter saw the small hole and the sign for the first time. It had been a most pleasant experience, and then he reciprocated in kind as the fellow put his muscle through. The doors were later opened and both went on about their business. There hadn't been a word spoken.

The same type of affair had happened several times during those three weeks, including the three times that very week. It was so much easier doing things in that way. No words, no introductions, no complications. Previously there had always been so much fuss made, especially by the bum boys who hung around the toilets expecting to be paid for their servicing. A quarter would have been too much for all of them. Then, too, they usually turned out to be troublemakers. And homosexuals like Carter Winston needed as little trouble as possible. Besides it was probably one of those type of creeps who thought up the hat pin routine. If he never saw another one of those gag artists, it would be too soon.

"You must like this picture," grinned the pretty ticket girl when she punched up his ticket and shoved it across to him. "It's the fourth time this week, isn't it?"

"I didn't think anyone was counting." Carter Winston didn't smile. But the realization of what she had said cut into his mind and stayed there. He thought of it all the time he was crossing the lobby then searching for a seat in the darkened theatre. It had been four times that week and the picture only changed once a week. But then maybe she did think he liked the picture. How could she possibly know that he spent a leisure two hours in the men's room performing the services of fellatio, and in many cases being fellated in return? "Damned nosey busybodies," he muttered to himself as he put his elbow up on the cushioned seat and buried his chin in his hand. He was looking at the screen, but wasn't seeing the movie. He never did! "She's much too young to know what that part of life is all about. But, then I don't know. These young kids! They know more than their own mothers and fathers these days. Or at least they think they do. They know the words, but what do they really know?" He pouted in his silent thought.

Any other time he wouldn't have sat that long in the auditorium. Usually he got the urge to get to the toilet almost immediately when he sat down. After all, that was his complete reason for paying the two bucks over and over again. He honestly hated movies, unless it was a sex picture. The Le Grande hadn't shown any of that variety as yet. Truth of the matter was he didn't even know the title of the picture his eyes were watching and not seeing.

The little bitch in her tight-fitting sweater and miniskirt had really turned him off and he didn't like that at all. He'd looked forward to that next affair all night. He'd hardly slept a wink. He'd even taken another day off work, and didn't have much sick leave left for that year. He felt he could strangle the blue-eyed blonde without any compunctions at all. In fact, he knew he could kill her and spit on her grave while she was rotting in it. He'd even add the worms. The stinking little bitch.

But in his prolonged anger he felt the steam going from his brain, down through his chest and centering in his groin where the fires heated up his testes, then shot through the shaft until his manhood stood rigid and throbbing in his pants. He put his hand down to it and realized that in his anger at the girl he had been really turning himself on. It had just taken a little longer, that was all. He'd never been turned on through anger before and the sensations were all new to him. Strange what will turn a guy on at times.

The only thing that could go wrong, or further wrong, was the possibility of no one going to the rest room. But there was always somebody who had to go sooner or later. All he had to do was wait them out.

His eyes roved over the theatre and there was a goodly crowd for that early in the afternoon. And there were several more males than females. Sooner or later nature was bound to call some of them. He rubbed himself and felt the thing throbbing, expanding and retracting in the demand for release. But he didn't hurry. He let his eyes move around the theatre several more times, attempting to pick out a likely subject to whom he could send mental telepathy messages. It had worked before. Several times he'd spotted someone that he found particularly interesting and, with his full concentration directed to the fellow, it was only a matter of a moment or two before he got up and made his way to the upstairs lounge and into the rest room. Carter figured he had a powerful mind.

But either the theatre was darker than usual, or his anger at the sweater girl in the ticket booth didn't permit him to focus his mind as properly as it should.

Once more he cursed her, then took his hand away from the front of his trousers and rubbed his eyes until he saw stars. When he opened the lids again he calmly waited until the pure black and the stars disappeared and moved his eyes slowly to the left of the auditorium, where a tow-headed youth finally captured his attention. The boy didn't see the action. His eyes were fastened to the screen action and his chin was cupped into both his hands. There was a complete tenseness about him.

No matter how hard Carter Winston concentrated on the young man, he did not twitch. Perhaps he was too engrossed in the film. Then again perhaps Carter's mind wasn't at its fullest concentration point. Incidents like that had happened to him before. At work there were many times he'd tried to concentrate on his business at hand but there were outside influences which hampered the ambitious drives. The blonde in the booth must have been the distracting factor. And once more he cussed her, and that time almost aloud. The mushy sounds came out as a bubbling of saliva in both corners of his lips.

He took his eyes momentarily from the towhead and looked carefully around. He knew he'd almost spoken aloud, but didn't really know how loud the sounds had been. He wanted to make sure no one had heard him and thought he was some kind of a babbling idiot. No one had heard a thing. But, also no one was heading in the direction of the stairs which led to the lounge.

Once more Carter Winston directed his eyes back to the screen. For the first time he was actually seeing the film. Slowly he came forward a bit in his chair. He rested both his elbows tightly on the arms of the seat. His eyes opened in pure amazement. The silver screen flashed back the scene of two handsome young men. One a blond and one a brunette. Both were stark-ass naked and their arms were around each other, their bodies tight together. Both had a full erection, and they looked at each other a long time before one of them lifted his hand up behind the other's neck and their lips met and their tongues slashed in a wild orgy-like kiss. Then they were sinking down to a black velvet covered bed.

Carter Winston blinked again and again. Was this the film which had been showing all week? Something deep in his brain told him it had to have been. A scene here and there registered in the void and he knew he'd seen them before. But they had never connected before. The owners of the Le Grande had not only redecorated the theatre, but had changed their policy of entertainment. They had switched to adult films. He was watching one of the roughest homosexual affairs he'd ever watched. He'd never seen such on the screen before. But there had been many *live* scores which had presented themselves to him.

First the two on the screen were tender, all loving, then they were as rough as two truck drivers or coal miners…. But the finishing climactic push made everything right.

The end title shot across the screen and Carter remained in the same rigid position, stunned, shocked, unable to move or speak. It was even hard for him to breathe. Then just before the film started again he noticed the towheaded boy get up and make his way toward the rear of the auditorium… back where the lounge stairs were. He'd only seen this through the corner of his eye, but he was positive his mental message had gotten through. Throughout the film his erection had remained rigid. The film itself had kept him turned on. But he also felt that much of the first message to the boy had remained with him, although he didn't remember it. All he could remember was the scene on the screen. However, the message had gotten through. The towhead had gone back toward the lounge stairs.

Carter Winston waited only until the end of the title credits. It was long enough to permit the boy to get into position at the urinal. That would be enough time to strike.

Carter didn't want to seem hurried. He measured his movement in getting up from the chair, then equally measured each of his steps as his light shoes sunk deep into the plush carpeting of the aisle. Then his hand lightly grasped the banister and his feet again sunk into the plush carpeting of the stairs. He was in the panic of need. But he fought down that urgency. He kept his left hand in his pocket so that the erection would not bulge out the front of his trousers… just in case someone was looking his way… like the mini-skirted one in the box office. That's all he needed was for her to see him and go off giggling somewhere, or make some sly remark to an usher or the manager. That would be the end of his new world. The end of the plush lavatory and the hole in the cubicles.

But no one saw him, and looking back from the top of the stairs, there was no one near the head of the aisle, or in the foyer below the stairs. He had once again made the move completely undetected as to his real purpose. Then the two doors confronted him. One on the left and one on the right. The ladies' restroom was on the left. He certainly didn't want that one. His eyes fell on the simple sign over the right door which read *"MEN'S ROOM."* He hesitated no longer than it took to think of the first step, then easily pushed open the door. He stepped quickly inside and let the door swing shut behind him. His eyes shot immediately to the urinals. The towhead was not there. No one was at the urinals. His eyes quickly shot across to the cubicles. The number two booth was closed and locked.

He pondered for a long moment as to the approach he should make. He knew what the move had to be. He had to take a chance. Undoubtedly the towhead was in there, and from what he could tell in the dark auditorium, towhead was fruit. However, it would be the first time he would shove his penis through the hole without the proper pre-affair signals.

Carter Winston was so completely steamed up by his own imagination there was just nothing else he could do. He pushed open the number one booth and swiftly locked the door. His fly was unzipped just as quickly and the throbbing manhood seemed to jump into his hand. He put it through the hole and the soft lips and tongue took it in an experience he'd never had equaled.... He was shot into orbit with a kaleidoscope of colors and sounds, and all was beautiful.

Then it was over. He wiped off and waited. But he was not to reciprocate. The number two door opened and closed. The affair had ended. Carter Winston opened his own door and his eyes nearly popped from his skull. The blue-eyed blonde in the beautiful pink sweater and white skirt was just putting "his" penis back into the pink panties "he" wore under the skirt. "He" winked at Carter and swished over to the restroom door and went out.

THE END

The Price of Jealousy

(no author listed)

Two + Two *Vol.2 #1 Jan./Feb. 1972*

DORIS THRILLED TO THE FEEL of Goldie's firm little body against hers. She fondled her small breasts, ran her hands up and down her smooth back, and pressed her naked body to her own. Goldie's fingers were busy, caressing the insides of the older woman's thighs, inching closer to the warm nest.

Lying back with her eyes closed, Doris let herself drift. The smooth skin on the girl's back could have been Irene's. The breasts could have been hers too, firm and perfect. The searching fingers were a bit too strong, too probing. But as she lay there, Doris could imagine that she was at home with Irene.

But this wasn't Irene.

This was a girl who was paying her for sex, paying her for lessons. The older, experienced dyke was giving the young trainee her money's worth.

Doris let her fingers probe the girl's box as the young thing's fingers were probing hers. It was all so easy for Doris, experienced as she was. Her powerful arms were tight about the little fluff of a girl. This is what they wanted for their money, to be dominated by a strong woman, an experienced woman, a dyke who was famous among lesbians… a living legend.

Men feared her… actually feared her with a physical fear. An emptiness in the pit of their stomachs. A trembling. Doris was known to have mastered every form of martial art. She could box with almost any man, wrestle, fight no-holds-barred. She had mastered judo, karate, jujitsu and savage. When she couldn't handle a man with her mitts, she carried weapons to take care of it. A stiletto in her garter, a pistol in her purse.

Doris was the terror of any man who might try to take away one of her bits of fluff.

But she was the darling of the dykes.

She skillfully worked Goldie over. The girl was one of those rich brats that Doris couldn't take anymore. But she was where the money was at. Doris hadn't cared much about money before, but now that she was living with Irene, married so to speak, it became important to her. Irene never bugged her about things. All she wanted to do was stay home and keep the house nice for Doris. But Doris wanted her to have things, pretty things, and that was as good a reason as any to go on making money off girls like Goldie.

From the sound of the moans, Doris was satisfying her customer once again. Then her thoughts turned to the walk home. From the hotel where she conducted her business, she had to walk a dozen blocks through darkness. There were dark alleys along the way. She liked to walk, but the walk was not something she looked forward to. There had been a wave of crimes, violent crimes, and the people of the city were terrified. There was a mad rapist on the loose.

Doris had to chuckle at the thought. Sometimes she hoped the rapist would try her. What a surprise the joker would be in for. It was the kind of thing men did to women, because they were defenseless.

But Doris wasn't.

That's why she half-hoped she'd run into the man. If he gave her half a chance, she'd nail him. As long as he didn't get a blade to her throat before she could react… wham! A little judo to throw him off balance and rid him of any weapons. Then a savage kick in the teeth to shock him. Finally, either her famous right cross or a stiletto in the gut if he really got tough. Then she always had the pistol… just in case.

She heard Goldie moan beneath her. Her head was nestled to Doris' cheek. She lay there peacefully while Doris caressed her gently. The girl had finished her orgasm now.

Rich brats were all alike, thought Doris. A thing about their rich dads, sex envy toward their moms, turned off by young men, lot of time to throw away, and a lot of money to send in the same direction. Doris would be glad to take it.

She used to enjoy making it with the girls who paid her, but now she was only turned on with Irene.

Doris went through all the motions with Goldie, caressing her all over, kissing her, whispering the sweet nothings the girl wanted to hear. She was gradually working her up towards another orgasm. It took time to do a girl right, but Doris was willing to spend that time. That's why she took fewer customers now, spent more time with each of them.

Doris lay there, caressing her happy young customer all over. She was worried about her lover at home, the way she sometimes got. It was the worry all dykes had. That they couldn't completely please the women they loved.

Because they were lacking something.

The one thing they couldn't have, that all men had, no matter how inferior the man might be to them in all ways as a lover. Whenever Doris was away from Irene, and her work took her away from her often, she got it into her head that... a man... some man... *he*... might be making it with her girl. Doris had talked about that to all of the bull dykes she knew, and they all admitted that it was something they all worried about.

Were they good enough?

Could they finally please a girl?

Without... without... without one.

It was ironic. Doris was paid to please women, and her worse worry was that she couldn't please the woman she loved. In recent months, she had begun to worry even more. Was there a man? When she was away from home? Irene was so quiet. She never said anything to Doris.

There wasn't anything Doris could actually put her finger on. Irene didn't have much to do, so she had a lot of free time. And Doris was away so much, finding customers, taking them to the hotel.

There was no man Doris had ever seen Irene with, not even before they "married." Irene was shy, the kind of girl who stayed home a lot. She was content to sit on the back terrace of the apartment, doing the charcoal sketches she liked to do.

Yet Doris could not help wondering whether or not the girl was true to her. Irene was a beautiful thing to see, and men loved her. She always claimed to be turned off by them, but... how could a girl be sure?

Doris wasn't young anymore, and she had never been pretty. Irene was nineteen. It had seemed to Doris that for the first time in her life she had met a girl she loved. Doris had enjoyed many a torrid relationship with a young woman before Irene. Yet, they were just flesh. She felt differently about this one, and in her heart she feared only that she would lose her. Irene had so much to offer... especially to a man.

Doris thought about that handsome actor down on a lower floor in their apartment building. Irene had said she despised the creep, disliked the way he stared at her when they got on the elevator at the same time. And there was the fellow who came to wash the windows. He wore a tight t-shirt, and he had quite a physique. He wasn't conceited like the actor though. He was a regular sort of guy, and even Doris liked him. But she feared him.

It might be some man Doris had never met. Somehow, she could not conceive of it being another woman. Doris was all that a girl could want. No woman could be more than she was. She couldn't imagine the competition coming from another woman. They were too weak, too feminine.

But if Irene wandered, it would be to a man. A strong man.

With… what Doris lacked.

A pleasure pole.

The thing she tried to imitate with a dildo but could never duplicate. It made Doris furious just to think about it. A man in bed with Irene… now… while she was with this bit of fluff. Doris was resigned to the fact that she would always live with jealousy, but she could not resign herself to the fact that she might have to give Irene up to a man.

She was finished with Goldie now, and she rose from the hotel bed. The girl stretched, yawned, and got out from the other side.

"When can I see you again, Doris?" asked the pretty blonde.

"Same time next week," said Doris casually. "And… same fee." Doris managed a smile. "You're lucky there's a wage and price freeze on."

The girl laughed.

The girl left, and after waiting a few minutes, Doris headed for home.

She passed unnoticed through the hotel lobby, and then out into the street. It was a nice evening, and she strolled up the street toward the apartment house where she lived with Irene.

She usually went back to the lez bars at that hour, for there was still a score to make. But she was nervous, nervous about Irene, and about him, the imaginary man. The lover. The one with the pleasure pole. She covered the twelve blocks quickly. It was a clear and moonlit night, not a very good one, she thought, for the mad rapist. He liked fog, haze, anything in which he could hide.

As Doris reached the lobby of the big apartment house, her mind was working overtime. That actor. Handsome devil, and so sure of himself. He would be up there with Irene at this moment. They expected that Doris would still be working the bars. It wasn't Irene's fault. She was innocent. It was that guy. He fooled her with his suave talk. And he had a pole. Irene was a young woman, and she had to be turned on by that.

Doris rode up in the elevator.

Or maybe it was that window washer. Damned nice fellow. Unassuming. Cheerful. And what a build. He would come up during the day to wash the windows, and maybe have a chat with Irene. They would get to talking. One thing would lead to another. And Irene would have to invite him in for a cup of coffee.

Then…

…on the couch.

Doris felt a lump in her throat as the elevator glided to a stop. She stepped out into the carpeted hall. She didn't like sneaking in on Irene like this. She wanted to go back downstairs, back to the bars. Maybe not even to pick up chicks. Just to have a drink and cool off.

She should trust Irene.

The girl loved her.

There was no reason for her to be like this. It was all in her mind. It was all because she wasn't a real man. She was an imitation. But she shouldn't have been jealous, because she was better than any man. She could whip any one of them. She was that tough.

She got to the door, her key in her hand. And then she heard voices. From inside. She heard the soft voice of her lover, so soft and sweet she couldn't make out what Irene was saying. She was talking in the sweet pleading voice she used when she begged for love, begged to be touched here or there or someplace special. And then Doris heard the other voice.

And she tensed up.

It was a man's voice.

A strange man.

Doris froze. It wasn't the actor. It wasn't the window washer. But it was a lover. It was the worst she had feared. Bored, alone during the day, a woman, Irene had found a lover. A man. A real man.

Doris had to force herself from bursting in. Why should she? She loved Irene. And the girl had her own life to live. She'd go away, to the lez bars, and then come back at the right time. They would have a talk, and Irene could pack and leave whenever she pleased during the next few days.

No yelling.

No fighting.

Irene was a free woman.

So Doris left the apartment door and returned to the elevator. Then she went down into the street and back to the bars. She sat and drank in the bars, and when it was time, she came home.

And she found Irene. Raped. Strangled. Dead.

She sat staring at the lovely body. The body of the girl she loved, the girl she could have saved.

Except for her jealousy.

THE END

Never Look Back

by "Ann Gora"

in Fig Leaf, *Vol.2, No.1 Gallery Press Jan./Feb 1973 on Ed's resume 1972, from the book* Short Wood

TERRY DIDN'T TAKE that advice because she was looking back. She was still looking back as she let her legs dangle for several moments over the side of the bed, and the feeling continued with her all the way to the motel shower.

It was a long hot shower, then a cold one which brought her slowly back to the living. And she didn't bother to dry off. She slipped into a terry-cloth robe and walked back into the bedroom where Robbie the young, muscled man still remained sound asleep and on his side, with his back to her.

She sat down on the edge of her side of the bed and once more let her feet dangle over the edge. A moment later she reached for Robbie's pack of cigarettes and struck a match to the end. She took the smoke in deep, like a professional who had been smoking for years. Actually, that might be a fact. She'd had her first cigarette when she was fourteen, and she was then seventeen. And who the hell cared? She certainly didn't. And who the hell cared if she'd been having a guy between her legs since she was fourteen either? She'd care if she didn't!

Terry was the most popular girl in her school, and she was about the prettiest, and she dressed at all times to show off her body and to turn on the guys who were always staring at her. She liked that, the guys staring at her. She also liked to watch that thing raise up the front of their pants. She knew what it was. And she knew what the guys were thinking and what they'd like to do with that thing. They'd like to get her somewhere private and strip off her panties after they had pulled up her skirt and they'd like to shove that pink arrow into her moist target.

She knew alright what every one of them wanted. And she knew she wanted it just as much. But she didn't give it to all of them. There were plenty she wanted nothing to do with. Some because of their physical attributes and some just turned her off from their personality. But the ones she turned down the quickest were those who didn't have the price of a motel room, and something extra that she could put into the cup of her brassiere.

At fourteen she found that giving it to the broke creeps was the biggest loss of all. First of all, most of them went around bragging how easy a lay she was and that she could be had at the drop of a hat. If they didn't have to pay for it, they didn't appreciate it. Terry made sure that anybody who got between her legs was going to appreciate it.

At that early age of fourteen the sessions were generally out in the park behind the bushes; over in the swimming pool in the dark of a cave which was carved there out of a hillside by the Indians. It was all such kid stuff. She didn't mind it so much with the older boys and their cars... like in the back seat. But she really didn't like doing it where she couldn't take her clothes off. It seemed to take forever to get the wrinkles out of her skirts and blouses. That's why during those times, she generally wore sweaters and wool skirts; they didn't hold the wrinkles. But there were also those times when some guy turned her on and her knees trembled and the insides of her thighs began to sweat and she just had to have the guy no matter how she was dressed.

But to her it was always that much better when she could stretch out in some safe spot and take it like the woman she knew she would grow up to be.

She didn't have much reason to worry about getting knocked up: becoming pregnant. Her mother had explained the facts of life to her very carefully during the early days of her fourteenth year. Perhaps all that explaining was what turned her on to the boys so heatedly. While her mother had told her those facts she could feel herself fantasizing, and the more the fantasy pictures captured her mind, the more the body heats swelled up inside her. They swelled so heatedly that she simply had to grab off the first boy who wasn't too frightened to take her on... which wasn't too difficult a task... the boys always had eyes for her... even though the younger ones didn't know what it was that was happening to them.

"It's just too bad that youth is wasted on the young," she remarked after the first older boy took her... he was all of sixteen during her fourteenth year. Then his hand lifted up the pink angora sweater she wore and pulled down the cup of her brassiere so that the youthful mounds and the ripe pink nipple came into sight where he could put his lips around them and play his tongue to the nipple.

The one thing her mother, as well as her father more recently, always told her just before she went out on a date… "Just be careful of getting pregnant. That's all we ask of you. Be careful of getting pregnant. You're much too young to be saddled with some bastard kid. You've got too much of a life ahead of you to be tied down like that."

"Don't worry. You've both taught me so much about keeping from being pregnant."

"There's those rubber things," her mother had often said, and a couple of times showed her the ones kept in her father's bedroom drawer. "Those things like your father uses. Make sure that your boyfriend has them around before you let him take you. I know there is no demanding that you don't do things like that with the boys. And then I suppose there is really no reason that you shouldn't. I was young once, and I guess I liked to do it with the boys as much as anybody. But I never got pregnant. You were the full product of your father, three years after we were married. You'll never have to go through life with the stigma of the name bastard connected to you. And I know you wouldn't want such a tag put on your own child. There will be plenty of time for you to have a child."

And her father would cough a few times before she'd go out, then look over the rims of his glasses as he spoke his small piece of advice. "Your mother has spoken to you?"

"Yes, daddy," she had always answered, because it was the same words every time she left the house. They knew she was going to probably make it with the boys and they wanted her to have a full life. They had read all the stories about the sexual revolution, and that the girl and perhaps the guy who didn't make out simply wasn't with the IN CROWD. All the kids wanted to be with the IN crowd, otherwise they would be what used to be called a WALLFLOWER. Nobody wanted to be a WALLFLOWER. Terry certainly could never be called a WALLFLOWER.

"Then just be careful, dear. We love you very much… and we want you to have all the good times you want to have. But make sure the good times will always be remembered as good times." Then still speaking, he would look back to his paper, or book, or to the news on television. "Good times, sometimes have a way of coming back to you as bad times. You just go out and have all the good times and leave the bad times for somebody else."

"Yes, daddy." And she would adjust a cardigan over her shoulders and head out into the pleasant street where her date waited for her.

By the time she was sixteen she refused to date any boy who didn't have a car... and didn't have the money for a motel. There were plenty of motels around who looked the other way when the boy signed the register... turned the other way so they wouldn't have to ask their age and get a lying answer... and if they had to lie... what the hell! They'd lie, that's all... and still the man would be looking at them through sightless eyes. It was best that way... besides, there was always an extra five bucks, clear profit, for him in such a transaction... and the cops never bothered him... he always kept a clean establishment... he always told everybody that... and he also bragged about being high on the list when voting for the *bed tax law*. He and a few dozen others situated around the county line.

Terry puffed away at the cigarette all the time she was deep in remembering. Then she crushed it out and lay back on the rumpled bed. The terry robe fell open down the front and she left it that way. The shower water had soaked into it and her skin was dry and the room was very warm. She really didn't need any covering.

Her eyes looked across to Robbie who had turned over and was looking at her. "Hi," she said, her face as bright as the sun light and her smile as warm as the outside summer air.

"Right back at you." he grinned.

"When did you wake up?"

"A long time ago. You weren't on this planet so I didn't want to disturb your thoughts."

"Oh. I was just thinking."

"About what? Was I in your thoughts?"

"Not right then you weren't."

"I don't know if I like that."

She reached over and kissed him lightly then laid back again with her hands behind her head. She was high up on the pillow. "I was just thinking about the first guy I laid... and some of the others."

"Now I know I don't like not being in your thoughts."

"Silly. That was a long time ago."

"You sound like the old woman of the mountains."

She let her hands travel first along the luscious sides of her curvy body, then they came back up to rest on her breasts. She held both of them for a long moment, then she let her right hand drift down to the soft angora-like qualities of golden pubic hairs. "Do I look like the old woman of the mountains, my pet?"

He rolled over on top of her. "Good Lord, no!"

"You like my body?"

"You bet! I always have! I like you all the time, even when you've got clothes on."

"Most of the boys like me with my clothes on. But not all of them ever see me without my clothes. They'll never know if they like me that way or not."

"I don't want anybody ever to see you that way but me… not ever again I don't."

"Now don't start that again, Robbie. I go with whoever I want and I'll undress in front of whoever I want… and I'll lay whoever I want. I'm too young to be tied down to any one guy. You know I told you that's the way it was going to be or I wouldn't screw you in the first place. Everybody's got to know that I'm nobody's personal property. Somebody gets any jealous ideas, then they can go get Mary Jackson or Helen Tensite. They're looking for somebody steady."

"I'll play it your way."

"That's the only way it's going to be played… with me as a partner in the game anyway." Then she took the hand from her pussy and raised it to tickle Robbie's nose. "Want to make it with me again?"

"I'm already in position."

She lowered her hand and helped him into place. A moment later they were locked in the *missionary position*, the major position for the sex act known down through all the ages as one of the most favored. And when Robbie began to moan his intentions of exploding into her, she grabbed both cheeks of his buttocks and spread them so far apart that he almost screamed with pain… "Wait for me, bastard… wait for me," she hissed into his mouth, over the tongue which was slapping at her own…

Then she released the pressure and pushed her pelvic region up high and tight against his. She didn't have to say anything more to him… the sweat poured from every pore of their bodies and they pumped into each other as if it would be the last time they were ever together… and they sighed and they moaned. They did not scream even though both of them wanted to let out their pent-up emotions, the joy of the moment, the excitement of the second in a long piercing scream. But they could not. That was part of the motel rules. There had been some kids who could not hold back their screams… and that was the end of their motel usage… and word like that gets around to the other places fast. No one wanted to lose the place where they could make their secret love acts.

Then Terry and Robbie did explode. They sent each other into the pink clouds of oblivion… the kaleidoscope of colors and sound… and as they started over the brink into infinity their pleasures subsided and they sunk back to earth.

Robbie rolled off the girl and lay panting for a long time. Terry once more reached over and lit another cigarette. She drew the smoke deep into her lungs. "Did you like that one, Robbie?"

"That was the best one yet. Where in hell did you learn actions like that… what movement, what grace, what rhythm."

"I have a very broad-minded mother. I guess they must have been born just on the fringe of the sexual revolution." She laughed heartily.

"Sometimes I wish my parents were that broad-minded," he almost pouted.

"You mean you never learned about sex from your parents?"

He shook his head. "Anything I learned I had to go out into the field and find out for myself. I guess I didn't do a bad job of learning though."

"You sure as hell didn't! You're alright! You make a girl get real hot… I mean real hot. But you got to always remember a girl has to be satisfied, too. You got to let her climax a couple of times before you explode. Get what I mean?"

He took the still sore cheeks of his ass in his hands. "I get what you mean."

"Sorry about that. I won't let it happen again. I was just afraid you'd explode and it would be all over and I wouldn't get my jollies. That is horrible for a girl."

"You know so much."

"Like I said. My parents were always frank with me. The only thing they ever worried about was that I'd get pregnant. You know, you're the first guy I ever let lay me without having a rubber on."

"You better not get pregnant. My parents would kill me for sure."

She swung her legs over the edge of the bed. "Not a chance. I know exactly what to do." She started for the bathroom but stopped at his insistent voice.

"Would you mind if I go first? I got to take the worst piss I ever had to take."

"Go ahead." She sat back down on the bed and watched as the naked Robbie went into the bathroom and closed the door behind him.

Inside he let the yellow stream go loudly into the toilet and when he was done he cleaned himself with the toilet paper and he looked at the chancre which had appeared on the head of his penis nearly two weeks before. He thought for a long moment then shook his head and spoke silently to himself. "Naw, it would only embarrass her. Hell, it's only a sore from so much sex. Besides, her parents told her everything there is to know about sex. She probably knows what to do anyway. I'll just say nothing."

THE END

THOSE LONG WINTER NIGHTS

by "Ann Gora"

in Garter Girls *Vol.7 no.1 Nov./Dec. 1972 on Ed's resume 1972*

SHEILA DIDN'T KNOW for the life of her why she chose a mountain resort for her vacation. The snow outside of her window was piled six feet deep and although her expensive room was well heated, just the sight of the snow made her shiver all over. She hugged her arms around the long sleeved, long waisted, pink angora sweater then let one hand drift down to the pink wool ski pants. Sometimes she could make the shivers leave her body by rubbing the palm of her hand on her crotch. It worked!

The shivers stopped, but she figured "why test the fates?" So she turned from the window and the sight of the snow beyond.

Just why in hell did she come to a ski lodge? She didn't ski. She was frightened to death of toboggan rides. About the only thing she did like to do was sit around the bar and watch the sex traps go by... there were certainly plenty of those around. But there were plenty of bars and plenty of sex traps in other resort areas. Why in hell a ski lodge?

"For one thing," she answered herself. "It's something different from the usual. A place to go, to get out of the city where most of her life was spent as an executive nurse at Mid-City Hospital."

She lit a cigarette and after a puff or two crushed it out. She crossed the room to a small bar and poured herself a stiff jolt and downed it. The smarting liquid felt good. She started to pour another but stopped midway in the move. She'd never been a morning drinker. But then it was a vacation and people did a lot of things on vacations that they wouldn't otherwise do.

However, why drink alone? There were always people in the cocktail lounge no matter what time of the day it was... even after closing time they sat around with coffee cups and tea things in front of them. Who was to tell on those who filled their mugs with booze?

She took up a matching angora cardigan just in case she went outside. But that was the farthest thought from her mind. She draped the fuzzy cardigan over her shoulder and left the room. The cocktail bar became her destination.

"Good morning Miss Everly," grinned the bartender who was in the process of polishing a tall glass. "You must have gotten up before the chickens this morning."

"I watched all night television."

"Couldn't sleep, huh?"

"The quiet kept me awake all night."

"Ahh, now, the best doctors and psychiatrists say that the cold mountain air is the best health tonic in the world."

"Then we'd better get a bunch of new doctors and psychiatrists. Let me have a bloody Mary."

She watched him start the mixture then looked down along the bar where the cute little waitress was writing something in her order pad before lifting a tray with a single drink on it.

The girl had caught her eye every time she'd seen her during the past four days. Blonde, petite and with a pair of love muscles the likes of which would be the hit of any lesbian bar.

Sheila had never been one to keep hands off of a fluff when she wanted her. But there was something about this girl which struck her different. Sheila wasn't sure if the girl would go that route. It was the first time in her history she wasn't able to read another girl's emotions: able to tell if she was strictly for the boys, or for the girls, or if she would play the game either way.

The one thing Sheila did notice was that she did have eyes for certain men. She had caught the sly winks and had watched as she gathered in heavier tips than any of the other girls.

She knew something was going on, but she really couldn't figure it. Yet she was delighted as the girl picked up the tray with the tall drink and started in her direction. Her voice was music to Sheila's ears as she said, "Good morning, Miss Everly."

"Hello there," smiled Sheila and she felt the electrical shock start in her brain then swiftly shot down to her pubic region and bounced right back up to the think machine again. She turned her head slightly and watched the cute little rump under the extremely short, tight waitress costume as it swayed across the polished wood floor and deposited the drink in front of an elderly man who reached out and patted her on the fanny, then tossed a bill onto her tray.

The girl didn't seem to object to the ass patting. In fact, she almost curtsied as she turned from him and started back toward the bar again.

Then she also caught the eye of a much younger man who was being serviced by one of the other waitresses. She winked at the man but the wink was not returned. Then once more at the bar she motioned for the bartender. Sheila strained her ears at the nearly whispered conversation.

"What's Mr. Henderson drinking?"

"You mean you've been hound-dogging him for three days and you still don't know what he drinks?"

"He's never been at one of my stations."

"Figure him for Scotch and soda… the very best Scotch, Babs."

"Make it two."

"That's Orley's station."

"I'll talk to Orley."

"And why two?"

"One for me."

"You know the management doesn't like you girls fooling around with the customers."

"I don't think Mr. Paul will mind," and she gave the bartender a knowing wink. He also grinned because he knew what the beautiful, sexy blonde meant. And he watched as Babs stopped Orley and talked a moment, then she slipped the brunette a bill and Orley moved to another customer in the far corner of the room.

Once more Sheila strained her ears. But she couldn't hear the conversation. However she was determined to hear it. She took up her drink and moved across to a table very near the couple.

"I didn't order that," replied Mr. Henderson.

"You might just as well drink it up, it's already on your bill."

The young man's face soured, but he sighed and took the drink which was placed in front of him. Then he watched as the girl put the second drink across from a vacant chair.

"Who is that one for?"

"Me! When I can sneak it."

"And I suppose that's on my bill also?"

"You wouldn't want a lady to pay for her own drinks at your table, now would you?"

He had to grin at her forwardness. "I guess I wouldn't at that… Tell me. Does the management permit you to drink on the job?"

"No."

"Aren't you afraid of getting fired?"

There was the knowing wink again. "No. I have a certain arrangement around here. But then I don't make a scene when I slip down a little juice." She lifted the glass and downed the contents, and the move had been so swift that anyone who had not been directly looking for such a move would have missed it. Sheila didn't miss the action.

But Sheila was also amazed that such a beautiful little piece of fluff could be so brash about her intentions. She was to be even more horrified.

"Want to meet me in my room when I get off at four this afternoon?"

"What would we do?"

"I think I could come up with some fun and games you might appreciate."

"I've had girls try that before."

She didn't get his full meaning. "I bet not like my fun and games." She winked again. "Want to try me on for size?"

"I'll think about it."

"Don't bend your mind too much. There are other, more enjoyable things to bend."

Sheila shivered in her frustration. There Babs was propositioning the guy as blatantly as she'd ever seen a proposition made and the guy was all but turning her down. She could only think, "The guy has to be dead or queer." But he didn't really appear to be either.

"See you just after four," fluttered the girl then went back to the bar.

The whole incident made Sheila angry. But she couldn't bring herself to get up and leave the bar. Her eyes feasted upon the girl every time she moved. She watched Henderson as he gathered up his skis and exited the cocktail lounge for the snow slope outside and that was one bright moment. She was glad he was gone.

However, she had been so engrossed in watching, with hatred in her eyes, to the exit of Henderson that she did not see Babs come up to her table. "Another, Miss Everly?"

Sheila looked up into the sparkling blue eyes. It was the first time she had realized that Babs had blue eyes. But it was the first time she had been so close to her.

"Huh?" Then full recognition. "Oh, Babs."

The girl grinned. "I didn't think you knew my name, Miss Everly."

"Call me Sheila!"

"Oh, I'd like to," came the musically pleasant sound of her voice. "But the management wouldn't like that."

Sheila thought deeply and the red of anger wanted to spread across her features. But she fought it down. For some creep of a male wet-head Babs could forget about management rules. But for someone who really had an interest in her there was only, "But the management wouldn't like that."

However, "I see," she said aloud.

"Would you like another drink?"

Sheila hadn't planned on having another. The previous scene had soured her stomach. She had planned to return to her room, get undressed, perhaps masturbate, and spend the rest of the day sleeping. But Babs was there. She was in Babs' station. And she would order another drink, and perhaps yet another and another. Because each time she ordered Babs would be there, and each time the drink was brought to her table Babs would be there.

She ordered, and the drink was brought to her. But then Babs shifted back to her original station and Orley once more took over. The frustration began all over again. Sheila couldn't very well simply change stations; get back into the one being serviced by Babs. The move would have been all too obvious.

The drink came into her hand and she only took a sip or two from it, then for the first time since her arrival she felt like getting out into the cool air. She had to get some of the heated anger from her system, and she figured the cold snow filled air should do that for her. She stood up and slipped into the pink angora cardigan and went out onto the cleared patio and seated herself in one of the patio chairs. And there she would remain the rest of the afternoon. After all the waiters out there would bring her drinks, and since they were waiters it might help to take her mind off of Babs....

But it didn't.

From just before four o'clock when she saw Henderson come in off the snow slopes until well after five she fretted and fumed and took double shots. She felt she knew what was going on in Babs' room. At five fifteen she went to her own room and threw herself down upon the bed and stared angrily, and frustratedly at the ceiling. At first she was going to masturbate with her fantasies of being with Babs…. But she needed the real thing… the masturbation wasn't to come off.

However, Sheila was to find out what really happened a short time later.

Henderson arrived at Babs' room at ten after four. She greeted him in a sheer negligee which did nothing to hide her lovely shape. And he was barely into the room before she threw her arms around his neck and their lips parted and their tongues slashed and smashed against each other. She was beyond herself for want of the man. He did little in helping to remove his clothing. But that was no obstacle for Babs. The clothing came off and laid in a pile on the floor… and from that moment on for the next hour the girl did everything she knew, everything she had ever heard of to arouse the sexual hots in the fellow. But even to the end he remained cold and aloof.

And all the while it actually seemed that he was trying. He took her lips, and he took her vagina with his tongue and his lips and his lips circled her breasts… first one then the other, then both of them at the same time. Babs was raised to sexual stimulation as she had seldom been before. He was built like a man, and she knew if he ever got an erection he would be one of the largest she had ever seen. But nothing happened to him… and she trembled with the unfulfiliment… and even her own fantasies couldn't give her any relief at all….

Then she tired completely. Naked she swung off the bed and glared at him. "Just what in the hell is the matter with you?"

"There's nothing the matter with me. It must be you. You've got to be the one that's at fault."

"Why you cheap bastard, I've turned better men than you on in ten seconds. We've been at this thing for more than an hour and you're as weak as a worm."

"Maybe I don't like broads like you."

"Like me! And what's that supposed to mean? Maybe you don't like broads at all. Yeah! That's got to be it! You don't like girls. You're one of those." She reached to a chair where she had put her clothes earlier. She first threw the panties at him and they momentarily covered his face. Then she followed the move with her brassiere, then the skirt and her cashmere sweater,…." There she screamed. "That's probably what you need. Put them on and I'll call Harry the bellboy. He loves to make it with men, especially if they're wearing my clothes. Oh, I've seen your kind come and go all the time. I get extra for the use of my panties and other things, buster."

"Why you dirty bitch," he screamed and got up from the bed and cuffed her back and forth with the palm and the back of his hand... over and over again until she fell unconscious back to the bed.

Sheila slowly got up from the bed at the knock. She was startled to see the bruised and beaten Babs standing there.... "Well what in hell happened to you?"

"Miss Everly. I know you're a nurse. I can't go to the house doctor like this. I couldn't explain to him what happened. I'd be fired. I had to come to you for help. Will you help me, Miss Everly... Sheila?"

Sheila put her arm around the girl's shoulder and led her into the room. There was a sudden glow to her cheeks. The frustration left her immediately. Babs had come to her. Perhaps it had been a rugged way to come... but she would soon rub all the hurt from the girl. "Of course I'll help you.... You just come in... get off those clothes.... I'll give you one of my nighties, and take care of all your hurts."

"I don't think I could stand a nightie. I don't want anything against my skin. I couldn't stand it."

"I had in mind something very soft... you do like soft things, don't you?"

"Oh yes... yes... something very soft...."

Sheila lowered the girl to the bed as soon as she had stripped her naked.

THE END

BIG MAN–LITTLE MAN

by "Dick Trent"

from Illustrated Case Histories: A Study Of Group Sex Practices
Vol.3 No.3 Oct./Nov. 1971 (on Ed's resume)

JOYCE LOOKED AROUND and the buildings were tall... all around her, tall buildings. Taller than she ever imagined any building could ever be. There had been one three story building in the small mid-western town she had come from. But buildings like those! They were straight out of a geography book. Sure, she'd seen pictures of them, but they did nothing to the mind like the real thing.

She'd dreamed of going to New York City ever since she could remember... she longed for the experience... but there was nothing in the stories which told her of the loneliness she would also find on the island of the giant cement statues. It was a loneliness which was nearly overpowering.

Back home she'd had Rickey and Jimmie and Fred and most recently Bill. They had been good to her. Ever since she'd realized what sex was all about and had had her first experience she found she couldn't get enough of it and those boys didn't know their ass from a hole in the ground when it came to sex. Only one had halfways pleased her and that had been Rickey, the first one. He'd broken her cherry and perhaps because of the pain involved she'd had a most delightful orgasm. Ever since then she had attempted to find that exotic pleasure again. There was none to be found with the small town hicks who were available.

But she was in the big city and there still were none to be found. None which could satisfy her. Three months... a small job in a department store, and still the small town type of clerks who lowered her panties, drove their shaft home and left her wanting... ever wanting.

Then there were the creeps who tried to pick her up on the street corners. Nothings which irked her even when they breathed near her. She

347

got more feeling using her finger than any of those could have given her, she was sure of that. She knew she got more feeling using her finger than out of any of the guys she did let touch her.

One would expect upon going to the big city that she was going to meet big city men. Instead the big city seemed to be comprised of small town men, no better than Rickey, Jimmy, Fred and Bill. Even their names rang the same tune. The only thing she found big about the big city were the buildings.

She did find some of the men built big in the chest and their shoulders and some of them were even tall. But that's as far as the classification *big* went. The rest of them were no different than any of the others. In other words, once she had seen one she had seen them all. At least that was her feeling....

Until Harry approached her in the lingerie department where she worked. He was a little man, and certainly not one she would generally turn to for any kind of gratification. But he did have a nice voice and his pick of words were astounding... especially those he whispered in her ear when no one was around. And whenever his hands were resting on the counter his fingertips would continually feel the cups of the brassieres and the crotch of the filmy nylon panties. The crotch of the panties was extremely fascinating to him even though he didn't look at the garments. And the sight of his hand doing that precise movement fascinated Joyce.

She finally found herself almost feeling his hands doing that to her brassiere and to the crotch of her own heated panties... while she still had them on. Then she felt her body quivering with uncontrollable shakes... not shakes that anyone else might notice, but shakes she could feel just under her skin. And she found her tongue attempting to moisten dry lips... dry from the body heats which traveled with the shakes.

It was then she knew she had to try this little guy on for size... just like she tried on her own panties for size. And the words he whispered in her ear were words she had heard from the boys when they wanted to talk *dirty* or make some girl think they knew everything there was in the world about sex. They knew all the *dirty* words and she had to admit she liked hearing them. She even liked hearing them when she was doing something in bed with a man. Sometimes it was the words, only the words, which gave her any pleasure at all in the affair.

Harry used them all in context to what he would do to her if they were alone. He used them over and over whenever he came near her. And after a couple of days of that she found herself waiting for his appearance. His appearance was only when the floorwalker was in another part of the building. She even found herself feeling the crotch of the panties on her counter, and when she had to go to the ladies room, she found her hand lingering at the crotch of her own panties. She would take a long time in lowering them and even longer as she drew them back up when her *duty* was finished.

But Harry never approached her with a definite date. It was always the *dirty* words and the feeling of the panty crotch. And then the day came when she could feel the body heats were going to explode within her and she came right out and told him to put up or shut up. Put whatever it was he wanted to do on the line and stop talking about it.

Harry did! He captured her at the time clock that Friday night and they went to his car and he drove for a long time out into the country. The clock, when she punched out, was five minutes past five, and when they stopped in front of the old house it was nearly eight thirty and it was very dark. Harry was no longer tender. He was a searing torch which had to be extinguished. And no sooner had they entered the hall of the old house than he threw off his clothing and reached up under her skirt to pull down her panties. These he put upon himself, over the largest penis she had ever seen.

He pushed her to a set of double doors which flew open and her eyes went wide when she looked into the pillow-ladened room. Wall to wall pillows and perhaps a dozen more of the most beautiful naked girls she had ever seen.

Harry slammed the door behind her and a moan of delight went up from all the girls. They had suddenly come alive and squirmed and writhed beneath each other, like snakes in a snake pit… and each reached up to grab the crotch of the panties he wore, and he brushed each aside. Then roughly tossed Joyce to the thickest of all the pillows. And still the hands reached for the crotch of the panties… a dozen naked, beautiful girls, and two dozen arms and two dozen legs squirming in anticipation.

"We have a new set of panties tonight, my darlings," he said to the girls. "They will have to be serviced first." Then he pulled Joyce down to him and his body covered hers. He had only to pull aside the panty leg and pull up her skirt.

Joyce found a big man!

THE END

SPOKES OF THE WHEEL

by "Dick Trent"

on Ed's resume 1971, from SWAP

"**MOTHER**," **HE SAID** for the really first time confiding in the woman, or at least about to attempt confiding in her. "I want to live my life as a girl." He was seventeen, and for all the time he could remember he had stolen his sisters clothing, her undies, her blouses, sweaters and skirts. And he dressed fully then stood before the mirror and masturbated... over and over again he would masturbate, and even after ejaculating he would continue pulling at the thing. How he hated that piece of muscle between his legs.

His mother brushed the subject aside. "You're going to college and you're going to become a man, all man, or else you're going to get out and get a job. Your father's been dead a long while and it's about time you became the man of the house." How he winced every time she uttered the word *man*. "It's going to be either work or college. I do hope you will select college. If you do, I'll find the money somehow. You should become a track star, or a football player... some kind of athlete. That would build you up and make a man of you."

And when later that night he stood in front of his mirror, safely behind locked doors, he wore the tight pink brassiere, and the form fitting pink panties and he viewed his thin body critically. He always filled the brassiere cups with rolled up stockings and prayed night after night that God would fill them with the real thing like his sister who was a year older. He'd seen her lovely boobies time after time. She had never made much of an issue about closing the bathroom door when she toileted or took a shower and she hardly ever closed her bedroom door when she stripped out of her street clothing and donned the sheer nighties she always wore to bed. The sheer nightie was something the young fellow, Ronnie, really wished he could get hold of. He had put them on a couple of times, but was never able to take one for a full night. She only had three of the nylon fluffs and she certainly would miss them from her closet where they hung.

But Ronnie was seventeen and he had learned much about the life he was living. He'd had several homosexual experiences through the force of the older boys upon his frail, girl-like body. He had been forced into the oral copulation the first few times. He didn't like it at all. Then later! It wasn't so bad! Then when the older boys made him dress like a girl for the action he was impressed and he knew the life he was about to seek.

The sex change was nothing new. It had been around a long time only he hadn't heard about such a thing happening until a few months before he had approached his mother with the startling revelation. He knew that going with the boys as he had been and doing what he had been was wrong. But if he were made into a girl everything would be alright.

His mother wasn't going to stop him, and after stealing two hundred dollars from a place of concealment in the house, and while she was at work the next day, he packed a small suitcase. There was little to pack other than a shirt and an extra pair of pants. But he did take a blouse, sweater, skirt, undies and finally one of his sister's nighties along with shoes and stockings. At least he would have one set of girl's clothing to start in his new life... a new life in the big city...

Where he took up residence in a small hovel of a room in a sleazy downtown hotel. After all, Ronnie was no dummy, and he knew the money wouldn't last very long. And he also knew that he would soon have to land some kind of a job. He also knew that would be difficult because he had tried back in the town where he came from and because of his pretty face and almost boyish/girlish figure he had been laughed out of offices.

The first night as he sat in a hotel lobby he was approached by a dapperly dressed man. Carney! Their talk was bright and Ronnie needed a friend more than anything else in the world. He was lonely and homesick, but he wasn't going to return to the life which he not only rejected but which rejected him.

"Hell, Ronnie," replied Carney. "It ain't hard to make money in the big city." Ronnie hadn't told him any of the reasons he wanted money. He hadn't even mentioned big money. Only that he needed a job. "Good lookin' kid like you! Why you got the chance to go all the way. All you gotta have is the right connections... you know... the right people." Then he invited Ronnie up to his room "for a drink."

Ronnie had tasted liquor a few times when the big boys forced it on him while they made him do things to them, but he had never considered it much for his taste in beverages. But this was the big city and he knew from all he'd read that the city people were always drinking in bars or at cocktail parties and the like. He accepted the offer.

The booze went quickly to Ronnie's head and before he knew it he found himself naked on the bed and the character Carney changed to that of a vicious sadist. The anal intercourse session brought no end of pain. The tears welled in his eyes and Ronnie wanted to scream out, but he couldn't. He was tied and gagged.

But then a strange thing happened. Once the pain subsided a certain thrill overtook him. He imagined himself to be a woman. And he was being taken from the front. After all, he did want to be a woman. And that was the way they took it. Of course they had a vagina and he only had that other. But one day that all would change. The only other thing he wished is that he wasn't naked. Perhaps later after the sex change he wouldn't mind being naked... he'd have the right kind of body. He wouldn't need any other illusions. He wouldn't need any illusions at all because the physical body would be there. But for that moment, that moment when Carney ravished him so ruggedly, so dastardly, he wished he had the clothing which was tucked away so secretly in the suitcase... at least even if he could have had the panties and the brassiere... there would have been more of the illusion... the illusion that he really was being taken as a woman by a man.

He was soon to have his clothing. Not only the small amount in his suitcase... but a few more odds and ends which Carney thought he might need in his new role as a prostitute... nighties and negligees. "And you try to get away from me before I want you to, bitch," Carney had sneered. "You'll find yourself in a dark alley with your throat cut."

Ronnie took them naked, clothed... sadists, homosexuals, lesbians... he took them all, anyone that Carney brought him and Ronnie found himself with cigarette and booze money and that was about all. There was no way of saving for *THE DAY*, there was no saving for anything, including saving enough so that he could simply run away, get far enough so that he was out of Carney's clutches, there were day and night clients. There was little or no time for resting. Carney knew how to use his prop, and use him to the fullest. So what if he died! Carney could always get another. But as long as he stayed alive Ronnie was going to be Carney's boy/girl… his tool… his means of livelihood… the pimp and his whore.

But Ronnie had turned eighteen and was well on his way to nineteen. True, he was living as a woman all the time, and he was being laid like a woman. But he was not a woman… and the months were not far in advance when he would be twenty. He had to make his move sooner or later, and that move would take money. And it would take the proper clothing. He couldn't escape in the nighties, the frilly undies and the negligees which were all Carney permitted him to have. Ronnie hadn't been outside that room in more than a year. Even the hotel clerk was on Carney's payroll.

Then the thought of how real pretty he was struck Ronnie again. Tired but very pretty. "I could earn a lot more money for you if you could get me something pretty to wear, then we could go out on the street and you could point out the proper clients and I could make the proposition. I know we could make a lot more if they could see me right up close before they bought. Right up until now all you've been able to do is show them pictures and tell them what a looker I was. We could go right into the joints and a real deal could be made."

Carney was convinced. And the first outfit was a form fitting angora mini-dress of shocking pink. And while Ronnie was slipping into it Carney left for another bottle of booze. It was easy then for Ronnie to open the back of a picture where Carney always kept three hundred-dollar bills. And Ronnie slipped it down into the "Y" of his brassiere. It would be a long time before the money would be discovered gone. Carney never went to that picture unless he was short of money. And there was no shortness of money that week. Ronnie had turned over twenty tricks at twenty bucks a head.

The door unlocked and when Carney came in they had two quickies. "That's all you get right now. You gotta be sober when you're out on the street."

And they left the small room where all the action had been for the past more than a year. Ronnie swore that he would never return. He had a warm, beautiful dress and a warm fur jacket which had come into the room the same time the latest bottle had been brought in. "The broad that owned it won't ever need it again," was all Carney had said.

Then there was the plush bar. Carney situated himself in a corner and Ronnie melted in with the atmosphere. His long hair and exquisite dress was all the introduction he needed if the lovely face and padded body wasn't enough. The combination was successful within moments. The attack was made and the deal was set. They moved to Carney's table and the money transaction changed hands.

"Would you mind if I visit the ladies room first?" and they excused *her*. It was only a guess on Ronnie's part. He had never been in the cocktail bar before. But it was a lucky guess. There was a window. And it wasn't sealed shut. He was out and *she* was on the street and ten minutes later on a bus to Texas, then crisscrossed back to Denver, then another double back to Texas before traveling on to Los Angeles.

The largest of the cities Ronnie had ever seen, and the loneliest and the scariest. Money was needed in such a place more than ever. The simple sweater and skirt he had purchased somewhere along the way couldn't afford him much of a job, and he had no male attire. He didn't want any. But there was always the street, and there was still the pink angora minidress and there were the males who wanted to possess *her*.

Ronnie had no beard. It was easy to pick up the unsuspecting males. And when they wanted intercourse he could always convince them that it was *her* time of the month and it had to be done *her* way or not at all. *She* was beautiful and there was never any argument. There were times when *she* even took them while they stood in doorways. *She* would take any and all comers and as many as possible. *She* was going to be a *real she* come hell or high water. The men paid good! It made a little difference if they paid good or little, Ronnie would take it all. The age of twenty crept up fast and Ronnie had no intention of spending another twenty years as a man in woman's clothing performing oral copulation on all except the homosexuals who he had let in on the know.

But the bank account was gaining rapidly. He didn't spend much, a few new clothes. Some fancy undies and nighties for those times when he undressed that far… and then there were some visits to the cocktail lounges where the homosexuals hung out and there he met several transsexuals. He learned of a doctor who would start him on the female hormone treatment, and with the powerful dosages his breast grew large. But he couldn't get any doctors to perform the necessary surgery to his lower quarters. He was under twenty-one.

But Mexico had some doctors also. They charged much more heavily than any doctors in the States might, but there was more and more of an urgency to become the woman he always wanted to be. He wanted to give up the life of prostitution. When he had the operation he swore he would never return to prostitution as a way of life. He had viewed so many secretaries and girls in other walks of life as they went hand in hand with their fellows and/or their husbands. How happy they were. Perfectly *normal* women going about their everyday business. He would be a *normal*, happy woman very soon.

He was accepted by the Mexican doctor. He never thought he wouldn't be. His breasts were already quite enlarged and with the continued use of the hormones they would gain even more, and within a few weeks the artificial vagina was formed. There would be pain for a time, but that would go away. He would have intercourse within six months after the operation, and he dreamed of that time. He would not return to any of those who knew about his past. There would never be anything which linked him with ever having been a male. He was born on that operating table a girl and that would be all he would ever remember.

There were men. There were lots of men. But only the ones that Ronnie wanted. *She, Ronnie,* kept the same name because it was as much a girl's name as any. But no matter where she went, she was followed by someone of her past, and she found that even with the men who didn't find out, she felt she wanted to tell them which she did. She was proud of what she had done… the operation… and they left… in disgust… She was alone in a world of many… She had to return to the people she knew, the homosexuals and the future transsexuals who stood in awe of her complete change. And the beauty of her figure made so many, including the lesbians, want to try her on for size. She granted those wishes. Her own wishes were for a straight guy to whom she could give her love. But when she found one there was always someone around to relate her past and they would drift off into the darkness from which they came.

She needed friends. She needed to be taken as the woman she had become. There were only those of the street who would take her like that because they would never be around long enough to find out that they had not been with a complete woman. They would be there from the time it took to complete their intercourse session, pay their money and leave. But at those times she knew she was a real woman because she acted like one and the men and the lesbians took her like a real woman and told her how beautiful she was. She was a real woman as long as she played the streets.

There would be no outlet for her with a home and family. There would be no secretarial job and the boyfriend to come home to at night.

The *normal* world wouldn't let her forget her past. They would shove it down her throat at every chance.

But those on the street need never know.

She was thirty, then thirty-five and the street grew longer and the customers grew older and Carney grabbed her by the back of the neck as she passed a dreary rooming house, and pulled her into his dank flat and threw her on the bed.

"A little older," he growled, "but the same Ronnie. Maybe there's a buck or two left in you yet…" Then he laughed a snaggletoothed yak… "Ever hear about the spokes of the wheel always returning to the same place… eventually?"

THE END

NEVER UP–NEVER IN

no author listed

in Garter Girls *Vol.5 no.3 Oct./Nov. 1971 on Ed's resume 1971*

JERRY SQUEALED with delight when Helen used her delicate fingers to squeeze him there. He was a rugged guy and not one to squeal in exalted delight very often. Perhaps a shout or a shiver or a moan, but never a squeal. However that's the way Helen affected him when she used those talented hands all over his naked body before they actually got down to the nitty gritty of the session.

But that's about all there was to it. They had tried for some kind of a completion five times in two days and once the preliminaries were over and the nitty gritty was about to commence, everything went haywire. There just was never the nitty gritty of the situation. When her extremely talented hands went to his male member or her lips took the place of the hands or her thighs closed around his, everything went down.

Damn, how much he wanted the beautiful, the luscious, the exquisite Helen. He wanted to run barefooted through her long golden hair. His eyes bathed in the light and the beauty of her pink skin. And her breasts excited him to a point where he was positive nothing could hold his explosion. But damn it all to hell, something did hold back that explosion. Not only held back the explosion, but actually eliminated all the body heats which had been built up during the preliminaries. His blood turned to ice and his nerves sent messages to his brain that they were not going to respond any longer. It was as if every muscle in his body had suddenly become tired and refused to respond. He became a wet dish rag all over.

All he could do was lay back and watch the girl working so hard above him. Every muscle in her body was hard, taunt in the reflexes of her straining excitement and illusions of what should be happening.

She tried, oh God how she tried! She continued until her body was glistening with the sweat of exertion and unsatisfied demands. Then all she could do was roll away, put her hands behind her head and lay her head on the stained pillow. She stretched her body hard and straight along the bed. It was the only way she could force the muscles to relax. The hard strain hurt her. But through the hurt she found a certain amount of release… certainly not satisfaction, but release.

She would sigh loudly and Jerry would moan pitifully. The sixth try was over and still there had not been the final upheaval of surging delights. There apparently was no longer any use in continuing. Nothing was going to happen! Slowly she rolled off the bed and slipped into a brown skirt, then let a soft white angora sweater drift down over her head. She wore no brassiere, but she slipped into a set of pink panties and fastened her loafers over naked feet. She stood up with her hands on her hips. She wasn't actually angry, but she was tremendously disappointed as she looked down at the Tarzanic build of the guy she had tried so desperately to make. Here was a guy who exuded sex yet actually had about as much sex in him as a striking rattlesnake. Good God, he didn't even have that much sex.

Jerry opened his eyes. He'd nearly gone to sleep again. "You leaving?"

"What's the use in staying?"

He covered his eyes with his right arm. "What the hell's wrong with me. You're a luscious dish. You make one see stars and pink clouds when you do those things to me. You've got the most talented hands and fingers I've ever come across. Even your toes do things to me. Your lips are heated entities of fire that burn me from the roots of my hair to the soles of my feet. You turn me on like I've never been turned on before. But then what happens?"

"You tell me, Jerry. Lord knows I've used every trick in the book that I know of and still… well, we both know what happens. What happens? Hell, nothing happens! Maybe you should see a doctor."

"I couldn't begin to put into words how much I want you, Helen. I have since the first day you came to work at the office. We both knew the way I looked at you. I could see right through that knit dress you had on. I could see you naked as clear as I've seen you naked these past two days. Things happened to me right there on the spot, that's why I never got up from behind the desk. Then there you are naked and I can have all of you and there's nothing to take you with. You're like a goddess to me… a goddess I've got to possess or I'll go out of my mind. I'll actually go mad. I've taken every part of your body except… except…." He took his arm down from covering his eyes and looked to her, then, naked sat up cross-legged in the center of the bed. "I never have gone to doctors much. Them and their knives and their pills."

"That's not the kind of doctor I'm referring to. Maybe you need a psychiatrist. You've got a mental block someplace, honey-bun."

"Why don't we give it one more try?"

"And get all worked up again for nothing? Nothing doing! I'm at the point of sheer exhaustion right now. In fact you'd better give me tomorrow off so I can rest up. Monday mornings are bad enough without something like this extra added attraction… did I say attraction? Misadventure is more like it."

"Stay with me a while. Just a little while longer." Helen sighed again. She let her hands drop from her hips then looked around the room. "Where did we put the whiskey last night?"

"Out by the refrigerator." He watched her turn toward the door. "You're not leaving? You will come back?"

She turned in the doorway and shrugged. "I just feel like having a stiff drink… something I don't usually do this early in the afternoon."

Jerry sank back on the bed and stretched out naked. Angrily he slapped his manhood several times then cursed at the grey ceiling to which his eyes had become attached. He was still cussing when Helen returned with two tall glasses of scotch and soda… hers with ice and his without. She handed him one as she sat down on the edge of the bed. "If that helps don't let me stop you," she said referring to his cursing at the ceiling.

"Just lets a lot of hot air out of my lungs." He sat up on the edge of the bed beside her and was the first to sip from the tall glass. Helen didn't sip, she took a healthy swig which made her momentarily gasp for breath. Then she said. "So what's the next step?"

He looked her over from head to toe and the corners of his lips felt like the drool would start all over again. "Why don't you at least take your clothes off? You must be hot in all that fuzz."

"It's not the sweater that makes me hot." She looked at his nakedness and saw the same reaction she had caused six times before. A lying reaction which would only show its true colors when her body laid on top of it. She followed through with that train of thought. "God, what a lie that thing is."

"I just can't understand it. This has never happened to me with any other girl I've ever been with, and that goes back to my school days and the young broads I took out beyond the football field and the gym locker during the weekend dances."

"They must have had a hell of a lot more than I have," she muttered as she once more lowered her panties and put them on a chair near at hand.

"None of them… none of them could compare with the end of your fingernail. You've got everything any girl would give half her life to have. You've got everything! I've been saying it ever since I met you. You're a goddess!"

She lowered her skirt and put it neatly on the chair with the panties. "I honestly don't know why I'm doing this. I sure as hell know how it's going to end again."

Jerry's eyes fastened on the soft mound of deep golden fur between her legs and he felt himself throbbing uncontrolled. He wanted to grab it, hold it down, but that would have been much too obvious. Helen would do that when once more she sat beside him and then the excitement would race through his body the way he wanted it to. Everything would have to wait for that moment. Besides, he couldn't take his eyes from her body. He raised them from her crotch upward and they continued traveling up with the angora sweater as it once more came up over her golden hair. He didn't see her neatly place the sweater with the skirt and the panties but he did watch anxiously as once more she sat her naked body down beside him and picked the tall glass of iced scotch from the floor.

"You're going to give me another chance?"

"The scotch is good. Kind of picks up my spirits. Strange how whiskey has a warming quality. Burns all the way down the first drink you take, then the burn is gone and there is only that soothing feeling left." Her free hand drifted to his manhood and Jerry almost jumped off the bed with joy.

He was positive this time he'd make it. But then he'd been positive six times before, and six thousand times, in thought, before that when he watched her going about the office duties at his place of business.

"I've never given any man this many chances before," she pouted, but her eyes drifted toward what she was doing to him. "I really don't know why I have this time… except you're about the most handsome, most well-built guy I've ever been with. Lord, how you turn me on. It would seem such a shame if I had to go elsewhere to finish my release."

"Don't talk like that." He almost lost his body heats with the thought.

"I mean it," she snapped back. "You can't just turn me on like this then leave me so completely up in the air that my eyeballs feel like they might pop right out of their socket. A girl has to have her releases too. I don't know why it is a man always thinks if he get his thing, his jollies, that everything is alright… to hell with how the girl feels. I've never met a man yet that doesn't feel that way. As long as he's satisfied that's all that matters."

"I'm not that way."

"How in hell should I know? I haven't seen any action yet to make any statement by. But you've got me so heated up I'm ready to explode and what the hell can I explode on?"

"You're my goddess."

"Goddess hell! I'm a flesh and blood woman and a flesh and blood woman needs what all flesh and blood women need when they're in bed with a man and they have done things like we have done all weekend."

"I want to! I want to so very much! I'd do anything in this world to please you. Anything out of this world if it were at all possible." He finished off his scotch and threw the glass across the room. It shattered against the far wall.

"Now that took a lot of brains. We'll be cutting hell out of our feet." But she finished off her drink and did the same thing. And when he rolled back onto the bed and stretched out she mirrored his move and came up close beside him, their hot bodies touching down the entire length of their sides, his left to her right. "Do I get the day off tomorrow?" she snapped.

"Take two," he growled. But the growl soon departed when her hand touched him again. Then he was once more all hot and bothered. "Hot damn," he expounded.

"I hope so," she muttered then rolled over and let her lips briefly brush across his. She was laying half on top of him and he expectantly waited for those talented hands and fingers to start their move.

The twinges started up and down his spine when her toes, those talented toes, found his own. It was only at such times he could completely comprehend that his toes were connected to the foot itself. Even his heels tingled. But it was the fingers which could drive him mad. Those goddess fingers and those goddess lips, and the luscious goddess tongue. But she waited, waited for an eternity, an eternity in which only her toes shouted of things to come.

The light sexy moans then started deep in her throat and her body began to twitch slightly. Jerry knew that it was only a moment away from the time when her fingers would start their magical trip over his skin... turning on every nerve ending in his body.

He fought down the fact that all the preliminaries would do him no good in the end. He fought so damned hard that much of the illusions almost left him as to what was happening at that time. But it was fact. Damn it, it was all too much fact. Then he gave that same squeal he'd given every time her fingers started their movement during those past two days. In fighting down the eventual end he directed his mind to that first moment, that first time he'd found her lips with his and her fingers drifted up and down the inside of his thighs when they stood just inside of his apartment door. That had been the first moment they entered on that wonderful day, two days ago. That was when he knew what those fingers were going to do to him and within a short time his goddess would be captured.

All the *witches*, the *tramps,* the *whores* he'd ever come in contact with could go to hell. Finally he had something which meant all the world to him. The untouchable was about to be touched, had, captured, taken as his own.

The wonders of that first meeting made him squirm with every muscle. And the hot sweats which poured from his body, wet the already dried bedsheets... dried from the sweats of the last attempt. "Squeal, damn it, squeal," he screamed silently through his tortured mind. He was determined that this time would be the time. But the same thoughts fought against what had happened before, and those happenings were more powerful. And still the talented goddess-like fingers worked over his body, turning every nerve into a fiery hell of demand, of anticipation and of illusions which trapped every thought.... Then she rolled on top of him again as he screamed "GODDESS... GODDESS... GODDESS... MY GODDESS... I'VE GOT TO POSSESS YOU... I'VE GOT TO POSSESS MY GODDESS...."

And his member fell away from him again. Helen slammed herself off the bed and this time the anger in her eyes at once more being rejected was real. "Goddess, is it... damn you, you bastard. This is the last time! There will be no more! You can take your job and go to hell with it. You can take your whole body and put it in a cellar trunk. You're no man! You're a sniveling idiot! Goddess! Why, you silly schmuck, you wouldn't know a goddess if you saw one. It's a word you saw in the dictionary once. Maybe you've seen too many Cleopatra movies. Goddess!" She grabbed her skirt and held it in front of her, in preparation for putting it on. "You lousy bastard. That's the last time you'll get me all steamed up and let me cry for mercy. You've got to be some kind of a sadist. Well let me tell you this, buster. There are a lot of guys where you come from and a hell of a lot of them pay high for my services.

"Goddess, is it! Well, you can believe one thing. I was a whore before I came to work for you. I tried to play it straight. But if it's a whore I must be to be satisfied, then that's what I'll be."

Jerry reached out and grabbed her. He yanked her violently to the bed. He no longer faced a goddess. He was facing the kind of woman he'd always had, always enjoyed. There was no longer the possibility of failure between them.

THE END

TRADE SECRETS

by "Shirlee Lane"

in Hellcats *vol.2 no.1 Jan./Feb. 1973 on Ed's resume 1972*

SANDRA MADE HER WAY across the spacious lawn; the well kept lawn. She fully expected to find Mina seated on one of the Marble garden benches near her favorite fountain, but she wasn't there. She put her hand on the smooth marble then looked off to the thick forests beyond the estate.

It was the only place Mina could have gone. Anyplace else, except back at the house, she would have been visible on the estate. She dug her hands into the pockets of her riding pants and took off slowly for the woods. If Mina were in there she could only be at one place. The cliff, overlooking the trinkling waterfall. And that's where she was... seated with her arms locked around her upraised knees, her long organdy dress skirt circled around her. She was a picture in that pose, in that setting.

Perhaps, presently, a pathetic picture. But a picture nevertheless. The white of the organdy dress. The pale pink of her skin. The blue bow hanging loosely from the bow knot at the back and then there was the blue of the sky and the green of the grass. The clear trickle of water from high above dropping noisily into a blue pool below. She was indeed a picture.

Mina hadn't heard her come up. She had been much too deep in her own thoughts. Sandra laid a light hand on her shoulder and the lovely young girl looked up. She tried for a weak smile.

"Sandra. I didn't hear you come up."

Sandra's smile was totally honest. "I know! I didn't want to shock you out of your daydreams too quickly. Bad for the nervous system I understand."

Mina reached up and put her hand over that of her friend. Two very smooth hands. Two hands that any artist would give anything to possess; any surgeon. "I had to get away from the house for a while."

"That's understandable." Sandra curled up on the ground beside her. "Something like this happen to me and I think I'd go out of my mind."

"We the living must keep on living. But one can't help it if they drift back into memories. I decided to come out here where he spent so much of his time. There was no use in my brooding around the house. It might affect everyone I came in contact with."

"Larry's dead, honey! You'll have to give him up, sooner or later."

"I know."

Sandra eyed the cliff and the long drop to the pond below, then she let her eyes drift back to the girl once again. "No foolish ideas, huh?"

Mina got her meaning immediately. "No, of course not. Even if the thought might have crossed my mind I know that Larry would never have wanted me to do anything like that...." Then she blushed. "And I guess I'd be pretty much of a coward.... I couldn't go through with it. The taking of a life, even ones' own seems so distasteful to me."

"Have you figured what you're going to do next?"

"Take a trip, maybe. Back to Europe.... Go to see the places once more where Larry and I went last summer."

"That's living in the past again.... You've just got to get used to the idea that he's no longer here. We buried him more than two weeks ago. Sure, go off somewhere if you like, but not to the places where memories will be brought back to you. That doesn't make for a good mental condition."

Mina reached over and took Sandra's hand again. "Would you go with me?"

"I'm not in the category of those able to afford such a venture."

"Silly! You'd be going with me. I'll take care of everything. Larry was very rich you know. He's left me very well off; very well off."

"I couldn't take money from you."

"You wouldn't be taking it from me really. Let's just say you'd be a tax deduction. You'd be traveling with me as my traveling companion, my accountant, my secretary, my something. You think up a title and that's what you'll be."

Sandra knew the title she'd like to accompany the girl with. But that was not the time to make any such suggestion or even to give rise to any thought as to her real demands. "Sure. I'll think about it." Sandra got to her feet and put both her hands down to take Mina's. "Martha's got a good lunch all ready. Shrimp, just as you like it."

"I'd throw up."

"You'll be sicker than just throwing up if you don't get around to eating something. Now this is just what the doctor ordered… and your favorite dish at that."

Slowly Mina permitted Sandra to ease her to her feet, then Sandra put her arm around the girl's waist and they walked back through the woods.

"Do you always say just the right thing at just the right time, Sandra?"

"I try to…. Sometimes I get bashed in the mouth for it, though."

"Now that I doubt."

Then a short time later they sat at the table in the massive dining room of the great house. They were one at each end of the long table. Sandra never liked sitting so far away from anyone… and she never did like that particular table. There had always been Larry on one end and Mina at the other, and anyone else who happened to be fortunate enough to dine there were spaced somewhere in between. Sandra also always felt that she needed an intercom system for conversation, and she advanced that opinion again.

"You always did say that, didn't you, Sandra."

"I've always said it because I've always meant it, honey love." Then the ancient Martha, the Swedish cook, brought in the steaming shrimp and dished it out for them in silence… and after, they ate in silence… then there was very little to do for the rest of the afternoon. Mina tried reading. But the words blurred. Sandra solved part of the situation by making them each a couple of martinis and that took the edge off until suddenly it was dark outside.

Masters, Martha's ancient husband - part time butler, part time handyman lit the large fireplace then left them alone again. The flames flickered across the great logs and the flickering shadows danced up and down the walls.

"Like little devils," muttered Mina.

"What?"

"The flame reflections." She sighed. "They're never the same twice. There is an entity which never repeats itself. Wouldn't it be so wonderful if life were like that."

"It is, in a way. We're all individuals. We come and we go and we're never repeated. We only come this way but once." She got up from the big easy chair and sunk down to the white fur rug in front of the fireplace. "Sorry, honey. That must have sounded rather morbid. I didn't mean it to be."

"No…. That's alright. I thought it rather profound. Profound, but ever so true. Perhaps life is like the flames of a fire."

Sandra looked across to the large chair in which Mina was curled up with her eyes staring at the flickering reflections. "Come on over and stretch out on the rug with me." Her rump was to the flames, but some distance away. "Heat feels good, you know where." She patted her fanny.

"I haven't laid on a fur rug in ages."

"Then it's about time you did."

She moved across the room and stretched out beside Sandra. Her skirt came up around her knees. Then coyly she looked again to Sandra. "You know what Larry and I used to do when we laid on this rug?"

"I'd hate to hazard a guess."

Mina also got that meaning immediately. "Oh," she said and feigned a slap on Sandra's rump. Sandra loved it, but tried not to show her emotions. "That too," continued Mina. "But we used to get all naked and let the fur capture our whole bodies… our whole skin. Now isn't that naughty to think of something like that?"

"In this case, no." Then Sandra arose and pulled her sweater up over her head and tossed it to one of the chairs. Next, she unhooked her brassiere and let the straps sexily drift down over her arms. The brassiere joined the sweater on the chair. Then her hands dropped down to the fly front of her slacks.

"What in the world are you doing?"

"I think laying naked on your fur rug is an excellent idea. Remember it was all your doing which has made me so brash."

Mina jumped to her feet just as the slacks fell around Sandra's ankles, and she kicked them loose. Mina's hands went to the back of her dress and slipped the knot, then she pulled the dress up over her head. "I think you have a very pleasant idea. It can do nothing but get my mind off of the other things, the unpleasant things."

"Now you're getting with it, kid," grinned Sandra and her eyes fastened on the girl's luscious, youthful, white mounds with the pink rosebud tip which popped out of her brassiere when it was unfastened. Her lips suddenly went dry and her pink tongue came out to moisten them again. "God, what this girl is doing to me. What she has been doing to me all these months," she said silently to herself. However, she tried to keep those thoughts from showing in her face. She wasn't entirely successful, but Mina was much too busy slipping out of her panties to notice any change in her friend.

Sandra let her hands slip down through the top of her panties and she lowered them part way then lifted each leg to step out of them. Her snapping pink twat, exposed, began to twitch as her body juices heated and melted through the opening. This time Mina couldn't help but notice. Yet, suddenly, it didn't matter to her. She remembered what her own had done when Larry looked at her, on those times just before he had taken her in their bedroom... on that very fur rug.

Mina slipped down and lay stretched out on her back. She opened her legs wide. Her eyes fastened on those of her friend, standing naked above her.

Sandra could hardly contain herself any longer. Her eyes went from head to toe of the girl... they locked for a long time on the heaving breasts, then to her twitching middle and the slight rumbling motion of her thighs. She knew that Mina was feeling something... the something that she should be feeling. But Sandra still wasn't quite sure... not entirely of just how to go about it. Then she made the first attack. She stepped over the girl and put one foot on either side of her, so that her fur lined crotch was almost directly over the girl's face.

"Larry used to stand like that, over me, when he wanted to do things to me."

There was that damned Larry again! Sandra wanted to spit the name into the fire where it would burn and be gone forever. But instead she grinned. "Bet he was good in bed."

"That's something between only he and I."

"Sure, kid, and that's the way it should be." Sandra lowered herself to the fur rug and stretched out very close to Mina. She lifted her head and leaned on her hand which was supported up by her elbow.

"Did he ever tell you how beautiful you were?"

"Often! But I think he was just getting me all hot and bothered, and that was his way of doing it."

"But you are beautiful."

Mina felt much of the thrill from those words that Larry used to give her. It was like a chill which started at the base of her skull and traveled swiftly down through her spine until it reached the region of her groin. It made not only her thighs twitch, but her leg muscles jumped spasmodically at the same time.

Sandra's hand went over and slowly began to rotate softly on the girl's flat middle. Then when Mina's moans of acceptance and enjoyment escaped her lips, Sandra rode the hand upward until it melted between the mounds of her lovely breasts. She would play with each of the breasts for a long time. Mina liked that. She remembered how Larry had always done it. Then Sandra lowered the hand until it fit smoothly, perfectly between Mines legs and Mina closed those legs, locked them over the hand while the fingers twisted and curled in the fine brush of her pubic region, then entered the walls of her vagina.

With heated lips Sandra leaned over the girl's body and took the nipples, one at a time, of each breast. She sucked at them as if she were about to drain them dry of all the body fluids they might contain. Sandra's saliva drooled over the mounds and it ran in a small, thin river down the length of her body. It was hot saliva; sexually heated by the fires from within them both.

Sandra's head, after a time, came up and she looked into the Angel-like face of her new lover. "I love you," she spoke ever so softly.

Mina's arms went up around the girl and tightened around her back. "And I love you, Sandra. I always have. Ever since we first met, I've always loved you."

Then their lips came together and their tongues lashed and smashed, and licked, and crashed within their mouths. Their bodies locked, crushingly together. The sweat came from every pore, on both of them. They slipped and slid into and against each other, but they never unlocked themselves. They remained pressed together, pelvis to pelvis, clit to clit until the sounds of the Angels took them to the clouds above and showed them where the horns of heaven were blown, then permitted them to witness a glimpse of eternity, before letting them return to earth, and the fur rug.

"I'm glad I killed him," said Sandra and she meant it with all her heart.

"I know you are," sighed Mina. "And I'm glad it was planned so well."

"So very well."

"No one has ever found out."

"No one will ever find out. And I will have you all to myself for all of our lifetime."

"And I will have you, my love."

Although their body heats had subsided, they once more locked in a tight embrace and their tongues locked just as tightly. They would remain that way for some long moments… then…

The two old, haggered women, got up from the fur rug and put on the clothing they had used every night since Larry was murdered more than fifty years ago. The clothing they had had on that first time… once more they had relived the ritual. And both knew there would be another night… perhaps many more nights.

THE END

Kiss the Pain Away

by "Shirlee Lane"

in Gemini *Vol.2 no.1 Mar./Apr. 1973 on Ed's resume 1972*

SHE CROSSED HER LEGS tightly under her short miniskirt and hoped he wouldn't touch her again. He had already pushed her to the filthy alley floor and her new, white knit skirt and matching turtleneck angora sweater were messed beyond belief. She wanted to scream, but there was only hot breath over a dry throat and no sounds came out except a whimpering which she herself could hardly even hear.

The rugged, filthy man in the ragged undershirt and soiled trousers who stood over her certainly had more in mind than to just throw her to the ground and mess up her lovely outfit. But for the moment, and for several moments since she had hit the ground and rolled over in the slime several times, all he had done was to stand over her with the drool… a grey-green drool, dribbling over the corners of his lips. His eyes were tense… looking directly at her but also as if right through and beyond her.

His hands played with the front of his trousers for all that time and Barbara could see the bulge quickly rising there… and when it looked like it was full, his hand movements… like the masturbation process, kept moving up and down with the object and the material of his pants held tightly in his thick fingers.

Barbara moved her injured arm up as if to rest it upon her forehead and the man gave an animal-like growl and indicated danger with his free hand. She let her arm drop back down to her side again and froze in the position she had assumed when she realized the spot she was in originally.

The man's free hand came down again and unzipped his fly. His enormous rod shot out. Nothing stopped Barbara from flinging her arm up over her eyes then. But it came away again when she felt the rough hand reach down to the bottom of her soft sweater and pull it far up around her neck… and her arm flew down again when the giant hand tore away her white nylon brassiere and her luscious breasts came into full view… heaving up and down with the frightened breaths she was gasping in and exhaling.

She was certain the crotch of her panties would be torn out next. Damn…. God…. How she wanted to scream out. She knew that the creep was going to jam that enormous rod into her and she would be soiled more inside with his fluid than she was outside from the alley filth.

But again he stood up. He gripped his throbbing muscle and began to pump it with all his might… his eyes never left the sight of her breasts, and her eyes never left his stare. She began to shake all over… and so did the masturbator as he strove for a climax. Again she opened her mouth to scream, and again nothing came out except some of her hot saliva which had gathered there.

There was no hiding the fact when he was about to shoot his load. She could see his face muscles tighten and the skin appeared as tight as the skin on a drum. His eyes widened… the drool at the corners of his lips increased. He arched his entire lower quarters forward… his hand movement went faster, and suddenly he swung his mammoth tool to a point directly over her face and it spurted… spurted as if he had been storing up for months, and the sticky white goo spilled over her eyes, her nose and into her mouth which was opened again in a dry scream… a dry scream which was quickly lubricated. And when the scream came, it was ear piercing… a terror stricken….

A door near the end of the alley suddenly flung open and several girls of all shapes, sizes and dress pushed their way out. The light from within illuminated the alley. They saw the girl in white on the ground and they saw the creep still shooting his load over her face….

"Get the dirty son-of-a-bitch," screamed the tallest and broadest of the girls, and there was a mad rush in the direction of the action.

The masturbator gave one yelp and with his cock still drooling and sticking out of his pants, raced out toward the mouth of the alley… several of the girls gave chase.

The big one with two of the others stopped beside Barbara. "It's alright, kid. He's gone."

Barbara came to a sitting position and took the handkerchief the big girl offered her. She wiped the sticky fluid away as best she could, then looked down at her clothing. She began to cry. "It's ruined. It's all new and it's ruined."

"I'm Beth," said the big girl as she took the handkerchief from Barbara's hands and looked to it. "That all he did to you?" She didn't wait for an answer. She reached down and pulled up the white knit miniskirt and looked at the crotch of her panties then let her hand rest there a moment. "Yeah… you're a little damp, but he didn't get to you." She straightened back up. "You can always get more clothes, honey. But you couldn't get a new pussy." She reached over and helped Barbara, unsteadily, to her feet. "Come on into my place. It's a bar. I live right behind it. We'll get you cleaned up."

Silently Barbara permitted the three girls to help her down the alley to the door, then into the dimly lighted beer bar. She nearly fell into the first chair she came upon. Beth disappeared a moment then returned with a bottle of whiskey. "Can't sell this hard stuff in the bar, but ain't no law says I can't keep some in my apartment back there. Come on, kid. Take a good swig. It'll do you good." She slopped the water glass half full and forced it to Barbara's lips. She spluttered and choked, but got most of it down.

For a long moment she gasped for breath, then looked to the girls as she tried for a smile. "I'll be alright now. Thank you for everything. I mean everything."

"Creeps like that are in every alley in town. Young and pretty girls like you get killed around here. What in hell's a fluff like you doing down this way in the first place?"

"I started to work over in the Gilmore building this morning. I couldn't find the bus stop in the dark. I don't know my way around yet."

"You sure don't, honey. Shit, you sure did get your clothes messed up."

"And I just bought it. A hundred dollars."

"Clothes don't matter none when ding-dongs like that want to beat their dork. Only when they get finished shooting all over the place they generally do a lot of other things to the girl. How come you didn't scream sooner?"

"Couldn't…."

"No voice, huh?"

Barbara nodded. "Well, you can't go home looking like that. Come on back to my pad, we'll get you cleaned up. Some of the girls leave some of their things in my place at times. I probably can find something to fix you up with so you can get home. Come on…."

But before they could move out, the rest of the girls returned telling of the chase… but the creep got away… and more than one wanted to go out and haunt the alleys and cut the balls and cock off any bum-bastard they could find… "poor little fluff like you getting tore up like that…."

Beth turned to one of the girls who had stayed behind with her. "Take over the joint for a while, Gus. I'll see to the little fluff here."

The one called Gus winked. "I bet you will."

Beth put her strong hand under Barbara's arm and helped her to her feet then led her to the rear of the bar and they entered the makeshift place she called an apartment. Barbara sat on the edge of the mammoth bed and was surprised just how soft it was. It had not looked so soft upon first sight.

Barbara watched as Beth picked up a sash basin and went into her bathroom, then returned with the hot water which she placed on a nightstand near the bed. "Come on, I'll help you get undressed."

It was a logical request but for some reason Barbara felt strange about it. She had undressed in front of other girls many times, especially at college… and there had been a couple of strange ones… but none of them affected her as much as the big woman who stood in front of her, hands on hips. But she slowly, almost painfully, stood up and slipped the once beautiful angora sweater up over her head. She let it fall to the one wooden chair in the room. She didn't want the mess of the garment to rub off on the clean chairs or the bedspread. Then she slipped the zipper-free miniskirt down around her legs. As she stepped out of it, picked it up and was about to put it with the sweater she caught that strange glint in the big woman's eyes… the same strange glint some of the girls had that she remembered at college….

Barbara stood there in her bikini panties which had matched the torn and discarded brassiere. "Them too," Beth said heatedly and indicated the panties.

"I don't hurt down there."

The woman grinned. "When I finish what I have to do, you'll want to take a bath." She lifted the wash cloth from the hot water as if in preparation for rubbing the dirt and the dried semen from Barbara's face.

Barbara shrugged then put her hands into the top of her panties and slipped them down. When she put them on the chair with the sweater and skirt she stood absolutely, but radiantly naked… and there was no longer any mistaking the glint in the big woman's eyes. But there was nothing Barbara could do about it then. She was naked. She moved to sit on the edge of the bed. She listened to Beth wheeze through tight lips and clenched teeth. But the wet cloth felt good as it cleansed her face.

"The filthy bastard," she muttered while she worked. "The friggin' filthy bastard. Men! All of them! Puttin' their stuff all over the face of a beautiful fluff like you... a real beautiful fluff." Then the wet cloth was put into the water again and when it came back it found its mark on her breasts. Beth took a long time with her washing movements there, and the fingers squeezed the ripe mounds and her fingers left the cloth at times to put her nipples between them. The nipples rose up, hard and in need. Barbara didn't want to think about sex at that moment.... It might be a long time before she wanted another man with her. "Dirty, rotten bastards," she hissed. "All the same. All they can think of is one thing...."

Then suddenly she threw the wash cloth into the basin and her lips went down to capture first one, then the other of Barbara's nipples... then before Barbara knew what had happened, each of the globes, one at a time, had gone entirely into the big woman's mouth....

Beth came away suddenly and pulled Barbara to her feet and clamped her mouth over hers. Her tongue searched in the dainty mouth and found her tongue. It slashed back and forth. Barbara again felt like screaming... but something else raced through her mind. There was something about the woman that reminded her of those strange girls at college... but with one difference. Beth was in a man's work shirt and work pants... the other girls had been dressed like girls....

Her mouth came away from Barbara's but the big woman held her arms pinned to her sides. "Do you want to scream?"

Frightened, Barbara shook her head.

"Good! Because it wouldn't do you any good, not in here... the girls out there will only be envious of me...." Then she shoved Barbara heavily back onto the bed. "Bastard men never know what a girl needs. Shot all over your face, did he. And what good... what pleasure could that do you? Now I'll show you what the son-of-a-bitch should have done to you."

The animal like growl was the same as the alley creep as she dove her face, her lips, her tongue between Barbara's legs and were buried deep into the pubic hair.

THE END

MORBID CURIOSITY

by "Dick Trent"

in Switch Hitters *vol.2 no. 3 Calga pub. Dec./Nov/ 1971*
on Ed's resume

"ALL RIGHT, SCREW YOU, CHARLIE," she screamed, took a big swig of her martini, dropped her glass then promptly fell flat on her face in the pool.

She remained that way, face down until Charlie reached over and dragged her by her feet back to the side of the pool. He sat there for several minutes looking at her stilled form and wondered if he should pump the water out of her. But then he thought better of that thought because she hadn't been in the water that long, and besides, if she had swallowed a little water it would probably be good for her… dilute the double martinis she had been swilling all evening.

"Why in the fuck do I get stuck with all the shit-heads?" he mumbled to himself, then stretched out on the tile with his hands up behind his head and his eyes glazed glaring up at the full moon. He'd had his share of martinis also, but then he had a tremendous capacity for alcohol of any kind. And no matter how much he drank it didn't seem to affect his staying power in the sex act. He could make it with any broad all night long and still ask for more when the sun came up. He was twenty-eight, tall, muscular and ruggedly handsome. A full parlay for any sex minded girl… in fact he had been known to turn on many a frigid one where lesser males had failed.

He rolled his eyes across to the naked girl next to him as she moaned once, then opened her eyes. There was a silly grin on her face. And it was apparent the dousing in the pool had done nothing to sober her up.

381

"Was I swimming?"

"Something like that."

"Another little drinkie?"

Charlie got up. "I'll get it. I doubt if you could stagger over to the bar and back here and still have the glass in one piece."

"I could do anything I have a mind to."

"That I'd bet on."

He turned from her and walked to his pool side bar and poured the already mixed martini. He drank the first one, then refilled the glass and took it back to the girl. She took it then set the glass down on the tile beside her. "Did we make the scene yet, Charlie, honey?"

"Twice before midnight."

"I don't remember."

"I didn't think you would."

"Then I have to do it again so I'll remember." She opened her legs and the split beaver seemed to wink at him and Charlie couldn't stop the erection which suddenly came upon him and stood out so prominently in front of him.

Shirley giggled and tossed her long, wet blonde hair out full on the tile, pulling it away from where it was sticking to the back of her neck. "You like what I got? You don't need to answer." She snapped the end of his penis with her forefinger. "I can see what I do to you. The other girls get you up like that?"

"I like broads. I dig them deep."

"With that, I bet you do." She wiggled her pink butt invitingly on the ground and with each movement her ripe for plucking nipples quivered on their beautiful, round firm bases. Then she reached up and wiggled her fingers. "Gimme!"

Charlie moved in closer to her and she took his large dork into her hands, and knowing what she wanted he knelt down beside her and she turned over to put her lips firmly around and along his shaft. He knew he was being had and he wanted it badly. The insatiable urge that always swelled up inside of him at such times could only be turned off by a complete climax so powerful he never knew whether he was being hurt or pleasured. But who the hell cared. Whatever it was he knew he wanted it. He only wished there was a never-ending release to the feeling.

But then he was spilling his seed and Shirley took a martini chaser. "That was good," she sighed.

"Which?"

"Both."

Charlie picked up her glass and carried it for the refill, then back to her. "You're starting to sound sober."

"Something like that," and she snapped his penis again, "is enough to sober anybody up. But don't worry. I'll get drunk again." Then she stretched out and opened her legs wide. "Just let me know when you're ready again."

And at that point he got his own martini.

Shirley turned over on her elbows and cupped her chin with her hands. Her eyes gazed out into the darkness and they searched for the darker shadows which were there. The darker shadows of markers and other remembrances like crosses and the main mausoleum. "Did you ever make it out there?"

"Where?"

"The cemetery of course."

"Do you think I'm some kind of a ghoul?" He actually choked on his martini. But when he looked up his eyes followed her gaze.

"You don't have to be a ghoul to think of something like that. Besides, when you have to go there it's too late to use that thing in your pants. I hear they break it off anyway. Maybe you're not supposed to use it anymore in hell or heaven. It's a thing of the past. You know if I felt there was no sex after death I just wouldn't go. Tell me! If you're not a vampire or a ghoul or whatever else hangs around cemeteries, how come you bought a house next door to one?"

"It's quiet and I can write undisturbed."

"You mean you aren't afraid of the grave creatures coming across that dinky little wall and capturing you?" She giggled. Then she stood up. "Come on. Let's go do it over somebody's grave. It might be real kicks."

"Too far to carry the martini jug. Besides I like that nice soft bed inside."

"I'll be extra special good."

"What makes you think so?"

"Because just thinking about it has juiced my pubic hairs and I'm quivering all over."

"Anticipation is sometimes more powerful than the real thing." He was serious.

"Sure it is. But I bet I climax so hard it will rumble the whole grave-yard."

"That would be something to see."

She stood up, raced to the bar, gobbled down another martini and raced back to him.

"It's dark as hell out there. We're liable to break our fool necks. Come on, Shirley, let's just go back into the bedroom and I'll bring the martini pitcher and we'll have a ball the way we always do. You always liked that white fur rug on your butt. We'll put it on the bed and take off for the tall timbers and the short grass."

She pouted. "That's the whole trouble. It's doing it like we always do it. Sometimes people should go through a change. It's like only a couple of years ago when we were in school all the kids liked to do it in strange ways. Like in the back seat of a car when they could go right out on the grass and be comfortable. And we did it in the shower and behind the football field. And I even did it in the front seat of a car with a boy named Pete."

"What's so strange about the front seat?"

"The car was in the garage and his father was mowing the lawn outside. Imagine the sound of that thumping motor combined with our own thumping on the front seat. The old man out front didn't even hear the horn when we hit it once. God damn, that was a thrill... any minute we could have been caught and all hell would have broke loose. But that's why the big thrill. The wondering as to what might happen. I tell you it was one of the most intensifying moments of my life."

"But there's no father out in the cemetery mowing any lawn. There's only graves and monuments."

"Perhaps there is father time."

"I do believe you've gone psycho." He paused, looked out into the darkness then back to her sex hungry, expectant eyes. "You know there are names for people who play around with the dead."

"Necrophilia? Nothing like it." She shook her head in emphasis. "That's like making the scene with a dead person. I know all about that shit." She shuddered. "But this isn't the same. This is like out under God's free sky, laying on God's sacred soil. Good Lord, Charlie. Reach for the impact of what I've just said."

"I'm reaching... I'm reaching."

"Say you'll do it."

"Maybe if I get drunk enough."

She raced across the tile, after snatching his empty glass from him, filled it and raced back. She shoved the glass into his hand. "Then get drunk enough." Her thighs twitched even as she stood there looking at him. She had an uncontrollable, slight forward and backward motion which also captured her fanny and thighs.

"The grave diggers were all over the place this morning. They might have left some open graves."

"So if we fall in we'll do it right there in the bottom of a grave where somebody's coffin will be set in permanently tomorrow."

"Nothing turns you off once your mind is set, does it?"

She shook her head. "Nothing." She prayer styled her hands and placed them at her crotch, pressing the thighs in tightly around them. She crossed and uncrossed the lower part of her legs as the heat flashed up and down her body seemingly to start nowhere but everywhere at the same time. "I'm on fire, Charlie. You've got to do something fast. And the same old way isn't going to do it for me this time. I'll die right here, all burned up. I just know I will."

"I don't like walking through places at night that I don't know. I don't even go down dark streets in the city."

"I'll guide you."

"Now who sounds like the ghoul?"

"Maybe there will be a Mrs. somebody out there who went all through her life sexually unsatisfied. And there she is laying in her satin lined box and she never knew what it was all about. Maybe she's looking down at us from heaven..."

"Or up from hell," he cut in once more attempting to dissuade her with a joke line...

"Or hell," she continued seriously. "No matter where her soul is, it's looking and it is seeing two mortal souls having sex on her grave, and they are doing things she never did in her whole life... possibly never even thought about in her whole life. Think about how many people in this world never thought about having intercourse, a good lay, on a grave."

"You think about it." He took a drink.

"I am thinking about it." Shirley had become dead serious. "I am thinking extremely hard about it and I'm turned on to a point where there is no turning back now. If I have to, I'm going out there alone and jerk off. But I am determined to have sex on somebody's grave before this night is over. I've thought about it ever since I've been coming out here and laying you."

"That's morbid. You mean you had such thoughts all the time you were using your mouth and when I'm in you. Thoughts of me wasn't enough?"

"Don't become jealous of a graveyard, darling. In all sex there has to be some kind of an illusion. You have yours. Just think about it. You're not always thinking of me when you're pumping up and down. I've seen you with closed eyes. I've seen you shoot off to your little pink cloud." She paused and looked out into the dark again. "This has been my illusion for more than two weeks."

"Look, girl, there's no Mrs. Smorgasboard or Mrs. anything else out there with a spirit which is going to be playing peeping Tom with us. It's just a wild cricket, mouse, maggot filled piece of land reserved for the dead."

"And the living who demand it. We demand it."

"You mean you demand it!"

"I demand it." The determination caused her eyes to narrow. "Charlie. It's either that or I never come back here again. If you want to make love to me you'll have to come to my place… next to the funeral parlor."

"Good Lord, I forgot about that." Then he remembered about his thoughts when she fell into the pool. "Why in the fuck do I get stuck with all the shit-heads?" But she was far from being a real shit-head. She was stacked to the hilt. And there was nothing in the sex line which she couldn't handle and turn in the best of the professional jobs.

He didn't want to lose her. And it was true she did live next to a funeral parlor. Possibly, deep in his mind, that was why he moved to the edge of the cemetery. Morbid curiosity. But it was different living near the cemetery. All was so quiet. Next to the funeral parlor there was always the wailing and the shouting and the crying, and the crazy laughter of the morticians as they went about their joyful work. The cutting up of the corpses and the bloodletting to make room for the preservatives along with the continual flushing of the tanks. It simply wasn't good inducements for sexual practices… except for the necrophiliacs.

"Alright! Let's go!"

Shirley gave a tremendous shudder. She fairly grabbed his arm and wanted to run. But he made them level and kept her to an even pace. He wasn't about to screw her at the bottom of some open grave. Topside of the grave he could take. Any lower than that and she wouldn't have to invite him to her place next to the funeral home. He'd simply find himself another steady girl. There were plenty of others around and probably just as good as she.

Then he didn't think any more until she laid her hot, naked butt on the slight rise of a fresh grave where the grass had been replanted.

"Take me," she breathed heavily and extended her arms up to him and her hands and fingers looked, in the dark, like skeletons and talons reaching out from the grave. But the mental image could not frighten him. He bent to her and his rigid shaft extended deeper into her than it had ever before accomplished and Shirley screamed with delight. She screamed and called him all the vile names she could think of. She was getting kicks she never before had witnessed and Charlie had to admit that he too found something more than he ever dreamed existed. And below them was a third party... sleeping... endlessly sleeping and still further below in the center of the earth... or about where the earth's crust was stirring...

Shirley gave one last scream of pleasure in her exploding climax and it had happened at the same instant Charlie blew his tool and to them the earth opened up in one shaking disastrous bounce... and sometime the following day the funeral procession moved in religious silence into the cemetery... and the casket was carried past the wide split across the grave... the wide split which went the length of the cemetery and through several other lands of many counties... and upon looking down the mourners found two more victims of the fantastic earthquake which had shaken the city.

THE END

BAITING MILLIE

By Ed Wood

on his resume 1973 from Hellcats *July/Aug. 1973*

MILLIE ALWAYS WORE PANTSUITS... not the fluffy or extremely feminine type, just the opposite, more extreme, toward the masculine styles and materials... but in this day and age of the unisex look few ever thought much about it. If she got angry her voice would go deep, but other than that her voice was little different than any of the other girls in the office, and she had a cute swing to her delightfully rounded fanny, she didn't try to hide it or disguise it... in fact she might even have emphasized it at times, especially when she passed Sharon's desk... Sharon, the new girl... not more than a month on the job... always in those tight or fluffy sweaters and the short miniskirts... always advertising her wares, her attributes... like she was out to make every male in sight, like every male in sight would flip over the slightest raised eyebrow on her cute little oval face, and her long red hair hung far below her shoulders. It was hard to see the lovely turned ankles under that desk, but Millie never missed them when they appeared and crossed the spacious office to the water cooler, or when they transported her to the desk in the morning and away from it when the five o'clock quitting time came around... she never missed that sight... she would glance over the top of her glasses, pretending that she was still going over some papers on her own desk, but she was really watching those luscious ankles, and the bobbing of the girl's titties under the sweater.... She knew that Sharon wore no brassiere... no titties in the world could bounce and sway like that when they were constricted in a brassiere.... Sharon was something else, and Millie could almost taste the crotch of the girl's panties every time she came within a foot of her...

and there was always that cute, almost inviting smile when they passed each other, but what kind of an invitation could it be?… the only ones the girl ever seemed to care about were the good looking men who strolled through the office all during the working hours…. Millie had seen her with a couple of them at times when she went into the cocktail bar which was on the ground floor of their Wilshire Boulevard office building… watching the men making their passes, and that crazy smile of the girl always turned Millie on and there were those times she got so hot she had to go into the ladies' room of the cocktail lounge, lock the door behind her and masturbate… she could never have waited to get home to her apartment where she could be more comfortable… where she had a set of dildoes… but she preferred her soft finger… there were few times whenever she saw any girl which turned her on that she could fully wait until she got back to her apartment… it was impossible… her inner thighs would begin to twist, then to quiver and soon they were throbbing and the pink lips of her vagina snapped at each other… and the heated moisture wetted the crotch of her own panties and at times of an extreme heat the moisture turned to little riverlets which drooled through the legs of her panties and down her thighs into the tops of her nylon stockings… outside she might have had the mannish pantsuits, but underneath her undies were always nylon and sometimes quite frilly and there were always the panty hose or garter belts to hold up the more conventional nylon stockings… she was not a confirmed butch, the aggressor, although she did prefer that role, but she hated men's underwear, they were too conventional, and she didn't dare wear men's outer clothes, she didn't really approve of the butches that did, it took everything away from the makeup that they were trying to produce, a girl should be a girl, even though she preferred having her love affairs with other girls, that was the way a lesbian should always act, she had to be a girl with a girl, if she wanted a man then she wouldn't be a lesbian, and if she wanted to be a man, then she was missing the whole point of being a lesbian… men were to be eliminated from the female love role… a lesbian could always do without a man, and the only reason she ever used a dildo, shaped like a man's cock, was because there were times she wanted something deeper within her canal than her finger could extend, that was the only reason for the dildo, certainly not for any male thought reasons… she had met many butches that were of the female transvestite lure, but she didn't approve of them, she never could be aroused by them, although there were many that had put the make on her

from time to time, the truck driver types, the lumber jack type, the steve-
dore type, the downright brash, street bum types. She couldn't be turned
on by them, so she never had a sexual experience with them... there was
no reason to try if she couldn't get excited from the first sight. Sharon was
easy to like, to get all hung up on... lovely redheaded Sharon. She was so
far from the butches she had met and were always propositioning her...
she disliked them more than men, because they seemed to be neither
male nor female, simply freaks which should be pitied... what could they
do for a girl except remind her of men, rough, tough, hairy, smelly men,
that's how the bull dykes affected her... but there in that lovely cocktail
lounge everything was different... there wasn't a lesbian in the place... at
least she didn't think so, and she was in on the know... and it takes one to
know one... she felt she was completely secure in the fact that there wasn't
a lesbian in the place... except her... and no one could ever class her, by
sight, as a lesbian... her clothing came from the best, the high class factories, the high class stores... high fashion... she made her face up with just
the right amount of makeup... she was always having passes made at her
by males... she dated a few... to keep up the pretext of a nice girl in the
office... but dinner, a show, or something like that was as far as she would
go... she didn't get as many dates as she might if she had let one or two of
them at least play with her lovely titties, or permit a hand to caress the
front of her slacks, or even slip down the waist band and permit the hand
to rub a bit on the crotch of her panties... but that would go against all of
her lesbian principles... she did let them kiss her a few times... at her
door... she never invited any of them into her apartment... tight lipped
kisses... and it was all a cold fish deal... seldom did the same fellow date
her twice... the cold fish would never have a hook in her mouth... at least
not a male.... Sharon might lower a hook... she might get caught on Sharon's hook, or someone exactly like Sharon... there had been Margie before.... Margie was a delightful girl... soft, wore see-through blouses
when she could get away with it, like at cocktail parties, and some such
affair and those glorious boobies just hung out there for everybody to see,
and Millie had to laugh in private as to the thoughts of the males who
oogled at those luscious globes and then probably went into the john to
jerk off with their fantasies as to how it would be with Margie... and all
the time Margie wouldn't have given them the sweat off her pussy... she
hated men with a purple passion... she accepted them because they were
in command of the world... in command of the dollar... and she went to

the cocktail parties to keep up a front.... Millie had always accepted the important invitations to cocktail parties because she had to keep up a front also... and she could carry on a conversation with the best, the most witty of the males in attendance, and with their wives or their girlfriends... they would be surprised to learn how many of their girlfriends were just like she was... lesbian to the core and playing the bastards for all they were worth, taking for themselves whatever they could get and laughing behind their backs.... Poor Margie... whatever got into her? She was insatiable where sex was concerned, she could go at it night and day, she said she got turned on to lesbianism by a school teacher as far back as her grade school days and it was in the toilet of the locker after the school had closed and she had to remain to clean up, it was her time for that duty... and it was by no accident that the teacher left her desk at the floor above, straightened her severe skirt and made her way down to the locker room... she knew it was Margie's time for the cleanup detail... she had hounded herself about that fact all afternoon in the class room when she looked across to the very young Margie in her fluffy white angora slipover and the light brown skirt, and there were times as Margie twisted in her seat that the teacher could see the yellow crotch of her panties, and the teacher could hardly contain herself, she might have exploded right there on her chair behind the desk if she had not had extreme control of herself, perhaps not her emotions, but her physical self, through the experience of years and years of such onlooking... dry lips, dry tongue, hot breath, stuttering, nervous hands and trembling inner thighs... the teacher had so looked forward to that moment when the others had left, and the janitors never came in until seven in the evening, their usual time, and there was only she and Margie in the building, and if there were any of the male teachers or students around they wouldn't dare come into the girls' locker room, and certainly there was nothing wrong with her being down there, she was only checking to see that all was being done well.... Margie looked at the woman and something about her eyes hypnotized her, and when the teacher took her lightly by the hand and led her into the toilet and sat her down on the bowl and locked the door behind them, and then using both her hands raised her skirt, and then lowered her panties, then lowered her eager lips to the fuzzy little snatch and her tongue protruded to the dainty, girl smelling, slightly protruding, youthful, soft clit... the first shock sent a gasp from Margie's lips and her hands grabbed the back of the teacher's head and held her into place until she found climax after climax... the boys were out from that time on, and the teacher had her new pet, and Margie found many of the girls who liked to do their thing that way... she watched the teacher and found out the girls who were left alone with her, and she watched the school to see how long it was from the time the school closed until the teacher and the girl came out... and she knew by how long they stayed in there as to which of the girls had become another pet, and Margie went to them and they always came around to her way of thinking, and Margie could never get enough.... It was Margie who approached Millie, not the other way around, and they lived together for such a long time, then Margie found a book that said that lesbians make the best whores because they have the best of two worlds, they make fortunes taking on men and they can do it so easily because they have no emotional entanglements to offer... they do not like men, but they can service them, and they can fill their bank accounts, and they can have a lesbian lover on the side to have orgasms, and true love... and they could have all the sex they craved, and never a care or a fear in the world, and that's what Margie felt she was cut out to be in life. With her insatiable demand for sex she would get all she wanted... therefore Margie was gone from the apartment, which they had shared, one evening when Millie came home from work... Margie had worked, of course, at the same office as Millie and it was Millie who reported her as sick that morning, but she would be alright in a day or two... and when Millie came home she found the note.... Margie had to write her feelings because she knew she couldn't bear to face Millie and tell her the facts, she was desperately in love with Millie, but it had to be her way because she would only hurt Millie in the long run if she went out time and time again to get her complete satisfaction... a satisfaction which would never be complete... then there was Shirley.... It was a bar pickup... but not one which might cause distress between either party.... Shirley was a delight to watch as she swayed in her miniskirt... she never simply walked, she had a rhythm which could only be classed as swaying.... Millie almost let her hand go up under her skirt and masturbate herself right there in the bar when she saw that swaying fanny... she did let her hand go to the front of her skirt, and slightly rub the spot... just enough, but not enough to be noticed... at least she thought she wasn't being noticed.... Shirley had noticed... their eyes had met and there was that spark which went through them... and that spark told them everything they needed to know, but even at that Millie wasn't sure... she never was the one to make the first move… except when she was definitely sure… she wasn't sure about Shirley… she rubbed the front of her skirt and she knew she had to go into the ladies' room, and what she had to do… she did… she stood near the toilet and pulled back the leg of her panties after pulling up the skirt and holding it in position with her free hand, and she inserted her finger… it had just reached the inner edge of her pubic hairs when the light tapping came on the locked cubicle door and the little voice asked to come in and Millie was shocked, but she opened the door and there was the exotically beautiful Shirley and Shirley told her that she would do that for her, only she didn't use her finger, she sank down on the toilet seat and inserted her tongue…. Shirley would last a full year with Millie…. Shirley would never work at the office where Millie worked… the opportunity never presented itself during that year… there never were any openings… none of the girls there got pregnant during that year so they never had to quit or take time off which would have permitted an opening where Millie might have slipped Shirley in… but then Shirley didn't like to work too hard anyway… she liked to sit on her cute fanny as a ticket taker in the box office of a movie theatre, and she was quite content there… she didn't make much money, but then she didn't have to spend much…. Millie was the head of the department at her office, she made enough for both of them, she took care of all the bills, the rent and the phone and the gas and the electric…. Millie could have cared less if Shirley worked or not, but then Shirley didn't like sitting home all the time…. Shirley was killed in a street accident when absentmindedly she went against the light at an intersection when she was racing to catch her bus across the street… it broke Millie's heart and she cried for a week, and she didn't get to her job for a week, illness, a death in the family… she wouldn't be fired… they depended upon her too much… then there was Sharon… the luscious Sharon who swayed when she walked… she didn't just walk, she swayed with each step… she glided… she was so much like Shirley…. Millie had to possess the girl, but she never caught her eyes in that spark, the way she did with the others and knew that there was the chance for a good make…. Shirley's eyes had met hers and there was that spark…. But Sharon… And then she was in that cocktail lounge in the building below the office and she was having a martini with one of the office managers… and her eyes did look across to Millie who was also having a martini… a double… and still there was not that spark, but Sharon did raise her breasts a little higher and it seemed that she was sighing and taking in more breaths than was necessary and her boobies bobbed up and down, and swayed like the cheeks of her ass when she breathed, and that did it for Millie... her hand rested on her crotch... and although she tried not to, her finger dug deep into the material being hidden by the rest of her hand, and still trying to control herself which she couldn't, the finger dug in deeper until the material was lightly rubbing against her clit... and the sweat appeared on her forehead... more so in the "V" of the pubic hairs beneath the crotch of her panties. She knew what she had to do. She had to go into the ladies' room, get into the cubicle and relieve herself and try to forget Sharon... it would never work... never an indication... never a come on of any kind... and then she was in the cubicle and she lowered the top of her pantsuit, and pulled the leg of her panties aside and her finger had just reached the base of her pubic hairs when the light knock came at the cubicle door and Sharon's voice said those same words about letting her do it for Millie... and it was all starting again... fate was no stranger to Millie... somebody was always baiting Millie... it had been that way all her life.

THE END

INSATIABLE

by Edw. D. Wood Jr

in Cherry *magazine Vol.3, no.1 Jan./Feb. 1974, on Ed's resume 1973*

SHE WANTED TO GET LAID, damn how she wanted to get laid... but Jim wasn't around and he'd been the only one she'd gone to bed with for the entire six months they'd been going together... he wouldn't be back for another week... six days to be exact... but she wanted to get laid right then, her whole body cried out for the sexual experience, and every time she thought of Jim it made the whole sexual process that much more terrifying to bear.

She hadn't always been that way. There was a time she could take it or leave it. But ever since she had been with Jim and his insatiable sexual demands she couldn't get enough either. There wasn't a day that they hadn't done some form of sex act... in the car... out in the park... of course, in the bedroom. Weekends when they could spend the whole seventy-two hours with each other they hardly ever left the bedroom... just to eat or go to the bathroom... they didn't even take time to shower off the sexual sweats which had enveloped their bodies during the actual action... there never seemed time enough, and Jim was one of those guys who needed very little time between sessions and Shirley could take him continually without let up and she climaxed with every one of his ejaculations... sometimes six or seven times. Oh, how she loved the feeling of the climax...

And even as she thought about it her inner thighs shook, quivered and began to sweat... she didn't have to worry about sweating up the crotch of her panties, she didn't have any on... she only wore her sheer nylon bed jacket, but she had a small fuzzy rug wrapped around her feet.

Her feet seemed to be the only part of her body which hadn't heated up… her hair was straggly from the sweat which welled in that area.

Her hand reached down and her index finger began to lightly diddle with herself while her mind's eye formed moving pictures of Jim and what he did to her when he was physically present… where was he, what was he doing?… she knew there would never be another girl in his life, not while he had her around. She was beautiful, there was no doubt about that… her mirror told her that each time she looked into it… she liked what she saw, and she knew Jim would never take a chance on losing her, but he was a long way away and he was insatiable… he'd taught her to be insatiable, if he was going through what she was going through, how much thought would he give to the atmosphere before he went out looking?… and Jim would certainly have no hard time in finding some girl who would lay with him, take the heat from his body, give him the release he needed, release all of his tensions in that one tremendous fiery gasp as he let loose into her on the bed.

Jim would be like that.

Why shouldn't she be like that? Who would ever know? There would be a cocktail lounge, and there would be a good-looking guy, perhaps not as good-looking as Jim, nobody could be that good-looking, but good-looking in that sense of the word, and she would look him over and she would pick him up and she would come right out and ask him if he would like to get laid, and he would look her over, not for very long, he wouldn't have to because she was that beautiful, and he would silently take her arm and lead her to his apartment, or she would take him back to her apartment and then she would get laid, perhaps it wouldn't be as good a lay as Jim would give her, but it would be a lay and she would have some measure of release.

Four days. Four days of pure torture. Jim had shot his load into her just an hour before she drove him to the plane, and an hour after he had gone she started building toward the torture she was going to feel for the next four days. But four days were enough. She couldn't go through another four hours let alone another six days.

Jim would never know. And she would never know if Jim had laid some broad out there in the wide, wide world of wherever it was he had gone, Chicago he had gone, but how long would he stay in Chicago?… how long had he stayed there once he landed?… his ticket had said Chicago… but there are planes out of there, and ten days is a lot of time, a person could go around the world in ten days and have plenty of time to stop off and screw any girl who might be willing, and they all would be, to lay up with him, that's how she got him in the first place.

Cocktail bars! What a pleasant place to make a pickup... only she hadn't been out for a pickup that night... she'd only told Harry a few minutes before to get the hell out of her life and stay out of it, what a bore he had been, Harry and his high airs, his stacks of money, his fancy car, his fancy house, his fancy clothes, his fancy words, and his dinky peter. It's a wonder she stayed with him that long. It's no wonder she got in the mood where she didn't care if she had sex or not any longer, good lord he had worked on her for nearly two hours, with his pubic hairs bouncing, brushing, rubbing, striking, tearing into hers all that time made her rough, raw, red, hurt so badly she wanted to scream by the time she rolled him off her body.

Harry had gotten her three times in the few weeks they had gone together and none of those times had he ever made the grade... she did everything for him, perfume, the fancy negligees, the stroking of him with fur, oh how he liked to be stroked with fur, that was supposed to turn him on, well it didn't turn him on for her, it still lay there between his legs like a limp worm, but he was moaning and groaning all the time she rubbed him with the fur piece she kept for that purpose, but still nothing, and then when he put it to her she felt nothing but that soft little worm, and then when he took it out he raced to the bathroom with his piece of fur, oh the bastard could take care of himself, but there was nothing about her body that could get him aroused, only that damned piece of fur, and even then he had to be out of contact with her body, she rubbed his face in that messy piece of fur when he came out of the bathroom that last time, and she told him where he could jam it and threw him and the damned piece of fur out of her apartment, and she got dressed in a sexy satin cocktail dress and went out for a couple of drinks.

But as she thought about it all over in her mind, she knew that deep down she really was looking for a lay that night, a lay that could take care of her, because Harry's hands had done something to her body, they always had done something to her body, a something which he couldn't satisfy, and she knew that she had to be satisfied that night or she would go ape shit right up the walls.

She knew that was what was needed on her third martini as she looked across to the bar and saw Jim, only she didn't know his name at that time, Jim looking across to her, his eyes riveted upon hers through the mirror, then she couldn't take her eyes from his… there was only one blank spot between their eyes and that's when he took them from the mirror and turned to face her, they were lost from her only in that turn, then they were locked together again, and he kept them locked as he crossed the room and sat opposite her in the booth and he snapped his fingers to the waiter and indicated both their drinks, and there still wasn't a word spoken, not until after the waiter had brought fresh drinks, picked up the nearly empty glasses and departed, only then did he speak, and the voice that came out made her inner thighs not only quiver, but shake violently, so violently that she thought that the whole table was shaking, maybe it was, she didn't give one damn, all she knew that there was a guy sitting across from her who was burning her up with his eyes.

Her hands trembled, she didn't dare pick up the martini glass, she knew she'd spill it and that would be most embarrassing for their first meeting, and she felt the sweat wetting the crotch of her panties and the sweat became rivers and it went down into the tops of her nylons fastened there by a fluffy black garter belt, she knew a lot of the guys were turned on by garter belts, another reason she knew that in reality she had searched out that cocktail bar so that she could entice some guy into laying up with her… she always wore panty hose on other occasions, they didn't need garter belts, only the long nylon hose needed garter belts, and they were going to get soggy long before she could take them off….

Then her whole body nearly convulsed when his hand reached over and took hers… the guy she had dreamed of all her life, all her life when she had just turned twenty-one, that didn't seem so old that she could think of it as all her life, but even during her school days she looked over all the pictures of the movie stars and wondered which one of them she would land when she met them, but there was never any movie stars in her life, even though there had been a lot of men, and had she ever met a movie star they would have fallen head over heels in love with her, but she had never met any movie stars, and she had never met any of those rugged sports stars, but she had also heard that most of those athletic characters were built like small worms like Harry had been, and that was one type of cock she could very well do without, she had to have them big, and long and fat, and they had to know what to do with what they had, even a guy with a big one if he didn't know what to do with it couldn't please her, and she was the one who had to be pleased, if a guy got his gun off he was always pleased, and most of them didn't give a good damn if she made her jollies or not, just as long as they were pleased that was all there was to the affair, they couldn't give a damn well if she did, and if the guy had a worm there never was going to be any pleasing her.

Where in hell was Jim? What was he doing at that very moment? He was out there and she was right there in the room. She had to get out of that room or she would be climbing up the walls as she had done for the entire past four days....

And who was there before Harry? It was hard to remember who was before Harry because there was just a blur of faces, indiscriminate faces that meant nothing to her sex life, but there must have been somebody... even though she didn't become insatiable until Jim had taught her how to become insatiable, but there must have been other guys before Jim, before Harry, before Bobby, oh yes, that was it, Bobby what a character, used to wear her nighties and negligees all the time, damn how many of these fetishists people would she have to meet before she met the guy who simply wanted her for her body like Jim had done?... and of course it was Bobby, who had been pretty good, there were times when he could bring her to climax even though he was always in her nighties and negligees and her panties as soon as she took them off and they were wet with her sexual sweats and he put them all on and stuck his pecker out through the legs and took her that way and he moaned and groaned and he pumped and sweated and he took her in his arms and their tongues always slashed and smashed in their mouths and they swallowed each other's spit, and that always tasted pretty good and she liked that part of the affair, but if he ever pulled out, like he did a lot of the times so that he could watch himself shoot off while dressed that way and he looked into the mirror, then she was left high and dry again, and she just couldn't be left high and dry ever again... and she wouldn't be as long as she was with Jim and Jim wasn't going to ever leave her, except for the trips he had to take some of the times, but that was alright, they were for business and business was business because he had to make a lot of money so that he could buy her all the pretty things that she liked, and besides they had to have money so that they could spend those seventy-two hours at a stretch there in the apartment and never have to worry about anything, they had to do that, and she had to understand that he had to be away those times or none of that could be possible, but why did he have to leave her when she wanted to get laid?... just because he had to go away, he could have found some way of getting back to her more often than he did… how long ago was it she met Jim…? Oh yes, six months, or was it six years?… or sixty years?… no, it was only six months, and it was there in that cocktail lounge, and that would be the cocktail lounge she would go to again if Jim didn't come back, and he wouldn't be back for six days, why did the number six always stick in her mind?… it was there and she couldn't shake it, but she knew it would be six more days and that would be Sunday, and then they would have that insatiable session which she had never known before she met Jim…. Bobby was such a character, watching him shooting his load at the mirror and him all dressed in her clothes, and she laying back on the bed diddling herself, diddling just as she was doing when she started thinking about Jim and all the things he could do with her body, and do with his tongue and his fingers and his hands and his tongue, oh that tongue, with his tongue, oh that tongue, and her thighs began to bounce up and down on the canvas chair, she liked that canvas chair, it wasn't as comfortable as the fur chairs and the fur couch she had in the other apartment, but Harry had so turned her off of furs, and every time she thought about fur she thought about Harry and how she could never reach a climax with him and his furs and that was enough of the furs, and she didn't mind Bobby, and then there was Fred and Billy, and another guy named Tommy, he wasn't so bad, he just liked doing it in the bathtub too much and that always wrinkled her lovely skin and she wasn't going to have her lovely skin all wrinkled, that would make her an old woman, and she didn't want to be an old woman, she was just past twenty, or was it twenty-five, she didn't know anymore, it was hard remembering anything, that is anything but Jim and his wicked prong, and his slashing, smashing tongue, that hot probing tongue, sometimes she liked that better than his prick, yes that's what it was called, that's what Jim always called his thing, a prick, what a hell of a name that is, she didn't know if she liked that name, prick, but if Jim liked to call it that, then prick it would be, anyway there were those times when she would rather have his tongue slashing at her little man in the boat than she did having his hard prick poking at it… but he never hurt her, except when he went away like he did, when did he go away?… was it six months ago?… six days ago?… there was something about six and she knew that she held the answer in her own mind but she couldn't bring it to the foreground, and pretty soon she would climax all over her fingers and the delightful thoughts would stop, that is until the next time she thought about Jim and what he would do to her when he saw her in six months… six weeks… six days… yes, six days, that was it, he would see her in six days and he would do all those things to her with his hands, and his tongue, and if he kicked her like he did that one time, that would be alright too, only it wouldn't be alright because Jim was gone, and he wouldn't be back, maybe for a long time, and why did she think of six days?… they put him in jail, that's what they did, they put him in jail for kicking her, and pretty soon after she climaxed she knew she had to put her nightie back on and put the bed jacket over it and she would have to lay down and sleep again… six days… they always had chicken on Sunday… and sometimes they gave ice cream, and the doctors always gave little speeches about not diddling one's self….

THE END

TEARS ON HER PILLOW

no author credited

in LEZO Vol. 5, No.4 Nov./Dec. 1971 on Ed's resume

PAULA DIDN'T LIKE the name *whore*. She didn't like any of the other names she had gotten around the school. She didn't like being thought of as an easy mark, even though she was. She didn't like it when the boys, in their cliques, told that she could be had for a nickel or a dime or for anything they had in their pockets. She didn't like that at all because she never took anything for her services. She simply liked sex. She liked to make it with the boys in the back seat of their cars, or wherever they might take her, even to those spots behind the bushes, behind the school and in the park.

She didn't like the names but she also didn't like giving up sex.

Many times she had said to some of the other girls who were 'easy marks' like herself, that she'd like to spit in all the boy's eyes. She'd like to jam a corn cob up their ass and watch them jump.

"Sure, I guess I like making the sex scene just about as much as any other girl on this campus. But why in hell do the boys have to say such things about me? They want us, and they even threaten to beat us up if we don't put out. So we put out then they go off by themselves and give us the whore-bitch title. Bastards! They're as much a whore as anybody I ever heard of. They get what they want and we don't turn up with names like that for them. They're the football and the baseball squad and they're supposed to be looked upon as heroes, and every girl wants to take down their panties and spread their legs for them. So the girl does and she might just as well go hide her head someplace.

"They grab off a girl once and she thinks she's got it made for a steady and all he does is start passing her down the line among his friends. Men are fickle. Men are apes. Men are no more important than the crap you flush down a toilet. If it only wasn't for enjoying sex I'd forget I ever saw a man in my whole life."

Then she'd go home, put on a soft nightie and cry for a long time… until she felt the wet tears shed on the pillow case, turning cold. Then she'd masturbate.

"At least," she'd mutter to herself through tear-filled eyes, "that's one way of doing it without the need of one of those male creeps. At least that's one way." Then her eyes would really cloud up and she'd speak aloud over a thick tongue. "But it just isn't the same. A finger, just isn't the same."

"You ever hear about two boys going together?" asked Sally, one of her closest friends, on a cold afternoon as they walked home from school through a thin sheet of snow which had fallen earlier in the day.

"You mean queers like the boys are always kidding about?" She was wide eyed about hearing any story of such experiences. Of course she had heard about boys getting together sometimes. And when they were found out, the other boys tried to laugh them right off the schoolyard, and were always trying to get them to do something with them.

"Give you a buck to do it to me," they'd scream, then laugh so that the pretty boys would run off in tears.

Paula knew well the feeling of tears. "What about them, the queer boys?"

"They do it without girls. You know how they do it, Paula… do you?"

"I've heard stories. They got a couple of ways."

"Well, they don't like girls any more than you and me, we don't like men. Yet we got to have our thing taken care of whenever we want and all most of us know is having it with the guys who call us names. Well, there are girls who do things between themselves, just like the boys can."

Paula really became wide eyed. "You mean girl queers?"

"The girls don't like to be called queers any more than the boys like to be called queers. There are other names."

"You know what the names are?"

"Sure. The boys are called homosexuals, and the girls who go together with only other girls are called lesbians."

"Lesbians? I think that's a better name than homosexuals, or queers."

"Sure it is. But lesbians are homosexuals too. Homosexual girls. There's a lot of other names, but lesbians is the most well known. Don't you like the sound of it! Hummmm! Just let it roll right off the end of your tongue."

"Lesbians." Paula spoke the word slowly, and her tongue rolled over every syllable. She did like the sound, and she somehow found a taste in her mouth that she liked. "What do girls do together? I know the boys stick their… their thing in another boy's mouth…."

"They do a lot more than that. And girls have things that look like a boy's thing. They strap it to themselves and they use it just like a boy's thing. One girl plays the part of the boy and the other girl is the girl, then they take turns so that both are happy. And they use their tongue… you know… use it down below."

"Do they really do that? Do they?"

"Of course. Girl, you don't know nothing for sure, and that's a fact. You sure don't know what it takes to make a real sex scene. Here you are talking all the time about how much you like the sex scene and how much you hate boys but in order to make the sex scene, you gotta have a guy. Well, here I am telling you what it's like to do it with another girl and thereby getting rid of all the boys and you go off like I'm lying to you or something. You sure don't know about the real sex scene."

"I guess I been too busy with the boys to find out anything else about sex."

"Didn't any of the boys ever go down there on you when you were making out with them?"

She blushed. "Yes."

"Didn't you like it?"

"I… I guess I did. But men are so rough. They get so rough and tough. All they want to do is get themselves pleased then they don't care if the girl is pleased or not. And they don't care how rough they are with a girl. Sometimes I wish the little queer boys would go for girls. They look like they might be softer on a girl. They would do things more easy and could maybe turn a girl on, where she could enjoy herself."

"Hell! All men are that way! Course I can speak about the gay boys, that's another word for them… the gay boys because they never go with girls. But the others, think they have to be rough on a girl. They think that a girl wants it that way. And they think that's the only way they can prove their manhood, and that they've become a man. Zim, Zam, thank you ma'am… without the thank you part. That's what the body of the male is made up of. Remember the rhyme? Snips and snails and puppy dog tails, that's what little boys are made of. Well, that really goes true for all the boys I've ever met and been with.

"But now I've tasted girls. And the other part of the rhyme goes. Sugar and spice and everything nice, that's what little girls are made of. And that's so true. At least that's the way I feel about girls. They always smell so good. They don't stink like boys. They always smell so good, and they're so soft and so gentle."

"You've been with girls?"

"Why would I know so much about it if I haven't been with girls? I've been with girls a lot of times. You know Jennie Partridge?"

"Sure! The boys all say she is the most beautiful blonde in the school, and she is the prettiest sweater girl in the school, and that her sweaters have a front that no other girl could come close to. They all want to make out with her, but she don't go with any of them."

Sally nodded knowingly. "Right! They all want to get into her panties, and the only ones of the boys whoever did get into her panties were the gay boys… the queer boys."

Paula was dumbfounded. "They gay boys were able to make out with Jennie Partridge when the other boys couldn't?"

Sally laughed. "Not like that. Not get into her panties like the other boys would. These gay boys actually put her panties on, as well as the rest of her clothes."

"Why do they do that?"

"That's when they go off by themselves, or with another guy so that one of them is playing the part of a girl."

"Why does Jennie give them her clothes like that?"

"Because she is in tune with them. Jennie is as gay as the boys. She's a lesbian. Can you imagine all those big campus shots, all in love, all wanting to make the sex scene with a broad who is really a lesbian? Now that's really a laugh. I sure say it is one hell of a laugh. They all want her and none of them can get her… none of them, but I've been with her. I've been with her right in her own house, right in her own bedroom, and we both got into a couple of nighties and I got right down between her legs and she got right down between mine, and we made lesbian love together. What do you think of that?"

"With Jennie Partridge?"

"Right there in her own house. That was a couple of months ago when her mother and father went on vacation. She made the pick up in our locker room."

"Pick up?"

"You sure are sex dumb. Pick up means she picked me up in the locker room after gym class. She knows about my sessions with the boys, and I guess she heard I was off them for life and that I had made the scene with a couple of the other girls, and she wanted to try me on for size. I guess I fit alright. I must have fit her just like one of her sweaters fits her because we've been making it with each other ever since. I was going to lay with Julie Smith a couple of weeks ago and Jennie got so jealous she threatened to cut my nipples off if I did. And you know? I think she could do it. But Julie Smith hasn't got any of the physical equipment that Jennie has, so what was the use in pressing my luck?"

"You and Jennie Partridge!!!" The statement was one of complete amazement.

Again, the girl shook her head and the long hair wiggled across the shoulders of the white angora sweater she wore. "I made out where all those football and baseball and basketball clowns couldn't. All the heroes of the campus drooling and doing things in their shorts and I got to her. Only you got to keep that from getting around because she's got an image to keep up. Remember she's head of the class and lead cheerleader. She likes to stay in that position. It makes her feel important."

"I wouldn't say a word."

"Want to try it on for size?"

"Her sweater?"

"Maybe mine! Damn, you are dumb! I mean how about you and me going over to my place for a couple of hours. I could really teach you something you never knew in all your life."

"Your mother might come in and catch us."

"She won't be home until after seven. But if you're afraid of my place we can always go to yours."

Paula shook her own head of long black hair, and it floated over the furs of her white shortie coat. "We couldn't do that. My mother is home all the time."

"Yeah, she doesn't work, does she! But we'll go to my place if you're willing to give it a try. It's all safe. I've done it there dozens of times. But you got to promise one thing. Once we get started you can't turn me down. I could get awfully angry if you turn me on, get me all heated up and then you back down. There's nothing worse than the temper of a girl who has been turned on and got all sexually hot, then she is left cold on the bed…

unsatisfied. You got to go through with it all the way. First I do it to you to show you how it's done, then you do it for me."

"I will! I will! Anything to get rid of those men. Get them out of my life forever."

"You'll never want to look at another man as long as you live. You'll never need one either. But you got to go through with it all the way. You know how it is with a girl when the guy has made his explosion and the girl hasn't, but he won't do any more because his sexual excitement has all gone. So the girl gets to hurting inside and she has to go home and use her finger. That's the feeling when it is with girl to girl, only worse. She really gets on fire and it burns the hell out of her entire insides if she isn't taken care of. First I take you, then when I make you explode, you got to send me into the pink clouds."

"I... I... I guess I'm looking forward to it." She didn't quite know what to expect. But she didn't want any more nights when the tears would stain her pillow because some guy had not given her the full release she demanded of her sex starved nature. She would go all the way. After all, once wouldn't matter that much. It couldn't poison her. Sally certainly looked healthy enough. And she had been with Jennie Partridge. That was something.

"If you're real good," said Sally, "pretty soon I'll take you out to Jennie Partridge's place and we can have a threesome."

"Do you think she'd really let me come... Let me join in with the two of you?"

"Hell, girl. She's already asked me about you... you especially. You better believe it."

"But why me?"

"Because next to her you're about the prettiest girl in the whole school. And she doesn't fool around with tramps. She could have any one of them and all she'd have to do is wink her eye and they'd coming running. But she chose me, and now she's choosing you. Only you got to be ready for her. She's like the queen... the queen of the school, and the queen of the lesbian society. That's something. But the queen has to be pleased. With me, you'll learn and it won't be long until you're as good at it as me. You just got to know where the real hair lies and I'm the one to show you that. Then on to Jennie. You're really in solid already, before you've even started."

Paula grinned. An inner warmth spewed through her body and she felt the crotch of her pink panties turn hot wet, then cold from the air which raced up under her short miniskirt. She loved the feeling. It was the first time she really looked forward to the sex scene in all her life. And she was thinking of laying with the queen of the school as much as other girls looked forward to laying with the football hero. Let the whores and the loose girls and the easy marks have the school football hero. She was going to have a lesbian. There would be no more tears on her pillow!

THE END

A Piece of Class

from Boy Play Annual *on Ed's resume (from Greg Javer)*

SALLY WATCHED HER YOUNGER brother through the keyhole of the door which connected their rooms. She had often watched him during the month after she found that one of her nighties, a frilly blue nylon, was missing. At first she thought it had been lost in the laundry and only made a brief mention of it to her mother that morning. But she had also caught a slight glimmer in Junior's eyes, and at any other time the look might have passed on. But something held that look to her mind.

It was the next afternoon, after school while her mother and father were still at work that she went to her room as usual to shower and change that she heard the strange sighs coming from Junior's room. She bent down and looked through the keyhole and there he was in front of a full-length mirror. He was petting himself through the nylon material which clung tightly to his youthful body. She watched as the hemline came up with one hand to a point just below his hips. And with the other hand he took hold of his penis and it was quite apparent he knew what to do with it.

But all the time he was masturbating his free hand was moving over the material. She also caught a glimpse of the pink panties he was wearing and she wondered where he'd gotten those, since none of hers were missing... but the sight began to turn her on and she found herself fingering her own pussy and she had to use all her will power to keep from making the heated sounds she wanted to. After all, it wasn't the first time she had masturbated. She knew a lot of the girls around the school who had been masturbating as long as she had. But her masturbation fantasies were different than the other girls. Always they had pictures of their male heroes... or they had mental pictures of those well-endowed young men, and what they could do to a girl.

Sally didn't. This lovely young girl of sixteen would stretch out on her bed with a well poised linger and permit her mind to drift over the pictures of lovely girls... of the models she saw in magazines... of the movie stars. It was the thought of being with another girl which turned her on and gave her the sexual responses she demanded.

That's why she liked to watch Junior after that first time. He was like a girl. He was fourteen and she could figure that he really was a girl who hadn't started to form as yet... just a lovely, youthful, clean body. Although she could see him working his small pole to an erection then ejaculation she could put that part of him out of her mind. She could completely concentrate on the dress and the panties... and she wanted to see him in other things. But she was also afraid to let him know that she had been watching. It might frighten him off... he might plug up the keyhole. Of course she could threaten him with exposure, but what good would that do? And then too, if he knew she was watching he might not be able to get a hard on.

But something had to be done, and the more she thought about making it with her own brother, dressed as a girl, the more she thought her mind was going to snap.

When the time came it was easy to see that Junior was no longer happy at simply wearing the panties and the nightie he'd pilfered. The demand in his own mind had caused him to reach out. He needed more and more clothing, girl's clothing to capture his sexual imagination.

Sally began to find things in her closet and in her dresser drawer in other places than she had originally put them. There was no doubt that Junior had been investigating her garments... and putting them on for his releases. She didn't mind him going through her wardrobe, in fact, even the thought made her hotter'n hell... but she did become angry that he was doing it alone... a waste of all that energy... all that sex stuff, when he could be doing it with her... and she would have her own little girlfriend to play with.

Junior always got home an hour and a half ahead of her because of the half sessions at the school. It would always give him ample time to get home, go through her wardrobe, select what he wanted, put them on, beat his meat and have the things back in her closet and dresser before she got home.

That's the way it had always been. He was getting away with it and having all the fun. Sally couldn't take it any longer. She decided to skip classes one afternoon. But she didn't go right home. She wanted to make sure he was completely dressed in her clothes before she surprised him. Although his door might be locked at other times, she knew it wouldn't be during those afternoon sessions. He had nothing to fear. He had that whole hour and a half of complete safety… and too he probably changed several times… going from Sally's room back to his own any number of times. There was no reason to take up any time locking and unlocking doors.

She was very careful coming in the back door, and more so when she put her books on the kitchen table. She took off her shoes so that there would be no noise on the kitchen floor. There would be none when she reached the rug in the living room, and the stairs to the second floor were covered.

She could see him when she was only halfway up the stairs. His door was open and he was in front of the mirror where she thought he might be. He was wearing her short sleeved blue angora slip-over sweater and matching blue miniskirt. There were her blue angora socks… the low-heeled shoes and even the blonde wig she'd gotten the Christmas before.

She froze in a sexual paralysis at the sight. He was more beautiful that she had believed in her wildest dreams. She fought to keep her finger away from the crotch of her panties where her body heats had already started the hot sweat rivering down the inside of her thighs. She bit her lower lip to keep from crying out in her excitement. She wanted to move, to continue up the stairs and to walk right in on him and stand beside him and do as he was doing. But her leg muscles wouldn't move.

Then she watched as he put his small erection back into the blue nylon panties and he straightened the skirt, and the bottom of the angora sweater over the top of the skirt and walked out toward the upper hall. He froze when he saw Sally.

He made several futile attempts at describing something with his hands… then he let them ride lightly over the bottom of the angora sweater and the top of the skirt as if he was trying to smooth out some nonexistent wrinkle… then his mouth made several moves with no sound issuing. He wet his suddenly dry lips. But in all of his fright he had not lost his erection. It pushed the front of the miniskirt out so that there was no doubt but what was concealed there.

Sally's eyes became fixed on that spot.

Completely embarrassed Junior reached under the skirt and pushed his thing back between his legs… then crossed his legs so that the muscle remained trapped there.

Sally was the first to find words. "Don't hide it, Junior." She also licked at suddenly dry lips.

"Hide… hide what?" He very well knew what she was referring to.

"Open your legs and let me see it. Show me what you've got under my panties." Then she moved forward and took him lightly by the hand.

She led him, stiff legged, into her bedroom and locked the door.

"Are… are you going to tell on me?"

"Why should I do that?"

"I got on your clothes."

"And they look sweet on you."

"You're not going to tell?" He sunk down the edge of her bed, still not quite knowing what to do with his hands, so he folded them over the lap of the skirt. He no longer had any erection, and some of the wetness was coming back to his mouth.

"I hated you as a boy. I've always wanted a younger sister… so that we could play at… things together."

"I thought you'd be angry… if you knew about me going through your clothes."

"You're much prettier as a girl, you know."

He turned so that he could see himself in her full-length mirror. "I like the way I look."

"And I know what you do when you get dressed up like that… even when you only have on the nightie and the panties."

The red of embarrassment crossed his features again and he couldn't help the move as his hand went as if for protection to his small manhood through the material. "I peeked all the time through the keyhole."

"But you didn't tell on me?"

"You got me hot doing what you do to yourself. It was like watching another girl doing that. It was fun. I saw you a long time ago doing it just as a boy. But when you got to putting on my clothes… you gave me hot and cold chills all over and then when I played with myself I got so excited I nearly exploded through the roof."

"You didn't like it when I was doing it dressed like a boy?"

"Did you?"

"No! It's much better when I have your clothes on." He stood up and moved to the mirror. There was no doubt that he was getting excited again. The talk about the clothes, and his own fantasies were beginning to work overtime for him... and for Sally.

"Do you feel like a girl this way?"

"I don't know what a girl feels like. But I guess I must feel something like that. I get all dreamy. And when I start playing with my thing...I hate to sweat... but I can't help it. I break out in both cold and hot sweats both at the same time. I can hardly stop myself. The only time I can hold back is when I want to keep changing clothes. Sometimes I put on three or four different outfits of yours before the right one suits me. This one I like best... like I like the white angora sweater too.

"I wish I could dress like this always. I wish I was like you. That's what I wish." He had pulled the panty leg aside and began to play with himself.

"Don't do that... not all by yourself."

She moved swiftly to him and took him back to the bed where he stretched out and she lay out beside him. Her hand drifted over to take his muscle.

"I don't think of you as a boy. I think of you as a girl. Sometime maybe when we get a little older we can leave here and we can go where you can live always as a girl. With just the two of us knowing the truth."

"Do you think that's possible?"

"Boys are changing to girls every day. You'd be surprised at how many stories I've read about boys putting on girls' clothes and doing what you do. And sometimes they go out and marry men. But I don't want you to go out and marry any man. I want you to make love only with me. Just like two girls making love all the time with nobody to say we can't."

She reached over and took his hand and laid it over the crotch of her pink nylon panties. Both their thighs were quivering uncontrolled. They knew instinctively that their climax was near.... Sally had the foresight to reach over and take a box of kleenex from the night stand. She put it between them in readiness.

"And I can use your clothes anytime I want?"

"Anytime... all the time. I'll get a job after school and buy you all the girls clothes you want. I'll turn you into a real girl. Do you know what a lesbian is?"

"No! But it sounds strange."

"I think I'm a lesbian."

"Why do you think that?"

"Because I've read about lesbians, and lesbians always go with other girls. I think about other girls all the time and they get me so hot and bothered. I always used my finger. But now I have you. And you look like a girl. But you got that thing like a man. Maybe it will feel good to me that way. I tried it with Jack Turney in his car once. I hated it. He smelled so bad. I don't want no man smell… or man thing. You don't look like a man… and I love what you look like…." And she rolled the soft youth on top of her and she showed him what he must do with his small hard muscle other than gripping it in the palm of his hands.

Once more instinct took over and the girl/boy plowed into his sister until the hot sperm stained the crotch of both their panties.

"I've ruined your panties," he said lightly.

"Nylon washes out easily. Did you like it?"

"I never done it with a girl before. Is that what it's really like?"

"I'd of had no fun at all if you were completely a boy. This is the best of all ways. I've never been so excited. All the time I've been watching you through the keyhole I knew it would be like this." Then she pulled down her skirt and turned so that she faced the extremely feminine youth. "Thank God you're not a man. How I hate them. How you should hate them. You will always be a girl and I will take care of you. I'll see that you have all the beautiful clothes you'll ever want. Next year when I'm seventeen I'll quit school and go out and work for you, because you're going to be my little princess. All the guys will drool over you when they see you and think about what a tremendous body you have under the sweaters and the blouses and skirts… but they will never touch you. You will be my girl… a girl for a girl… and we will be so happy. No man shall ever know the feminine beauty under your clothes. And you'll grow your own hair long. No one will stop you. Long hair is the style. But that will not be enough. I'm going to start training your body… you will need a training brassiere… I'm going to make you into the girl I want you to be."

No one ever came into his room at night once he had gone to bed. He slipped into the very frilly, long sleeved nylon nightie of Sally's which he had so much admired, then he stretched out under the sheets and permitted both hands to drift up and down the soft, slick material. Truly he was happy and he had made Sally happy, and she couldn't have made him happier. For a time they would have to be careful. But there were so many clothes which were girls' clothes that looked a bit boyish. Lots of the boys wore them. He would be careful, but he would also be the girl he wanted to be... that Sally now wanted him to be.

He visualized the lovely breasts and let his fingers caress the small nipples on his chest... then a hand found his middle, and furthered down to the crotch of the panties through the nightie. There was no man muscle there at all. His mind told him that it had disappeared as soon as the flowing, frilly nylon melted over his body.

There was no he there at all. There was only the lovely girl stretched out in her finery... but a girl didn't want another girl for her love affairs. Sally must be some kind of a silly. There she was, a beautiful girl with all those beautiful clothes and all she wanted was another girl. How silly. But Junior, June, wasn't going to be like that... not when she had such a beautiful body and could wear those lovely clothes so well.... June was going to have a man... a man who would know how to make love to her.... June would feel a stiff erection, and she knew as a girl she could make any man happy.

THE END

Detailed In Blood

by Edw, D. Wood Jr.

in Garter Girls *Vol.6 no. 2 May/June 1972 on Ed's resume 1971*

There was no blood!

However, blood or no blood, the sight the witnesses beheld was the most gory sight for any of their memories. The blood had all been drained out at the mortuary hours before the body had been so neatly dressed and placed in the silver casket with the pink lining. Pink had always been Shirley's favorite color. It was inevitable that she would be buried in her favorite color… and her dress was her favorite pink cocktail gown.

There were those at the funeral parlor who said at the time, how beautiful she looked… perfectly natural… like she was simply asleep and would soon wake up.

None could say that on Monday when her remains were found near the opened grave.

The undertaker had done such a beautiful job on her. It was impossible to tell on Monday.

There was so much of her body missing. There were no hands or feet. The breasts had been sliced from the chest and the upper arms had disappeared along with the wrists and the hands. The eyes had been taken from the skull and only deep black holes remained in the skull. The tongue, the kidneys and other innards would also be found to have disappeared later when she was taken to the coroner's office. The heart and the liver had been removed by the undertaker. It was part of the law which required such removals before burial of the cadaver in that town.

There was no need for a trained eye to see that the entire operation had been done with a skilled hand… necessarily a doctor… or a butcher... preferably a butcher... the cutting had been done with a surgical knife. All had been so perfectly separated from the main torso... not a deviation in the perfect surgery. Even the bones had not suffered in their amputation... all had been cut in the right spots... the knuckles.

There had been four others that month. Shirley had been the fifth... and the bodies had been from several other cemeteries in the city... all young... all beautiful young girls, and all had been left in the same condition.

Undoubtedly the work of some fiend, the newspapers were having their sensational headlines which told of fact and of speculation... the work of a fiend... but undoubtedly a fiend who knew the human anatomy to perfection.

Lieutenant Pat Crane reviewed his notes and could only remark to his sergeant subordinate, "Too many cemeteries to put men on every one of them. Besides, they have their own security forces. If there's a ghoul running loose taking these bodies from the grave, then... well damn it all man, the laws are difficult when cadavers are extracted from the grave. Our job is to protect the living and make sure that a cadaver-maker is apprehended."

"But that's just the point, Lieutenant," muttered the sergeant. "We gotta grab the shithead off n' lock him up in the rubber room at the happy farm before there aren't enough dead bodies to go around... pretty soon he's going to make his own cadavers from the living... make his own dead bodies to order."

"Hell, man. Look the word up in the dictionary. The freak-out is probably some necrophiliac."

The sergeant nodded. "A guy who likes to make it with the dead. But in all the years I have been on the force I ain't never heard of a necrophiliac who went around cutting the corpses up like that. And where are all the parts taken?"

"Ghouls have been known to eat their victims."

"Sure... but the bones are always left. I tell you, lieutenant... we better get him before he starts making them to order. He runs out of the dead ones he likes and he's going to start supplying his own."

"So the question is... where do we start?"

"Looks like an impossible task."

The entire operation was an impossible task, but the pinions of the law were right in their figuring... the freak with the surgical knife wasn't going to be satisfied very long with the ready-made bodies. Decay set in much too swiftly... too easily. For his purpose he needed fresh bodies. The limbs which he could control. The vital organs which could be removed, even at times while the victim still lived.

The first in the ready to acquire bodies was Regina Oatmere... just two days after Shirley's body had been discovered at her graveside. Regina, well-known to the police, was a prostitute... a streetwalker... nonetheless beautiful, but one who found walking the streets for her John much more interesting and much more profitable than waiting on tables or holding down a desk job. Often she had been heard to say, and it was on her last arrest record: "Why settle for peanuts when you can have the whole elephant?"

There was little left of her body on the blood-soaked bed in her small one-room, pull-down bed apartment. She had not been known to take her clients to her apartment very often, thus the killer must have been someone she knew and trusted.

She knew and trusted the wrong client!

However no one in the apartment building, even the next door neighbor, had heard the slightest out of the way sound. There was, however, the report that her television set had gone suddenly loud for a moment... but just for a moment... then went down again.

There was nothing strange in that!

Often television sets throughout the building went loud at times. Perhaps someone went to the bathroom, or into the kitchen and the set went loud. It would take them a moment to return and adjust the set. There was nothing strange about a television set being loud for a moment or two.

The television set was turned off when Regina's body was found!

The maggots would have completely captured the body had not the girl been long overdue in rent and the manager feared her disappearance and used his passkey. He had planned, upon leaving, to plug up the keyhole.

The sight which greeted his eyes caused him to throw up on the spot before he could turn and summon help.

"Hell, man," related Lt. Crane to the horde of newspaper and television reporters outside of his office. "There's no doubt but what we've got a fiend on our hands." But he had little else of information to offer.

And later Sgt. Hendrix stretched his long legs across the lieutenant's desk. "He did just like I figured," he informed. "He got tired of the dead ones. He wants them made to his specific order now!"

"One thing for goddamned sure... this gets around the way it's going to, we're going to have a panic on our hands." The lieutenant thought for a long silent moment and Sgt. Hendrix sipped from his great cup of coffee. The lieutenant swung on him. "Get those reporters back and give the general statement. Ladies keep off the streets from dusk on until daylight unless they got some tough guy accompanying them... somebody who can protect them... that goes especially for the young ones... and they shouldn't pick up any strangers. That might protect some of the hookers like Regina."

Hendrix grinned. "Sometimes I think you've got a real heart, copper!"

Crane smiled back. "My heart might keep another heart beating."

Hendrix frowned again. "Lot of good that will do for friends."

"I don't get you?"

"Everybody's got friends... even creeps... all he has to do is start picking on *unsuspecting friends.* Women are gullible to friends... and it's women he's after. Let a friend give them a line and they put their own neck in the grip of the knife... under the knife, in this case."

"You can't protect all of the people all the time. All we can do is issue bulletins. There are always those who won't take our word for anything."

"Yeah," sighed Hendrix. "It's always things like this happen to other people... it never happens to them."

It happened next to Paula Takkasy, a beautician who left her shop just after dark... she had heard the reports and that the girls were not to walk the streets after dark, but then she wasn't walking... she was driving... what could be more safe?

Naturally she had read about the mutilating killer.

But who would want to kill her?

"What in the world would anybody gain in killing her?" she thought silently as she briefly rubbed her ample breasts through the neat white nylon uniform. She would not give it another thought except when she read the newspaper articles, then she dismissed the whole thing from her mind... each time she put the paper down. Hell, there were nuts scattered all through the town... but if one wasted their time worrying about the nuts and what they might do next, there would be time for doing nothing else. Nuts were nuts... and *they were always someplace else.*

The someplace else proved to be the back seat of her car on that fateful Friday night. And the *somebody else* didn't rear its unmasked face until she pulled into her garage. Even then the attack didn't come until she moved to the garage doors in preparation for going outside.

The doors closed in front of her.

And she was trapped inside the garage with the fiend.

Where she was found...

Where what was left of the body was found. There had been no scream. Not a sound of terror or distress, but she had not been taken without a struggle.

The lights in the garage were blazing and the blood from her spliced body had splattered the walls and the car. She had not been easily sent into the afterworld... yet still there had been no cries heard, no outcry... no scream....

Then she was simply another dead body with no limbs attached and very few insides... guts... all had been removed.

Carla Henries was the first to be completely drained of blood. She was AB NEGATIVE!

"What in hell's that supposed to mean?" It was Hendrix talking.

"Very rare... a very rare type of blood."

"Sure. Some creep walked up to her, cut open her veins and walked off with a bucket full of blood." The sergeant lit his cigarette. "What in hell would a creep want with a bucket full of dead blood?"

"So maybe we got a Dracula on our hands."

"Or a blood bank!"

"Who was this Carla Henries? I'll tell you. A dental assistant. She remained late at the office. Dr. Hallicourt the dentist, her boss had gone more than an hour before. There was all the equipment in the office for a blood transfusion... the airtight bottles which would be necessary to take the blood and preserve it. All blood is saleable.... Man, AB NEGATIVE has it going the second it's in the bottle... out of the veins and into the bottle where it can enter somebody else's veins."

Mary Lou Denton became the next victim. Fell is more the proper word. She fell from the sixteenth floor of an apartment building... her apartment... she landed in a deserted alley... dark... foreboding... a place no one ventured after dark... after the sun went down... and like all the others... there was no scream... no outcry. If her body made any sound when it squashed to the brick of the alley floor, it was not heard... any sound would have been covered by the freeway traffic less than half a mile distance.

There was always the noise of speeding cars… the bad mufflers… the big trucks and the screeching brakes….

Only Mary Lou Denton's right hand and right foot were taken!

Only the hands and the foot were taken as the rest of her body had been much too crushed and broken to be of any use. The bones of her legs and her arms had acted like spears when they were broken… splintered and jammed through her internal guts, and the easily penetrated skin… even her face, the once lovely face, had been left nothing but a bloody pulp… the once exotic body was nothing more than maggot fodder.

The panic in the city was on and the women and the girls realized that they were in trouble. "The street isn't the only danger zone," replied Sgt. Hendrix. "He's been grabbing them in their own garages… their own apartments… he enters wherever he wants!"

"Which is where his downfall might come."

"How so?"

"He enters wherever he wants! Remember what we were talking about the other day. Friends? I've got a strange feeling that this CUT-UP was known by all the victims… he was known on a personal basis with each of the girls."

"I think you're coming up with something, Lieutenant."

The lieutenant was coming up with something… but that something didn't prevent Patsy Walker from falling victim to the bloodletting and the mutilation. She was cut up alive and there were dried tears still staining her cheeks, having rivered down from the eyeless eye sockets.

Her panties had been jammed into her throat and was secured there by a nylon stocking knotted around her head and over her mouth. She could have screamed at the top of her lungs and not a sound would have been heard more than a foot or two away.

She had died horribly.

Only her head was connected to her torso which also had the breasts removed with exacting perfection.

"So what have we found that makes any connection between them?" The sergeant was bewildered.

"Just one thing. He knew all of them."

"You figured that a couple of days ago."

"But I know for fact who it is now."

"You really think it is him, then?"

"I'm positive of it."

"How are you going to prove it?"

"He's convicted himself."

"Do we go through his office again?"

"No need. They were all his patients."

"His house?"

"Right!"

"What put you onto him?"

"His house is too big for the kind of loot he makes. The three expensive cars. Much too large a bank account. Wild parties... orgies, to say the least. All that kind of stuff costs money. He's got to be in the business like I've listed."

"I remember an old Boris Karloff, Bela Lugosi movie that had something going for it like this."

"Just about the same thing. In the movie they were collecting cadavers for medical students. This creep has a much more ingenious plan."

"We won't take him easy."

"Then we take him hard."

Dr. Hallicourt met them at the door. And he knew what it was all about... and he knew what he had in the cellar, in the cellar laboratory... and he knew that Dena Washington was right then strapped to his operating table. She had been such a quick date for such a wealthy man. Then suddenly she found herself asleep and when she awoke she was tied and gagged to the operating table. The knife had already sliced through her upper arm to the bone.

Dr. Hallicourt made no fuss. He invited the two detectives in and ushered them to the basement where he quite readily explained the operation of his parts bank. He would supply a perfectly good hand... guts... eyes... whatever was needed he had the supply....

And he also had more tricks of the trade. The metal net fell over the two men and they were trapped... and the doctor glowered at them as he kicked their guns aside.

"There is not always the call for simple parts of the female body...." His eyes glistened. "I have also been commissioned for parts, healthy parts of the male." He lifted the sparkling knife. Then sprinkled ether generously over the two men, struggling under the heavy metal net on the floor.

THE END

ONE DELICIOUS MOMENT

from Pussy Willow *vol.3 No.2 Apr./May 1971 (no author listed on Ed's resume)*

PAULA LOOKED ACROSS her martini to the crystal clear mirror behind the back bar. She had situated herself on the same bar stool for an even week… her eyes continually drifting up to the mirror where she could see the deep purple padded front door. There was nervous expectation in those eyes. She knew the beautiful blonde would come through that door at any moment. It had been a nightly entrance… and a nightly churning of Paula's sexual expectations. Paula wasn't backward when it came to fulfilling her sex demands, but the blonde who had turned her on so violently from the first moment she'd seen her was something different. From that first moment, Paula had placed her on such a high pedestal that she went watery all over every time she wanted to make the approach. It was something which had never happened before. If Paula wanted to make a conquest she simply did it.

The blonde was different… Paula didn't even know her name. But whenever the girl came through the door and Paula went hot from the top of her head to the soles of her feet, she mentally undressed the girl naked. All the time she watched the girl through the mirror reflection and she was getting up her nerve to make the approach, there were mental pictures so vivid that Paula could actually feel her hands unfastening the buttons or tugging at the zipper… then the removal of a satiny brassiere. She could imagine the full breasts which always filled out the front of her dresses. She wanted to experience the pointed nipples which she knew to be there because they were so outlined when the blonde wore tight knit dresses or sweaters. Her mind dwelled on the globes for a long time before the mental pictures lowered and her hands had slipped into sheer pink panties and lowered them down around the girl's well-turned ankles. She never let the girl kick them free. Always she bent down to remove them, and took her time getting back up… time in which she let her tongue start at the ankles, first the right, then the left, and the tongue slowly rivered its way up the inside of her leg and paused a long time in the sweet smelling pubic patch where a pink clit winked at her.

It was as her tongue attempted to capture the sensation-seeking object that the mental pictures blasted her back to reality and she was still at the bar and the blonde was still in a booth, fully clothed in one of the darker corners of the bar.

Paula figured the girl must have known it was a gay, lesbian bar… and if she wasn't "one of them," what in hell was she doing in such a place? But she never spoke to anyone… made no advances that she wanted a lover or would be accepted as one. She simply entered the bar, the chunky waitress took her order… Scotch and soda… then sat back with her drink and stared into space as if she had drifted off into a world of her own where no one was allowed.

That was the part which kept Paula off… the aloofness… the singleness of the girl… the inner attitude.

But with all of that beauty going to waste Paula knew she had to bring the girl into the fold… it was pure criminal to let anything that luscious go to waste. If any of her friends knew about the reluctance in her conquering tactics they'd laugh her right out of the lesbian world.

"Not our Paula," they'd say between gruff laughter. "Not our Paula who knows every approach there is! Not our Paula with the insatiable tongue!" Then they'd laugh some more and the one thing Paula couldn't stand was being laughed at… laughed with… but not laughed at.

Paula's eyes took a different direction momentarily as she checked her man-style wrist watch and the big clock at the end of the bar, both of which proved the blonde was much later than usual… and this brought on the inner panic trembles as her mind fought back thoughts that perhaps the girl was not coming… that she had disappeared back into the nothingness from which she came one week before.

The more the hands of the clock turned, the harder Paula fought back those thoughts until she was suddenly, silently cursing herself for not having made a move before. Even if she had been rejected for one reason or another, at least she'd have tried. All the girls figured it was better to make a pass and be shorted than never to have advanced at all.

"You miss more good stuff that way," she had often told her girlfriends when they had mentioned such episodes. "And who in hell of us wants to miss out on any good stuff? You see it, you take hold of her shoulders with both hands and use your teeth to tear off her panties. Don't ever let any of the good stuff get away… life is too short."

Paula's hand drifted down to the crotch of her nylon slacks… both the slacks and the long-sleeved blouse were thin enough to be pajamas… but the new pant suits called for the revealing of the under body. Her hands found the heat she knew was there, and she knew her bikini panties… white… were damp. But none of the dampness had soaked through the slacks. Nylon wouldn't show the dampness much if it did finally seep through…. Besides she didn't give a fiddler's damned if it showed or not. There weren't many people in the cocktail lounge that early, but everyone who was there had hot pants for somebody… or something. One more damp crotch wasn't going to make much difference.

She let her hand rub the sensitive inner thigh muscles, and then forced her fingers to push the thin material deep into her vagina. But that was too much! Anymore and she'd have an orgasm right there on the stool… the pressure of her slowly moving finger and the thoughts of the beautiful blonde… it was too much. She snapped the finger away and grabbed up her martini which she downed quickly.

It was as the burning fluid went down her throat, and her eyes fastened on the mirror again that the blonde floated in and took her usual booth in the dark corner.

Paula went dry all over. She knew she had to wait until the waitress brought the girl a drink… at least that would be more polite… so she ordered another martini from the gay, dyed blonde bartender and held on until it was put in front of her before she turned on the stool and fully faced the girl.

Their eyes didn't meet immediately. Paula had felt they wouldn't because the girl always stared so vacantly off into the further darkness of the bar… she didn't even look to the tall glass when she drank. But Paula knew from experience if one stares at somebody's back long enough they will eventually turn around. The old case of "unseen eyes" boring holes in the back of your head. But when she did finally turn around there was no "come-on" to the look. It was a simple glance, then back to her own day dreams…

"However," thought Paula to herself, "it's a start. At least she finally looked at something beside the walls." She didn't change her own stare. It hung right on the back of the girl's head, right where it connected to her shoulder blades… although she couldn't see the connecting point because of the long blonde hair which cascaded there in deep waves.

"Ohh, how I'd like to run barefooted through that silk," continued Paula's silent thoughts. "I'd pay her a buck a mile plus travel time." Again her hand went to the soft nylon at her crotch… the heat had become more intense, and the wetness in the crotch of her panties made her legs tremble with building excitement.

The approach was near… but just how to make that approach. The blonde wasn't one of those run-of-the-mill bar broads, she was class… real class… the baby blue knit dress which encased that tremendous body absolutely oozed class… and the sensuous lips, full red, called out for capture.

Paula could take it no longer. The trembling in her legs had turned to quick twitching movements. It wasn't unpleasant but the heat which caused the twitching shouted for release, and Paula knew only one way to achieve that release.

Slowly she slid off the bar stool and the moisture in her panties turned cold. She'd had sexually wet panties before, but never had she found these turning cold… not when she was as hot inside as she was.

The blonde hadn't turned around again… only that one time. And she didn't turn around when Paula stood directly behind her, still looking at the same spot on the back of her neck.

"You have beautiful hair," muttered Paula. It was the only thing she could think of to say at the moment. There had been many other things she'd planned to say… dreamed of saying… but they were all lost in an infinity of the moment. Her throat felt dry, but the panties had become warm, moist again as the perfumed fragrance of the girl rose up to greet her nostrils. More than ever she knew she had to nuzzle deep into those silken waves… those tresses of pure gold,

She didn't look up, nor did she change the direction of her eyes. Her only movement was to lift the glass and daintily sip of the amber liquid.

"I wish I had hair like that." Still she couldn't think of the other thing she had planned to say although she did follow up with: "I'm Paula. That's my name. Paula. Everybody knows me around here. I… I stop by nearly every day. I… I even have a tab at the bar. Not many of the broads around here can say that. Think I might sit down…? Buy you a drink?" Paula didn't wait for an answer. However, she couldn't help but notice the girls eyes had finally glanced in her direction as she moved around the table to sit in front of her. The girl's eyes followed the entire movement… there was no welcome in them, but neither was there hostility. "I've seen you around a couple of times this week… But you're new here, aren't you?" Still there was no answer.

Paula played her next card. She snapped her fingers in the direction of the chubby waitress and when confronted she ordered her martini with a Scotch and soda for the blonde. "You do take Scotch and soda, don't ya?" No answer. "Sure she does," snapped Paula and the waitress moved off.

Paula didn't speak again until the drinks were served and the waitress moved off with the blonde's empty glass… emptied while waiting for the new drink. "You don't like people?" Silence. "You don't want anybody around… me?" When the silence overwhelmed the situation again Paula sighed and started to get up.

The girl placed her hand lightly on Paula's and for the first time the mask cracked and the beautiful face smiled softly. "I guess I'm a prude. Aren't I?"

"Oh now, I wouldn't say that." Paula had almost said something like that. Had the girl let her fully stand up, she'd have said a hell of a lot more and probably spit in her eye saying it.

"Please, drink your martini." The smile still hung there.

Paula sank back to the cushioned chair again and picked up her martini. She sipped from it without taking her eyes from the girl's blue pools of delight.

"I've seen you looking at me… in the mirror," the blonde remarked as she indicated the mirror behind the bar.

Paula grinned. "I didn't think you saw anything except the dark walls over there. You're new in town, aren't you… at least, you're new around the neighborhood?"

The girl nodded. "And you're a lesbian, aren't you?"

Shock set in immediately, but then Paula wondered why there had been any shock. She knew what she was, why did it sound so rough coming between those lovely lips? "I've been called worse."

"I didn't mean to offend. But you don't look like a lot of the… the others I've seen on the other end of town where I come from. I mean you're not as hard as some of them."

"It takes all kinds to make a world," Paula grinned. "You do know what kind of a bar this is, don't you?"

Again the lovely blonde head nodded. The smile came back to her luscious red lips. "Isn't that why I'm here?"

"Honey, I wouldn't know why you're here. All week I couldn't figure you out. You come to a place like this... you say you know what it's all about... yet you don't even bother looking for any action. You just sit down and stare at the walls... walls you can't even see because they're so dark. Are you looking for some action, or are you not?" Then before the blonde could answer, Paula decided she was playing too soft. She should plant her demands in and let hell freeze over if the blonde didn't like it. There had been too much mental torture for seven days. She doubted if she could take another week of hemming and hawing around.

"Would you make homosexual love to me?" Paula hadn't had to open her mouth except to gape at the girl's request.

Paula was out of her chair in less than a second and captured a side of the padded chair next to the girl. Her arms went to the girl's nylon covered knee, right on the edge of the blue knit miniskirt. "Good Christ, girl... if you knew how many times I've wet my panties over you during the past week... You have to ask me a question like that... I've sat on the bar stool drooling over you like a school girl and I haven't done that in years."

The blonde winked her eyes, "Will you?"

"Right here on the rug of the cocktail lounge if that's where you want it. Or in the silk bed I know you come from... or a fur rug I have in my apartment five blocks from here... On top of a mountain with or without snow. You just name the time and the place, honey... better yet. I'll name it... we can take off right this minute." Then she cooled her words. "What's this all about? I don't even know your name."

"Shirley." She started to say her last name but cut short with the letter "E." "I guess last don't matter in affairs like this."

"Who knows where affairs like this will go? You never can be sure. Not a beautiful little thing like you. You want to be the man, or is that my end?"

Shirley shuddered. "Please don't mention the word men to me ever again. I've had all I want of men for the rest of my life. I hate all of them."

Paula grinned. "So that's it. Boyfriend trouble?" Paula didn't give a damn what kind of man troubles Shirley had. All she knew was that the blonde wanted an experience, and surely Paula was going to give it to her.

"I was married. He fathered two children."

"Then you should be home with the kids."

"Not by me… with two other women. Will you?"

Paula let her hand slowly run up under the ridge of the knit dress and it went along the smooth nylon of her pantyhose until it reached Shirley's crotch. There were no panties under the pantyhose… only the same heat Paula had found when she investigated her own pubic region. Shirley didn't move except to close her legs slowly over Paula's hand and wrist, locking it at just the right spot… the spot… the clit which has always escaped Paula's mental vision just as her tongue was about to pull it in between tight lips. The pink knob was not going to elude her again.

"I want to know," started Shirley, "I want to know for sure."

"Of course you do, honey. We all want to be sure. And I'm about the right one to show you. Drink up and we'll go to my place. It's only a short way."

Shirley pushed the glass slowly from her. "I won't need any more of this. I don't drink, you know. Only when I'm nervous. I'm not nervous anymore. Besides, I don't want to miss a single moment of… of what we will do." She slowly opened her legs and Paula waited anther moment before extracting her hand… she gave the covered clitoris another couple of tickles… proof of other things to come, then she looked into the girl's eyes as they stood up. "Don't worry Shirley, honey… I won't let you miss one delicious moment."

THE END

THE GREEKS HAVE A WORD FOR IT

by Edw. D. Wood Jr.

Menage *Vol.1 No.2 June/July 1973 (thanks to James Pontolillo)*

ETILE BEAT HIS MEAT, beat his wife Ledom, beat his Captains, beat his Lieutenants, beat his subjects and necessarily beat his meat again… then he retired to the massive dining hall and ate a full supper, burped and went to the bed chambers where he climbed in beside the luscious form of Ledom.

"Do you wish me to take my negligee off?" she questioned of him immediately after she felt the brush of his strong erection.

"I'm too tired."

"What I feel pressing against me does not tell me you are tired."

"My cock is willing but the rest of my flesh is weak. I could not promote the exercise that it would take to hump over you… and further, I could not promote the exercise it would take for my guts to spew forth the sperm of enjoyment. I fear that such exercise would surely see me to my grave… and you would not like to see your husband, your ruler, dead and stretched out cold in the tombs… would you?"

She was quick with her answer, the only answer she could give if she wanted her breasts to remain where they were attached beautifully to her chest. "Of course not, my sire. I too would die if you were to pass beyond the great dark river of the dead." Those were her words, but her mind raced to earlier that evening when she was with the handsome Captain of the Army, Ythgim. It was comparatively safe for them at such times. It was directly after the prayers when those sentenced for crimes against the Ruler, or the state, were punished. There was always two to three hours of

437

beheadings for the most vicious crimes. And then there were the loss of one or both hands, or feet for the thieves… and there were the loss of one or both breasts for ladies of easy virtue or adultery, and the amputation of penis and testicles for the male participants… rape saw the testicles go first… then the penis… then each finger was pulled from the socket one at a time, and if the fellow survived the shock his tongue was cut out, his ears sliced off and then his head was neatly decapitated from his shoulders.

One of Etile's newest innovations of torture was the pouring of molten lead, via a wooden funnel, into the hapless victim's anus. It was a sure cure for the crime of sodomy.

But those were the two to three hours in which Ledom and Ythgim could have their weekly sex scene. They never took a full two hours let alone three. Neither one of them wanted to suffer the tortures which they would receive if they were caught. They limited their engagement to one and a half hours, and that gave them plenty of time to clean up and return to different parts of the castle and/or the courtyard, whichever gave them the most distance apart.

But as she looked to Etile as he closed his eyes, she let her hand float down over the sheer material at her crotch and she permitted her finger to indent itself through the material just enough so that it pressed between the lips of her vagina where it paused to lightly tickle her clitoris… she knew the finger movement along with her mental thoughts of Ythgim would bring on another much needed climax… but she also knew that she must not move another muscle… she must not scream out in climax, or even sigh with the release. Except for himself, Etile had ruled that all forms of masturbation were punishable by the cutting off of penis and testicles or the filling of the woman's vagina with scalding wax… along with shaving of the pubic region and the hair of the head.

She climaxed three times and she guarded the light flow of steaming breath which did escape between her lips. It had been so hot that she couldn't retain it in her mouth.

Etile didn't open his eyes. "Did I hear you sigh? For why did you sigh?"

"Just the thought of such a pleasant night this is, and that I am so safe here beside my husband, my lover and my Ruler."

"Yes. I am all that." He burped from the massive supper and wine he had taken. "And for your lovely words to me, your exalted Ruler, I shall give you a present tomorrow. I shall decree something else as a crime and invent a new punishment for that crime… all in your honor."

"You are so good to me."

He let his hand drift over and captured one of her breasts. His hand was hard and strong and he hurt the girl, but she could do little more than take the punishment until the punishment of his snores offended her ears. Merciful sleep was not easy for her to come by.

The following morning after her bath in warm water sprinkled with perfume she joined Etile at the breakfast table in the great dining hall. It was the only meal she was permitted to eat with him.

"I have had more than an hour's session with our court physician already this morning."

"Are you ill, sire?"

"Of course not. I'm as healthy as a stud bull, and I can continue as long as a stud bull. One day we will have a showing of that. We will get the largest stud bull and a cow, and I myself will compete with the best maiden in the court. Is there any man or woman who will say that the bull will not drop dead while I am still mounting?"

"No one would dare." She had finished her breakfast. "But the physician?"

"A new torture. One to honor you. As I spoke of before sleep overtook me last night. Ah, what a glorious torture that will be… for young boys."

"Young boys?"

"You have heard my words. I do not repeat myself, dear woman." He burped and gobbled at his wine.

"What will you do with these young boys? And for what crime would the young boys be convicted?"

"Since when is it any of them have to commit the crime? I will select whom I wish and invent a crime for them to be punished with. It is that simple. Have not I always seen fit to rid myself of enemies thusly?"

"But the young boys of the land certainly can't be your enemies, sire."

"They will be so if I decree it. Who is there to dispute my word?"

"And the punishment, in honor of myself, is to be?" She felt she needed further wine for what she was about to hear from Etile's fat lips.

"I've heard that the Greeks have practiced sodomy for ages… since the Greeks are my enemy I have outlawed sodomy throughout my lands, thus the pouring of molten lead into their asses. But the thought has entranced me for sometime. Why would so many risk such a torture? Those of the multitudes who watch are little affected. Others have gone out and done the same thing, and I dare say that there are hundreds, perhaps thousands of others whom I have never caught. There must be something in it. Therefore I deemed to give it a try."

"You've had sodomy with a young boy?"

"Not yet. I tried it with one of your hand-maidens. She screamed with the pain... then the screams became screams of pleasure and her hands clawed at my vitals attempting to drive my shaft deeper into her brown hole. She simply could not get enough of me, nor I of that delicious new sport. It is much tighter than doing it in the usual way... and perhaps to its newness for me... it was a very thrilling experience. I do suppose it would be the same with young boys... except that while I was perform-ing sodomy upon the young lady she was at the same time masturbating. Even under threat of the ultimate punishment decreed to fit that particu-lar crime she could not help herself. Her finger continued to diddle with her clitoris until she screamed with all the pleasures of both heaven and hell. She will receive her punishment today, directly after prayers."

"But if she gave you such extreme pleasures, why punish her with such horrors?"

"Simply because she defied me. I told her to stop masturbating and she did not. It matters little that she could not stop... she committed a crime. Her ass will receive molten lead and her vagina will receive the scalding wax. She will be completely sealed off until her death."

"Which will come quickly."

"The boys will receive no such thrills... they will not be able to mas-turbate."

"You will amputate their manhoods."

"No. Of course not. I am told by a Greek prisoner that that is all a part of the joy. Sodomy might be alright with the maidens, but it is much more powerful with boys... and to be boys they must retain their pole and their sacs."

"But if you excite them, they will surely do as the girl did... mastur-bate along with the sodomy."

"The physicians has given me a sure cure for that. He has sworn by his head that his process will work. What is to be done is that the boy will be stripped naked and he will ride a horse bareback daily for ten hours, then he will be committed to masturbate at the same time... continually... and when the night hours come he will continue to masturbate or be masturbated by handmaidens until he is permitted to sleep a few hours. Then the process will begin all over again when he awakes. This will be continued over and over again for months, a year perhaps, until his tool is so withered... so completely useless and his sacs nothing more than skin hanging between his legs that no longer will he have the sexual faculties of a man. I am assured he will become quite effeminate... he will act much like a maiden... dress as such... but in the bedchambers there will still be the sight of the young boy and the thrill of the real Greek sodomy."

"By your own orders masturbation is a crime."

"I shall be using it for science."

"And sodomy is a crime?"

"I will change that law... but only to include my highest officers and myself as participants. It's much too good for the rabble. And the masturbation... besides, it will not be used for enjoyment.... I am also assured that there will be no enjoyment felt by the boy as he masturbates thus... there will only be the pain... as if punishment.... for masturbating... until he becomes girl-like in all his modes. The Greeks like boys to be boys. They are my enemies therefore I could not have boys being boys. I would not do as they do. But being there is such pleasure in such an affair... it was not difficult for my physicians to show me the girl/boy... they will live with the handmaidens... and learn many tricks of their trade from them... they will be bathed in the warm waters and perfumed and powdered daily. They will be at the service of all my officers who have earned some reward from myself. It is better than dipping into the treasury, my treasury, every time. And they will appreciate my generosity because they are elite and will know that only they may participate like their Ruler. All the others of the army and the rabble are excluded on threat of the usual lead in the ass punishment."

"You are indeed a cruel man, sire."

"Thank you for your kind words." He burped again and stood up. "My army will begin collecting these youths late this afternoon, after the punishment period." He folded his thick velvet robe about him and walked from the great dining hall, leaving Ledom to ponder over the state of affairs. She bit her lip nervously, then she got up and walked to the sun porch, her sheer gown trailing out like a cloud behind her.

She looked down to the courtyard and saw Ythgim who could only acknowledge her by a quick look. He was in command of several men who were marching a group of prisoners across the courtyard toward the gates where they would be taken to the town square and there to receive their punishment. Ledom recognized the handmaiden. It was Nwodnus who had befriended her so many times. Nwodnus who knew of her love for Ythgim and had protected her absence to Etile several times when the punishments were over too quickly and Ledom hadn't returned. But Ledom also knew that no matter what the torture, Nwodnus would die before revealing that secret. And Ledom also knew there was no hope that she would be spared....

"She is to be the last punishment," told Ythgim when they locked arms around each other for their first embrace.... "Perhaps an hour from now. There are not so many prisoners today. We have little time."

"Little matter about the time. I cannot bring myself to a sex mood with the horrors I have upon my mind, even though my love is most powerful for you, the horrors today are more powerful." And she told Ythgim of Etile's plan.

"The man is a monster... a madman... he is totally insane. This is the final hilt of the sword. By God I will not be turned into a Greek boy-lover and neither will my officers. I can assure you this will not come about. If the soldiers of the army were to hear of this they would go up in arms. He has gone too far this time. We have heard that we were to round up a hundred or so young boys this afternoon, but it was for masturbation crimes... but this... he has gone too far."

"But he is the supreme Ruler. His word is law. His Priests back him up by finding scriptures that deem a crime whatever he says is a crime.... And they have proven it not to be sodomy for those of high rank as long as the boy looks and acts feminine."

"By the Gods... he would have us a land of freaks so feminized that the smallest of countries could overrun us... take us to task... make us slaves. There would be none of the youth in the land who could handle or would handle a sword." Then he spun from Ledom telling her to return to her chambers where she would be safe and to gather her handmaidens around her so they also would be safe....

And within the hour Nwodnus was sent with a special messenger to her. The messenger told her that Etile had fallen... taken by the officers of the army.

"What has happened Nwodnus?" she asked when the messenger had gone, and she was told the story of waiting her doom and seeing so many of those lose their heads and their hands and their vitals. But suddenly Ythgim appeared on the scene and from a high platform he told what Ledom had told him. "En masse they surrounded Etile and dragged him to the ground. No one raised a hand to help him until the watching rabble started to make a riot. They were going to stone Etile to death and then dismember him, feeding his parts to the barnyard cattle and the pigs. Ythgim stopped them. He told the army as well as the rabble that it would be better to permit Etile to live and suffer. He shouted to them, 'What is it that Etile prides most about himself?' and they answered, 'His cock.' And then they wanted to cut that off and feed it to him, but once more Ythgim screamed that the punishment must fit the crime."

"And they punished him?"

"He is undergoing his punishment. It will take a long time I am told… and the rabble are all along the road and the corral watching… they will watch… and there are old, ugly peasant women who will do what they must do at night…."

Then Ledom knew. Etile would suffer the punishment which was to be held in her honor… and when she locked her naked arms around Ythgim that night in Etile's bed she felt the honor of that punishment really pleased her. Etile had finally given her something she could enjoy… and Ythgim had other enjoyments for her.

THE END

CEASE TO EXIST

as "T. G. Denver"

in Horror Sex Tales, The Jumbo Book, *1972, on Ed's resume 1971*

LIKE THE DAY he first saw her at the office. She was wearing an extremely tight, yellow sweater and short white miniskirt which showed every ripple of her buttock cheeks as she moved. She wore no brassiere, that was apparent. The nipples poked so enticingly against the tight yellow wool and the mounds jounced excitingly with every step.

From that moment on the girl spun him like a top. She gave him wet dreams during the night... something which had not occurred since he was a small child just entering puberty. And he always woke up just at the climax...while the dreams of her was still fresh and her face and naked body still hovered in the vacuum above the bed.

At such times she had been very real. Almost like she actually was right there, laying with him, kissing him, feeling his stiff member and running her tongue over every inch of his body. She was as real as when she walked past him in the office corridors and he wanted to reach out and gather her into his arms.

He had made no such move, either physical or with outward indications. It was all stored up inside of him, a streaming mass of molting sexual fires just waiting to explode.

Damn, how he wanted that broad. She turned him on as if his body would go up in smoke at any moment from the fires which burned within him. There never had been a girl which affected him quite the way she had. All he had to do was look at her and he would have to sit down and cross his legs to hide what was happening to the front of his trousers.

But then it was too late!

There was the graveyard... the cemetery... the foreboding dark brown hole beneath the flower-covered pink casket. And there was the preacher and he was saying her name over and over again as he described the lovely creature who was to be interred there on that ever so rainy day. Even the black clouds and the flashing lightning seemed to be crying out for her release from the sealed box.

One so lovely should never die so young.

He held back the tears with all his might even though in reality he wanted to let them flow... show everyone how he felt... show the others gathered around the grave that he more than any of them cared about that girl.... Shirlee was her name... how very much he cared about her. But he only stood there with nearly bowed head, his eyes glued on the end of the casket where her head would be... his hands folded in front of him.

His stomach sank and he felt like throwing up each time he thought about the dirt which would fill in that hole, over the pink casket in so short a time. He desperately tried to think of other things, of pleasant things, but he couldn't. How could one think of pleasant things when the horrors of the funeral were right there in front of him. There is no pleasantness at a funeral.

He couldn't see her walking in front of him any longer. All he could visualize was her stretched out in that pink satin lined box, her body dressed in a white satin bride's dress... the way he had seen her an hour before at the funeral home. She was so still... so silent... so dead... but having lost none of her beauty.

Death is always so final!

So terrifyingly final! So absolute!

He honestly couldn't realize why he hadn't made a pass at her while she was alive. He had had so many opportunities. He'd dated many girls before that. He'd never been bashful about approaching some girl of his choice, and he was a pretty good looking guy. His mirror told him that every morning when he shaved, and whenever he combed his hair. The girls went for him... generally. Perhaps Shirlee would have gone for him also. She had smiled many times when they passed each other. And she had offered the usual good mornings and good nights. Other conversation was unnecessary because their jobs were not in tune for closeness of operation.

He did manage to brush against her a few times in the elevator and in that closeness her perfume nearly drove him insane. But the only insanity on his part was that he didn't attempt making a date with her in all those weeks since she came to work at the office.

He never dated any other girl from the moment she first walked into that office and captured his imagination.

Then the service was over and the crowd of co-workers and friends moved away and were soon driving off in their individual cars. Some would return to their offices. Others would go to cocktail lounges and relive the events of poor Shirlee who had been so brutally murdered and stuffed under the back seat of her own car.

She might never have been found, except that it was a very hot July day and warm blood attracts flies and it is only a matter of time until the maggots take over and let loose their stink, and it is only another short time until that stink will engulf an entire neighborhood.

That was how it happened!

That was why her garage door was forced open by the authorities when they arrived. She had missed work for more than a week and all during that week her phone went unanswered while the employer attempted to find out the reasons for her absence. So no one really thought about dropping by personally. An unanswered phone simply meant that she was not home to answer it.

But she was home!

She was dead and she was stuffed under the back seat of her car in the garage and the maggots were having a stinking feast... a stinking feast upon the lovely remains of Shirlee who had been so untouchable in life... so completely untouchable... as untouchable as the Angels.

He did not leave the graveside for a long time... until he saw the two men in blue overalls as they approached riding on a scoop shovel vehicle. That's when he turned and made his way swiftly to his own car. He knew he couldn't face the grave filling actions. There was a morbid fascination which attempted forcing him to turn and look back at the operation. But he successfully fought that demand.

Then he himself sat in a plush cocktail lounge. He was not returning to the office that afternoon. He couldn't face being in that office and knowing he would not see the beautiful Shirlee and her glowing smile... but he would see the pink casket and what was inside of it. He saw the same thing there in the cocktail lounge. But at least there he had the martinis to deaden the pain and blur the objective. It took a lot of martinis before that blessed state coveted him.

"After hours in the cemetery, long after the cast and crew have gone," he mumbled to himself, then grinned, but it was a grin of irony, not of humor. There was no humor in any of his thoughts. There was only Shirlee in his thoughts. Shirlee and her dead body. "She has ceased to exist," he added to his mumblings and the bartender thought he was ordering another drink. He served another to the very sad man. There would be more, and more and more, and around closing time when he got into his car he didn't realize it.

There was only the dead, dull, lifeless feeling of movement, but movement almost without direction. He was a mechanical man running on alcohol. His glazed eyes were fired by the same fuel. He realized the starter, and he realized the motor turning, then the wheels beneath the framework also realized the dazzling lights of the city, then the darkness of the highway…. and he fully realized the tree near the entrance of the cemetery as his headlights captured the massive bulk of the trunk.

His head pained terribly as he climbed out of the wreckage but suddenly he wasn't drunk any longer. He was as clear as when he had entered the bar late that morning. All the thoughts of Shirlee came back to him… all the damning torture… and he realized those thoughts must really never have left him… perhaps they had been deaden a bit by the alcohol, but they couldn't have completely left him because he had driven, unconsciously, to the cemetery where she was buried.

He didn't bother to look back at the mangled wreckage of his car. Instead he moved toward the gates of the cemetery which stood open, inviting entrance. And he wondered how that could happen. The cemeteries were always securely locked at night. He had often wondered why the gates were locked… was it to keep the live population out or the dead population in?

But the gates were not locked. They weren't even closed. They stood open quite wide. Wide enough for him to pass through without having to touch the metal.

The dull of the night raced his body and the rain started slowly. Perhaps it had started before he'd crashed into the tree, but he didn't remember. He only knew that just as he stepped through the gates and entered the cemetery proper he felt the rain for the first time. Certainly the rain must have started before. His clothing was already soaked. The clothes couldn't be soaked if the rain had just started that moment.

But he didn't hear the rain hitting the ground… and the lightning flashes were unaccompanied by any sounds of thunder. That happened sometimes. Not often. But there were lightning storms which produced no thunder sounds.

He was thankful for the lightning. It helped him to find his way off the path and through the maze of big and small headstones and monuments, and remembrances. He fell a couple of times when the earth sank beneath him… and he stumbled over several newly filled graves. But he knew in what general direction he was going. It wasn't as if he hadn't been there before. Only that morning he had been there. The direction was fresh in his memory. And if it wasn't, Shirlee was calling to him and her voice was like a magnet drawing him in that direction.

He didn't even know she knew his name.

But she was calling his name.

At first it was as if from some tremendous distance. But as he neared the grave where he knew she rested, the voice was louder… soft, singing, sweet, but louder.

Then he stood looking down at the fresh mound and the glistening headstone which spelled out the legend of her name, birth and death dates. That was all! There were no sweet lines of devotion… of love, of remembrance. Just the cold facts of her name and the date of her birth and the date of her death. It did tell him, however, that she was twenty-three years old… so and so beautiful to die.

His mind drifted back to her lovely form in the white satin bride's dress when he saw her at the mortuary, and as he looked down on the new formed mound with the freshly planted grass he could see through the ground as if with X-ray eyes and she was laying down there just as he remembered her last.

And there was something else on the ground. One of the workmen had forgotten his shovel. It would not be a tremendous task to dig open the grave. It had only been filled that morning… late in the morning. The dirt would be very soft and with the rain… muddy.

It would be an easy removal.

What he could not have in life he would take in death. She was there… down there and he would open the grave… open the casket… open it wide and he would pull up that white satin bride's dress and take her as if she were his bride on their first night. The casket would be their motel and the grave their secret covering.

He would not have to approach her with any of the usual propositions. She would simply lay there and he could do anything he wanted to do with her luscious body. He could kiss her silent lips. He could peck at her closed eyes. He would play with the unfeeling breasts and his tongue would run rivers over the stilled stomach. And then he would investigate her brush and he would know the feelings of those soft hairs against his own naked frame… for indeed he would dig up the grave and then he too would become naked when he entered the box with her.

He was in a fury… saliva dribbled over the corners of his lips and his shoulders ached but in time the shovel hit the hard top of the pink casket… then he was on his hands and knees to brush the remaining dirt from the top. He breathed heavily as he stripped naked to the night and the rain and he tossed his clothing out of the grave. Nothing must mar the fact that he would have naked contact with Shirlee. Every fiber of his body and mind strained toward those thoughts.

The lid opened easily once he had unfastened the outside locks. He opened first the bottom portion then the top. It was very dark inside. But the streaks of silent lightning brightened the scene every so often… momentarily. It was all he needed… simple quick glimpses of the Shirlee he had loved so long from afar.

He knew he had to recapture some of his strength before he could make a successful affair out of the situation. The digging had taken so much strength out of him and he breathed heavily and deeply for a long time. He raised his head to the Heavens and let the cool rain refresh that area.

He heard the moan and snapped his head downward to look at the wide, staring eyes of the dead girl. They had been closed the last time he'd seen them. But they were open again… all blue and shiny… glistening when the flashes of lightning streaked across them.

Then he watched, transfixed as her reddened lips drew back and her white teeth shined like pearls in a clear sea.

His mouth went dry. He had expected no resistance from the girl. She was dead. She couldn't see.

She couldn't smile her way back from the dead.

Nor could she lift up her arms inviting him into them. But she was doing that, and her knees slowly raised up so that the white satin bride's dress fell back along them to her stomach leaving that area of desire open for him. It was impossible! But he was seeing it! It was impossible for her to resist him. But she wasn't resisting him. She was accepting him like the *whore* she had been in life… like the *whore* who demanded money from him when he had taken her home that night during the rainstorm and he had cut her heart out and then stuffed her under the back seat of her automobile which had been incapacitated several days before.

Even in death she was that same *whore* and she was demanding his body in return for taking her life… and when her arms encircled him, and with all his bloodcurdling screams he found no strength to pull away.

He felt himself locked in those claw like arms, those taloned fingers pulling at his manhood, his member, pulling it down and into her… and her salivaless tongue smashed against his own… cutting down the screams to tortured gasps and groans… and the smell of the maggots was only added to by the horror of the maggots themselves as they began to swarm all over his own body….

Then all went black….

And they would find his smashed, broken, dismembered body crushed in the wreck of his car where it had come to a grinding, splintering stop against the tree at the cemetery gates, that cold and rainy night….

He had suddenly and simply ceased to exist!

He felt himself locked in those clawlike arms, those taloned fingers pulling at his manhood, his member, pulling it down and into her… those fang-like teeth piercing through his lips almost locking them together as her salivaless tongue smashed against his own… cutting down the screams to tortured gasps and groans… and the smell of the maggots was only added to by the horror of the maggots themselves as they began to swarm all over his own body….

THE END

www.ingramcontent.com/pod-product-compliance
Lightning Source LLC
Chambersburg PA
CBHW070748030726
47504CB00003B/471